The answers you seek swim in the river of your subconscious thoughts. The deeper you dive, the more there is for you to see. Open your eyes and discover the power of the reflection others already know you to be.

NEMECENE

THE GADLIN CONSPIRACY

(EPISODE 2)

KAZ LEFAVE

Enjoy the continuing journey

luv Kaz

AGUACENE PUBLISHING, INC.

NEMECENE

THE GADLIN CONSPIRACY

KAZ LEFAVE

www.NEMECENE.com

An Aguacene™ publication
Published 2016-2017 by Aguacene Publishing, Inc.
Toronto, ON, Canada • publish@aguacene.com

Distributed by NBN (National Book Network, Inc.)
15200 NBN Way, Blue Ridge Summit, PA, USA, 17214

Printed in Canada

ISBN-13: 978-1-988814-01-8
ISBN-10: 1-988814-01-4
10 9 8 7 6 5 4 3 2 1

FSC
www.fsc.org
RECYCLED
Paper made from
recycled material
FSC® C103567

Paper:	FSC® certified
Cover:	Supreme Recycled Silk 100lb, 55% recycled with 30% post consumer waste, made without the use of chlorine gas, manufactured using cogeneration energy
Pages:	Roland Enviro Print 50lb text, 100% recycled, 100% post consumer waste, processed chlorine free, manufactured using biogas energy
Press:	Variquik PC15, web offset

Cover art by RUKE. Edited by Sylvia McConnell. Page layout by Karen Lefave.

NOTES ON THE TEXT

THE NARRATORS

Each chapter is organized into three sections, each section consistently assigned to a single narrator.

Section I - NEPHARISSE
Written in the third person in Nepharisse's voice from an out of body point of view.

Section II - ELIZE
Written in the first person as a running dialog inside Elize's head. If she does not think it, hear it, see it, taste it, feel it, smell it or sense it, neither do you.

Section III - KEETO
Written in the first person as diary entries to his mother. One section represents one journaling session.

THE TIMELINE

The novel, as a whole, moves forward in time, although sections may overlap as the different narrators offer their experiences during the same time period. A note at the beginning of each section states when that segment begins relative to Chapter One of Episode 1, *Nemecene: The Epoch of Redress*.

Flashbacks and fanciful musings are enclosed between the following symbols:

▼ ▼ ▼ and ▲ ▲ ▲

Gaps in the story, where the text jumps forward in time are preceded by the following symbols:

✂ ✂ ✂

GLOSSARY ENTRIES

Since the characters are living in the *Nemecene* epoch, they are intrinsically familiar with their futuristic world, its technology, and its language, therefore they would not naturally explain the meaning or significance of words, foreign to our 21st century society, as they relay their story to you.

I encourage you to read the glossary at the back first, in order to immerse yourself in their world.

THE MYSTERIOUS *they* OR *them*

Who are *they*? That's a well-guarded secret. In fact, only one person knows the answer to that question and I'll give you one guess. ;-)

Feel free to share your theories with me and each other by following *Nemecene* on social media. The answers shall be forthcoming … in due time. Muahahaha.

For all who dare to be more than their perceived limits.

MEET NEPHARISSE

*She captivates wandering minds with
lyrical incantations*

No human can resist the sparkles that dance on the wings of her words. When chaos worries the thoughts of men, she sashays in step with her calm intensity to soothe their angst. But if their actions interfere with her heart's desire, a master puppeteer slices through the veil of her verses.

As it was with Nathruyu, Nepharisse's voice emanates from a deeper place. Her body serves as a host for a larger presence, while she glides through time by the grace of her kind. The sweet innocence behind her eyes is hers to wield when matters call for a little mischief, wrapped in a sheath of trust.

You need someone to trust. Trust is key. You can trust in me.

MEET ELIZE

*Her restless tough-girl attitude betrays her
splintered mind*

Keet is such a pup. Honestly. There's nothing mystical about my nightmares. It's a scientific fact that dreams are just our brain's way of processing things. And in my case, it's simply trauma nothing more. Keet's afraid I'll get lost in some mental void like Mother and that Father will commit me to the GHU. That's where Mother died. Wipe that image. No more tears. Good. So we're keeping everything hush. Crazed, eh? Anyway, I hope he's wrong. Better keep the voices to myself. Everybody hears some. They just won't admit it. It's not considered normal. Right. Normal. At least, we'll be gone soon and maybe even … Crap! No. Not now.

Breathe, Eli, breathe. Here he comes. Breathe. Act normal.

MEET KEETO

*His courage hides inside the cocoon of an
armchair archaeologist*

Time has not filled the void you left when Eli and I were just nine years old. As I cloister myself here, sprinkling the pages of another journal with my emotions, I image that you see through my eyes, and write through my quill. It is this insanity that keeps me sane while my days spent digging for answers to questions that constantly change consume my sheltered life. If only your spirit could materialize into the Mother I need you to be once again. But reality reminds me otherwise. My only hope is that connecting with you, in these quiet and sometimes not so quiet moments of reflection, will uncover truths that liberate us all.

But will they come soon enough?

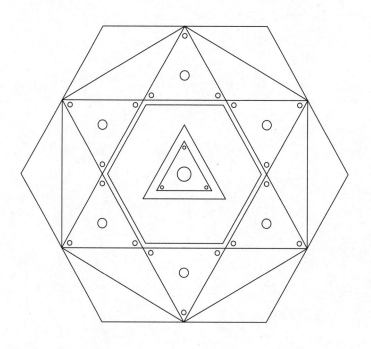

CHAPTER ONE

NEPHARISSE

Day 363: late evening

Nepharisse hesitates. The moment is hers to shine, yet a split second delay in her decision collapses the star of her grandiose illusions into a black hole of insignificance. What life can she salvage from her deflated aspirations? She leans back against the yellow-dusted wall separating the ventilation shaft from the stagnant waters holding the city of Eadonberg's history hostage and closes her eyes for a glimmer of inspiration. Only her breath knows how to shape victory from this failure, so she draws wisdom from the sweeping draft dancing in the wake of a tattered cloak, and moves into action once more.

The flitting of heels that chime through the main duct, hasten, then vanish with a whip into the thickening air. Nepharisse's hopes are escaping just as those of the prey take flight. She tightens her lungs and resolves to temper her pace. There is an abrupt end to this path. A draft will soon blow past again. She slips into a notch in the tunnel and hones in on the incoming panic. There will be no third opportunity, of that she is certain. Still, she hesitates, and a cloud of yellow dust flicks its feathered tip at her chest.

The words Nepharisse fears to hear vibrate through her bones as thoughts, reminding her of her limits. Perhaps she was unrealistic when assessing her capabilities, and now she will be ridiculed in light of her ambivalence, unless … she rises above the footsteps now swooping towards the nearby hatch and stops them as they close the gap. This act, she decides, could be the requisite proof that she is indeed ready for the stage. Could be. Could be.

Once again, the tattered cloak cuts by Nepharisse, who is tucked inside a dark nook, her weapon hungry and expectant. Her shoulder slides past the edge of the wall then leads her body out from the shadows. She has a clear sight line, but her right arm carries the weight of uncertainty. It falls to her side as quickly as it secures its aim. The target has already collapsed. The blue beam charging through the shaft from the cloaked body now lying motionless below the hatch stops short as it infuses a weapon activated by a black glove, a meter away. Someone else has stolen Nepharisse's limelight. It seems that doubt has its price. No doubt. No doubt.

Nooooooooo.

The sentiment is mute but no less resonant than if it were bouncing off the walls of a grand canyon. Nepharisse sinks to the ground in her mind. Were it not for the determined charge of boots heading her way, she would surely craft a sweet harmony of deprecating notes on how incredibly undeserving she is. To thrust responsibilities upon herself, when she clearly is not yet ready or even suited for the venture, as her inappropriate dress for the circumstances demonstrates, is presumptuous on her part. She looks past her long curvy thighs down to her sapphire blue shoes and watches them kick puffs of gold dust as she retreats to the dark nook.

The footsteps approach. They stop. Nepharisse exposes an inquisitive blue eye and the fingertips of a white glove to the back of the evocative candy-red mane. The pounding in her heart awakens the loneliness she harbors inside. He will sense her, and he does as he stands over the prone body. Sothese chuckles, hoists the fallen mark over his left shoulder, and walks back towards Nepharisse, smirking while at the same time intrigued. He invites her to reveal herself as his eyes revel in sensations of his own. She struts out, weapon in hand, its meal as yet unfulfilled. She says nothing, for her words have no power over his kind.

Sothese admires the ginger-auburn curls in Nepharisse's disheveled bun, flirting in the tendrils of a forthcoming blast. He glances at the empty containment cartridge, clipped to the immobilizer in her hand, puckers his lips in a self-satisfied smile, and utters: "I thought as much."

The arrogance infuriates her enough to incite her to react with a bold statement that was really intended for someone else: "You will learn to show me more respect." Nepharisse aims at his crotch and lifts her right eyebrow at him, as she slides the muzzle from one side of his groin to the next and adds, "It all comes down to a choice, my dear."

His response further aggravates the tension between them. Sothese gropes her frustrated body with his eyes. Her desire for him is immersed in a poisonous cocktail of hatred, lust, and guilt that drowns the deep sorrow she feels whenever he is inside her exterior world. She knows his ravaging ways and has succumbed to them in the past, but, she is determined, no more. Yet duty still binds her to him, even as her love for another mirrors the offense he has done to her.

Sothese brushes past her, humming a familiar lullaby, with the limp body swaying against his shoulder. Nepharisse casts her eyes to the weapon, resting empty in her hand, as the melody fades down the shaft, glowing with the accomplishment she could have donned. A sulfide-rich smoke bomb comes barreling straight for her. The toxic cloud pastes a noxious scent to her despair and fogs the betrayal that belongs to a sister she can no longer trust.

▲ ▲ ▲

A flash illuminates the deserted hallway long enough to draw attention to her white glove holding the emitter's hilt. Nepharisse pulls her focus back from the negative memory interfering with her current assignment. Reliving the past does nothing to ensure success in the present moment.

The power surge is her cue to move into position. She adjusts her crisp uniform, picks up the food tray, and approaches the medic staffing the night shift with a warm herb infusion, a delicacy that only high-ranking GHU employees have privileges for.

The doctor raises his sleepy head from the diagnosis board to meet twinkling sapphire eyes and a gentle smile. Nepharisse offers the prized beverage to him and yawns purposefully while he savors the treat. Her mouth regains its friendly curve then pauses, with lips slightly parted, as she strings together some enchanting words. The man listens, mesmerized.

Nights were made for dreaming. Dreams are beautiful

things. Everyone loves to dream.

Nepharisse breaks the cup's fall with her right hand a split second before the medic's head plunges through the holographic brain floating in front of the board and lands on the desk. She places the intact antique china piece back in his hand and positions it palm down in his lap. Dreams fill certain hearts with passion. Nepharisse stifles a giggle as the liquid drains into his pants.

A second electrical surge overloads the photovoltaic cells in the sunshaft, and the center tower of Osler Hall goes dark. Auxiliary power puts in an appearance, but this also quickly fades. The hallway becomes a black tunnel. A faint light, coming from a crack under the entrance to a surgery cell, points the way to that which she came here to witness for herself.

If her intuition proves correct, or rather, when her intuition proves accurate, she can boast a higher consciousness and progress to a more exacting task. Until then, her attention belongs in a vertical shoot on the east-most side of the floor. Nepharisse points the frequency emitter at the east wall of the shaft and creates a temporary rift into the building framework, from which she drops onto a sub-floor, one meter below.

Last year's abominable experiments in the east tower of the double-helix-inspired medical building had stopped as expected once the perpetrator was clamped, but Nepharisse knew something equally, if not more, disturbing had taken its place. She just did not have any physical evidence to trade if such a need should arise as her plans develop. Tonight, she risks her own freedoms for the pleasure of uncovering such a felonious exhibit.

Willfully trapped in the space between the amethyst exterior facade of the tower and the holowall decoy playing on the opaque interior wall, she drags herself on her stomach counter-clockwise around the outside of the hidden ninth floor until she reaches the west-most point adjacent to the room she seeks. Through the amethyst wall, she has a translucent view of Elize's room at the northeast corner of the adjacent building, Van Billund Hall's J tower. Similarly, if Elize were to glance her way at the illuminated gemstone medical building, she would see Nepharisse's petite silhouette interacting with the prerecorded shadows acting out a research scene inside a fake laboratory, an ingenious illusion fooling all but the most astute.

Nepharisse faces the interior and emits a frequency for molding uniportals. She keeps her profile as small and as low as possible and spies into the blinding room revealing itself through her own personal one-way spy gate. She is well aware that the holoscientists have all but dispersed in the massive shower of photons coming from the secret cell, leaving the crisp contours of her body visible to whoever strolls in the orchard below. This is surely her moment to shine.

Framed by this particular spotlight, however, is not the vision of stardom Nepharisse wishes to manifest. Her hope is that the eerie intensity to the usual sparkle Osler Hall creates off the campus pond will redirect accidental watchers to the north clearing, instead of up at her impromptu debut as a holowall stand-in. A glimpse into the violations under way by the three jittery forms drenched in sweat, dissecting what appears to be the head of a steaming male corpse covered in crusty lumps, confirms that this is no ordinary autopsy.

A sudden twitch on the operating platform suggests a half-life still remains on the slab. Nepharisse senses the remnants of fear creeping inside the refrigerated trench where the triad is working one meter below the cell's retracted false floor, but life, as they know it, has left the subject. The rhythms of that deep vibration consume the burning flesh, the scent of which has yet to fade. Beads of sweat from above drip and sizzle as they hit the body, releasing the soul of each cell to a wispy plume.

The female perpetrator reaches for a thermostat, but the more androgynous one stops her. A frozen specimen does not respond well to the procedure. She pulls a sopping cloth from her pocket and starts to shake. The third member, a male, races to a sub-zero chest in the corner beside stacks of monitoring equipment perched on energy beams, yanks it open, pulls out a frozen beaker, and pitches it to the woman. She chugs its content as it liquifies and the frost on the outside of the jar vaporizes. Her two accomplices syphon off another two beakers of viscous crimson fluid, which seems to settle their nerves somewhat, but not enough to cool their sudoriferous skin.

Their suffering floods Nepharisse with delight. If they could only sense her presence beyond the frequency tight walls of their own design, they would feel infinitely more comfortable, that is, until she intends otherwise. This architectural anomaly is what drew her to this level in the first place and now their ingenuity is their undoing; they are mere shadows fumbling behind a mist of steam, tinted by an amethyst glow that breaches the rift Nepharisse opened from the space between the frames.

▼ ▼ ▼

Filtered smog hangs over the Central Core within the tall biowall grid posts framing Eadonberg's majestic skyline. From a gyroscopically balanced ocean barge, Nepharisse surveys the network of diffuse amethyst lights, saturating the brume where small crystal structures, the sajadums, are strategically positioned. The boat moves northeast around the campus oval and into the eastern canal, flanked by the central walkway to the west, and, to the east, an impressive monument leading up to Ministry House, the seat of fear for the fewer than one hundred thousand residents.

The gateway sajadum, the one with a direct connection to the private meditation quarters of the Pramam himself in Ministburg, floats on a thin pure-water outdoor courtyard on the mezzanine level above the grand foyer. It radiates a vibrant purple dome that penetrates any fog that Earth's onshore winds can beat into a monstrous mass.

The satellite sajadums are open for general use as quiet spaces for contemplation, while the thirty minute Unified message loops continuously throughout the day and the night. Their tetrahedron shape gives their smokey amethyst construction the ability to focus transmissions, thereby projecting an almost solid holographic experience.

Nepharisse safeguards her thoughts as the barge continues northwards to the transport station hostel. When the midday sun burns through the morning fog, her anticipation turns to trepidation. She looks back towards the campus oval and at the nine square towers of Van Billund Hall, the residence complex. Her fear tunnels down the central walkway and into the northwest window on the top floor of J-branch. All she knows is that whatever happens today will change the course of time forever.

Fear grows in cycles, to a versal rhythm of planets and stars. Some civilizations shrink, others expand, and still others lack the awareness to recognize the signs in time to remedy their ignorance, and thus vanish into the dark unknown where monstrosities await. What sacrifices are the chosen ones prepared to make in order to break the seals of fate? Nepharisse closes her eyes and projects her soul's desire into the future.

▲ ▲ ▲

The mist behind Osler Hall's gemstone veneer is clear now. The secret room is sealed, and contrast has returned to the silent actors against its solid walls as they continue their fabricated research. One of the troupe puts down his instruments, walks around Nepharisse, and feigns interest in the open lotus flowers on the pond in the clearing below. Another one tweezes a worm-like blob which only someone at close range would recognize as part of the human cerebellum, the vermis, and smirks at his colleague. He then stares through Nepharisse at the one enjoying the view to the outside and laughs. The silence has been broken. Nepharisse is incensed. She has already seen enough blatant disregard for human respect with the real medical staff to substantiate her suspicions, although the means by which they have acquired their victim eludes her. When the so-called twisted child collector was free to roam the orphanage, the sacrifices came fully researched, but since the Ministburg penal island is the serial killer's new home, someone within the URA must be feeding this new campaign.

The day the incarceration was publicly announced is still present in Nepharisse's thoughts, along with the assigned rehabilitation facilities, proclaimed as such in the official Unification rhetoric. They are nothing of the sort.

▼ ▼ ▼

Nepharisse follows the whispers inside her heart to the cell where the murderer is to commune with They and repent, in order to become one with They. Her journey impels her across expansive waters that are seething with virulence and charged with anger. Although she is not the object of the ocean's fury, her resolve is duly tested. She disembarks at low tide, slices through the vertical cliff comprising the compound's liquid foundation, and swims into the ventilation system's exhaust biotubes. Once in the shafts, she glides to her target.

As she nears the correct location in the detainment catacombs, a far cry from a humane environment, she rifts inch by inch into the meter thick stone partitions as she travels along it from the inside. Once in position, the granite softens for the recorder that is poised to bring her some notoriety, within a certain circle. The voice beyond the transmuted rock, repeatedly knifing the resigned tenant with its verbal attacks, is as clear as the last pure water source on the planet. This purity also lives behind a fortress only a select few can access, although its keepers exhibit a much greater level of respect for their ward.

The whimpering scorched charcoal figure in the corner still shows some spirit in the face of her insolent assailant. Nepharisse and her recording device digest it all, except that, in her case, the drama results in nausea and judgment. So this is what happens when one acts in a manner that invokes the holy Pramam's displeasure. These violations are not in keeping with the avowed clemency of a messenger of the Unification's divine mission. Mysterious are Their ways indeed, but perfect They are not.

▲ ▲ ▲

The unsettling sound of stenopods upon stone scuttling towards Nepharisse seem strangely misplaced, until she realizes that her body and mind are in two different locations. In this instance, she quickly deems it best to let the body be the instrument of the mind and crawls at a supernatural pace, leading the immobilizer carrying crabbot into a frenetic chase. A quick peek behind to assess her advantage reveals a gloved hand releasing a second eight-legged soldier in the opposite direction. She is trapped.

The situation demands a prompt assessment. Rifting a hole in the holowall is suicide. Considering the atrocities that just transpired in the operating room, which she is positive are grossly beyond the URA mandate, the disturbance would immediately activate the second line defenders. Her chosen course is, therefore, not the lunacy a naive observer would regard it as. Nepharisse faces the amethyst wall, takes a deep breath, aims the emitter, and swan dives into the night sky.

Her blue sapphire shoes finesse a body roll onto the east spiral tower, and, with another fluid leap of faith, Nepharisse emerges from an airy tumble into the north clearing for an unscathed escape through the orchard. The furious echo of pincers, snapping nine stories above her, fades as she approaches perimeter security at the north gate of the Schrödinger University campus island. She smiles her way past the guard to the Victory Bridge and stops. Her heart races.

A soul piercing feeling pulls Nepharisse's focus to the ninth-floor window in the J tower of the student residence complex, the same feeling of dread she had on her first day in Eadonberg, almost nineteen years ago. Elize is staring back at her. The evil has returned.

E L I Z E

Another hot night? Don't I have a fan around somewhere. Good. There it is. It's nothing too fancy, but it does the trick. Giggle. I feel like a princess with this flutterbot flapping its wings at me. Oh, I like that thought. Come to think of it, I've had a lot of good thoughts lately. Sigh. I feel great! Except for these random heat episodes. Hang for a sec! Is that who I think it is?

What is she doing over there? I thought the counsellor told her to stay off campus. Or rather, "his holier-than-the-Pramam forbade her further contact with us," according to Keet. Speak of the pup.

"Hey lo, Keet."

"Happy birthday, Eli." Ohhhm gee, he's singing. Don't quit the archives. Not that he'd ever consider that. He was born with a book worm up his butt. Hehehe. OK. Long enough.

"Thanks, p— POP star." At least I think that's what they're still called. I'm not much into dazing anymore. That was Caroline's little obsession, not mine. I'm past all that now, or so I hope.

"Eliiiiiiiii, you were going to call me *pup*!" Hick! How do I *weedel* my way out of this one.

"No, I wasn't. I was just imitating that p-pop sensation. Th-the g-group f-from A-Albaraaton th-that d-does th-that d-double-take th-thing. You the know the one, eh?" He's quiet.

I think I hooked him.

"You mean the t-t-triple-take th-th-thing. Trimorphic Rhythms is their name."

"Yeah, right. Well, our birthday is not until tomorrow."

"I know. I just wanted to beat Stitch to the jab." Will these two boys ever get tired of the one-ups? I honestly don't understand why Keet seems so threatened by him. It's that self-confidence issue again, I fig. I thought he got rid of that after last year's adventures. He's regressed back into his cocoon. Spending hours on end digging into ancient civilizations and such.

"It's 11:43, Keet. I'm sure he's busy tearing the soul out of some unfortunate piece of technology and morphing it into something useful." Stitch never seems to run out of ideas.

"Yeah, annoyingly useful." Maybe it's his resourcefulness that Keet envies. "Anyway, I meant to comm you earlier today, but the curator has me working on a new shipment of artifacts that are just the most fascinating timepieces I have ever seen or even read about. They have all sorts of gears and pins and gold faces and—"

Here he goes again. Jabbering away about *more* relics. It's hard to believe we're related let alone twins. I'm more interested in exploring, going places, talking to people, the outdoors … you know … living things. Like those weedels over there by the pond, vacuuming up the weeds to keep the stone paths nice and tidy. They're quite the little swimmers. They clean up the pond lining voraciously too.

I wonder what would happen if the hybrid architects amped their production line and started some weedel warfare with the oceans. They could eat up all the junk at the bottom, and then we wouldn't need biowalls anymore. Hmmm. How many would we need. Trillions? Pica trillions? Ziga trillions? With no predators they'd have a feast. But what about when they're done cleaning? All these cute little furry sucking machines would go after the flowers. Not good. I like the colors and fragrances all over the city during the day. And they remind me of Mother. Especially that indigo one on the pond right there. Whoa! It's so huge and bright tonight. It looks just like Mother's jewel but … tonight? What is it doing awake at this hour? Sigh. I miss Mother.

"Eli? Are you here?" He sounds worried. He thinks I've started blacking out again.

"Of course, fishy." That's good. Be the strong one. Or maybe that was too harsh. We're in this together. We promised. "Sorry, Keet." He's quiet. "I'm fine. I'm just thinking about Mother. I can't believe we've been here almost a year and still no answers."

"It's all juicy." Hehehe. Better leave that one alone. "I can't believe we've been here almost a year and Father hasn't found us yet. He's up to something."

I wouldn't put it past him. "Do you think we made a mistake, Keet?"

"What do you mean?"

I'm feeling even warmer. When will these night flashes stop! "Coming here. We're fugitives in plain view of those who hunt us."

"They don't know who we are." And neither do we, apparently.

"How can you be sure? They seem to know a heck of a lot about us." Even Stitch does. I know he's a genius, but if he can find private information on our background, then the Ministry certainly could. "Besides, Father is on the inside. And he knew the killer."

I can't help but feel responsible for Mashrin. She didn't deserve to have her brain ripped apart like that, the poor girl. No. I'm not to blame. It was no accident. No. I did *not* choose her. Shudder. Sick wack! I have to stop replaying the fight. But still. I wish I could remember babysitting Mashrin. It would be easier for me to wipe the flash of her lying there. What I need is a happy memory. Like I have of Teddy. Thank the little baby prophet — he's safe now. "Huh?"

"Eli, are you paying attention?"

Did my pocket just stick to my underwear or something? "Yeah … barely … ummm … not really." I need some sleep. I feel like … the walls are closing in … Someone's out to get me.

"Get some sleep. Mother will always be with us." In my dreams he means. Wipe that thought. I don't want those nightmares again. Never again. Don't even entertain that thought, girl. What's in this pocket? Crap!

"Goodnight, Keet. And Happy birthday, officially now."

It's the rock. Did I put it in there? It's been locked up for months. How could it be in my pocket? I specifically programmed my privyshelf to bite if anyone reached for it. And no bite marks on my hands.

Stitch? At this time of night? Quick. Back to the privyshelf for you, little rock. Can't have you in my pocket. Don't want

Mashrin on my brain anymore. Geez. The thing is all gums. No time to pick through the shag for it. Just don't toss it around, OK?

"Way, Eli. Happy birthday!" Keet won't be happy to know Stitch beat him to the gift.

"Ta, chum … I think … What is it?"

It's a nice enough blue crystal urn. Not sure what's in it though. He looks very excited to give it to me. Bouncy even. His wormy hair would be doing a calypso right now if he hadn't chopped it off and dyed his new haircut, ugh, fluorescent red. Better go easy on my squished frog face. Just the same. I have to ask.

"What is it?" Stop tickling my toes, you little tentacles. Something cold. Crap! The rock! I hope Stitch doesn't see me fidget. Maybe if I bury the piece into the rug with my heel …

"It's called a sleeping—" I'm jam. That nasty rock. Ouch. He got to it first. Kick the shag. Traitor. "Is there something you want to share?"

This is just like during the quake at Tir-na-nog last year. Mashrin's rock is in my pocket, and I have no clue how it got there. Well, it's not Stitch. I haven't seen him all day, and I distinctly remember my pockets empty this afternoon. Not even a wipe for the drippy flyer bake I ate. Juicy. I feel guilty now for suspecting him in the first place. Oh, stop beating yourself up, Eli. We really didn't know him then.

"It's just a rock, Stitch." Grab it. Creeps! His hair is turning black. What has he done with it now?

"It's not just a rock, Miss Elize." Hey give that back … or not … Yeah you can have it. Whoa. He's blowing. "It's red

Aswan granite!" His hair is turning red. Now he's happy. I guess. "Where did you get this? It's very rare." He is engrossed by it.

"Red ass what?" Oh, that sounded wrong.

"Aswan. Trip. Where did you get this?" He flips the rock back to me.

I fumble. The shag is happy again. Right, you play while I *weedel* another story. Here it goes. "I found it in the ..." quick think fast, "actually Keet found it in the ..." oh no, Stitch's roots are black "the ..." Stop staring at his hair! "Ummm. Your hair!" What's so funny?

"You're not a very good liar, Eli." His hair is blue now, and I'm way dunked on this one. He notices my squashed frog face. "Mood hair. I recycled the wriggly frequency sensors. I was tired of washing their mud off my scalp." Dizzy. That deserves a tongue out. His foot is tapping.

Just switch to your toes. No. Heads up, girl. You can trust him. No. Don't. Keet will stomp. I can't decide. Just focus on your feet, and maybe he'll let it ride, like he's done before. He steps towards me. So it's a shoe to toe now. Here comes the chin raise with his finger. Look away. At what? The window. Imagine drawing smiley faces on it. That's better. And a heart. No way. It's getting hot in here. Keep your eyes shifting, girl. To the door. Back to the window. It can't be! Blink. Look again. Phew. Nothing there. My imagination is too vivid. And he's still staring. Eli, you know what happens when you look at him. Concentrate. Oh, what's the use. Let's get this over with.

"Trust, Eli. That's what chumbuds do. Trust."

Control it. Don't fidget.

He stretches out his hand towards me. That's my cue. Down comes my fist and slap goes his second palm flat from above. The chumbud salute seals the deal, as always. The blue in his hair saturates. OK. Time for some honesty.

"It was Mashrin's. And no, I didn't steal it. It just showed up in my pocket."

"Just now?" Cringe. How can I frame this. "You found this last year, didn't you?" I'm mute. Come on words. "And Keet told you to keep it a secret, didn't he." Double-cringe. Back to black? No? Gold? Now *he's* speechless. Hmmm. That's not a bad color on him. Have I seen him as a blonde before? "I don't know whether to be angry or hurt. But I'm trip with it. You two have been through a lot. You're still my chumbuds." There's that big smile of his, followed by the familiar poke on the arm of course.

What a relief! I smile back. "Slap me, Stitch." I duck. "It's creepy how this stone keeps showing up. You know, I've been stable for months now, ever since …" I don't have to finish that. He was there. He's always there for me. And here I am keeping secrets. Sigh. Who's in charge up there anyway? Yeah. I'm talking to you, brain. Don't answer. It was a rhetorical question.

"Well, if it's so rare, too bad the thief who took my mother's jewel didn't know any better and take the broken piece of ass wand instead."

"Aswan." He tries to look serious but bursts out laughing instead. "You're cute." Another poke and a smile. Hehehe. Relationship rescued. Yuck! Not that kind. "The jewel will show up somewhere. It's just a matter of time. A gem like that just doesn't assalam without a trace. Someone is going to fence it and get some major credit for it. I sent a flare in the maze. The Gadlins will be wanting their hands on it, yeah." His hair is developing a pinkish hue now. "So … you're blanking out again."

"No, I'm not!" I just told him I was fine. "I didn't take it."

Stitch hangs back. "Ease, Eli. I'm not accusing you, yeah?" He looks up at the patch job in the corner of the ceiling. Oh right. The hole Keeto used to escape campus lockdown last year after the creepy three found Mashrin's body.

"It's sealed. No one is getting in again." Or out for that matter. "I made up a story for building maintenance and they took care of it. It's just like new."

"Perk. Your room is not frequency tight anymore." He stands there looking at me, like I'm supposed to know what he means by that. Am I missing something?

"And that' s important because …"

"I'm dunked on that one. All I know is that your room used to wipe out the background noise in my biochip. It was pica calming, until you cut the ceiling open. Then the interference came back. I fig there's frequency broadcasting that messes with my biochip."

"I had no idea, Stitch. Constant noise?"

"A high pitch. I get migraines. As long as I have Odwin's herbal magic potion, I'm trip." We wiggle our fingers for a spooky effect. "I've had them as long as I can remember but it's not like hearing voices, yeah?"

He has a point. But in my case they're just episodes. The

humming in his brain is constant. "How come you haven't gone completely bent yet? On second thought. I take that back." Ouch. I point to his hair.

He pokes me and winks. Here comes a purple mane now. "At least, you won't have to squirm anymore every time I get too close to you."

Register that. Purple equals mushy. Let's play coy with this. "Oh reaaaaaally. Well, should I be wary of a certain telltale hue?"

"That would depend on what you want to be wary of, chum."

OK, right. This is getting awkward. Say something. "So ..." Something else. Help me out here, Stitch.

He clears his throat and his straight cut turns green. He notices the shag lobbing the Aswan granite chunk around the room, picks it up, and hands it over. "Interesting choice of colors."

He's referring to my new decor. "I was looking for a challenge during the break." I guess my adrenal glands were wanting after things settled down. "I figured out how to program my room selector and discovered that most of the virtafurniture is from the Stew Über Home Collection. I couldn't decide which of three palettes I liked the most, so I tapped the merge and shuffle option and this is what I got."

"Pica eclectic. Pica trip! Remind you of someone?" Ohhhm gee. He's not ribbing me. Stitch blends right in. "Flip me the room controller, Eli." I'm not so sure about that. "Chumbud?"

"With my life, not my decor, Stitch." I know he's up to something.

"Perk. I could rig the device to key on your mood instead." He sidles up to me and whispers covertly. "Then I'll know when you're being sneaky, when you're keeping secrets."

Zapped. I fell right into that. That still deserves a snare. And why not a shove too. Yawn. "Time for me to lie low, Stitch."

Stitch picks up the present he brought and places it on the neon orange and fuchsia polka-dot virtatable by my moss-textured four-poster virtabed. "You can't let anyone know you have this, yeah? It's not strictly speaking legal."

He must be ribbing me. "A jar full of flyer mud is going to get me clamped?"

He signals for me to hush and gets secretive again. "It's soil." My jaw drops. Not literally of course.

"Whoa! You mean ancient soil? Where did you—?"

"Shhh. Remember who's next door. Keeping this quiet is pica crit!" He smooths over the dirt to make it level. I think there's something inside it. "Don't touch it and tomorrow morning, I mean, this morning you'll see something special. Chumbud swear you won't be digging anything up?"

Dig? Me? That's Keeto's craziness. I won't be putting my hand in that stuff. "Chumbud swear."

"Pica trip. Sweet dreams, chum."

And they will be sweet not sweat. I'm finally sleeping straight through the night after over nine years of torturous nightmares. Now I can give myself permission to relax. No more tears.

"You too. Ta for the sleeping surprise." He grins and dances out.

Well, little red ass wand, no more magic acts. "Open up, privyshelf." You're back on duty. "And this time keep your mouth shut." I didn't mean now. Stop gritting your teeth. Fine. A piece of flyer bake then? That's it, yum it up. Now if I can just sneak the rock right between the incisors. There. Hmmm. That's odd. The granite crystal bits are glowing? It must be a reflection from my virtalamp. I'll need to adjust the intensity.

All right. Off to a peaceful and serene dreamland. But before that, some last minute reading while I brush my teeth. Juicy. I get to try out my new geckohold. "Stay still, Mini-Lizzy, while I paste the slipbook on. What a nervous hybrid. Now for my pajama pants. What? Please tell me these things don't have crabseat attitude. So you want me to follow you around the room, is that it? That could be fun for a while but then quickly become incredibly annoying, like right now. "Get back here!" Ouch.

Face plant. "Thanks for the soft landing, shaggy." Ok. Now where did that geckohold go? Oh no. "Stay away from the privyshelf. Crap! Run away!" Whoa. I've never seen old toothy one snap so fast. Phew. No serious damage. The tail will grow back. And here comes the lizzy. If I can just reach the slipbook then … and there he goes. This creature seriously has a death wish.

Didn't I dim the light? Yeah. So why all the shadows. I'm not chasing the lizard this time. Let my snarly shelf have a go at it. No more hybrids for me. "Wait! My slipbook. No, not *behind* the shelf." That's strange. A light? Since when? Forget it. I'll deal with it all tomorrow.

✂ ✂ ✂

Eyes open. Aaaaaaaaah! Get off me!

KEETO

Tonight is a special night for journaling in many regards, not the least that it was nineteen years ago today that Eli and I shed your protective bubble, but also because this is the day Father's tenure at the URA has finally been revoked.

As I think back to last year at this time, Eadonberg was a mere dream in our hearts, and a bold plan in our minds. I could not have foreseen how much this city would change me. Eli, however, still regards me as a pup with a nose for the kind of adventures safely buried in books. There is a shard of truth in that statement, this I will admit, but only you, Mother, know what new thought processes my waking hours are entangled with and invade my sleep.

One such thought process has been more of a feeling than a concrete idea, the feeling that the beautiful stranger with the gemstone eyes, whom I bumped into on the hovertrain platform our first day in Eadonberg, still has a grip on me. I do not dare share this with Eli, as I suspect she will emphasize how easily Nathruyu manipulated me. "A puddle of mush" are the words I recall her using; nevertheless, I still hold fast to the belief that we had, and still have, a deep connection beyond the physical, a dimension Eli still does not acknowledge. But you understand.

The myrrh is what joins us, that much I sense quite literally, since olfactory frequencies appear to have a VIP ticket to events evoking intense memories. At least for this pup they do. Unfortunately, for Eli, the connection is not quite as pleasant. The nightmares are where her visions of you lie, which involve Nathruyu in complicity with scenes that had haunted her for nine and a half years.

I say "had" because, for the past six months, Eli no longer suffers from the nightly terrors and the morning tremors. The dreams, the voices, the blackouts, and the hallucinations have finally ended. And all the panic I felt, paralyzed with the fear that she would end up as you did, in a padded cell at the GHU, subsided. Coincidentally, this transformation immediately followed the capture of the woman I continue to sense. Or could it be serendipity?

This morning I shot out of bed at six, to the sound of Sparky barking and my comm playing the tune of my favorite archeologist. It was Eli. She was screaming. My instantaneous reaction was that her nightmares had returned. My heart sank at the thought of my worst fears manifesting. When I recognized that her voice was not only shrill but also wavering between inaudible and intolerable, my heart shattered. She was fighting for her comm, while someone, or something, was assaulting her.

I exploded out of my crypt, with barely one leg in my pants and my satchel dragging behind me, and crashed into the J-tower lobby. As I blistered by the guard, a hunch came that whatever Eli was battling had best be kept hidden from campus security. My intuition did not fail me although my ego readily did. The gift with which Stitch had preempted my own birthday surprise was manhandling, or should I say leafhandling, my sister in a way that suggested a territorial dispute. My personal challenge was to blanch the vivid fantasy of throttling Stitch from my mind, and to focus on subduing his recklessness in leaving Eli alone to deal with an ornery hybrid. Privately, however, I gloated. My thoughtful present was far superior.

If I had known ahead of time how harmless a behemoth this botanical frankenstein was, I would have rivaled Stitch in a howling match. The green abomination, with a monstrous pink flower as its thinking center, was bowed over Eli, muffling her screeches by playing a leaf-to-hand slapping game with her mouth. Its stems served as arms with grippers securing its blue urn from tilting.

Although there was much flaying and swinging, it did not have the strength to drag its base to the floor. After getting to know the creature afterwards, I appreciated that it was not lack of power, but finesse that kept its roots well protected, for the shag had flattened and had opted to let gravity be the judge in the event of a fall.

Out of my satchel came the Swiss army knife that I bought from Mr. G. He always carries the best antiques. I have become quite a patron of his Tir-na-nog shop. I even run errands for the curator at the Museum of Antiquities. And since Mr. G keeps no records of his suppliers, that tactic keeps me dependent on him like a junkie. I wager that the means by which he acquires his distinctive inventory do not comply with Unification trade laws, which gives my indulgences all that much more cachet.

Upon seeing my folding scissors, Eli rejoiced in a state of gratitude for what she would normally refer to as a useless relic, but the insolent guest had the opposite reaction. It pasted its body of stems against the wall, and resigned itself to my tiny weapon. Apparently it was petrified by the sight of its own fluids, a psychological trait designed into its DNA as a security feature "just in case", as Stitch later confessed. That boy is reckless.

After the ordeal was under control, I managed to step back and breathe in Eli's new room decor. As unpalatable as this is to accept, Stitch's shop of horrors addition to her new environment was right at home, once the plant had surrendered to its subordinate rank within the Simone homestead. The sleek minimalistic furniture with its low profile, the well-manicured shag with its tentacles pressed and raked into interlocking swirls, and the precisely placed water features, complete with sound effects and a hint of quince blossom, provided a calm canvas for the elegant monstrosity. I found the floor to ceiling waterfall particularly soothing. Eli, on the other hand, just sat up on her sleeping platform stunned and confused.

We had planned to exchange gifts first thing in the morning, yet in my haste, I had forgotten to bring hers. She assured me that she was fine, just rattled, so I ran to my mausoleum living space, in the back garden of the Museum of Antiquities, and rushed back with the big surprise: a personal viewing tent large enough to house two adults.

Eli loved it. Not only did she rave about the immersive quality of the holographs, she also valued having access to any flashes she wants, without having to plan ahead to reserve a viewing room in the V-wing of the residence complex. I was right on credit. Sometimes I know my sister better than I know myself. And other times? I suppress who I am, afraid of what I may become. A foreign consciousness is always trying to reach me, or rather trying to lure me into reaching for that towards which I am bound. I fear the fate I am fleeing is the same fate you were seeking. Then, there is Eli. What is she fleeing?

As my eyes rest at the niche in my crypt, where your spirit lives inside worldly possessions, a thought is flowing through my quill. If we could trap our future in a treasure chest to consult whenever we feel doubtful, just like we do with the past through lullabies in a box that recapture our childhood when we long for comfort, then Eli's present to me, a songstress inside an exquisitely carved case, overflowing with your melodious voice, would be inside that chest, for I consider no treasure a future without you in the depths of my soul.

Please forgive my smudged script while I pause to wipe those same tears Eli and I cried this morning, when we listened to your ballads, together.

Now I continue.

A few songs into the collection, we discovered that we were not the only ones connecting with the music. Stitch was an obvious audience, but the plantrocity which, just minutes ago, was sprawled against the wall, resisting any attempt for us to move it away from the virtabed, was also eavesdropping. It softened and even responded playfully to a spontaneous game of peek-a-boo with Stitch, who was shocked at its enormous stature. He called it a toy lo-flower, but he figged Mr. G had sold him a standard one by mistake.

Eli was still not impressed. After a night wondering whether

her Mini-Lizzy would spring from behind the privyshelf and drop a Wayne Dyer slipbook on her head, she was not warm to the idea of a gigantic blossom, with multiple eyes, watching her while she slept. Stitch assured her that once it became acclimatized to its new surroundings, it would stop staring. Apparently, it is also quite the sound sleeper.

The lo-moth qualities are simply aesthetic as opposed to functional. And yes, Eli did say *Wayne Dyer*. I almost fell over onto Stitch's lap. Shudder. Clearly she is not the same splintered spirit who has masqueraded as my sister, for the past nine years. Where she found a slip version of this twenty-first century book is a mystery to me. Fulfilling wishes is not what the Unification preaches.

I feel compelled to share with you, and you alone, that as much as Stitch and I maintain an undercurrent of competition, and I personally have trust issues with him, he has an uncanny talent for winning you over, including in the worst of circumstances. I think this is due to his generous and attentive nature, because the birthday gift he gave me was absolutely perfect. In fact, I am writing in it at this very moment.

The journal is leather-bound, with the same etchings as my new songstress's case. Eli categorically denies having colluded with Stitch on the purchase. Regardless, I added an appreciative highland hug to our usual chumbud salute. When you look through the page towards a light source, you can see an image referred to as a watermark with the year this particular journal was created. In about three weeks, Mr. G will be receiving a whole shipment, each of them originating from different eras. Juicy! Guess where I am headed.

Stitch was genuinely moved by my enthusiasm, as was evidenced by the pale blue hue to his hair, but this slowly faded to the grey his anxious foot tapping generated.

Odwin is missing.

Stitch's Gadlin mentor is no longer responding to any communications in the maze, which implies that something, or someone, is driving Odwin underground. No one is talking. The chumbuds network has been quiet, too quiet. Although Odwin regularly practices inward retreats, coincidentally just a few months before Eli and I arrived in Eadonberg, this time the hiatus is uncharacteristically long. When I pressed Stitch to be more exact, that old inkling of distrust thickened the space between us. Musings behind his eyes hinted at suspicion, as if I had a hand in Odwin's disappearance. A brand of conspiracy theory was no doubt floating around underneath where his squigglers used to be.

Although Eli habitually feigned revolt at the wormy mess on Stitch's head, she had come to enjoy terrorizing them. Today, all she could do was poke fun at his bright pink strands. But Stitch was not bantering back, for the matter remained disconcerting. The day Nathruyu was clamped marked the day his friend and master went silent.

The woman who has assumed temporary leadership of the underground network, in Odwin's absence, has locked Stitch out of the inner circle. He is not comfortable with the new direction, or lack thereof. His queries attract vague responses, and Wakanda's Pramam-like communication style breeds distrust between the Gadlin and non-Gadlin members of his chumbuds community. Her motives are unclear.

Stitch has only met her once, very briefly. She lurked in the background during a private meeting Odwin had summoned him to, silent but watchful, like a kittybot before a strike. I personally have not met this woman and should really form my own opinion, but my radar raises its antennae whenever Stitch utters her name.

The shakeup in the maze is not the only shift happening these days. On the day Odwin went into solitude, the meteor showers, which had started three months before we arrived, left as quickly as they had come. Eadonberg's population also seems to have expanded in the past six months.

The walkways and hovertrains are no more crowded than they were, nor are the queues at the Snack Shack for the world's most delicious flyer bakes, but I just get a twinge that space is closing in. I notice it most when I am really present, like I am now with you, in my journal. Ridiculous, I know, but maybe the paranoia I wrongly assumed Eli was exhibiting as Nathruyu drew closer has decided to attach itself to me instead.

These events occupied my mind as I walked back through the orchard on my way to the archives. If it were not for the feathery brush on the back of my neck, I would not have seen the red GHU emergency craft racing towards me, sucking up pretty much every student in its path.

I whipped behind a tree just in time to avoid a quick trip to the "special" quarantine cells they have for "irresponsible citizens" with unresponsive biochips, who apparently put the whole city at risk for potentially terminal viral infections. What they actually mean is that they throw people they cannot trace into their sub-level dungeons and perform brain experiments on them until they die. But somehow, you were spared and were upgraded to a padded cell for non-invasive observation instead. I, for one, had no interest in taking that chance.

A GHU convoy swarmed the campus. It was a full search and seize operation, and I was stuck right in the middle of it. I ran to the East Gate of Rubrique Court, dodging a red energy tube fortunately three steps behind me. There, I witnessed a fallen student at the Nook, trapped in the energy beam meant for me and sucked into the hull of a GHU slider.

I commed Eli for help. I told her to keep a low profile, to sneak up to her corner window, and to talk me through a flyer's eye view of the mayhem below. From her vantage point, she was able to direct me away from the GHU vehicles. Then, she whispered a shriek. Both the north and southeast gates off the island were blockaded. I was trapped.

I ran back for cover in the citrus grove and paused to think. I quickly remembered that, last year, Sothese's hounds had chased the dark figure while I was hanging off the lower link between the J and I branches of Van Billund Hall, escaping lockdown, and they were left unconscious in the south clearing, near a sun catcher in the shrubbery, while their prey had vanished. So I trusted my instincts, and bolted for a secret entrance to the Schrödinger University ventilation shafts I was convinced I would uncover.

And I did. The GHU caught sight of me, running through the northwest gap; however, their zigzag maneuvers proved too slow to catch me, and, for a fraction of time, I could smell the myrrh guiding me to my salvation.

I dove into the sunshaft head first and rolled. As I lay there on my back, stunned, breathless, and shivering, I could hear the hunters flying back and forth, confused. Once I was certain they had resigned themselves to my escape, I summoned my inner compass to usher me northwards inside the dim steaming labyrinth. When I reached the tunnels beneath the north gate, I realized that there was no way off the island from below. I had to wait out the blood-curdling screams, echoing through the shafts, so I focused on the voices blocking my exit.

GMU guards were speculating as to whether the GHU could contain the virus. A doctor working the night shift in Osler Hall had succumbed to strange lesions on his body, which suggests a form of accelerated decay. Interrogations and swabbing the ninth level of the central tower, where the medic was working, have not revealed any probable external causes. They believe a malfunction in the biochip might be triggering DNA deformities of some sort.

That is about as scientifically sound as the hearsay got. They added that their best defense against a full scale epidemic was to screen every single resident, starting with those most at risk, the students. All I could think of at that point was *Eli*. But then I remembered about her room saving us from the GMU sweep last year, and relaxed.

If you ask me, paranoia is the real contagion here, and the GHU has plenty of it, never mind their fair share of stupidity as well. There is no logic in screening. No. This is a pretense for more sinister intentions. But what?

I wish I could blame this on Father. It would certainly clarify my mixed emotions for him, and tip them onto the side of hatred, which is all he deserves, after what he did to you.

However, responsibility for the draconian measures that the Unification's Global Health Unit is exercising, most likely lies with the acting URA director who, by happenstance, is none other than the Pramam's advisor. We still do not know what treachery Father is now leading.

My crystal!

Phew. I thought I had lost it in the shafts. I had hidden it under my mattress. Given that Nathruyu wore one just like it, except indigo not blue, it might attract Ministry attention towards me. Not that I am paranoid or anything, but I was getting the impression that strangers were staring at my neck. Not that I am paranoid or anything.

Who's there? Who's talking?

Soon.

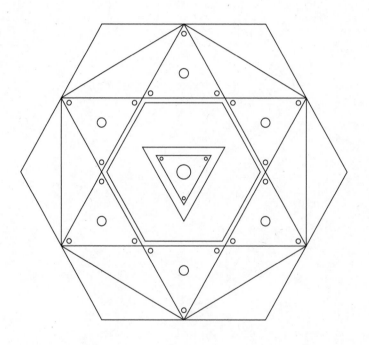

CHAPTER TWO

Day 372: daytime

An epidemic? Nepharisse titters. The GHU is quick to concoct all manner of excuses to keep themselves busy. She fills the next bowl with today's nutritional broth and places it on a disgruntled cafeteria attendant's tray. Her endearing simper enchants the indignant look on his face. He responds with a boyish smile and returns to his hospitality duties as her eyes float back down to the cauldron, to scoop another ladle full and offer it to the next cafeteria attendant.

The newly imposed pandemic protocol precludes direct contact with the medics and administrators that Nepharisse requires for her aims. Personal access to the buffet being newly restricted hampers her ability to impress the hungry patrons with her lyrical voice. Her revised tactic must breech the distance between the food counter and the seating area, which, for such mesmerizing eyes as hers, is not as onerous as one might think. A focused intent always returns the undivided attention she seeks, and a directed gaze, with three subtle flutters of her lashes, is all she needs to penetrate an open vessel.

The Unification has resolved to trap the source of the recent accelerated decay through sweeping measures, which are but vanity. Decay does not exist. It is merely one manifestation of the manmade construct of time. The fog in their brain is as thick as that which lingers along the coastal cities. Centuries still reflect the inner world that is within all those who have chosen to remain inside the mist of unconsciousness. And now, memory loss has joined the ever-growing list of consequences, perversely misconstrued as symptoms.

The real culprit here is humanity. This ill-fated breed will no sooner cure the affliction than Earth will have managed to eradicate the infestation that they are, no matter how much testing, confining, and cutting they perform. The disease, at its core, shall remain and continue to evolve at a predetermined pace, sometimes slowly attacking the skin, and other times consuming their host within minutes. There is no cure. The GHU will discover no antidote. A complete sub-cellular reset is the only remedy.

As Nepharisse drifts into thought, the emerging hysteria in the dining room extends into a methodical choreography executed in time-warping detail. GMU operatives seal the exits. Chaos becomes order as bioshielded GMU guards target several high-tenure medical staff, shackle them with reverse bioshields, and rope them into a protesting chain-gang, presumably for their personal safety and that of those fortunate enough to have escaped the current roundup. Their turn is nevertheless imminent, as is Nepharisse's.

Now that the Pramam has ordered the Global Military Unit to contain the contagion, efficient large-scale sweeps have infected the city, allowing the GHU to concentrate its efforts on collecting blood samples, analyzing their DNA structures, and updating the corresponding medi files. The official Inner Council position is to screen all Eadonberg residents, as expeditiously as possible. The holy decree, however, excludes whoever has foregone Unified life and subsists inside the Restricted Sector. These are the lost ones.

They are the ones who cling to their freedom from a biochip prison by voluntarily caging themselves within a hydrogen sulfide infested fortress that the Ministry would rather strike from historical records.

They are the ones who lurk in the ventilation shafts, looking for opportunities to surface when situations of special interest to them present themselves.

They are the ones that the GHU has, as of yet, been unable to trace and are a potential source for concern far worse than the current manufactured emergency, suffocating the liberties of the impressionable Eadonberg residents. Nepharisse knows their kind all too well.

A GMU unit corals the catering staff into the kitchen. Inside a silver case they carry are reverse bioshields, one for each of their captives. These portable quarantine devices are the pride of the Unification Research Arm's director, presumably leading a secret project at a remote test site, and today is their first deployment in a real world containment operation. Their usefulness cannot be overemphasized, for Eadonberg's current state of emergency is now able to unfold in secret, while intercity business and trade flourish amidst a clever camouflage that the Ministry can blanket the political landscape with, as the Pramam crafts health and prosperity propaganda for public broadcast.

Ignorance and misinformation are the Ministry's choice weapons in this psychological battle that stymies potential civic unrest. The Pramam knows that his self-proclaimed divine authority prevails unchallenged only as long as the veil of serenity endures. The contagion need not be announced, for those who must know already do, and those who should not will find out through covert channels.

A systematic medical assault begins. The lead tagger binds each employee, while the nurse acquires the blood samples, until the final vial is marked for Nepharisse, who, in turn, winks at her co-worker and leads her captor into a light and frivolous conversation that ends with a pat on his lapel button and a "targets neutralized, samples secured."

Nepharisse's smooth ivory skin remains unspoiled. She smiles at the attending nurse's fleeting confusion as the tube that could have preempted her evening plans drops into Nepharisse's open palm, along with two more, and all three promptly disappear into her pocket. The staff are released.

Back in the cafeteria, Nepharisse tunes in to a muted discussion between two female intern students from Dr. Tenille's special crew. The soft vibrations, tickling the inside of her ears, carry a jumbled message of relief, perplexity, and discontent from the fidgety one, Elize, at the far table against the slip racks. Her classmate is blank. The ordeal has left her trawling for thoughts.

The restless one, on the other hand, relays her shock that the GMU should suddenly abandon their maneuvers, and she silently entertains paranoid theories that perhaps their unexpected retreat is a tactical gambit designed to trick her into a false sense of anonymity, only to ready her cell in the psychiatric wing, by special request of her father, the URA director and secondary advisor to the Pramam himself.

Nepharisse would love nothing more than to be the one to help Elize understand what is really happening to her, and to explain to her what she really is, but it is not her place to do so. This Nepharisse must remember. She is not to initiate direct contact, lest she is willing to suffer his ultimate reproach.

Those who interfere with the unfoldment meet with a stern teacher. That fact is unequivocal. She must accept her passive role, as surely as Elize must uncover her own answers. Nepharisse's duties as carrier pigeon must supplant her desire to liberate the inner hawk, for the power and stealth of a bird of prey lacks the docile qualities necessary for subtle influence. This is the talent with which she is gifted and for which she is valued.

Notwithstanding, passive complicity in matters which could actively benefit from her captive intensity does not satisfy her visceral longing for praise, and for the second time in a fortnight, the wings in her heart transport her back to her first visit to Schrödinger University.

Nepharisse's fear tunnels down the central walkway and into the northwest window on the top floor of J-branch. The sun has already invited the moon to lull the white, rose, violet, and blue petals, resting atop the milky lavender waters of the central canal, into a deep peaceful sleep. But on the campus oval, there lives a pond which refuses to turn down its bedding for its solitary indigo tenant, which blooms with a brilliance that suggests a light source shinning from within. This oddity is the concern for which Nepharisse was summoned, and which creeps inside the shivers in her veins.

From a distance, three cloaked figures, emerging from the foot of the Victory Bridge, appear to move as a unit, yet once they subdue perimeter security at the north gate of the campus oval, they fan out into the orchard. Haste is the force which impels Nepharisse to brave the noxious compounds lurking below the cloudy stagnant waters bathing the Central Core. She disrobes and dives naked into the eastern canal, her long powerful strokes leaving a euphonious ripple of bioluminescence in her wake.

As Nepharisse resurfaces at the perimeter woods, along the island's southeast gate, she adjusts her curly ginger-auburn bun, dawns a tailored suit and sapphire blue shoes from a waterproof chest she pulls from the channel, flattens the box, neatly arranges the beverages it housed, and presents herself to the watchman at the entrance, impeccable and dry, as if she had just drifted down from a hired slider. Her passage is granted, as expected. The musical click of her heels dances its way past the ivy covered wall and towards the side entrance to the J-branch lobby of Van Billund Hall.

Muffled screams from the ninth floor travel the silent night and shatter her hopes. Nepharisse loses mastery of her imagination as she projects a vision of loneliness and wanting into the dark. A cloaked figure parts the curtain of her lucid dream and urges her onwards. The physical presence soothes and frightens her as two more gather to salvage what they came for.

The brief moment she so foolishly wasted, relinquishing the lead to her anxiety before plunging into the murky waters, may have cost her the favor that she aches for. Today, as always, she is to embody the distracting accessory that she wears so well. She bows her head in quiet compliance. Let those designed for the task assume the risks involved.

A bright flash from above signals that the situation will soon reach the point of no return. Nepharisse regains her focus and smiles her way into the lobby while, in plain view, the three shrouded infiltrators rush the lift shaft. The guard's hand pauses midway between her thigh and her secure belt and relaxes to the pleasantries replacing the confrontational tone that had opened the exchange.

The lobby is quiet. What a calm evening. Such a tranquil shift.

Relegated to the sidelines, Nepharisse underestimates her importance and her value. It is true that what comes to her with proficiency delivers potency through intention, though she presumes that the ease with which she penetrates the porous human psyche restricts her role to that of an eternally subservient deputy. If only she could enchant the self-doubt, the wizard of hesitation, into relinquishing its obsessive need to protect her, she could transcend the limits masquerading as truths. If only. If only.

The battle, nine floors overhead, echoes through the entire residence complex, oblivious to the J-wing guard whose serene thoughts serve to create a veneer of tranquility. The alarming reality is anything but.

Students flee from all floors, through the inter-branch links. The tower seals itself off. The photovoltaic cells in the lift overload with an inferno that melts the community board in the lobby. Nepharisse scoops up the confounded guard and crashes through the main entrance, narrowly missing three fireballs bursting out the ninth floor window and incinerating the broken glass, as they plummet onto the north clearing and explode.

The ensuing roar is only dwarfed by a meteor shower beating against the city biowall. Sirens blare as emergency crews fly to the southwest frequency generation tower, conveniently keeping all eyes away from the pandemonium on campus. Some distractions are clearly more memorable than others.

Nepharisse crouches to check the guard's vital signs and smiles. She comforts her companion as she subtly glances up at the tall balletic woman who is teetering on the ledge of the broken window while bouncing two little blue balls of light with her fingertips. Paloma Yarkovsky is in their hands now.

▲ ▲ ▲

Elize's eyes glaze over at Nepharisse for an instant, then resume their conversational state.

The clock announces the evening shift, but no exodus occurs.

Nepharisse looks down at her hands and wills them to steady the tray as she walks down the hallway. She enters the nursery, equipped with special delicacies for the nursing staff reeling from an unusually long day with nine deliveries. Their duties will continue into the night, for the GHU has reassigned half the regular staff to the DNA screening labs, leaving the devoted birthing team overworked and prone to potentially irreparable mistakes, a hazard which Nepharisse expects to reframe as divine providence.

Grateful tired faces greet her and her food tray, while she surveys the area for the newborn monitoring station. Her gaze drifts to a small room, connecting the infant ward to the delivery cells, which in turn lead to the recovering mothers, at the far end of the obstetrics level. Under normal circumstances, physical contact between mother and child immediately after birth is encouraged, but the insanity invading the private lives of GHU employees has also spread to the care of its patients, splintering the primordial bond between love and creation.

Until the baby's immune system is deemed intact, a holographic feed plays in the mother's cell so that she may virtually bond with her child. The long term effects of this emergency protocol are unknown, but, in the words of the Pramam himself, "the immediate health crisis outweighs the minor disruptions in Their natural processes."

This poisonous reasoning is what drove humanity to war, to famine, and to environmental collapse. Now the blight of illusion rules the world, and the future will rightly follow that which results from the application of universal law. Further analysis of his entire Holy address also discloses that the quiet transfer of parental rights, in the name of "the greater good", will ensure that the Unified religion propagates smoothly to subsequent generations, through the cooperation of the GHU.

Nepharisse aims to disrupt the Pramam's sanctimonious aspirations and secret ambitions. The three vials in her jacket pocket are ready for the sleight of hand. She draws information from a particularly exhausted nurse, who leads her to an incubator near the monitoring center. Her hands tremble inside her skin, as she watches the tiny human squirm with a spasmodic heart rate.

Alarms sound. Carebots take flight. Medics swarm. And Nepharisse slips into the observation room.

There are eight active boards relaying images between each mother and her infant. On the middle one, there are two cribs, as moving overlays, linked to a single woman. Swift is the word Nepharisse replays in her mind as she replaces the corresponding blood samples for these twins with two vials from her jacket pocket. She chooses a third child at random and quickly replaces that tube, as well. Satisfaction for a task well executed flows as a shiver around her body, announcing that it is time to recharge, yet something unnatural takes her attention away from her waning focus to the mother's image, connected to the smaller live feed on the board closest to her.

There is no one else in the scene other than the infant. A quick glance back into the actual nursery reveals that the medical emergency is still creating mayhem. Anger turns the key to Nepharisse's heart while she assesses the situation. The feed is looped as are the other eight. Insidious violations are no doubt taking place here without maternal consent, and her suspects have arrived.

Hers is not the only artful hand in the nursery.

Three members of the Unified clergy require no permissions to enter the realm of the newly landed. They waltz in, waving the staff out, and head for the blood sample display, but not before Nepharisse flicks on the recorders centered on the twins. She pauses at the doorway on her way to task number two of three this evening, and breathes a prayer for the little ones, whose souls have been bound.

The soundproofing in the new mother's cell cannot contain the despair unleashing itself in the woman's voice. Nepharisse smiles her way past the GMU sentry and enters a chamber of suffering she shall never know. There is no time to explain. Nepharisse's thoughts follow the wailing mother as the woman rushes for the open door and stops short, calmly turns back around, and gathers her belongings.

They are coming for you. You are coming with me. Your womb is a threat as your twins shall be.

Nepharisse leads the mother into the GHU underwater level, the dark confinement awaiting those who officially become a threat to themselves and to others. She is fully aware that she is currently helping a Ministry threat escape from the clutches of the GHU. Her only lament is not having formulated more blood sample decoys to further disrupt the Unified crusade. Regrettably, that confrontational position serves only to thwart the movement she defends towards the universal good.

A secret exit into the ventilation shafts opens as Nepharisse attaches a bioshield to her intellectually bound captive. The ducts are no place for a lady to linger. With the woman in tow, Nepharisse races south to the base of the Victory Bridge, making note of the shadows lurking in the nooks. She lures her torpid passenger, whispering verses to numb the senses, onto a Gadlin barge idling in the eastern canal, and transfers her charge to the cloaked merchant poised for a prompt departure, just as three officials cross the western canal. The watercraft vanishes southbound for its treacherous journey along the virulent coastline, with its captain's hooded face visible only in memory.

While Nepharisse celebrates her third success this night, with contained enthusiasm, the three officials await her next move. She vacillates.

Although she appreciates the joy her protective role bestows upon her with every woman she saves, she refuses to believe that her sole purpose is to assemble a collage of simple lackluster successes, while larger and more exacting assignments pass her by.

His approval is, nonetheless, an impelling motive for her to continue as directed. She chooses to flee with the thunder of six rabid boots on her sapphire blue heels.

ELIZE

Day 383: early morning

"We've been in here since 6 a.m., Eli. What are we looking for?" Keet is bored.

I don't blame him. I'm getting a little fidgety myself. Better control that or he'll think they're back. I don't want him to worry. Why not? Let him. It'll be good for him. You know it's coming. You know it's only a matter of time. Go ahead. Tell him. He'll find out anyway. No don't listen to her. She's destructive. She's trying to break you. Keep it secret. *Oppose no evil and it shall recede into nothingness.* Whoa! Give your head a shake, girl.

"What?" He's giving me that look. See what you've done? The silence is irritating, welcome, *emptiness.* "Stop peeking. There's no room for you in here." I'm talking to a plant now? At least it's not talking back to me. I do quite well with that on my own.

"Why don't you just tell Stitch that your room is too small for it?" The lo-flower is after Keet now. "Hey! Stop slapping me!" Hehehe. Saves me the trouble.

"Maybe you're right. We'll need to sneak it past the sentinels though. They always seem hungry."

"We could just dig it up." Yeah. Sounds like something Keet would suggest. Where did it go? Oh back in the corner, hugging its urn.

"That would just kill it." Juicy! Who needs a needy hybrid

anyway. What am I saying? I don't kill things. Yeah, that's right. You just choose who dies and forget about it. "Shut up!" "Just poked a rib. No need to blow, Eli." Crap! Did I say that out loud? If they could just leave me alone. He's giving me that look again. Quick. Change the subject before he asks.

"I've been flipping through the views since our birthday, and I should have found something by now. But nothing."

"What do you mean? We found the amethyst eyes. That's what Father was topped up about, right?" He grabs the controls and forwards through the cubes.

I really like having my own viewing tent, but the flashes were much easier to navigate in the viewing room. Just the same, it's safer to be up here rather than the V-branch common area. I just have to get used to moving the holographs through me, instead of moving through the scene. It's a bit bending at first though. Almost like being possessed by the ghosts of our ninth birthday guests. And when I switch to a different point of view, my own body passes right through me. Crazed. What's he doing?

"Keet. Don't switch so fast. You'll jam the projector." Crap. "Look what you did. You broke it, fishy!" At least it's better than calling him pup.

"It just stalled." Even he doesn't believe that. He's fumbling with the controller. Geez. Where's Stitch when we need him. Keet has more know-how in his head than anyone I know, but reading about it is not the same as living it.

"Right. Let me have a go at it." It does look stuck. OK. So let's try a less scientific approach. Arm up and—

"Hang. Don't bang it!" Whoops. Too late.

Juicy. It looks like a jumble effect. Better tap the pause button. Yum. Time for some holocake. I can still taste it. Even Father is licking his fingers and he's not even into sweetness … of any kind. That was so much fun. I miss the friends from our circle. It was our first party at the new home. The whole circle showed up. Jenny, Carmine, Yannick, Pascale, Babbel, Jiah, and the new kid. I forget his … and Keet and I, of course. And. Groan. Fath— "What the—"

"Maybe there was a cross-frequency, and we ended up picking up someone else's recorder."

"At *our* birthday party?" If Father is in the scene, then whose point of view are we playing in? Keet looks just as confused as I do. I don't remember anyone else there except … but she was outside the kitchen window, not in the study, and certainly not standing beside me. That's strange. Jenny's squiggle tails keep flipping around, but her head's not moving. And Jiah keeps slapping his neck. Why haven't I noticed this before. Oh right. Our eyes are all on the cake. Jumpers! My face is huge. It's like the lens is right up against me … upside down.

"Nice profile." A little playful nudge.

"So this is the part I remember. Turning to the wall, but seeing nothing." Whoa. My face is right side up again and even bigger. Why am I wiggling my nose? Ugh!

"Sure glad you're a hologram. Ewww. You used your sleeve."

"That's what kids do, Keet. What about you? Did you forget to tie your pants?" Hehehe. Bunny bum. Look at him hop hop hop. Ooooooooo. Smash face. Hehehe. Now I remember *that* part.

"And so do I." He's still embarrassed after all these years. Insecurities.

He's weak. He can't help you. Stop it! You know it. Look at him. Beakish, you called him. He's afraid of living. He says so himself. That's not true. Leave me alone. It's true and you know it. He's weak. Nathruyu got to him. She's a liar. Maybe … no … You're the liar. Go away.

Oh no. Oh no no no! I feel like my hands are going to explode. Slow down. The blood's pounding too hard under my skin. Oh no, it's happening. It's happening again. Breathe, breathe, breathe. Good, Keet's still focused on the flashes. Actually, he's focused on his butt. A little vanity perhaps? Hehehe. Was that a snare?

"Perk, look what happens when I slow down the playback." Perk? He's spending more time with Stitch than he admits. And all I see is more Keet caboose. Hehehe. OK. That's enough. "Look!"

"Keet, I get it. Now you've desensitized yourself to the trauma and have acquired a strange sense of pride." Another snare face. Seems like he's stealing everyone's trademarks now.

"No, fishy. Someone pulled my pants down. Gravity doesn't yank and pull."

"OK. Show me." This better not be another rib. Eye roll for effect. But … Ohhhm gee. He's right. "But there's no one there!" Double jumpers.

"Jumpers! Someone's in the room." Just a quick peek. If I can get away from Keet's death grip.

"TEDDY'S MISSING!" Phew. It's just Stitch. No panic. Or panic?

"Ease, Stitch. Whoa! Your hair is blacker than black. Why so topped up?"

"Teddy's missing!" I think part of his brain left with his squigglers. Is Keet still inside the party?

"He's hiding with the Gadlins, remember?"

"No. That's just it. He's not there, Eli. The Gadlin who adopted him is gone too." There must be a mistake. But it takes a lot to rattle Stitch, so maybe it's true.

"Hey lo, bud." Keet's done admiring his butt now and ready for a chumbud salute. This really is serious. Stitch is just going through the motions. Now Keet's worried. "What's wrong?" I'd better jump in. Stitch can't seem to come out with anything else.

"It's Teddy. He's missing. Stitch says—"

"Perk. There's more, chumbuds. Three more abductions. All kids Teddy's age. Nine-year-olds." That's horrible! Keet doesn't seem as disturbed by this as he should. A swift kick might coax the empathy out of him.

"Ouch! What was that for?"

"For being insensitive. Weren't you listening?" I hope he's not thinking about *her* again.

"Yeah. Of course, I'm upset." A pause. He *is* thinking about her. "That means they caught the wrong killer."

I knew it. I'm going to put an end to this right now. "Honestly! You are infatuated by her. That's why you didn't come for me yourself. You would have had to choose right then and there. It's so much easier to sit back in your comfy chair and let others take responsibility. When are you going to grow up, PUP! She's a liar and a thief and she murders children! She's still toying with you." You tell him, Elize. His loyalty is to her not you. You need to win him back. You need to be more like her. Are you bent? What's come over me?

Keet is speechless. Good. Don't even dare argue with me. Eli, let it ride! Who are you? Let Stitch take over. The blonde hair is back. My outburst is testing his loyalties too.

"Truce, Eli. I fig Keet cares about Teddy, yeah? But Eli has a point. In case you forgot, Nathruyu was pica cryptic with information, yeah? She can't be trusted. So —"

"Neither can the GHU, or the Ministry. Certainly not the Pramam." Or Father. But he's off somewhere. Hopefully, he won't surface. "Who knows what the real story is?"

"Exactly! We don't. So don't let your feelings get in the way of the facts, Keet." The facts, not what you want to believe.

"I'm not, Eli." Stitch knows what I'm talking about. An eye-lock confirms it.

Hair green and bopping to bioRhythms. The symptoms of normal. As normal as Stitch can be, that is. "Perk. I cleared you with the network. You're in."

"Juicy!"

Keet is still a bit miffed. "What took so long?"

Stitch tries to ignore Keet's apparent lack of gratitude, but it's hard to hide behind his new hair statement. At least with the wormy mess, they were always busy moving around so we could miss subtle mood changes. He fishes through his three million pockets and hands Keet a slipnote. "We have a creed, Mr. Keeto." You deserved that Keet. "The chumbuds had to be sure you would qualify. You have a board now, Eli?"

"Yeah, the plantrocity is guarding it." Top funny, Keet. Just read the slip.

"It's beside Cyd."

"Cyd? A surrogate boyfriend?" And that's even funnier. Stitch sneaks in a quick chumbud salute with Keet.

"I fig it's short for cydonia oblonga, yeah? That's the original blossom the hybrid architects used. Trip. Honing your chumbud sleuthing skills." A poke and a smile.

Stitch tickles Cyd on the way to my board. He whips up a quick sketch, and he's into the underground network. Pretty soon Keet and I will be able to pick through high council packets like Stitch does. Juicy! Keet is excited now. He has been after Stitch about it for months. It takes digging to a whole new level for him. And for me?

I can send out a sketch the second I have a nightmare. I always forget so quickly. I just relive the same pain over and over. If I can get even the slightest detail out in the maze … Maybe one of the chumbuds will have something for me. Anything. They don't need to know the context.

Keet hands me the *Chumbud Creed*. A quick review and … done. "We're ready, Stitch."

"Trip. Now you sign your souls over to me." A huge grin and a twin poke. "Right here. Use your alias. Never use your real name, just in case."

"In case?" Ohhhm gee. Keet is having second thoughts. There's caution, there's paralysis, and then there's Keet. I can't resist.

"In case Father is posing as a chumbud and sends his scary

friends to throw you into a dungeon and torture you for hours and hours." Hehehe.

"Yeah and my dying words will be: Eli took it, Eli took it!" Zapped. Right back at me. Crap. Now I'm jumpy. You should be, Eli. Many creatures hide in the dark. They are waiting for you. No. You're a fearmonger. You are the one afraid. Afraid I'll find out what you really are. I will. We shall see. Come back, girl. Don't get sucked in by them. Stay calm. "Just a rib, Eli. You seem a little hormonal today." Huge snare for that comment, my dear brother.

"Let's not manifest that, yeah? We use aliases to protect the Gadlins in the network." And that same protection is good for Keet and me as well.

"So no one knows anybody's real name?"

"Not only the name, the alias. The creed forbids any disclosure. You must keep it private. The chumbud who vouches for you creates an empty alias as a placeholder and once you swear, you pick your alias and valah! You're in." Top juicy! As long as I keep my packets clean of identifying content, I'm a ghost flying through the maze.

Keet likes the idea too. "Juicy! Where do I swear?"

"Right here. You have to say it out loud so I can witness, yeah?" Sounds simple enough. Go ahead, Keet.

"I do solemnly swear that I am of sound mind and have read and understood the Chumbud Creed, and I further pledge that whatever happens in the maze stays in the maze." One stroke from Stitch. One from Keet. And now he picks an alias. Crap. Cyd fancies himself a security guard. I'd love to know what Keet chose. I'm next.

"I do solemnly swear that I am of sound mind and ..." You hear that up there? *Sound mind*. " ... have read and understood the Chumbud Creed, and I further pledge that whatever happens in the maze stays in the maze." One stroke from Stitch. One from me. And my alias. Hmmm. *MysteriousMazeMonster*. "OK, chum. Show me how to spy on the Ministry."

"Ease, rook. Let's start with something simple so you can learn how to navigate in and out of packets, yeah? Master that before risking your alias. The high council uses bait-and-trap. If you don't know how to poke into friendly packets first, you'll be riding with them to the cleaners." Gulp. Getting scrubbed off a dirty packet and into a wash bucket is not my idea of fun.

"What about the flyer mud pile, Stitch? Would that be the latest Ministry poop?"

"You got it figged, bud. Eli, sketch a scoop and stoop." Rip. No mystery who designed the controls here.

Ewww. I dropped some. Scoop again. That's better. "Where do I drop the stuff, Stitch?"

"I usually spread it on my wall, especially if it's really dark like the mud you have. That means it's pica dense."

"Meaning?"

"Pure flyer mud, piled higher and deeper than most." I'm still looking like a squashed frog. English please. He's laughing. "The Pramam himself is involved. His crap has its own hue." And pee-ewe as well I'm sure.

Stitch directs me to the wall. A quick flick of the scoop and let's see what sticks. It looks like the medical lab. But where? Some sort of hidden floor, three surgeons working on ... No! It's not him. It can't be him. How can you be sure? You don't remember. No. It's not me. Stop saying that. Hold back the tears. Don't look. Focus on the viewing tent. Don't listen. Stop think—

—Whose talking? Oh. Stitch. It sure is warm in here. Where's my flutterbot? In my pocket? No. Keet has it. Good. I'm not the only one feeling it. So what's in my pocket?

"We have to blow the lid on this one, chumbuds. The Pramam won't be able to jabber his way out of this. Keet, you have a clean slip on you?"

"No, but you can wipe this one. I can get another copy. What's the plan?"

I know these pants were empty.

"We need to contact the broadcast mick at *Oye Amigos*. We can use the anonymous alias. By morning, the whole world will know. He's jam!"

What on earth is in my … Crap! I distinctly remember storing this in my privy shelf. I wager it's Cyd's doing. Hybrid humor again.

Stitch is staring. Oh, he wants a chumbud salute. Actually no. His hand is palm up. "And the red Aswan granite, Eli?" Keet is confused. So am I. It keeps jumping into my pocket somehow. I might as well take out the rock. Hands off, Keet. "Ease, bud. I know about it, and no, I did not steal it from Mashrin. This stone seems to want to be known. It needs to return to its home." He examines the smooth point, the right-angled edge, the polish, and the rough chiseled edge. "I fig it broke off some sort of ancient artifact."

"Won't Odwin have an idea? The Gadlins peddle this kind of stuff." Stitch shrugs and hands it to Keet.

"You're the apprentice curator. This thing is out of the maze. I already sent a sketch out. Nothing." The room is cooler now. Keet turns the rock over a few times between his fingers and puts it in his pocket.

Stitch peeks inside the viewing tent. His hair turns orange. No, red. No, orange. "You want me to fix that?" Our birthday scene is flashing between multiple points of view now. None of them I recognize. Keet gives me the don't-you-tell-him look. Well, we could do our own sketching now. Stitch is on to us. "I thought we chatted this out, Eli." Stitch storms out.

"Wait!" Grab the flashes. Push Keet out of the way. "Here. Let's talk later. You trip?" Back to blue with a poke and a smile. He leaves. And for me, back to Keet with a tear in my eye. Silly emotions. Get a grip, girl. Keet is blowing. "We just swore, Keet."

"That's not what I'm blown about." He reaches over and wipes my eye makeup. Crap! I can't hide anymore.

"They're back. I didn't want to tell you. I didn't want you to worry … I can handle this!" He's patronizing. "Once Mashrin's killer was caught, they cleared right up. I focused on my studies and everything was going well — until all the buzz around campus about the new URA director got me thinking of Father. That's about when the dreams came back. If we just drop it and move on with our lives and be content with just not knowing, maybe they'll go away again." Geez. Now I need a another touch up under my eyes.

Keet freezes. My makeup tube! "What kind of heat did *this* to it?"

KEETO

I do not recall ever seeing Stitch that furious, even more so than last year, when he condemned the cavalier attitude towards Mashrin's death. The term "collateral damage", to a series of biochip removal experiments, sent his hair at the time into a rampage. And based on what happened today, I am not even sure any of that intel was even true.

We were easing in my crypt around midi, listening to the midday news interlude and munching on flyer bakes that Elize had grabbed from the Snack Shack on her way over here with Stitch, anticipating a world outrage for the kidnapping coverup, or so we thought. This was to be the hour that the archives would record as a public opinion disaster for the SIF, and especially for the Pramam's advisor, Sothese. Their "superior investigatory skills" were so broadly praised for the killer's capture, that we were positive the evidence Stitch leaked to *Oye Amigos* would cause a global uproar.

Stitch is quite upfront with his motive. He blames the GHU for his cousin Zbrietz, who at the age of nine, was found murdered, with a piece of his brain missing. Vindication is what impelled him to form the chumbud underground in the first place. His aim was to create a safe haven for others, like him, who wanted to build a community where honor and honesty are the chumbud's word, where lies and deceit become transparent, where respect flourishes for all living souls on

Earth, including the planet herself. The Pramam, according to Stitch, does not qualify for membership. I am inclined to agree. Not that I agree with everything Stitch concocts, of course.

For Elize's part, she had no strong attachment to the outcome, either way. In fact, before the announcement I am about to share with you, she was quite ambivalent. On the one hand, she hoped that the deceit lay outside the Inner Council and that the Pramam simply was clueless, to which Stitch added, "I'm trip with that!" — the clueless part that is. Yet on the other hand, she loved the idea of putting the Pramam on the spot and seeing how Sothese would manage to slither him out of the scandal. She even "reveled" at the possibility of the political unrest and complete anarchy, which would infallibly result from a massive collapse of the Unification, were it to unfold. For a moment there, I wondered where my logic-minded sister had drifted off to. Pandemonium would make it much more difficult to get the answers that we came here for.

As for me, I suspect that the mick Stitch sent the flashes to (of what appeared to be a medical cell in Osler Hall with a secret subfloor filled with classified monitoring equipment), either never received them or decided to take credit for its discovery. And I do mean the kind of credit that enhances the comforts of daily living.

Elize is convinced that the apparatus the three scientific assailants were using was the same she had seen at the GHU, when she snuck into the guarded cell where Mashrin's body was being held, the reason for which we only have nebulous theories.

Regardless, our motives are of no import, since the result

was born from disinformation and overripe with the matter of the peculiar hue Stitch so enjoys scooping out of the poop pile in the hidden chumbud layer in the maze. The voice that cut through the morning fog, via the *Oye Amigos* broadcast, was not that of a trusted anchorman challenging the SIF's competence with respect to last year's murders, but that of the Pramam himself answering carefully orchestrated questions, which might as well have been recited by a holopost advertisement.

The so-called messenger of the Unification's divine mission was no doubt plotting a clever campaign to pervert the facts and strengthen his hold on the ignorant masses of Eadonberg. The official Holy Address is scheduled for tomorrow morning and will include visual evidence of the perpetrators in action. Viewer discretion is advised.

"The twisted brain collector was not acting alone" was the headline falsehood. The lies went on to explain that the new abductions were not disclosed in order to avoid a panic and to enable interrogations with the prisoner to expose the terrorist circle responsible, all the while tricking the accomplices into believing that their efforts at concealing evidence of their transgressions have been effective. The Ministry's real world bait-and-trap tactic apparently rivals its virtual cohort.

This is the point in the transmission when Eli became annoyingly smug. She has maintained all along that Nathruyu cannot be trusted, and her willingness to turn in her confederates for personal clemency, proves it. As you know, I believe otherwise, which, according to Eli, does not allow me to think with clarity. She predictably re-accused me of being in love with the killer, or at least under some sort of spell, which I find amusing, since Eli does not give credence to anything crossing the boundary between the physical realm and imaginary dimensions. The witchcraft reference, however, I find worrisome.

The last moment Nathruyu and I were together in the sub-water level cell of the GHU sent a cool rush traveling up my arm with her touch. For an instant that lasted a lifetime, we had shared eternity. I cannot escape the scent that fills my heart with the memory of her amethyst eyes on the station drop platform, and the pathway it opens directly to your heart, forever fused with mine.

If this is sorcery, then let me burn at the stake, for I too am guilty of the craft. There is no earthly explanation for the sensations only I can see, hear, smell, taste, and touch. But I know that you have the answers that we seek, whether they come through Eli's nightmares, in the private journal of Dr. Tenille, or through the quill in my hand … when you are ready.

No. The newscast was not the Unification's undoing we had expected or, at the very least, a call for the Pramam to step down as leader of the Inner Council. It became an opportunity for him to play the card of fear in a game of chance he is masterminding with the brains of orphaned children.

The official fabrication recounted a tale of youngsters, aimlessly roaming the open country outside the protective biowalls of the cities and highland circles. It reported the courageous rescues by GHU paramedics, ill-equipped to handle the dense walls of charging poisonous fog prevalent near the coastlines. It claimed steady progress towards the imminent clamping of a well-connected terrorist group, thanks to cooperative discussions with the prisoner within the new rehabilitation framework at the Ministburg penal island, which fosters forgiveness through spiritual release therapies.

Another excuse surfaced relating to the body and mind decay spreading throughout the city. The Ministry had planned to announce all their findings with respect to the kidnappings three weeks ago, but when the first infection appeared, a unanimous Inner Council decision postponed the communiqué until after a secure plan to contain the contagion was implemented. And in good Ministry fashion, may I add, human and civil rights violations abound, all in the name of "the greater good," of course. Surprisingly, part of those measures include something I am actually grateful for.

The city's blowers will now turn on at first fog and operate until fog lift, which naturally occurs around midi, although the reasoning for this new schedule I find suspect. The GHU hopes to mitigate an airborne spread by keeping the city dry and removing residual fog, presumably in case the virus frequency is outside the biowall filtering range. The advantage I see in all this, is that Father, or any authority, will not be able to sneak up on us like guerrillas in the mist. It is all a matter of perspective. Hehehe.

All ribbing aside, the suffocating white in the morning really made me anxious. I never knew whether I was being watched, or being followed, nor whether noises and voices belonged to real people, as opposed to holowalls or even holocasters blistering overhead. Eli was not bothered by it. She said it was a breath of fresh air, which is debatable, compared to the blackness of her dreams. As for Stitch, he had every gadget imaginable that could help him navigate, and when he lacked one, he would contact his itinerant merchant chumbuds in the underground. They can acquire gizmos for him. Perhaps it is their acquisition methods that the Unification have qualms about. No. That is not quite the right word. How did Stitch put it?

"The Pramam has Gadlin envy!" Eli and I almost ripped and rolled on that one, but Stitch was beyond furious. The "terrorists" the Pramam was referring to were none other than the Gadlins. I, for one, have never seen the explosive side of our hip-jiggling, smiley, dweeby genius bud, and counted myself fortunate to have Sparky to protect me, as much as a satchel-sized canine with one centimeter long teeth can bark out, but Eli seemed to have the situation under control. She simply uttered a few sweet words, which I do not remember enough to rightly paraphrase, and his hair slowly shifted from black to blue.

Not too long ago their roles were reversed, Eli hyperventilating and tormented by the voices you are all too familiar with. And now that the nightmares are back with a vengeance, I fear that the debilitating episodes will return with even greater intensity. Well, no sooner had I entertained that thought than Eli started rubbing the silver pup on the chain I gave her last Unified Day. What you fear most will come upon you. I read that in one of your books.

Stitch had shown Eli some remarkably effective coping skills that he adapted from his neuropsychology and neurolinguistics courses. Nothing in Stitch's life is off the shelf. A quick rub of Eli's metaphorical anchor and she immediately counts down from ten, stays quiet for another ten, then she is right back with us, completely relaxed. I am not sure what she sees while she is gone, and neither is she, but the routine works. If only she could extend this control beyond her waking hours.

We have agreed to keep the nightmares between Eli and me for now. Luckily, Stitch entered a meditative state of his own while Eli was dealing with her psychotic interlude. Strike that thought. I am not really fair to you or Eli. The suffering you went through, and what she is currently experiencing, deserve more awareness.

In truth, I admire Eli's resourcefulness. She says she wants to drip some questions into the maze and piece together some answers on her own before burdening anyone with her problems. As much as I encourage her to PLEASE burden us with her problems, she insists. She fears that what she learns might make her a threat to the Pramam, and that ignorance of the facts will keep us safe. I sure hope your book is not always right.

There is also the Dr. Tenille connection Eli can pursue. Now that she is a member of his crew, our local pirate wannabe might share with his beloved Belle the private journal entries he kept when you were in his care. He does feel partly responsible for your death, though he is unsure why. That is likely the reason he has kept Eli's presence in Eadonberg buried, so to speak. As far as the university administration and the GHU internship program are concerned, she is just some rich kid from Blarney Way.

If the mystery as to why Eli's symptoms cleared completely,

only to return like a night flyer possessed, were not enough, the strange machinations of her makeup tube, and whatever other unnatural behaviors are transpiring in her room, keep life interesting, in a creepy way. What kind of heat can reshape a thick polymer into a mangled mess without causing a fire?

My newfound boldness gave Eli an ultimatum. Either she tells Stitch something sometime soon, or I do.

I realize it is not the strongest of ultimatums, but it left an impression nonetheless. I am learning. Even though we are now officially sworn into the chumbuds network in the maze, it will probably take a couple of weeks before we make sense of it enough to realize its nearly unlimited potential. We could definitely use Stitch's guidance here, but as long as we play this ridiculous trust tug-of-war, our progress just hobbles along.

Whoa! The "we" I am referring to is the ancient "royal" version. I have been the hindrance! I have been the acting monarch, projecting my doubts onto someone who has extended his full trust in us, thus, in me. I have been the one succumbing to unjustifiable feelings, based on no evidence whatsoever of deceitful conduct on his part. The crap from Father's constant lies about you is still polluting my mind with more of the same. No longer. I am not the same person from the night we left the highlands. Notwithstanding, habit wins out at times, and worry paralyses action. I trust that this is just part of the process. Interesting. I trust.

I wonder if Father would be proud, or threatened, by my bourgeoning self-confidence, wherever he is. Who cares anyway? For all we know, he could be dead. Whether his body is or not is immaterial, his soul always has been. Yours, however, lives on without a physical presence. My wish is that Eli's and mine will as well, and the three of us will be together again, in a better reality. But that is just a dream I escape to when I feel small, a fantasy in a dreamworld that is also changing.

A couple of nights ago, I endured a nightmare for which I cannot recollect any details, except that you were in it. Its meaning is unclear to me. I had actually fallen asleep in the artifacts room, finishing off some late night classifications. Could your sickness have discovered a trigger in me now? Or maybe Eli is right about manifesting our own nightmares. "What consumes your thoughts controls your life," she hums to herself, from time to time.

I have been obsessed with knowing what happened to you even as Elize had accepted the past and moved on. I seem unwilling to let you go. Part of me still finds comfort in all that pain, and I need to keep digging, and digging. The moments of reflection you and I share at night bring me so close to you that I have trouble accepting your death. I want proof, a witness, a grave, a bone even, but all I have is a board game, some books, and a crystal which I know now was yours as well. A voice inside keeps whispering "wake up." Or is it a ghost from the midday broadcast saying "Oye, Amigos."

There is a witch hunt going on, and I am still seeking the cocoons of the archives and right here, with you, in my crypt. The Unification has essentially declared war on the Gadlins and their descendants, for good measure. Their complicity ostensibly resulted from debriefings with Dr. Tenille, after a particularly intense regimen of the aforementioned spiritual release therapy.

According to Stitch, the whole concept is flyer mud. I was not entirely convinced of that, but was cautious not to challenge him while he was blowing fury out of his eyes. For my liking, he seemed to be making too strong of an argument in favor of the Gadlins when he interrogated Eli about her fake bathroom sessions at the GHU, spying the borrowed contents of Dr. Tenille's medical slippad. He is hiding something with his interminable vocal defense.

Geez. There I go again. Trust.

It turns out that Dr. Tenille keeps a secret slippad, of sorts, that he never lets out of his sight. Smart. Once, when he thought he had lost it, he, well, lost it, like Stitch was doing during the broadcast. For a taste of levity our conversation so desperately needed, Eli speculated that the journal contains top secret design plans for Captain Snook's mighty sailing vessel. We all had a good laugh. The new nickname is a rip. He is a bit scaly and he also acts a little fishy, so Eli aims to sneak a peek at the captain's logs somehow, just in case.

The interview ended, leaving Stitch deflated and the future disheartening. Kids are still having their brains stripped, a virus is threatening everyone else, and GMU law is upon us. Some days, I wonder what would have happened if Eli had not tripped over that girl's body in the arcade.

Would Mashrin's fate have been different? Was our meddling ultimately responsible for her death? And what about the other kids? I had to know, so as Stitch was leaving, I asked him if any new information on the young victims had dripped into the maze, and what he divulged confirmed the horror story that had been unfolding in my mind since yesterday.

Mashrin's parents reportedly perished on the transport Eli and I fled to Eadonberg on last year, information which we already knew as false. The parents for the other child abductees also died in various accidents, and none of the victims had defective biochips. The news that healthy children were being orphaned and their brains mutilated was disturbing enough, but it was the names that Stitch read to us from the slip he had imprinted that ejected the contents of my stomach in Sparky's food dish. All the nine-year-olds murdered were kids Eli does not remember babysitting. But I do.

We concluded that we really needed to get our hands on one of their biochips. I took a labored breath, for the reality of what we were considering nauseated me further. We were about to enter into contract with the Gadlin conspirators.

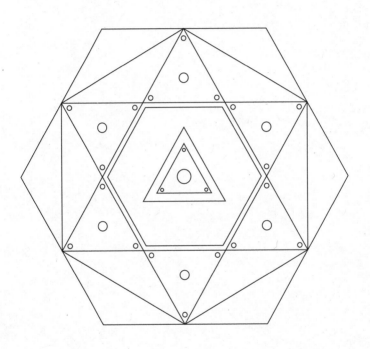

CHAPTER THREE

Day 384: evening

The moonlight charms a snake of mist from a gemstone cup on a silver tray, balancing atop the edge of the crystal fountain, marking the entrance to Ministry House. The polished limestone facade of the mansion reflects the whimsical symphony of light, color, and sound, playing amongst sleeping blooms, tethered to long green stems in the milky lavender waters of the Central Core.

Tonight, the city rests at the edge of a precipice as a tide of vengeance rises from within. Tomorrow, the floating walkways, plazas, and platforms will stage a new backdrop at the morning rush, for the first time since The Great Smoke. A blast of oppression will force the dense fog upwards, where it will hover over the new order of things.

Nepharisse tucks a few stray curls into her unruly bun, smooths her overcoat over her hips and buttocks with her white gloved hands, and picks up the beverage tray. Along the perimeter scaffold of the mansion, a GMU unit forms a human chain of nine bodyguards, virtually linked as one through hidden frequency transponders inside their lapel buttons. Sothese, the master of subterfuge and seduction, is here.

Her heartbeat races. She steadies it. Her breathing hastens.

She calms it. She is ready. Time and circumstances have retained a tattered shroud on the sizzling memories that refuse to fizzle out. The last lustful encounter they savored together seems more distant now than a childhood tragedy, yet no less vivid, or near. Intense emotions do not obey the passage of time.

Nepharisse conjures a beguiling smile and saunters across the wide buoyant mosaic, edged with intricately crafted glasswork lit from below. The air displaced as she walks touches small holes in the guardrail spindles, announcing her arrival with a delicate melody. The spellbound sentries at the perimeter gate relinquish their station to a gentle caress and a lyrical swoop of sapphire blue eyes. Nepharisse struts into the palatial foyer.

The great hall is curiously vacant of GMU personnel, except for two especially menacing thugs, flanking the sides of the grand curved split staircase, a fitting ascent for the one with a forked tongue whose face dominates the tapestry hanging from the vaulted ceiling, the Pramam. Sothese's hounds are also strangely absent. A more focused look at the guards reveal two men, grinning from across the stone floor, the cells of recognition in their brains unmistakably excited.

She pauses, but this is not hesitation. Her eyes inhale the purple glow emanating from the glassed-in courtyard at the mezzanine level, then quickly shift to her marks, erect on the first step. She sashays toward them, skillfully balancing the warm beverages on her tray, and places an index finger on the darker one's mouth, just as he puckers to welcome her by name. Hush.

It is a surprise. Sothese loves surprises. You love surprises. Everyone loves surprises.

Nepharisse offers the guards each a small sample of the herb infusion, which suffuses the air with a calming aroma, and watches them swoon as she strokes their shoulders in passing. The way is clear for tonight's hunt. Her intent is to uncover evidence connecting Sothese to the mutilation she witnessed at Osler Hall, and to hold it as further proof, not only of Sothese's incorrigibly sadistic nature, but also of her improving competence. Furthermore, producing a copy of the hidden surveillance recording that she suspects exists from that evening will serve to incriminate the Inner Council, as well as bring the bearer of the message much praise, which is of special interest to Nepharisse.

At the far end of the south wing, Nepharisse slips into the suite where Sothese lives when in Eadonberg and performs most of his official duties, as well as his secret ones. One such duty is to flank the Pramam wherever he may be. Rarely does the Pramam even breathe without his trusted advisor, nor does he grant interviews to broadcasters not directly in the Ministry's employ, but the unprecedented reportage on *Oye Amigos*, today, only gave an overview of the new measures he is implementing to ensure the safety of law-abiding citizens worldwide, which of course excludes those directly, or indirectly, involved in the newly announced Gadlin conspiracy.

Just as the fog is banished from within the confines of the Eadonberg biowall, an invisible shroud creeps in. The Gadlins may be acting in matters of their own devising, but the so-called "regrettable affront on personal liberties in Their name" is inconsistent with the teachings of the Divine Trinity.

The populace seems all too ready to forget that conspiracies abound, when Church and State are one. Nepharisse's thoughts, however, are not so easily governed. The power of influence is her forte. The power of pretense, on the other hand, is that which defines the object of her larceny.

Voices carry from the activated sajadum in the mezzanine level courtyard. They travel the thin veneer of water, reflecting the smoky amethyst brilliance, and enter the realm of thought. Nepharisse's mind is drawn to the conversation which is honing tomorrow's Holy Address.

"Greetings all. And may They grant peace upon you."

Nepharisse muses over the short pause. A Unified acknowledgment, from all those who practice, will reverberate around the world as: "They are one." Those inside the three-person sajadums for their scheduled meditations, will give greater potency to that utterance, and their vibrations will ripple throughout the universe for They, who listen.

"Not ten months ago, unspeakable atrocities befell the glorious city of Eadonberg for which They feel great sorrow. A human tragedy. An assault on our children. The illustrious Pramam sought Their counsel, and imposed restrictions on personal liberties, which, however regretful, were necessary in order to secure the city, and apprehend the perpetrator of these unconscionable crimes. The soul responsible was found and confined. Perfect are They."

Another pause.

Nepharisse strokes the blue sapphire fountain centerpiece from which Sothese draws pure water, a luxury only bestowed onto those whose Unified virtue is beyond reproach, according to *The Book of They*, channeled through the Pramam, in agreement with Their counsel. Speculation leads her to distrust the morality of this insatiate Inner Council member. She can only assume that the Ministry extends particular privileges to its high ranking agents, regardless of their questionable ethics, or in Sothese's case, complete lack thereof. And it is this deficiency that she has come to expose.

"Absence of open communication had led to misleading rumors and had compromised trust in the messenger of the Unification's divine mission. This shortfall the Inner Council now aims to correct, with today's Holy Address. As an act of good faith, and to uphold Their commitment to transparency, it behooves the Inner Council, through the word of the venerable Pramam, to announce a temporary infringement on the welfare of certain young members of our global Unified family. However, before I proceed with the details of this resurgence, please join me in a moment of silent meditation for the three innocent Unified spirits, who pass now through the darkness."

And for the fourth? Nepharisse strokes the silk-covered feathered throw on the bed. Her emotions flutter with intense confusion. They impel her to slide her hands under the slippery sheet, and to fondle the smooth sheath wrapping an all too familiar shrine to Sothese's seductive powers in the physical plane, maneuvers which have earned him a reputation in private circles.

"May their Trinity join with Their light. Perfect are They."

Nepharisse anticipates the words "They are One," unaware that the present moment does not yet express tomorrow's

Holy Address. Once again, her undulating feelings collide with the reality which brings her here. Her probing fingertips hover over the mattress at a point where its firmness bends. A dip she would expect, but a mound seems inconsistent with the pleasures which arise in Sothese's quarters. Perhaps his escapades required a quick flip of the mattress, in order to conceal his coital compulsions.

In contrast, the Pramam is attempting to remove the veil of secrecy that lurks in the morning hours, thinking that, perhaps, living in plain view might expose certain misdeeds, whereas, in reality, it is in full view that the worst offenses often go unpunished. That is until someone draws attention to them. Nepharisse smiles to herself as the Pramam pauses his recording and discusses its dubious motive with Sothese in the courtyard.

"There are two matters of importance to announce, Sothese. The speech is to overlay the confiscated footage, duly edited of course, and to broadcast over all holobands. Our official position, just so we are both clear on this, Sothese, is that Nathruyu has been graciously rewarded for her open and cordial cooperation in offering us her direct Gadlin connections in these crimes. Since the accomplices still live amongst the populace, They have guided the Inner Council's hand in implementing extra measures — in order to safeguard our children."

"Of course, my Pramam." Sothese has lost none of the sarcastic arrogance Nepharisse has learned to despise. The otherworldly guidance which leads her hands uncover the source of the atypical protrusion in Sothese's nest. There is a treasure waiting to be discovered under the bedding of a snake, but it is not the one she seeks.

The Pramam resumes the recording to a faint tapping sound, which summons fragments of timeless echoes ticking through the night. Memories splinter into sensations as yet unrealized. Sothese is no longer alone.

Nepharisse concludes her thievery, pulling an envelope from between the bed frame and the mattress. As she hurries to open it, her ears continue their attentiveness to the speech being crafted from inside the courtyard sajadum.

"Regrettably, certain personal freedoms must once again be suspended. The biochip location protocol on all our precious children, at or below the age of nine, will be activated in order to pinpoint any future kidnappings as promptly as possible, lest the perpetrators effect an unspeakable terror upon fragile brains. Please accept Their most humble apologies for subjecting us to the images about to haunt our sensibilities. Avert the eyes, if one must, but pay heed to the message they carry.

"As one can see from this confidential SIF surveillance footage, recorded at a Gadlin stronghold, the specimen retrieved from the young body lying on the platform in the operation pit is the child's vermis. Yes, shock has given way to sadness, as They, through the Pramam, regard all parties as casualties in such transgressions, the recipients in body, and the contributors in spirit. Let us bow in silent meditation for the Trinity in them all. Perfect are They."

Nausea washes over Nepharisse as a wave of tomorrow's "They are One" chant assumes a more visceral meaning, upon realizing what the package she found contains. These images are not the raw footage in the nature that she has presumed. They do not represent proof that the visuals, planned for the Holy Address, originate from Osler Hall. The sapphire in her eyes sends shards of blue hatred through the walls that separate her from the courtyard traitor.

How dare he! Her fury challenges her composure as she mutes her reaction and the speech continues.

"The truth be known, to those who seek it. Further measures are necessary in order to identify the itinerant criminals in our midsts. Years have passed with them hiding on the fringes of society, whilst the Ministry tolerates their dissent, but that charity has expired. With Their permission, all hovertrains and intercity transports will immediately acquire scanners, and the GHU will enhance all biochips with bioTravel. All those who accept the upgrade, before the payment system is fully operational, will receive one month free travel for their contribution to universal safety.

Furthermore, in good faith, and as humble messenger of the Unification's divine mission, I, myself, the Pramam, will obtain said upgrade and mandate that all GMU and Unification employees also receive it, at once. There are no special immunities. We are all one in the fight against terrorism. Perfect are They."

Perfect They may be, but humanity was not made in Their image.

The Holocene extinction was certainly not born out of perfection. An overblown self-image was responsible for the greatest multilateral genocide in all of Earth's history. A mere bloated grain of sand in the hourglass of eternity blocked the flow of life for countless species not of their kind as man drank the nectar of his own magnificence, and indulged himself inside a sugar-coated reality with a flaky crust. While civilization fed its natural resource sweet tooth, their confectionaries stripped the planet of her oxygen source, her oil, her minerals, and ultimately the water that cleansed her, leaving their life support system jonesing for a serious fix that would never arrive.

The earth shook, as she attempted to fill the void left by the deep holes her riches once filled. Pacifying her with man-made waste did nothing to satisfy her structural needs and the refuse became poison to her underground rivers and reservoirs. Death began from below, just as life withered on the surface.

The air fared no better. The mesh underpinning all of human existence collapsed. The cards civilization played had no foundation in wisdom, and all hopes that were placed upon that deck of chance fell, dragging along countless creatures, strung to them in an enormous ecological web.

The animal kingdom thrives in the absence of man. When these beings are left to their own self-regulating nature, the verse rejoices in her blue child's abundance. But when humans were flung upon the land, the balance shifted. When they claimed the oceans, more suffering ensued. When they mastered the air, the heavens choked. And finally when they breached the atmosphere, it was time.

Surprisingly, the human virus, the parasite ignorant of the long-term health needs of their generous host, was resilient. What they did to themselves, and between themselves, became their salvation as they eliminated their own viral load on the planet. The distant ancestors who survived bred the likes of the Pramam, whose apparent benevolence is their hope. However, the shortcomings which lay dormant through the ages, with occasional resurgences of insanity, are pressing up against the frosted glass of Ministry House. And those with keen vision see.

Nepharisse's intellectual interlude manages to clear her mind of reactive thoughts that ultimately lead to misguided actions. Still engaged with her find, she contemplates her next move as she witnesses the holograph of Sothese's virility rising between the aisles of a stockroom filled with bonbons.

His repeated thrusts immerse her body into a fog of reluctant ecstasy, tempered by disgust. A soft ginger curl wafts into the frame as his hand releases an already disheveled bun with a sensual tug and draws her onto him, moaning. Nepharisse bites her lip to anchor herself in her current reality. She is not the mirage cavorting with rapture. She must concentrate on a response befitting this deceit.

Encounters of this nature belong to private eyes. The revelation, although hurtful, will serve her well, but someone else has seen this. She casts her eyes in the direction of the voices, one final time, as the Pramam wraps up his grand scheme.

"Together we shall remedy the great tragedy that has befallen us. The criminal, currently held in lockdown for last year's offenses, was herself a victim. Her children were held hostage as a means of coercing her into executing the Gadlin plan. As a demonstration of Their mercy, she has been pardoned and has entered the criminal rehabilitation and the witness relocation programs, but there shall be no clemency for the Gadlin conspirators.

"A reward of five thousands credits stands for information leading to the capture of any Gadlin, or a descendant thereof. Treachery calls for austere measures. Your safety and that of your families are the Ministry's primary motive. Please contact your local GMU headquarters for details.

"The Unification's progress has been delayed too many years, due to Gadlin subversion. Now their dissent includes a further threat beyond that to our children. The epidemic of accelerated decay that we have experienced for the past three weeks is clearly an act of undeclared chemical warfare against Eadonberg residents. The new bioApp will restrict suspect individuals, while making travel safer, simpler, and more economical for the honest commuter. The Ministry expresses its deep gratitude in response to your prompt compliance."

Compliance by the masses perhaps, but not by Nepharisse. Approaching footsteps announce her departure. She gathers the skin flashes and quickly scans Sothese's quarters for her original quest. An energy signature betrays their hiding place, and a second bounty is acquired. As confirmation of her suspicions take the stage, she finds it inconceivable that no one will notice the extent to which the images are doctored, even to the point of the perpetrators being unrecognizable. The most archaic recorders have better resolution.

Moreover, that kind of lawless behavior from the Gadlins is unfathomable. They may have an aversion to, and an inherent distrust of, the Pramam's version of peace and prosperity, but it is not in their creed to condone acts of terror against a passive public. Their immunity to the epidemic does not convict them of originating it.

Regardless, the public shall be fooled, and time must leap forward.

><< ><< ><<

Nepharisse smiles at the sweet shop owner, as he chastises a young female clerk. His eyes scowl over the display case upon noticing the familiar blue gaze. They seem to say "you have some nerve coming back here," if only as a passing thought, for his demeanor returns to that of an eager merchant offering his wares while Nepharisse suggests a simple request.

Your stockroom is open for your special friends. I am your special friend and love your stockroom. You always invite your special friends to your stockroom.

He leads her inside and leans presumptuously against the closed door. He pulls her towards him to test how badly she wants the camera feed. A call from outside ends his dangerous gamble, with Nepharisse's gentle caress and parting words: "More than your insignificance can conceive."

E L I Z E

Day 385: morning

"What are you up to?"

Jumpers! Who's there? Not in my face, Cyd. Will you let go? Geez. What's with the death grip? "Back to your urn." Well, he's almost learning.

There's no one here. Just a dream. It sounded so real though, just like my voices. But that wasn't one of them. Oh no. I hope I don't have four now. Honestly, three are quite enough.

Crap! I slept in. No, I distinctly remember waking up drenched at six a.m. Brrr. Still wet, but cold. Better wash up and put dry clothes on. Now where's my spongysuit?

Whoa! Did I redecorate in my sleep again? It looks like some interior design virtuoso lives here. Certainly no Stew Über. I don't particularly like his home collection anyway. Look at all this artistic yet completely functional virtafurniture. And such intricate detail. It's as if a master craftsmen magically appeared. The pieces pull elements from the items next to them like they are symbiotically bound. Juicy! My very own ecosystem.

"Cyd! Enough with the slapping already." I thought I told him to go back to his urn. OK. He's hiding something behind those big leaves crossed over the front of the urn like that. Crap! Did he get into my privy shelf again? "Share, Cyd. I know you're covering something up." His bloom is drooping.

Embarrassment? I'll have to separate his leaves myself.

Wow, what a beautiful crystal vase! I've never seen one like this. I'm not even sure it's crystal. Whatever it is, I have no clue how it got here. I need a closer look. "Oh, don't be silly, Cyd. No need to look the other way. It's not like I haven't seen roots before." There's something swirling around inside the glassy substance. It's like fog. No. Waves. No. Clouds. Stars. It keeps shifting. Could this have been inside the blue urn? No blue flakes on the floor. Hmmm. Strange.

Ohhhm gee. It must be me. The blackouts. They're getting stronger. Where did I find this? Check my credit. No purchases. Gulp. No, I'm not a thief. Oh yes, you are. No, that was evidence. We needed that. It was for Mashrin. Nathruyu was the thief. If you say so. An eerie deep giggle. Leave me alone. Breathe. Where's my silver pup? Quick. Rub it. Breathe and count. Ten, nine, eight, seven, six, five, four, three, two, one. Quiet for ten. Calm. Breathe slowly, in … and out. Phew. Time to focus.

First, off to see Mr. G about my lo-flower. Cyd is still acting a little big for his urn. There must be a training guide I can read. Then, I need to be at the GHU by one. I have to put an end to Keet's constant nattering about Nathruyu's innocence. I am going to expose her for the murderer that she is. Dr. Tenille did the official psychiatric evaluation. There will be something in his secret journal. That will wake Keet up. And maybe there are answers about Mother as well. I'll just borrow it for a while. He won't notice. An eerie deep giggle. Thief. Shut up! *Judge not with the mind seduced by the senses and peace will fill your heart.*

Out the door, Hey lo to my floormates, down the lift, and out the lobby. The orchard is twinkling. Juicy. Sun sparkles are reflecting off Osler Hall's amethyst towers. Better hurry to the main gate. Hang a sec. Where's the fog? It's not midi yet. Maybe there's a festival today. I'd better ask that couple on the Victory Bridge.

"Excuse me. Is there a special event scheduled for this morning? The blowers are on." They're looking at me suspiciously.

"Did you not hear the Pramam's Holy Address at nine?" Crap! I forgot. Need a quick comeback. They seem anxious.

"Oh! Of course. I was trying to listen and study at the same time. *Oye Amigos* mentioned it yesterday as well. Preoccupied, yeah?" Juicy. I just made things worse. I should have kept my mouth shut. "Thank you."

I'd better leave. The woman is whispering to her match. Stay calm. Walk slowly with purpose. Hick. I might as well just wear a sign on my forehead: "No biochip. Tag me and alert the GHU." Pramam forbid I would be free to walk the city without being tracked.

The Central Core looks stunning in the morning sun. Ministry House especially has an ominous glow to it. I might not be able to sneak around in the morning anymore, but neither can Unification officials.

Is that Sothese? Creeps. His three officials as well. I hope they didn't see me. Don't even think about it, girl. Back to task and Tir-na-nog. Right by the sajadum … Wow! It's glowing bright amethyst, almost like it's lit up from inside. So this is what's been hiding in the early mist. Nothing scary really. Oh, dear Keet. Still a pup. Hehehe. Everyone is pretty much going about their daily routine. No spies watching our every move.

The glass courtyard at last. Splash the holorider for fun and off to Mr. G's shop.

"Hey lo, Mr. G." He really is a gold sculpture that man. Sigh.

"Greetings, Miss Elize." A flirty smile at me. Am I that obvious? "I have a beautiful vase to show you."

Maybe later. I'm in a rush. I'm here for—

✂ ✂ ✂

A table. A tray. No food. Right. Off to the buffet. Dr. Tenille is there having a conversation with a woman. Let's hope he's suitably distracted. Hehehe. I'm starting to get used to these memory lapses but I wish I could control them. Who knows what I've been doing for the past hour or so. I really need that journal. OK. Here I go. Thief. Not now. Go away. Pause. That seemed to work. Back on task.

"Top of the afternoon to you, Captain." He's squinting his left eye at me. Oh right, the patch. Slip it on.

"And to ye, sweet Belle. Early at the mess today, me lass? Model crew member, ye be." Giggles from the cafeteria staff. I feel one coming on myself, but best just ease on it. I be a model crew member, eh?

"Aye, Captain. Ready for my shift." And a little piracy of my own. Well, he encourages his students to act the part, so no sense disappointing. Hehehe. I see the edge of a journal sticking out from his case, his effects I mean. Good. He's back talking with the pretty redhead at the counter. Her voice is so soothing, almost calming. My voices are quiet now, and no brain fog. Just reach over while he is all smitten. Be the silent storm and no one will notice.

Juicy! No one watching. Nab the booty, pop it into my satchel, and valah! As Stitch would say. Not even a twitch of a nerve. And Dr. Tenille is still romancing the redhead. He's holding up the line. His eyes are looking down her uniform. Geez. She's bending over the food on purpose. Whoops. I'm staring too. Here come her sapphire blue eyes right up at me. Huh? So *this* is where—

The book? Yeah, I'll find it. Find the book. Got it. Off to find the book now. Brrr. Must be a draft in here.

"Are ye with me, me Belle?" Dr. Tenille leans over and squints. "Autopsy. A mystery, aye. The body was just released from a three-week GMU quarantine for a radiation scare. They say the corpse glows in the dark." He winks and chuckle snorts. "Walk with me."

He's reaching inside his pouch for something. Oh no. He's frowning. I hope I'm not busted. The pretty server at the buffet waves at him, smiling. He smiles back and fastens the case. Phew! Close call.

"Here's a free seat, Captain. Right by the exit."

"Good eye, me lass. Easy escape." He leans over the table and whispers as he spears a piece of flyer bake with a fork. "The skin is covered in welts, blisters, and burns." Crunch, crunch, crunch. "Care to assist?"

I look down at my plate. Dizzy. I'm not sure I could stomach that right now. In fact, I'm not sure I'm going to eat this fried up flyer either. He's waiting for me to say yes. Well, I wanted to act the pirate, tough as nails, so here it goes … Crunch. This is not going down easy. He's almost done. Crunch faster. "Aye."

"That's me Belle." He raises his cup and shouts. "To the morgue!" I feel like crawling under the table. He really is crazy. Who are you kidding, girl? You argue with voices in your head. Zapped. And I'm wearing an eye patch too. Follow the leader.

No GMU skulking about the GHU this time. The epidemic must be under control. I've been down this hallway before. This is where Mashrin was kept! This is the morgue?

"The morgue is being cleaned. Precautionary measures, considering." He opens the door and that's my cue. Fake an upchuck. "Haven't found yer sea legs yet, aye?" Another chuckle snort. I guess that means I stay then. NO! It's the kid from the leaked recorder feed. I have to know. Teddy? I feel a little ill. Right. No more faking. Clip out! Washroom? Crap. Here comes the flyer. Run.

Yuck! Just made it. Hold it together, girl. Stop crying. It's not him. It must be a transport crash victim. Thank the little baby prophet there's still hope. I need a moment.

"Miss Elize? Eli? Are you all right?" It's Dr. Tenille. "My apologies. You did well, considering. Take your time. The crew meets at two, but you can join us in progress."

"Thank you, Dr. Tenille. I'll be fine. A little fresh air is all I need." His footsteps are fading. Good. OK. Now for this pirate's treasure. Juicy! Keet has to see this. Whip off the patch. I have thirty minutes.

Head for the nearest exit, through the air lock, and freedom, of sorts. Deep breathe in. I feel much better now. A brisk walk to the archives will get me shipshape for two.

"How was your appointment, miss. Is everything normal?" Jumpers! "We didn't mean to startle you." They've been tracking me since this morning. Are they biochip spies or something? Ease, girl. I have this under control.

"Yes. Much better, thank you. It was humming something awful, and the medic had adjusted the levels down so I could sleep." Show them the makeup under my eyes. The nightmares have a use after all. "It's finally fixed." They nod in approval. "I've felt so disconnected the past couple of days and with the lack of sleep? You can well imagine."

"Of course! That's why you missed the Holy Address." They nod again. Creepy couple.

"Yes." Play it up. Look upset. "I only have secondhand fragments. The Gadlins. How horrible!" Not like what I just saw at the GHU. They seem genuinely empathetic now.

"It happened to my father once. He was so lost. We are glad you're better, so now you can accept bioTravel. You get a free month!" Pretend you know what they're talking about.

"I will. How generous of the Pramam." Liar. I'll give you that one. Thief. OK, stop right there. Mind your business. You are my business. Quiet. Good. Wave to the couple and smile. There they go and off I go. Anyone else on my tail? All clear. Comm Keet.

"Hey lo, Keet. I have it. I'll be there in three minutes. You ready?"

"How long do we have?"

"Thirty minutes. No twenty-seven. We need to work fast. I'm almost at the marble gate. Is there an old copy device we can use?" If there's one place we can find one, it's at the Museum of Antiquities.

"I'm on it, Eli. See you soon." More like now. There he is. Check behind me one last time. All clear.

"Mme Beaudoin is busy investigating a malfunction in her V-line skirt. Come in quick." Rip. He didn't! "Gotta love Stitch's O2-Line gadget." He did. I wonder if she wore real underwear. Hehehe. "Her panties were scanty." Double rip. My turn.

"Valah! A relic secret journal." His jaw drops. Just the effect I was looking for. "It's almost as ancient as your elderberry." Giggle. Ouch. Where did his sense of humor go? Ohhhm gee. Back to *her* again. "Dr. Tenille's journal will not lie, Keet. Let her go."

"I did! I have." You're not very convincing. You and he both: liars. You watch. You'll see. The hounds will come out of your little pup. Enough!

"What are those, Keet?" He snaps a stack of little discs, one by one, at the back of the pre-slippad technology .

"They're storage devices." Squash my face. "The pad is off grid. Top juicy! Can I keep it?"

"No! I didn't steal it, I borrowed it." You hear that up there? "We have eighteen minutes now." Tap. Tap. Tap. Hold still nervous foot.

"All the information is on the device itself. It's more private than an antique journal. There will be password protection on it." Crap. I wanted to read it now! "Hang a sec. Juicy, He forgot to lock it. Whoa! This goes back a long time. We have no way of viewing the entries without the display. We need to plug the disks into something of the same era, and there's nothing like that in the Museum, or even in Mr. G's shop." He clips out the disks, hugs Dr. Tenille's secret journal, and looks at me, sheepishly.

"Not a chance. Fifteen minutes." Think. Of course! "What about the printing device on display in the exhibit room. It still works, eh?"

"I just can't take it."

"Of course you can. Tell Madame Scanty Panty you need to catalog it, and then put it back when you're done. And aim the O2-Line at her top if she needs time to think." Hehehe. "I'll do a quick scan of the contents while I wait here."

"It's a touch screen. Work it with your fingers like this. I'll rush back."

Got it. It's well organized by date. That's good. Let's start the day Nathruyu was clamped. Swipe. swipe. swipe … nothing. He didn't debrief the killer at all! It's all a big Unification cover-up. Keet will never shut up about her now. Groan.

"What did you find?"

"Nothing so far." He raises an eyebrow. Well, technically that's true. Look at him blister. He fishes out a stack of paper, feeds it into the printer, plugs a disk in, and here come the words. Brilliant! Exactly what I was looking for.

"It's the day he found Dr. Yarkovsky dead in Mother's cell!" I can feel Keet's tension. Heart slow down. Are we ready for this? We lean over the printer together, holding hands, and speed read as pages fly out.

"He quotes a transcript journal he stole from Dr. Yarkovsky's pocket." You mean borrowed don't you, Miss Elize? Ignoring you. "It claims Dr. Tenille sent her in to see Mother, but he doesn't remember doing so."

"Right. He doesn't remember signing Mother's release papers either." My sentiment exactly, dear brother. Something smells here. "He has to keep the transcripts from the GHU or he'll be accused of complicity to murder." Ah yes. The look of an imminent treasure hunt.

"No mention of plans to discharge Mother. The next entries are empty." Keet and I lock eyes. A real memory lapse? "Then on the supposed discharge date … GMU operatives transferred the patient to Level 3 Ministburg lockdown."

"Operatives? That was overkill? Why was Mother so important to the Ministry? I wish I had had three more minutes with Nathruyu. She was ready to tell me—"

"Absolutely nothing, Keet! We need that transcript journal." Whoa! The pages are flying out everywhere. Keet can manage. What's this? His research sleeve. Artifacts, building, monuments, all of red granite like "The Stone!"

"Hush! The walls aren't soundproof. I know I saw what matches the stone, but I'm still digging." He'll find it. He loves digging.

"Gotta blister. I'll meet you at your crypt after—"

"Find the ship."

"The what?"

"The Galleon's sails. It should look something like this." A slipnote from the image archives? Hmmm. I wonder. OK.

Stuff it in my satchel, highland wave, and run.

Pant. I need to get back on the slick. Keep running, no thinking. That was fast.

Quick, before Captain Snook gets out of autopsy. Crap! A guard. Juicy! He's busy with the pretty redhead. Slip on by, girl. Too easy. Hmmm. His office is completely empty. He must have his controller with him.

"Feeling better?" Jumpers!

"Aye, Captain. I took a walk. I thought to wait here instead." Look queasy. "But nowhere to sit." He animates the room.

"Clean office policy, me lass." There it is! The Galleon floating in mid air. Wind in the sails. How did Keet know? Oh no. He's looking for something and I've got the goods.

"Now, where is my …?" He squints at me. Gulp. Huh? He gazes past me. It's the redhead smiling by again. Geez. Eye roll. He's a puddle of mush, which is good for me. "Oh yes! It's in my other office." Perfect. That's where I'll drop the borrowed journal. Brrr. What a chill. "You are still pale, Eli. The smell of a scorched body can be particularly hard to stomach. Here are some flashes of the procedure for you to study … unscented." He chuckle snorts. "Dismissed for the day, sweet Belle."

"Thanks. I mean. Aye, Captain."

Now I can slow down. The images are still disturbing though. I have to know for sure. Gasp! The vermis is missing. It's the seventh—

✂ ✂ ✂

—victim. Huh? O'Leary Hall? And it's dark already?

I'll just tiptoe past the counsellor's door, hand in satchel, and into Captain Snook's cabin. Almost there.

"Miss Elize! May I have a word with you?" Crap! Busted.

K E E T O

I have not slept for three nights. I feel like I am suspended in a dimension that Eli has no access to, as if the fog that cleared Eadonberg's walkways has collected in my brain. She is not responding to any comms. Any!

Stitch's hair is stuck on bright pink, and that means worry to a ziga pica degree. Add to that his blood-shot eyes from round-the-clock investigations and desperate attempts to contact a still absent Odwin, and he causes quite the scare on campus. Considering the mysterious decay virus is still spreading, Eadonberg residents are quick to call the GHU on those who appear to be losing their mental capacities, which even under normal conditions, Stitch could easily qualify to be.

Fortunately, he can still think clearly, despite acting like a twentieth century fat melting jiggle machine on overdrive. His regular bioRhythms selections were not pumped enough to flush out his mounting anxiety, so he created a phantom calypso feed, in the maze, where he loops *Oye Amigos* at triple speed. He is quite the sight! I managed to convince him, however, that standing apart from the masses in this time of Gadlin terrorist crackdown is not advisable, so he now sports a millenary creation, that he whipped up in a frenzy trying to stave off a nervous explosion. He is still a bopping oddity though.

The scent of fear, emanating from Stitch, is so strong that

my own panic is locked onto his frequency. I am aware of how powerful thoughts can be, especially when they are anchored in emotion. If events are to progress in a certain way, let it be the way in which I want them to. Part of me prefers to diminish into a cocoon of self-pity and self-blame for directing her to the Galleon's sails. I dread the notion that her current fate could be entirely my doing. How could I have been so impetuous?

, My throat aches with unexpressed sorrow, for the lion in me does not wish to attract more of the same. What I want is my sister back! What I want are the answers that will cure her! What I want is that Galleon! I will have these things. I fully expect my demands to be fulfilled! And I put my faith in the power that makes this so.

As a result, short of filing a missing person's report with the GMU, trust in Stitch and the chumbuds network's tracking experts, of which I am quickly becoming one, is the inspired action I must embody. By day, I am an apprentice curator, and by night, an apprentice bloodhound, nose to the ground for Eli's trail.

Strike the thought of Eli's blood as the bait. Captain Snook and the rest of his crew are missing as well. Surely, they cannot all have vanished.

Even though she has not been back to her room since she borrowed Dr. Tenille's relicpad, as she calls it, she is safe wherever she is, of that I am sure. Rather I hope. Strike that thought twice!

Hope is a poor excuse for timid faith. Hope merely appeases doubt; faith obliterates it. Faith is a decision. It is my decision. Your daughter is safe. I expect her to comm shortly.

Expectation leads to manifestation. Repeating these thoughts in my mind, and internalizing them in my heart is key. In the meantime, let me fill you in on my progress.

For the past three days, I have been sifting through the paper copy of Dr. Tenille's secret journal I am assembling, and I am left with more questions than answers. Madame Beaudoin is also losing patience with my insistence that the antique printer still has a few delicate areas to restore. She has threatened to alert the curator of my incompetence if by the time she waddles in tomorrow morning (poetic license here), the display case is still empty. The truth is that the volume of private notes he has recorded since his first day as a medic comprises several thousand pages.

Disk by disk, I have been secretly printing, right here in a corner of the artifacts room, and sneaking out the contents in my satchel. I even had to "purchase" ancient paper and ink from the chumbuds network, at ridiculous credit values. Gratefully, Stitch helped out by trading in a few favors. His gamble paid off in validation because, as far as I can tell, Dr. Tenille had not a single spiritual release session with Nathruyu, which means that either the Ministry is lying, or our eccentric Captain Snook is a crook. In essence, the Ministry's credibility may be debatable.

Stitch still maintains that the Inner Council is up to something, even though the maze has been clean, too clean for his liking. It is almost as if someone has sketched a monstrous scoop and scraped all the poop, he says. There is absolutely nothing flung on anybody's wall.

At least the chumbuds network is still secure. The hidden

alias mechanism is brilliant. Even when someone watches you navigate through packets or access your personal space, your alias is invisible. There is no way to attribute any activity, any sketches, or any queries to a real person. Stitch created a virtual world where chumbuds can live the anonymity prevalent before the Unification biochip invasion, the Pramam's humanitarian health and safety innovation.

I challenge whether genuine concern for the well-being of humanity was the Pramam's motive, as much as I suspect Nathruyu is not enrolled in the witness relocation program, but very much still a prisoner in the dungeons of Ministburg's penal island. Eli keeps telling me to let her go, and I truly have ... but you know that *she* has not let *me* go. Somehow, I sense that Nathruyu had a grip on you as well. Visions come to me, as vividly as the scent of myrrh still lingers on my blue tunic. And these mirages are no longer confined to late night journaling sessions in my crypt.

Recently, when I work in this quiet room, surrounded by ancient objects in and out of shipping containers, I feel a sharp pain in my heart. With each shard, I see Nathruyu's face, contorted in pain, her black eyes pleading, her naked body shivering. I wish they were nightmares that the morning would chase away, but I am awake when she reaches for me. Even now, as I confide in you, her mute screams cry a foreign name, the same name you cry in my increasingly vivid nightmares. Siufflah. Only the breath it floats on changes, a faceless emotion in a chasm of darkness.

While Eli's night terrors have shifted away from you and towards a presence unseen yet alarmingly invasive, your agony continues in me. The answers we seek may not be forthcoming in Eli's dreams, but my version of them looks promising. I am documenting the bits I remember when they jar me out of bed, and soon I will have enough snippets to organize into a story. Mostly they echo the fragments Eli has already relayed to me, after her particularly turbulent nights. I wish … I must stop now. My vision is blurred. Where is she? My heart is breaking, Mother. I …

My eyes are shedding. My whole body is shaking. All the strength I have been anchoring myself to, for the past three days, is exhausted, and the timing could not be any more perfect.

She commed me. Eli is alive! She is fine. She is coming over.

I need a few minutes, likely more, to let it all flow and clean myself up, before I cross through the archives to my crypt in the back cove. Tears never felt so good. I anticipate quite a stream to pour out of my quill later this evening. She is safe. My twin soul is safe.

What a night! The hour just turned one, as we capped the evening with sworn-in version of the chumbud salute, fingers tight and thumb out. If the theory about canine pets adopting their master's energy were simply hearsay, I would attest to the contrary. I require no scientific proof to make that claim, because Sparky literally flew across the room from the ground and into Eli's arms, when she walked through my door.

And yes, I did turn into a big puddle of mush, but not for any old girl, for my Eli … all for Eli. She tried to poke fun at me, of course, as she does whenever she feels overwhelmed with emotion, but I refused to let that ride. A huge hug was on back order, and it finally got delivered.

Stitch was not far behind, but he was still behind, albeit by just a few minutes. Eli had come straight from the GHU after she commed me. Only afterwards did she contact Stitch along the way. I do believe he broke the sound barrier getting here though. Hehehe. Between you and me, the reunion would not have felt complete without him.

Nevertheless, I fully enjoyed that window of glory over Stitch for the affection for my sister. Sparky was also lapping it up, and refused to leave her side during the entire account of her disappearance. Stitch's hips were given the reprieve they needed at last. His full attention was on Eli's report, as was mine.

The attempt to return Dr. Tenille's off-grid journal did not succeed as planned. She also was not able to stomach the autopsy procedure, but took advantage of the pass her Captain flipped her to familiarize herself with the victim through fragrance-free flashes of the procedure. She paused, as the memory of her encounter with the body rekindled the cinders of a flyer bake she had eaten, a few hours prior. Once her plumbing quieted, she happily declared that the child was not Teddy, then produced the evidence to our satisfaction.

I cringed as I noticed a distinguishing birthmark on the blistered leg, while Stitch focused on the mutilated brain. My silence was enough to attract both their attention to my demoralized face. Not Teddy, true, but still a child I recognize, and Eli forgets, which brings me to the subject of her memory lapses.

Prodding by Stitch regarding the hours between the morgue incident and Eli's second attempt to return the journal hinted at another blackout, but she found a way to fill it with a fabrication that seemed to satisfy his curiosity, for the time being. She made a scene of imitating the counsellor's tone, as he intercepted her in the corridor at O'Leary Hall, which put the matter to rest. A raised nose, flared nostrils, and a haughty "Miss Elize" brought some bright red back to the greying tips of Stitch's hair, and our interest turned to Eli's discussion with the counsellor.

The word he asked to have with her was more of a confession sprinkled with dust, like a packet in the maze rendered unsearchable. I suppose there were valid reasons for him to guard certain facts, but what he did share with her simply mystifies his involvement with our family.

He told her that he knew about her affliction, and that he knew you. Presumably, he was also aware of your sickness, although he did not specifically disclose as much. When prompted as to whether he was a boy at the orphanage you lived at, he replied, "It was a difficult time for us all," and contemplated the blooming vines on the back garden's thatched gazebo.

Eli's inquiry into Father evoked a less congenial response: "I have had dealings with him." And nothing more was offered, except for a terse: "Change is life, Miss Elize."

It is difficult to argue with that "statement of the obvious," but it is of no value to us. All clues we collect from our various sleuthing attempts add more credence to our hypothesis that your fate and the history leading up to it entomb a truth that everyone, including the Pramam himself, is afraid to exhume.

As I reflect on the potential anarchy gathering support in the underground, I debate our decision to put a query out to the chumbuds network for Mashrin's biochip. However, we suspect it was stolen, along with the grody worm in the blue goo Nathruyu had saved, and if that proves correct, it will certainly make an appearance on the black market. That small triangular cerebral shackle could crack the seal around your tragedy.

On the other hand, Eli's untimely meeting with the counsellor may actually work to our advantage. Caroline had vented about his special interest in Eli's wellbeing as the reason behind Caroline's banishment from campus, but the accusation did not make any sense to me until now.

"There are those who are watching you and those who are watching out for you," was the statement that reminded Eli of the run-in she had had with the three officials on campus last year, the hand he had extended to her in the shafts under Almedina Square, and now the promise to keep her journal theft in confidence.

His candor about disliking the Pramam, and particularly his advisor, Sothese, demonstrates intentions that, on the surface, align with our own. He aims to avoid any direct contact with either of them. This is likely the reason the counsellor keeps his schedule clear of official assemblies. His affinity for Eli, and for me as well, he disclosed, stems from his relationship with you, and reluctantly with Father, of which he spoke no further, and upon which Eli preferred not to dwell.

Eli was understandably emotionally drained, which she

offered as the reason that the rest of that evening was a blur, and that she just fell asleep, without getting back to me as planned. But I know better. She had a second blackout, I am sure of it. Anyway, we respected her wishes, and concentrated on her account of the next day, when she realized she had slept in, and ran to the GHU, late for Captain Snook's weekly surprise hands-on lesson for his crew, the top students in his human systems program. Had she delayed by a mere minute, the ensuing assault would have had no intact witnesses.

Before the crew could say "Aye, Captain," the SIF swarmed the nursery ward, in which that day's lesson was scheduled, and all within the obstetric wing were quarantined. One by one, students were tagged and processed and somehow lost all recollection of ever having attended the lesson in the first place. Dr. Tenille kept a squinted eye on Eli as she fidgeted continuously in a corner of the room that the GMU guards had sequestered them in. GHU staff received no immunity. Within less than ten minutes, the windowless prison was full.

Surprisingly, the situation did not aggravate Eli's anxiety. The effect was quite the opposite. Once the catering staff who were doing their morning rounds arrived, she remained calm throughout the mayhem, with not even a whisper of dissent from inside her head. It was as if her voices had lulled themselves to sleep. At nighttime, there were no nightmares, no night sweats, and no unnerving demands from the strange vocal addition to her dreams. She simply followed her Captain everywhere, and all was well.

Dr. Tenille was a point of much interest and amusement to her, as she recalls him flirting with a pretty redhead. He never left her side, the poor woman, or perhaps she enjoyed the attention. Eli remembers him teasing her — something about the mess getting into her hair? — pirate humor I guess. But what I find puzzling is that neither Eli, Dr. Tenille, or the woman were taken to the padded cell where unfathomable interrogations transpired.

The SIF have a reputation in the underground that is contrary to the image the Ministry portrays. Ideally, Eli would have used her time with the doctor to probe further into your case, but the risk was too great. The ordeal ended up being a test of resolve, which I am infinitely proud to announce: Eli topped it.

There is a question as to the Captain's age, which he has coyly answered as "old enough to know not to mention it." Based on his medical "novel," Stitch proposed that he may be an elder. A junior medic would certainly not have been assigned to you, he argued. Well, he is obsessive about sailing vessels. Bent compulsions tend to affect certain elders, and he might be dyeing his hair and his beard … and his eyebrows.

Could this also explain his occasional shift in writing style, almost as if an expert forger appropriated his secret journal? I might be over-feeling this. It is atypical for elders to boast a special connection to any otherworldly spirit.

My own pen, at times, will express a thought foreign to my hand, as if channeling a higher consciousness, but Eli just laughs and teases that I must be possessed by childhood soul suckers. I personally think I am in harmony with your vibration, and that one day you will tell me everything. Sigh. Would that it be so, tonight.

One finding in Dr. Tenille's notes did spark some discussion though. He writes about a woman with amethyst eyes, claiming to be your sister, visiting you the day before your planned transfer. Eli had her fun with that one. There was also mention of a cleaner who arrived after your apparent discharge, and that fortunately the doctor had already taken *it*. But taken what is the mystery, which I do believe hides in the Galleon's sails. Are you guiding me, after all?

The doctor's GHU office has a Galleon holograph, but the real miniature is at O'Leary Hall. I have to break into Captain Snook's cabin somehow. Geez. Did I really write that? Last year at this time, my organizer would have a list of all things murphy, keeping my nose safe in the archives. I need Stitch for this caper ... No, I can. OK. Settled. Sparky's the family pup now.

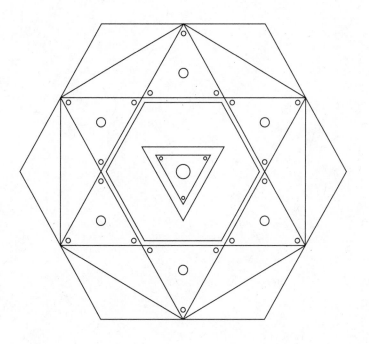

Chapter Four

Day 388: morning

As vibrant sun rays energize the grand foyer of Ministry House, Eadonberg residents swarm the central walkways, negotiating the best vantage point for today's festive occasion. From the northwest corner of the hall, where Nepharisse and her catering assistants orchestrate the final details, Nepharisse breathes deeply. She scans through each of the ten meter tall open archways, forming a U-shape around the front of the building, and into the Central Core for familiar faces.

GMU guard pairs, stationed at each point of entry, receive official word, and in unison, they lock into their designated orientation, one facing outwards towards the canals and converging crowd, the other monitoring the guests inside the cavernous lobby. Statuesque, eyes fixed in space, they occupy the center of each arch and are prepared to neutralize any potential threats to the ministerial function.

Sweet somethings and herbal infusions form mountains and streams on the exquisite display, honoring the Unified elite and the infants about to enter into the light of Their Trinity. Nepharisse feeds off the excitement of the congregation. Expectancy has been mounting since the early hour surprise communiqué from Ministburg, announcing an accelerated schedule for the event that all practicing Unified members regard as their most prestigious spiritual celebration. Consequently, the Pramam's holographic replicas will lead the ceremony in his stead.

Projecting from the apexes of the city's sajadums is the gargantuan head of the illustrious world leader, welcoming all who care to rejoice in Their Trinity and open their hearts for the new souls about to enter Their realm.

Curiosity is mostly satisfied upon hearing a feeble justification, which has become an Inner Council staple, as of late.

> The viral threat still beds amongst us. The GHU Minister has informed us that its seed has claimed the life of a young mother of twins in our current stock of newborns. I have sought Their counsel and have been assured that a speedy inauguration into our Unified family will protect their delicate bodies from the accelerated decay, as yet untamed. Such is the reason for this impromptu community baptism and the regretted physical absence of myself, the Messenger of Their Holy Trinity, on this joyous occasion. Perfect Are They.

Nepharisse senses the heat of fiery eyes as she fakes the customary "They are One" chant, pointing the number three to the sky with her right hand, then back into a fist. Her awareness directs her gaze at a female official, retreating from view onto the outside ledge nearest the Mount, where babes shall be baptized, and souls shall be stolen. Appearances at Ministry House are never what they seem. Nepharisse's presence here is no exception, neither is that of Sothese's trio of hounds, pacing the scaffold and hydrating incessantly.

Whether agendas lie on the side of reason or that of treason is of no concern. Two nights hiding her own intent from Dr. Tenille and Elize during the SIF pretense at the GHU has solidified Nepharisse's temperance. It has also granted to Elize's mind a desperately needed reprieve. The voices are punishing to someone whose intentions are still rightly guided, yet they form part of who Elize is, and who she is destined to become.

Gratefully, a sweet word or two still has the calming effect it is designed to. Were this not the case, urgency would require a fragmented alibi, fused together with falsities. That is a situation Nepharisse is loathe to encounter, for her services would no longer be of value, and that would destroy future chances to demonstrate her true worth.

The ceremony has begun. The parents of the infants position themselves along either side of the split staircase, awaiting their turn to receive their child, the mothers ignorant of the secret nursery visits that the Unified clergy inflicted upon the little bundles. Nepharisse criticizes the presiding minion from the Global Spiritual Unit and her two attending lackeys as walking ignorance, trifling with knowledge they are too stupid to comprehend.

The ointment lands between the boy's eyes and quickly infuses the pineal gland, where it begins its metaphorical journey as the embodied Trinity. By the count of exactly three, the child is whipped on the buttocks, held upside down by the ankles, to release his newly blessed Unified voice, as "They are One" shakes the Central Core, drowning out the child's agony.

Once again, appearances deceive those who gather in Their trust. The proud parents embrace their treasure, a second infant is received, and the holy heist continues. At the orphaned twins, a moment of silent meditation honors their stricken mother and the unfortunate loss of their father in a late night cooling plant explosion. The GSU cleric invites Master Chung, the head sage at the Almedina orphanage that is to be their home, to anoint his new wards.

Nepharisse readies herself for evidence of a victorious nursery room breach, but she is not the only aspiring disruption in the Unification's divine mission. Sothese's three officials have channeled their nervous footwork towards the first drop from the sage master's vial. A dark-skinned stranger, leaning against the archway in the southwest corner, harbors anticipation under his wide-brimmed hat. Time stops as Nepharisse summons the vibrations of a past success.

▼ ▼ ▼

She sits, quietly focused, at an empty table, hovering her right hand just above the surface. Her tilted ears listen to the doctor speaking slowly and methodically, as he introduces his female colleague.

"Dr. Yarkovsky, this is the patient we were discussing earlier."

Nepharisse's reality shifts as her wavering fingers move a game piece forward. Her opponent's hands heave the game board upwards in a childish fit over defeat, inciting a derisive row from the family circle watching. Grace does not flow through those who lack equanimity.

Time slows as she collects each token and stick in mid-flight, to clear a view to her playful titter. The padded cell, however, echoes no laughter atop the silent vibrations of a world only she can feel. Nepharisse's simper charms the hidden rival and bedevils the doctor scribbling furiously. She lowers her eyes to the floor, raises them, and smiles through the woman across from her, whose shoes angle towards the exit. This medic is known to her, but a formal introduction does not exist.

Questions. All these silly questions. An eerie deep giggle becomes her fleeting response, and Nepharisse's interest in the present wanes. Immaterial are the answers that find their way into the human vessel's notes.

Trapped ... again ... always. A void opens inside her, while the three realities she currently juggles suspend each scene in her mind. The task before her is one that must negotiate with failure. The risk of loss is real, as real as real can be, when *they* watch ... and *they* are watching ... *They* are always watching.

The game continues. Nepharisse challenges her next sibling, but this is a distraction that has become an obstacle to her duty. She must go. *They* are blocking her path on the bridge between thoughts. No place becomes her destination as she realizes she has said too much. Frustration mounts. Elize needs her.

Purposefully and slowly, Nepharisse extends her left arm towards Dr. Yarkovsky's chest. Her open hand snaps shut, and whisks back to a tossing match with her right hand, content with the intangible prize she has seized. The unwitting prey follows the dreamy dance, that the invisible bounty traces, as it plays in the space between Nepharisse's gentle touches. With each enchanting flick of Nepharisse's wrists, the hair on Dr. Yarkovsky's body becomes more rigid, until one thick swallow and a cool shiver overtake her, and Nepharisse lays claim to the moment.

As an added measure of protection, Nepharisse moves a cupped left hand to her open mouth and clamps it shut, while the right simultaneously slams the tabletop. She stares with distant intensity at the empty shell of a woman sitting across from her and smiles.

Dr. Yarkvosky's fear inches back with a clearing of her throat, but the fear clings to its host.

More questions. The answer comes with a roll of the dice and a scowl from Nepharisse's new imperceptible opponent. The answer is the magic number that the doctor cannot see. This lack of vision elicits scorn from Nepharisse, who watches her oblivious victim labour to remember and to write.

Soon, it will come back. It will all come back. All will come back soon.

The sound of a racing heart introduces questions not so trite, at last. The doctor's breath trips at her own words. "Are you playing a game? Who are you playing with?"

The answer she seeks is on the table. It was there from the start. Nepharisse's board game win crosses the chasm between metaphor and fact. The contender was Dr. Yarkovsky.

The victory fades with Dr. Yarkovsky's head sliced open on the floor as it clips the sharp corner of the table, and receives a soothing farewell.

"Sweet dreams."

▲ ▲ ▲

Dreams as sweet as the delicacies on display are what Nepharisse envisions at present. She amplifies the triumphant feelings that her death-dealing game brought forward, and flows with the moment.

The drop hits the mark. Master Chung hangs the baby from her ankles, in proper GSU fashion, as he counts the seconds that stretch between the three officials, the mysterious fedora man, and Nepharisse. The sage master misses his cue by a window only heightened awareness can detect. The ointment switch is confirmed. But to whom does the glory belong?

Nepharisse pierces the brim of the unexpected challenger's hat with her eyes. She senses her intensity reciprocated, while her peripheral vision monitors the reaction from the threat she predicted. The filtered onshore breeze teases the air while they endure an endless pause, waiting for the imminent verdict.

The next instant announces the champion. A faint resonant wave from the miniature vermis at the Mount radiates through the booming chant. Nepharisse's relief triggers a muffled curse from the mystery man. The twin sibling's baptism further solidifies Nepharisse's claim, which provokes more muted profanity from the far corner. She follows the stranger's line of sight to Sothese's third official, who points her nose at Nepharisse and smirks. Nepharisse returns the insult, whilst she notes the drenched uniform and the glistening skin.

The hounds are testing their boundaries. Sothese does not know they are here, and they do not know who they challenge.

▼ ▼ ▼

A scintillating blue fireball illuminates the dense morning fog and disappears beneath a pair of amethyst eyes. The gemstone lenses retreat as the sound of four dozen sharp claws upon stone intensifies, and the rising mist reveals a pair of sapphire blue shoes escaping onto a barge moored on the lavender canal. Three officials hang off the edge of the Victory Bridge, foolishly planning a drop attack, unaware that the entity they are chasing has switched carriers.

Nepharisse hedges her survival with a secret weapon. She knows precisely where they are. Together, they can be defeated. What they gain as a unit, they lose in flexibility. As long as she can deny them her stabilizing influence, she can strike them down as individuals, bound to their physicality.

The waters become her shield. She plunges beneath the flat bottom of the boat as the triad drops from the mist to land together on its empty deck. Soon the sun will burn the rising brume and their offensive will attract Ministry spies. A brisk swim to the edge of a watery cliff will provide the backdrop that will reward the audacious stalkers with a virulent grave. Nepharisse harnesses their panic to propel the barge past the campus oval, trapping her witless kill on a seemingly self-guided flat torpedo.

Three simultaneous sunbeams, focused through a clear crystal, swoop through the sky in Nepharisse's outstretched arm as she breaches the water, leaving a crescent trail of her flight over the canal's quieting surface, where the three officials last existed before an explosion of flesh and fire sprayed them through the biowall and into the toxic tide below.

They should have known better than to hunt without their master's support.

▲ ▲ ▲

Sothese's officials have learned enough to fulfill their immediate needs, but the scent of their brazenness pollutes the festive floral incense. News of their double-dealings has certainly expanded Nepharisse's repertoire of successes. Soon, she can boldly state her desires, by showcasing her glowing portfolio of talents. Effecting a perfect sting operation, however, is not one of them.

Although the swap itself went to completion, competing interests invite concern. The man slipping behind the south staircase, still shading his eyes after a failed bid for the twins, complicates her follow-up visits. The yellow film, imbedded into the stitching of his somewhat carefully dusted coat, and his rudimentary grooming habits betray his origin.

Nepharisse presumes that his informant has ears inside the GHU, and speculates that he must have ties to the chosen pair as well, since the peril he chanced leaving the anonymity of the Restricted Sector, and the credit he must have provided for such an opportunity, are obstacles his kind consistently shun. His motivation is a matter best addressed as soon as the reception concludes.

A gentle tug on Nepharisse's neatly pressed blazer interrupts her machinations. A toddler offers her a rag doll, with the seam ripped at the base of the braided hairline. Her imaginary friend said that Nepharisse could sew her back up and protect her. The little girl skips back to her parents, jiggling and giggling, as if chased by a ghost with a tickling obsession, while her mother hushes the child for fear of GHU intervention.

The torn human facsimile rests in the natural cradle that Nepharisse unconsciously forms with her arms. She stirs in time to spy a fedora poking from behind the south staircase, then retreating.

The celebration can continue without her. Nepharisse entrusts the craft services to her assistants, and slips past the social protocol, to find the shuffle of her target's boots receding inside the ventilation system. Her resistance is short-lived. She shifts her priorities away from the attractive sapphire sparkle of the shoes that compliment her attractively appointed ensemble. The brilliance within is what comprises her charm. She enters the underwater generator level.

The shaft-level entrance guard is down. His stiff body shows all the predictable signs: complete organ failure, absence of puncture wounds, and ghastly white skin. The rumble from the hovertrain, passing over the central walkway, rattles the ductwork, yet it evokes no concern from the black eyes staring straight at her from across the shaft connecting the main artery to Ministry House. His ivory hand mocks a highland wave, and he speeds northward with Nepharisse in urgent pursuit.

The words she cares to speak have no command over him, and no diplomatic flair, so she chooses silence, to give space to her thoughts. This Restricted Sector miscreant will learn his place.

A strong backdraft pulls the pin from her manicured bun as she desperately scans for a hatch. She knows what menace behind her is stealing the oxygen before her. A fool's laughter presumes the battle won, but pure wisdom knows it has but begun. Nepharisse takes solace in the order of things, which does not always explain itself in the moment. His ego-driven disclosure, at this juncture, will prove to be a dark hole for his ambitions. There is a more immediate thorn to blunt. Nepharisse leaves the injured doll in the path of the yellow storm blasting to the east-west tunnels and hires a private slider to Tir-na-nog for a rejuvenating water treatment.

As the falling sun dims its light across Eadonberg, so shall the light dim inside the son of a perverted trinity. Tonight, Nepharisse vows to accept the sweet shop owner's lecherous challenge, without interruption. She sprinkles floral hearts onto the head of Oisin's horse and whispers a wish that all but the one whose favor she seeks would deem impossible.

The inviting aroma of cherry-flavored jellies, attached to her unsanctioned assignment, wafts past. She loiters at the fountain a further thirty minutes, then crosses the glass courtyard to Tir-na-nog's residential community. A light shines in the man's bedroom. Her target is set. Nepharisse rifts through the wall furthest from view and finds her surprise visit usurped.

The blackmailer points a large serrated blade towards the silhouette revealing itself. Sothese leads his drooling snarling hounds into the room and stops at the sight of the disheveled ginger-auburn curls and the sapphire blue eyes.

Nepharisse interprets his initial emotion as shock, thinly laced with remorse. However short-lived, its presence teases her hopes, as Sothese questions the hapless criminal as to what he was intending to extract from her. A lustful glance at her thighs ignites Sothese with a flash of anger. Nepharisse is conflicted ... he still loves her ... but the recordings ... she ... she must not succumb to his charm. He is not to be trusted, yet her judgment weakens at Sothese's choice of words.

"Delicious."

Furious yet curiously drawn to him Nepharisse remains. Nonetheless, there is no denying the betrayals that weaken his position, although "no worse than your own" is the quip his tongue lashes out with. Nepharisse and Sothese stare each other's defiance down while the hounds get anxious.

The man with the knife looks tasty to all but one of the canines, who narrows her eyes at Nepharisse instead. However, the meal must wait since Sothese instructs them to stand down. The words he selects to cede one of his sadistic pleasures to Nepharisse, highlight his arrogant nature.

"You do the honors, my dear." He and his pack back away into the shadows.

Nepharisse saunters invitingly up to the foolishly relieved man, grabs him behind the neck, and plants a long suctioning kiss on him. He fades to white, stiffens, and drops dead of complete organ failure, without a single puncture wound.

The sound of clicking on stone behind her fades as she turns around to face the female official from Ministry House, who is sweating profusely. Sothese calls the woman's name, and in a flash, she is gone.

Day 388: midi

"Perk. The recording is out of phase." Juicy. Stitch slides his portable viewer over to me right during a flyer bake drip.

"Whoops!" He pulls a huge cloth from who knows where he stores all his stuff, leans over, and wipes the viewer and my chin. He must have no body parts. He's mostly just the contents of his zigazillion pockets. Hehehe.

"So you don't use your sleeve." A poke and a smile. "I figged there had to be someone else in the room with you, watching but invisible." Really? Invisible? Added some fancy fungus to your flyer, eh?

"I don't see anyone."

"Invisible, Eli. You wouldn't see him, yeah?" Send him a snare.

"Or her." Or it. Rip. He triple-staccato-looped Keet's butt hop. "Trip, Stitch."

"Yeah, ya fig? I was dunked on this one. My brain needed to ease a bit so I had some fun. Perk, I added a b-b-bopping tune." He taps the volume way up. Ohhhm gee. Top funny. Best tap it back down though. There's too much attention on us.

"So when did you get the portaviewer?" At least I think it's a portaviewer. There's no pop-up feature on it.

"I call it a ghostgrabber. I smashed an ancient tablet to a slice-and-dice invention of mine." I thought as much. "It dissects

the flashes' cube-shaped frames into slices. Like an autopsy."
Dizzy. And just when I was flushing those images from my
mind. Nice try, Elize. I will not let you forget. Hush. Chomp
on some flyer bake. That will keep your imaginary mouth shut.
Silence is next to Godliness. You mean Pramamness. Hehehe.
It's cleanliness, fishy. Mind the flyer drip, Elize. Shut up.

"How many slices can you make?"

"Enough to see the quarks in your birthday cake."
Impressive. "If there is someone at the party, I'll find him. It's
just a matter of chopping time."

"Inside the atoms of my cake? Really." He's definitely
doing the funky fungus. "And how long will that take?" Sooner
than later I hope.

"Hard to fig. It depends on how long he sticks around
for. Could be weeks." What? "Or years. We're dealing with
calculus, chum." I don't have years.

"So what you're saying is, it really is random luck that will
find the voyeur." Oooooo. Sounds so salacious.

"Yeah. It's like a particle in the quantum field. It could be
anywhere … or everywhere."

"Well, if it were everywhere, you would have found it by
now, eh?" Is that a hint of a smirk coming on? "Face it, Stitch.
You've been zapped. Muahahaha."

He just grins, freezes the cube at Jenny's squiggle tails and
flips forward a dozen or so slices.

"Right here." He explodes in. His fingers trace the outline
of a hand holding Jenny's hair in mid-air.

I roll my eyes. "It's just a shadow from across the table
caused by the sun through the window."

He leans over and whispers. "Do you believe in ghosts, chum?" Honestly! Grab his flyer bake. "Ease! What are you doing?"

"Looking for fungus. Nothing. Show me your forehead. Maybe you caught the virus."

He slaps my hand away. His green hair turns brown at the tips. "Until I get a more fine-grained modulator working, you just have to trust me on this one. But we both know how that goes."

He has a point. I still think he's wasting his time, but it's his time to waste, so just let it go, girl. "OK. You may be right, but you must admit, it's a bit bent." Add a little innocent shoulder shrug and he'll come around to blue. There. Turquoise is good enough.

The whole premise of omnipresence though is one I have difficulty believing. It sounds too Unified. Shudder. Everywhere would mean anytime too. I'm feeling a little warm. Let's change the subject.

"I prefer the Snack Shack. The red flyer bake is better." I can see Ashton from here. Wave back. He looks sad. There used to be queues, but since this Snack Barge moved in with bigger portions, business has shifted. Shifty like this new concession owner.

"They taste fine to me. They have their own spice that's all. Your taste buds are just glued to the other one." He gulps down the last bit of his. "What about the rock? Did you test out your sketching skills with the chumbuds?"

"Keet has a sleeve of various research results. I found pretty much the same stuff." Except the reason why it keeps showing up in my pocket. I shudder at the thought of it, but I must be having micro memory lapses. I don't even notice the time gap. "There are very few places left where you can still find red granite ... above water at least." And no one would risk venturing below. No one sane anyway. "Keet's now looking for artifacts that come from those regions so we can try to match up the composition."

"Do you have it with you?"

"I put it somewhere safe." So safe in fact I don't remember where it is. Oh. Keet's comming me. "Hey lo, Keet."

"Do you have the stone with you?"

"N—" In my pocket again? "Yes, I have it with me." There goes Stitch's eyebrow.

"Juicy. Bring it to the museum. I found something. You need to come now though. There's a private function this afternoon."

"OK. See you soon." Hehehe. I'm giving Stitch white hair. Oh no. All white. I shouldn't laugh. Why not? He laughs at you. Always poking. Always smiling. You know what he is, do you not, Elize? Stop denying it. That is why you do not trust him. Enough! Yeah, I know what he is. My best friend. You do this with Keet too. Always trying to cast doubt on them. You cannot trust them. Right. And I can trust you? Of course. Flyer Mud! Stop meddling. Stitch is staring.

"I thought you said it was safe."

"It is. Right here in my pocket. Safe with me." I hope that was believable. It's not entirely false. The question is whether it's safe or not. It can disappear just as quickly as it appears.

"Of course ... when it wants to be found, yeah?"

"Let's see what Keet has for us. Finish up." Chomp. Gulp. Gag. Next time it's back to Ashton's.

Stitch is lagging behind. Wave him on.

"Greetings, Miss Elize, Mr. Zafarian. Be aware the archives close early today." Mme Beaudoin is unusually pleasant. "Silence rules are still in effect, however." She glares at Stitch. Now that's more like her.

There's Keet poking his head into the hall. Yes. We're hurrying. We sneak straight into the artifacts room.

"Stitch, you monitor the one-way mirror to make sure Mme Beaudoin stays clear."

"I'm on it, bud."

I haven't seen Keet this excited since Nathruyu made first contact. He rushes to the back of the room where articles get packed for their next tour stop.

"I cataloged it just over three weeks ago. There were so many fascinating objects that day I simply forgot about it." I try to peak over his shoulder but he's too tall for me. "The curator didn't trust me with it, so he stored it himself. He was paranoid that I might drop it." He takes a deep breath to steady his arms shaking with anticipation. He pulls out a case from inside the box and tiptoes to the work table. It seems somewhat heavy for its size. He sets the valise down very slowly and gingerly. "The curator said it was priceless, more so than anything else in the museum." That's quite the claim. "He also warned me to keep my distance."

Stitch peeks towards the table. "Still clear." He returns to scout duty.

"Thanks, bud." Keet picks the lock?

"What have you been learning from the chumbuds, dear brother?" He just grins at Stitch and acts all innocent. Not bad, pup. Not bad at all. I slip my pirate patch on him. He chuckles. "It was headed for another museum, but then it wasn't sent. I don't know—" He lifts the clear display box out and nods. "I see. It's broken. There's a piece missing ... Hang a sec. Where's the rock, Eli." Now where is it? Right pocket. No. Left. No. Right. I've nabbed it. Keet's looking a little confused. "This wasn't broken when I cataloged it." He lifts the protective cover. I clip the stone in place and—

"Whoa!" The fragment got sucked out of my hand. It's melting right into the gold-capped granite pyramid.

Stitch leaves his post. "Pica ziga trip!"

All three of us watch with our mouths open. Mashrin's rock is a perfect fit! It must be at least— "Watch out!" Crap! What the— "Keet! No! Stitch, he's hit!" Run to him. Not now. Close your eyes. Breathe. Count. No. Forget it. No time to count. Get a grip on yourself, girl. "Keet! Talk to me. Please!" He's not responding. What do I do? No tears. I can't see with tears. Stitch starts CPR.

"Ouch! Way bud, I was trying to save your life." Stitch is relieved.

Keep breathing. Calm. Keet's fine. What a scare!

"Slap me, Stitch. It's just a reflex." A shoulder shrug as Keet struggles to sit up.

Stitch is laughing. "Trip, bud. A jittery pink-haired mick leaning over with an open mouth would have jumped me too." He helps Keet up. "Did you see that plasma arc fly right at you?"

"No. It was too fast. I just felt a strong pressure on my chest, and I guess passed out."

"You flew across the room, fishy." Check under his shirt. "I'm glad you decided to start wearing your crystal again. It just might have saved your life. It took the brunt of the hit and not a scratch. Crap! Mme Beaudoin might have heard us." Look out the one-way glass. No. Just a young academic looking up from his research. I must be seeing flashes now. No, it's just the sun reflecting off his eyes from the skylight. He must have turned his head slightly. Hallucinations. Geez. Are they back now too? Shake it out, girl. You're fine. It's a plasma arc echo that's all.

"He has no access, Eli. He'll just stick his nose right back down. There. Told you. He's here every day." Phew.

"How are your eyes, Stitch? Are you all right?"

He blinks a few times. "Yeah. Ta, Eli. I didn't go blind, but it was pica bright. I'll see spots for a while." He's already trying to figure out the physics of it. Keet is staying clear of the pyramid. Good idea. Stitch and I had better not touch it either. "I fig it's a defense mechanism. The curator must have known this." That makes sense.

"Are you sure it wasn't broken already, Keet. How would anyone get near it?"

"I guess they could throw another rock at it, or something harder, or maybe even drop it."

"OK. That's plausible. Then how did Mashrin get it? The timeline doesn't add up." Mashrin died almost ten months ago. "There has to be a second one."

"I think Eli has it figged, Keet. Someone must have

swapped in a broken decoy and then swiped the original."

"And whoever did the switch might be connected to Mashrin somehow."

"And it could be the same person who put the broken piece in my pocket last year at Tir-na-nog." We found nothing on the recording Keet was taking at the time, but that's the only place it could have happened. "Stitch, be careful, don't—" Huh?

"Maybe it was just a charge build up. It seems innocuous now."

Should I? Sure. Just a little tap. He's right. "The seam is completely smooth. Come and feel it, Keet."

"I'll take your word for it." He gives the artifact a wide berth and comes around the other side. "It looks dull compared to when I cataloged it. And I was able to touch it then. What are you doing?" Stitch is snooping through the museum packets and surveillance system. "I don't even have access to that and I work here."

Stitch flashes a cocky smile then frowns. He copies the security feed onto a flash he pulls from his bottomless pant pockets and starts bopping through the purchase orders. He stops. He stares. His hair flashes black for an instant. "Trip. Pass me a blank slip, Eli."

"What? None in your picazillion pockets?" I stick the slip on the board for him. He moves it to the right spot and rips it off. "Who's the seller?"

"We have to leave. My supervisor's coming." Keet's pacing. "Quick. Clean off the board, Stitch. And uh—"

"I'll put it away, Keet. You go and stall Mme Beaudoin."

He takes another wide semi-circle around the table.

"Thanks, Eli."

Juicy. The academic is asking for help on his personal automated librarian. Keet waves us out. Stitch seems anxious to get back. His hair is a complete beacon. We quickly nod, and he heads for the foyer. No chumbud salutes in public. Keet and I sneak right past Mme Beaudoin to the back exit. To the crypt. Now!

Keet freezes. He stares for a split second into the water under the marble bridge to the cove of mausoleum replicas. I beat him to his crypt. Tap tap tap. Hurry up, Keet.

I hear Sparky in canine protection mode. Hehehe. "Watch your ankles." Oh, show some humor. Keet slowly creaks the door open. He pulls me in. Slam! He leans up against it. "Keet? Are you feeling OK?" Hmmm. Maybe a bit louder. "KEET!"

"Shhh." He's just standing there shifting his eyes around. What's with him? I think the plasma arc got his brain instead of his crystal. Snap to, Keet. Snap. Snap. SNAP!

"Right. What were you saying?" He takes his crystal off and examines it.

"What are you thinking?" I know what I'm thinking. I'm thinking that the crystal was the cause of the whole attack in the first place.

"You might be right. I felt a sting just moments before the thunderbolt." He puts the crystal back on.

"Maybe you should leave the crystal off in case you find the original pyramid."

"No. My gut tells me to keep it on."

That's because your brain is fried. I don't think I quite deserved a snare for that. Hang a sec, how …? Hmmm.

"Let's go to Tir-na-nog." Huh? That's sudden. He puts Sparky in his bed and rushes me out the door. "We can take the hovertrain. It's faster. Race you there." Is this my brother? The private function has started. We need to work our way around the outside scaffold. Ouch!

"Pardon us. The hovertrain is coming." The two girls bump their way through the crowd onto the central walkway but no hovertrain in sight.

"Do you hear one, Keet?" He shrugs. Apparently, we're the only ones who can't hear it. Right. It's the new bioTravel enhancement. Here comes the sucking slider. "I guess we'd better walk to Tir-na-nog then."

Keet whispers back. "And everywhere else for that matter. That should keep you away from dazing in the Restricted Sector again, eh?"

A snare is not enough for that comment. Jab him.

"Ouch!" Keet's off in some other dimension. His focus certainly is not on where he's walking.

"What's so urgent?"

"I need more journals, like Stitch's present. Mr. G ordered some for me." Ah. The motive explained. He must have a lot to say these days if he needs a new journal already. "I want to be prepared."

That sounds more like Keet, planning ahead. Prepared for what though? He's hiding something. Of course he is. He can't be trusted. Not you again. Can't I just have some peace up there? *Peace belongs to a mind which accepts life as it is, rather than as it thinks it should be.* Fine, keep talking then. We're almost at the jade fountain anyway. I'm going to sit here while Keet … just stares at it, apparently. Juicy. A juggler.

"Keet … Keet! Can I borrow your recorder while you shop?" Tap it on.

Look at those crystal balls fly. Whoa! He almost dropped one. Stop wasting time. What? You're wasting time. Find the book. Time is wasting. The book is what you must find. Close your eyes and find the book.

✂ ✂ ✂

"He is watching you. Caution, Miss Elize. You are thirst provoking."

Did I not ask for peace? Oh. I'm dreaming. Open my eyes. They are already. I'm awake. It's a holoadvert winking at me. "A drink?" Roll your eyes and keep walking. It's dark already? When did we leave Tir-na-nog? Sigh. What a pair we make. Keet is off in his head too. Wait! Did he call me by name? No. I'm always a bit foggy after an episode. Geez. The advert's following us.

"What do you want!?"

"To offer you a sample of my wares, my dear."

"You're not real." No less real than I am, Elize. And I as well. *The reality within creates the reality without.*

"Perhaps not, but my voda is … by 20%, in fact. The legal limit. My word is my brew, and this it will do. Your thirst it will quench, my darling wench."

A snicker from Keet. "What happened to the guarantee by the roots of your hairs to relieve all our cares?"

"Change happens." He points to his receding hairline and

disappears. We cross a bridge to the next building scaffold and there he is again. "You both are new to the city, barely a year." "How do you know that?"

"There is nothing and no one I do not see." He winks again. "Versal shame I am but a holograph, eh?" Keet and I secretly shudder. The persistent peddler peeks past us. "Curious choice of friend." He vanishes.

Stitch is running at us. He is completely grey. He throws me a wig. "Quick. Put it on." This looks ridiculous. He's serious. Put it on. Done. And?

"You're wanted for murder, Eli."

Keeto

Three days have passed since my little plasma party in the artifacts room, and I am still clueless as to what transpired there. I have been moonlighting, through the historical section of the archives for any oddities attributable to a granite pyramid with an attitude, but no such enchanted object exists ... officially, that is.

Stitch sent a flare through the maze. As usual, the chumbuds slap theories upon theories, which all make sense to a certain degree, given an initial assumption. However, the more aliases join the quest, the further interim conclusions deviate from the facts. What we need are two or three solid thinkers to rein in the rest and discover the golden fleece through the maze. The contending hypothesis, as of earlier this evening, is that our ill-tempered relic is a new covert GMU weapon, and that I was the unfortunate soul who unwittingly set it off.

Fortune flipped a pass on Eli as well. For three days, she has been sporting a short curly blonde wig underneath a plain colored hijab, a clever disguise offering a facial shroud at a moment's notice. The head wrap further acts as an expression of style that people she already knows can readily accept, without probing questions. Although a niqab has more coverage and is common enough, it is most often associated with a female sage, which Eli most definitely is not, though she likes to think she is.

There is no public announcement citing foul play in the sweet shop owner's death, only a statement describing his passing as premature heart failure. Mention of the flash flood of a thief, who broke through cabinets, closets, and even walls, looking for something important enough to kill for, only hides inside SIF packets.

Under normal circumstances, Stitch would enthusiastically re-fling this kind of mud all over the network and wait for karma to unfold. Not so in this instance. The Ministry veils are working in Eli's favor. The only ones who can identify her as a suspect are a few SIF agents, misguided by the testimony of one questionable witness.

Since the flash of Eli that the classified SIF packets are wielding has dust on it, even if it were aimed at the community wall, it would just slip right off. Leave it to Stitch long enough and he finds a way, even to recreate Odwin's dust filter. But my greatest concern is the image itself, a cropped version of the one I took, using an off-grid recorder, of Eli and Stitch terrorizing the holorider at Tir-na-nog last year.

The current calm I am experiencing, relative to my journal entry three days ago, is not a testament to Stitch's costuming abilities. Today we gratefully discovered a reversal in the eyewitness's position. I admit that I have my own prejudices, as Stitch would no doubt attest to, but I believe they would stop short of accusing someone of a crime, with but a tainted vantage point. You see, that day, while I was checking the status of the journals on order at Mr. G's shop, your impetuous daughter decided to update her look. I guess her fidgeting required more creative outlets than a morphing room decor.

Eli arrived at the shop with her hair tied back into a loose bun and wearing the latest French lace shrug and pencil skirt, the kind only high credit worth Unified elite can reasonably afford. The exclusive uniform branded her as a trading class matriarch, generally mistrusted by the common resident, whose malicious gossip provokes whispered insults as the rich strut the walkways. She likely attracted such slander when she decided to act the part as well, quite convincingly may I add.

While I was examining a hand-carved small table, curiously identical to the one from Eli's newest room decor, she sashayed into the shop demanding a refund for the dysfunctional Mini-Lizzy Mr. G had the "shameless gumption" to sell her. He just laughed at the futile chase efforts she went on to describe, and offered her the vase stand I was admiring to replace the other one. "All sales final" never applies to those with the credit that perpetuates the double-standard that angers those who feel discriminated against. That very conviction validated the reasoning that withdrew Eli from the SIF's suspect list.

Today, the private man-hunt was terminated and the official heart failure obituary remains. The investigator assigned to the case received an anonymous tip that the accusation against Eli may be born from bigotry. He conducted a second eyewitness identification session, presenting images of a dozen female Tir-na-nog shoppers that same day, but edited so that a different woman dawned the tell-tale shrug, skirt, and bun. The bystander picked some other woman dressed as the unpopular elite. She looked absolutely nothing like Eli.

As a further precaution, Stitch attached a scrubber to the packets containing Eli's picture, which in hindsight may not have been the best course of action. Now we have nothing to dig deeper into that could indicate where the image originated from and when.

Rogue recordings seem to be a theme this week. The security camera in the artifacts room was the after-shock from the thunderbolt that whipped me across the room. This morning, the curator called me into his office, extremely concerned. He was quick to itemize his displeasure at my delinquent behavior. First, I invited unauthorized museum patrons access to the artifacts room. Second, I handled an object that he had clearly instructed me not to touch. And third and most importantly, I had endangered my life in doing so.

His genuine regard for my safety surprises me. It goes beyond that of an employer-employee or even a mentor-mentee relationship. I sense there is an outside commitment that binds him to my well-being. After watching the feed with him, I agree that paying heed to his advice is in my best interest. I still shudder at how the surge I apparently provoked from the short-fused rock picked me straight up off the floor and blasted me a good three meters away.

All I could think of was, "Crap. I should have asked Stitch to clean the evidence," but, in the moment, my brain was not in a coherent state. Since then, I have felt somewhat disjointed. It is almost as if I no longer have a consistent awareness of the uniformity of space, whatever that means. The curator has also noticed a change in my focus, which further worries him. But why?

In talking with Stitch at midi today, he suggested that my mentor may have entered into a Gadlin contract in order to ensure my welfare. That would have been Odwin's doing, whose own safety is currently threatened by accusations of terrorism. My dealings with the itinerant merchants are what allowed Eli and me to flee to Eadonberg, quietly and safely. Even our transfer chests arrived intact. Odwin has shown nothing but the utmost confidentiality, honor, and reliability. The Pramam would serve his constituents well were he to adopt the same qualities, rather than underhandedly work to vilify a culture that has consistently bailed humanity out.

Fortunately, Odwin is still on retreat. And if he were not, the GMU would still lack any intelligence on his whereabouts. No member of any clan would offer up the Gadlin leader and live to reap the contractual rewards. The leader embodies the creed, and, as such, his life is protected as a matter of honor, priority, and survival. Stitch expects decoys to appear as the ridiculous Ministry accusations spawn a world-wide infestation of credit-seeking community informers, like the couple who followed Eli around last week. Perhaps this is why Odwin remains incommunicado, even through his alias in the chumbuds network.

Wakanda, the acting Gadlin leader, refuses to assemble a meeting of chieftains for fear of unnecessarily creating unrest, or so she claims. She reasons that although a spiritual cleanse lasting more than nine months is highly unusual, it can happen, especially if the selected sanctuary is substantially remote. In any case, Stitch is looking forward to Odwin's return. The temporary mistress is no bastion of serenity, in his opinion, and now I am inclined to agree with that assessment.

Just after closing, I was volunteering my time setting

up the front garden for tomorrow's dawn social as a way to make amends for worrying the curator, when I overheard him receiving a woman in the Great Hall. Her greeting was unmistakably Gadlin, and particularly distinctive in its tone. Stitch's repeated mockeries proved to be more than frivolous entertainment at her expense. They were well-executed and timely.

The curator was visibly distraught by Wakanda's accusatory language. She barked something about him being irresponsible for having broken it. Then I almost dropped my end of the buffet table. She snapped about her poor judgment in having ever leased it to him in the first place. Wakanda owns the granite pyramid!

The Gadlins are a savvy lot when it comes to dealing in antiques and knowing how much their client is willing to pay for such merchandise. She, no doubt, could smell the large purses of the museum network's donors and took full advantage of the competitive nature of said modern bourgeoisie. Each city museum has its own local supporters, and when something exotic surfaces, the highest bidder lays claim to fame, as the artifact tours other cities.

I seized an opportunity to retrieve the music stands in storage down the hallway while tracking their conversation up to the archives. I swear to you that the stone floor shook when this woman stomped towards the artifacts room. Albaraaton must have an overabundance of food, and this woman must have a ravenous appetite for delicacies that rivals the one she has for shiny objects. I wager that she engages an expansive and loyal network to source her treasures. Perhaps even certain individuals who feed her morsels of information? Someone who has access to a large network? Someone who knows her fancy weapon has been unexpectedly deployed?

I rushed through the final orchestra setup and then blistered to my crypt, to grab my recorder with the original image that the SIF had mysteriously acquired of Eli. You can guess what was smashing around in my head while my satchel flapped against my butt as I ran to the campus oval. I spared Eli a sermon on the comm and simply told her that I was on my way over, and strongly suggested, almost insisted, that Stitch join us there. Her lack of words emitted an aura of awe. She complied without even the slightest verbal poke. Juicy! I could get hooked on reverence. Hehehe.

Well, I threw such a cargo transport of questions at Stitch that Eli could have swallowed a shipment of raw flyers in the time it took for the steam finally to clear my ears. Did you call in Wakanda? How do you know so much about the Gadlins? Who is this new Gadlin, really? Have we been set up from the start? What strings are they pulling on the curator? And finally, what do you, Mr. Zafarian, have to do with all of this? I made it clear to Stitch that he could take that smile of his and poke it somewhere else, if he so much as turned one strand of hair red, grey, black, brown, or anything but green or blue. Secretly, however, I hoped that it would all turn grey, but he managed to stay calm, with just enough temple massaging to satisfy my ego.

Odwin was his uncle Sauri's best friend, the one whose son Zbrietz was kidnapped and murdered at nine-years-old after living with Stitch for almost as long. Odwin felt responsible for his friend's infant, and when Zbrietz disappeared, Odwin vowed not to let the same happen to Zbrietz's cousin, especially as they were the same age. Stitch's parents sent him to live with Odwin, to keep him safe, and Odwin took him on as an apprentice. That is why Stitch has a wide array of covert skills, an aptitude for gadgetry, and an even stronger reaction to Ministry attacks on Gadlin integrity than just being half-Gadlin by blood.

With regards to Wakanda, Stitch was quite direct. He does not trust her. He has only seen her, in person, on a few occasions, but more than enough to get a sense of her. He also emphatically denies having directly contacted her, or discussing any of our findings in the archives with anyone inside or outside the chumbuds network. Wakanda found out about the granite stone through some other means, but from whom or through what means is the puzzle.

As expected, once my hostility tempered, Stitch was quick to make light of my newfound boldness. He tugged at a roll peeking out from my satchel, and before I could stop him, he unrolled it. The look he sent my way, when he uncovered the Galleon's sails, was obnoxiously fair. It was my turn to share, and the only explanation I could offer was that I had been compelled to take them.

A quip about my caper being a highland excuse for kleptomania enticed a giggle out of Eli although she admitted that she was impressed. They were both prodding for the details so I called them in closely, and whispered: "I opened the door and fear was no more." I had a good laugh at their wonderment, then admitted the truth. The door to his O'Leary

Hall office was unlocked. I simply walked in.

What was that?

Has fear come knocking at my door now? It sounds more like howling. Sparky has a ridge of fur all the way down his back, and he is staring at the niche, where my shrine to you lives. If I were not pasted to my bedsheets, I would hazard a peep through the slit, just to ease my nerves. Who am I kidding? This fresh bravado of mine comes and goes, and I would say that it has pretty much vanished right now. No head of mine is looking up that air vent. Jumpers!

Sparky! Ah yes, my fearless protector. He may be tiny, but nevertheless, his sharp teeth are still effective.

There it is again. Send some courage my way, Mother. I sense you cultivated an abundance of it … for our sake. And a sliver of something inside me knows you still do, albeit in a form I rarely glimpse. Only the pages of my journals incarnate your essence. Please infuse my quill with words of comfort and release the twinkling melody from your crystal hair tresses into me.

All will be well soon, my dear.

I did it. I finally harnessed enough power to squeak open a gap in the door and survey the cove. The lights in the other eight mausoleums were off, giving the blue glow under the floating floral centerpiece dominion over the night. The mist over the water played tricks with my eyes as did Sparky with my nose. He must have let out a silent killer because the scent was overpowering. And then the crawling under my skin started, then the heat.

Fear entered as I raced for a temperature sensor and

stuck it to my skin. The mirage-like movement through the vapors meant either I was crazy, or I was coming down with a hallucinogenic fever or virus. A faint blowing sound had me slamming the door shut. Whether it be my imagination or not, whatever was attempting to come in from the cold met with a hard stop. Then I heard them.

Adrenaline shot through the tips of my fingers and toes, until the explosion settled and blood returned to the fantasy factory in my head. Night flyers. They were just night flyers enjoying swoops and dives in the generator-lit darkness. No temperature, no monsters, just paranoia, which is a new development — in my case. Even my last trip to Tir-na-nog inspired conspiracy theories in the most harmless, yet annoying, devices.

I remember escaping to the jade fountain while Eli and Mr. G negotiated her refund. Dozens of creepy holocasters snuck up on me and whipped their holographs in my face, trying to sell me on Ministry propaganda, or crazy products like Mr. G's bug repellent coats. Lucky for me they are mute, but for almost all those with biochips, they are pests not too dissimilar to night flyers in fact. The Unification Media Council should tighten up their broadcast licensing rules.

The commotion must have disturbed the waters because I saw movement in the fountain, suggesting that water had a hidden awareness, if you believe in that sort of thing. I know Stitch does. Everything has a soul for him. Real or not, time appeared to have stopped, and I could absorb every detail of the entire scene. Of course I recorded the phenomenon, but all that I caught was proof of my industrious imagination. There was nothing there.

I now question whether I even saw Caroline's curly ginger hair and sapphire blue eyes, smiling at me through the fountain spray. Eli interrupted my expectant gaze with a rib about at least having Nathruyu off my mind, to which I whipped back that at least my sanity keeps me from manifesting Stitch wearing a silk suit. A snare came my way, predictably. Eli is still upset at Caroline for disappearing again without a word. "Who needs a friend like that?" she grumbled.

I too have misgivings about Caroline's conduct, with Sothese in particular, not only in that way, but also because I suspect she told him where the anonymous tips came from … me. Eli still does not know that I gambled our freedom against Nathruyu's capture at the Snack Shack that day.

I hear your soothing melody twinkling. So tired. I can sleep soundly now, with you in my heart.

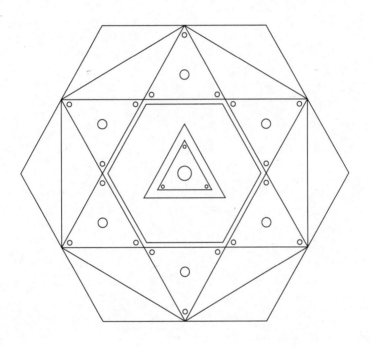

CHAPTER FIVE

NEPHARISSE

Day 391: late evening

Sing me a lullaby
Chase all my demons away
Stay with me here awhile
Make all my fears go away

Nepharisse hums a soothing melody as she hunts for tales of strange sightings in the maze. The versal energy within her has shifted. That distant yet eternally familiar feeling, with the faint scent of failure, weaves its way through the cracks of her resolve. If only she had access to the hip jiggling half-Gadlin's underground network, she could take advantage of virtual anonymity to expand her power of influence. But the permissions Nathruyu had borrowed from the Gadlin leader have been revoked. A new leader, wise to the workings of Zafarian's genius, has exploited the leverage her temporary assignment enjoys and has reset the alias. As a member of the GHU catering staff, Nepharisse is blind to the secret packets and chumbud community walls.

Darkness seeps into her veins. Still, she wills herself awake. The light flickers. Nepharisse risks reaching her breaking point through her tenacity as a cool wave ruffles the surface of her ivory skin. To persist in her research, in such a state, could open the gate for the shift to advance unchecked. This would negate all gains she has made in solidifying her position of worth. Regardless, her love and hatred for the man who betrayed her instructs her shaking hand to clip in the flashes she has so far resisted to watch.

His naked mirage drives himself into her, in repeated forward thrusts. His arm reaches behind her neck, while his body slowly drops away, revealing the carved reliefs in the ceiling of his Ministry House quarters. The plush silk blood red bed coverings rise and fall at her sides, whilst ivory holographic hands, a lock of ginger hair wrapped around the left thumb, pull his head towards her lips. A shiver of ecstasy, mixed with pain, overwhelms her as Nepharisse propels her chest forward in an attempt to stop her fall. Her body fails, and she lands flat on her back, wrapped in the coldness of her empty reality. A tear freezes on her quivering blue lips.

▼ ▼ ▼

The desert air whips the soft skin on Nepharisse's face, like ten billion microscopic arrows made of ice. Her horse fares better in the night, as does his delicate passenger, while they race to the river bank. The unfortunate yet critical timing, that could end in catastrophe, propels her towards a sanctuary they must attain, before her lips darken to rival her sapphire blue eyes. Movement in the waters forestalls their intended passage, and the lead horse forges a new path across the delta. There is no camouflage that can cheat the hounds that chase them, leaving few options for escape.

Equine speed is their best defense against the fork-tailed beasts. Nepharisse leans over her charge and into the steed, pressing her cheek against his neck, and whispers: "Fly like the wind." The bundle she carries stirs. The ordeal has weakened him, but his breath is steady still. Success is but nine days away, as long as they reach the haven which appears over the horizon. The black stallions rage towards the hill crest, shrouded in a whirl of dust.

The riders sing their victory as the doors slam shut and the hunters meet with a hard stop. The boy's absence duly noted, Nepharisse prepares for an overnight vigil. The boy must not return with images that can speak. He has seen too much.

▲ ▲ ▲

The morning sun caresses warmth back into Nepharisse's lips and she rises. Her experience with Sothese last night tapped feelings she had hoped were long sealed and stowed. It is time to confront him. Yes. Tonight she will disrupt his little kingdom and rip out his royal rug from underneath his arrogant feet. But first, a trip to the archives will confirm her readiness. And then, the cocky smirk will slide off Sothese's face faster than he can slither up anyone else's skirt, or into their pants, for that matter.

As she dresses herself in the GHU-issued tailored uniform, the abuse she recorded from Nathruyu's Ministburg dungeon plays on the board in her bedroom. This is the version she must triple-check, to ensure her edits are unrecognizable, for certain truths are not yet ready for the ears and eyes she aims to share this with. Satisfied with her masterpiece, she copies the interrogation onto a flash and places it in her satchel, while a copy of the original uncut footage rests safely against her breast, inside her fitted shirt, for later. More than one can play on the field of deception.

Her newest living arrangements suit her quite well. The restrictions imposed with the bioTravel implementation have prompted a change in environment since automated checkpoints are not amenable to her influence. Furthermore, she is accustomed to, and expects, unlimited freedom in her work, in so far as third party meddling is concerned. From where she receives her guidance, the Pramam's decrees form no part to any party. A quick hop over the eastern canal and across the central walkway is all she needs to reach the Museum of Antiquities' hand-carved marble gate.

The orchestral entertainment at the dawn social is offering a last dance to its delighted audience. Nepharisse swoops by, smiling at all who recognize her, and caresses her way past the greeter in the Great Hall. She elevates her thoughts above the weak-minded souls who cross her path, as she glides to the large round table under the crystal dome, inviting sunlight into the infamous Round Room. PALs buzz throughout the archives, ferrying sleeves, parchments, and books around as their directors sit comfortably and attend to their research, except for the youthful academic rummaging through the stack that forms the northernmost spoke of the wheel-shaped library.

Before Nepharisse can survey the room for her mark, the academic already has eyes fixed on her. Regardless, she sashays into position and brushes up against Keeto's shoulder, as she drops the adulterated copy of her Ministburg cinematography into the satchel strapped over the back of his chair. The hair behind Keeto's neck shows signs of alertness, while he feigns interest in the research before him. Nepharisse smiles. She leans over and examines one of the slips he has imprinted, describing a rocky city bordering a submerged quarry of red granite.

The pleasant surprise in Keeto's bright eyes replays the images from Sothese's sexcapades at the sweet shop. Nepharisse momentarily loses her ability to craft the right words, while her heart beats out the confusion in her mind at triple speed. What exactly are the relationship expectations hidden behind that child-like intensity? Nepharisse flirts with speculations, delaying her even further. The lapse nearly costs her quiet passage through the archives. She places her right hand on Keeto's shoulder and whispers as her delicate touch caresses him into a blissful trance.

"Great place for a vacation. You need a vacation. You deserve a thrilling vacation. You will find the tide quite breathtaking."

Keeto meets Nepharisse's warm smile. Impressions of pristine waves lapping four small pairs of feet on a sandy shoreline, running carefree in the setting sun, come alive in Keeto's dreamy gaze. Nepharisse savors the innocence that once was as she leaves her own investigatory handiwork, arousing the interest of the suspicious academic, who is scanning today's obituaries, and eliciting Keeto's curiosity towards her coifed ginger-auburn bun.

She pauses to greet Mme Beaudoin with a slight show of teeth until the draft behind her signals the impending moment of truth. What happens from this point forward will either empower her, or cast her spirited aspirations into a shatterproof glass box.

Echoes in the Great Hall from the early morning social around the Fountain of Bardo in the front garden now belong to memories in the walls. Nepharisse contemplates the silent footsteps, inviting her to the exhibit room before the doors open for the general public. Security cameras do not concern her like they do the hooded scholar, who assumes an austere position in front of a beautiful gold statue dating back to the Roman Empire. What does worry her, however, is the confrontational demeanor already apparent in her partner's stance.

Nepharisse's emotional being removes itself from her physical body, as a measure of temperance, and hovers over the pair. A well-appointed woman, drunk with anger, would make for good entertainment, but not discrete dialog.

Nepharisse breathes the vision of her eventual success, and the oral sparring match begins.

"What are you doing here?"

A split-second's hesitation could give the bully an edge. No matter what history they have shared together, all that is over. Nepharisse has now entrusted her heart's desire to her ability to claw the ground with the talons of her resolve. She is the chosen one. She is the one to bring balance to this volatile situation. She answers swiftly and decisively. "We must contain this."

"Leave it to me, Nepharisse. You are but a simple

messenger."

The quip was uncalled for. Nepharisse states with clarity that past relationship dynamics are no longer acceptable. "Yes. And the message I have for you is *we* must contain this." Confidence is an admirable quality that Nepharisse is putting to work through her insistence, but over-confidence leads to errors, which, if not promptly corrected, result in failure.

And what of failure? Clemency does not exist for negligence of this magnitude. Nepharisse finds the lack of will to cooperate disconcerting. All sacrifices will be for naught if *they* find Keeto, including those of a tormented mother whose allegiance has always been her grounding force.

"You don't own messages, you relay them. What did you slip into the boy's satchel?" Silence becomes the whisper that turns to anger. "Denial is futile. I was watching."

"That particular message was not meant for you."

Such unprecedented boldness releases the scorn that finally triggers an emotional reaction.

"Remember your place."

The volume trips the sensors, which brings an irate Mme Beaudoin to the entrance, demanding an explanation for such disrespect towards the tranquility of her shift. "The special privileges you currently enjoy, my dear scholar, are not entitlements. And who are you?" She charges towards Nepharisse, with her hand primed over the button on her lapel.

Nepharisse deflects the rage descending on her by releasing her own upwards. The time for fury shall come, but now is not that time. She bows her head respectfully to Mme Beaudoin and smiles as she slowly raises her eyes. The would-be GMU informant returns her hand to her side and mirrors the greeting.

Donors are always welcome in the exhibit room. Donors are respectful of patrons. Donors understand the virtues of silence.

"Always a pleasure to meet our generous donors." Mme Beaudoin bows again and exits into the hallway.

As the footsteps fade, Nepharisse reflects on the near catastrophe her counterblast could have created had reason submitted to the deliberate provocation that had consistently bested her in the past. Surface honor and loyalty obscure a self-serving and opportunistic spirit, which manifests itself as a patronizing personality that tramples collaboration, but if she is to request a reprieve from historical behavior, then she must bequeath the same.

With continued poise, befitting a devoted competent envoy, she recaptures the silence and offers her arm as a truce. The two walk side by side as they discuss their options.

"You must not contact him again. That is my task. You must not disrupt the order of things, Nepharisse."

"A new order forms when chaos appears."

Only a fool would deny that truth, and there are no fools in the exhibit room. The subject closes in peaceful consensus and the conversation circles back to the beginning.

"We must contain this. Continued resistance produces no positive results and stunts any progress. Divisiveness is an attitude which feeds our enemies and starves our allies."

"We must find them first, Nepharisse. I have been searching without success, which is fortunate. The situation is still controllable."

"The situation is fluid. They can slip through at any time."
A fear unlike any that Nepharisse has ever experienced pumps
through the blood she has grown accustomed to. The mystery
man she tracked into the ventilation shafts bores his solid black
eyes into the back of her own. Any threats that can complicate
or even delay events, as they are designed to unfold, could
invite a future neither of them wants.

The touch of a small rolled-up parchment against her
fingers disrupts her musings. She scans its coded contents.

"There are more immediate tasks to concern yourself with,
Nepharisse."

"But ... Nathruyu is ... I—"

"You will not be alone."

Emotions fall from the carved ceiling of the exhibit room,
but Nepharisse is prepared to accept the surge. They meld with
her and settle quite comfortably, proving that she is ready for
her surprise visit to the Restricted Sector, tonight.

Mme Beaudoin lifts her head from her board and frowns
as Nepharisse walks past the Round Room entrance. A subtle
bow and warm glance clears the confusion, and she slips into
the Great Hall, through the front court, and out the marble
arches.

Freshness permeates the clear blue sky. A rejuvenating
rest by the water's edge, with the sun burning strong, will
smooth her nerves while tonight's plan formulates in her mind.
Murmurs skimming the surface of the central canal call her
southward through the morning rush of makeshift bandanas
and shifty eyes. The titter she attempts to muffle draws fleeting
suspicions from a couple scurrying past.

Although the past six days have uncovered no new infections, the current cases progress with steady decay, as yet unchecked, a fact prompting over-caution as a means of protection. Anyone not acting defensively raises questions as to their ethnicity, since the GHU postulates that Gadlins are immune to whatever ails the general public, hence the Ministry accusations of viral terrorism.

Nepharisse charms her way to the Victory Bridge and onto the campus oval. Her boldness would likely turn a few heads, so she dawns a head scarf and swoops through the orchard, past the pond, along the ivy wall, and back out the southeast gate, with a congenial salutation from perimeter security, of course. Once in the forest fringe, she continues her journey southwards, until her footing teeters on Eadonberg's liquid escarpment.

Happiness, sadness, love, hate, generosity, greed, kindness, malice, forgiveness, revenge, … centuries of sentiments churn from the ocean's depths, with every tidal surge. The memories of millennia haunt every drop, their voices growing louder and louder with each passing civilization. Only those who really listen can hear, but soon, the silence will create a void for all to behold. Until then, Nepharisse retrieves whatever comfort she can glean from the drifting mist, through the palms of her hands, as they rise and fall with her body like the empires of human history. The retreating tide transports her healing thoughts to distant suffering, and kneeling back on her heels with her thighs sheltering her chest from the cold, in meditative prayer she rests.

✂ ✂ ✂

The red door opens to Nepharisse's sapphire blue eyes, scouting the dazers for familiar faces. A smitten bouncer radiates his delight that she has come alone. Her fingers leave a cool shiver on his lips. He escorts her to a private high-backed bench near the cocktail chef.

Nepharisse sips a warm drink while she lounges with crossed legs, teasing several admirers with a flirty sapphire blue shoe. As devised, Sothese accepts the invitation. He leaves an indignant young man and winds his way over to his favorite redhead.

A party favor is all she has become to him. Her ire catalyzes an urgent intervention. As it was in the exhibit room, ferocity acquiesces to reason. Nepharisse suspends her reactive impulse above the fire between them.

"More important careers have ended with fewer indiscretions." She glares at his young guest in the corner and whips some flashes at Sothese that he recognizes as tantalizing. "Can nothing satisfy you?"

Sothese smirks and playfully reaches up her skirt. Nepharisse can only control so much. "Your thighs are quivering. Why not enjoy a more refreshing drink. Sooner or later you must quench that thirst of yours."

The words slip off his tongue and onto hers. They linger there, a breath, as she reaches inside her form-fitting shirt for an abrupt response. "Entertain yourself with this." She throws the copy she made of Nathruyu's interrogation recording at his diversion for the night, still sulking at the back table.

Sothese's laughter is imbued with arrogance. "Succulent Nepharisse, the Pramam is our most avid fan."

This is the moment she braved the virulent seas and risked her body inside the lockdown walls of the Ministburg penal island for. This is the venue at which she has chosen to terminate her ambivalence. This is the consequence of his abhorrent behavior.

Nepharisse leans into Sothese and draws one last rush from him.

"I wager the Pramam will find this one particularly revealing, especially the insights you share about your brother." The entire club speeds by as time clamps down on Sothese. "Darkness is the dagger which carves out hidden demons, my dear Sothese."

The passion that drives him feeds the fury that blinds him. Nepharisse's gamble, with a prison far worse than the Ministry can concoct, has triumphed and Sothese knows it. He grabs her chin and pierces into her with a silent challenge, but it has no power over her. The magnet between them has reversed. She has released the grip he had over her and the guilt she had carried for the feelings she bears for his brother. She is whole again.

The affair is over.

Sothese charges back to his newest conquest and rips the evidence from him. The smile Nepharisse walks out of the club with contemplates a drink with the hapless dazer, who has chosen to follow her into the ancient subway tunnels.

She could really use that drink.

Day 392: afternoon

"Caroline?"

Is she ignoring me? Why is she in such a hurry? I'll cut her off at the ivy wall. I'm sure it's her underneath that head scarf. This will be a conversation long overdue. What the —

"Pardon me, Miss Elize." Shaplo! Ah crap! She's gone. "Where's your fancy scarf?" It was a hijab, fishy. And I don't like that tone, Mister Shaplo. Or your slits for eyes.

"I got tired of it." Think fast. He'll start sniffing around. It's hard enough keeping him from peeking into my room when I go in and out. Is there something poking out of my satchel? Crap! Phew. Saved by the comm. "No time to talk. Late for a meeting." Out of earshot? Good.

"Hey lo, Keet."

"I found the location. Can you come over?"

"I was just leaving for the Snack Shack, but I can grab a bake on the way back. Are you at work already?" I'd better blister — through the orchard, off campus, across the Victory Bridge. Wave at Ashton. "I'll stop on my way back, Ash."

"Back at the crypt. Are you already at the Snack Shack?"

It sure feels hotter without the morning fog. Here already? That was fast.

"It's Eli. Open up." He's still holding his comm. Now he's giving me that you-belong-in-a-jar look.

"Who were you talking to, Keet?" I know I don't have

three heads. "What?" He's staring. "Did I forget something?"

"Only the laws of physics. How did you—" He slaps his head. "Rip. Nice try. At the Snack Shack. You almost had me." He chuckles.

I have no idea what he's talking about. I'm not sure myself where time went. Best be speedy. I don't want to miss Professor Snot's lecture. "So you found where the rock's from?"

"Yeah. I don't remember where I read it though. It was early this morning, during the social. It's a good time for quiet research before the morning rush. With all the commotion I guess I got distracted."

"What commotion?"

"Do you remember the quiet academic who hangs around the archives all the time?"

"The one with the permanently raised eyebrow?" Or maybe he plucks it that way. Hehehe. He's constantly throwing his own look at us.

Keet chuckles while he serves Sparky his breakfast. "This morning he had a visitor." Now it's my eyebrow. "He was *not* happy to see her."

"Anyone we know … like Wakanda?" She's not someone I would be wiggling any hips over.

Keet's trying to remember. "I don't think so. I didn't see her face." Her face? You can see that woman coming from across the planet. "I would have recognized the thuds." More chuckling. He sure is in a light mood today. He must have really found something. He's always more relaxed when he digs something juicy up. I'd better check his arms though, just in case. Everything clear, no blisters, no oozing.

"Maybe it's brain decay then."

"Hahaha. Just look at the sleeve. I found a map as well. It's just outside Albaraaton. We could make a mini-vacation of it. Two nights should do it."

Whoa! Did he just suggest an adventure? "Indie would be proud." Grab some slips and paste them on. "We can leave Friday. Are you sure about this?"

He looks excited, with a tiny hint of fear, but that's good. He nods.

"Juicy! I'll throw these images on the community wall and see what the chumbuds come up with."

"Should we ask Stitch to come along?"

Is he serious?

Both brows up. Keet finally wants to include Stitch, but I'm not entirely sure about that. It's not the best time to be traveling, with the SIF, the GMU, and the GHU on alert. And Odwin is not around anymore to arrange safe passage for us, and then there's bioTravel. We could really use Stitch's help but ... "He'll just try to talk us out of it." With good reason. I would to if I were him ... but I'm not so ... "Let's see what kind of plan we can put together on our own."

"A plan sounds juicy to me." I thought it would. OK. Stack all his papers in my satchel and get to class.

"Be careful with those. If Mme Beaudoin finds out I snuck them ... The curator only just recovered from my last 'misdemeanor'." Hehehe. My brother the archive anarchist. "I'll need them back before the afternoon rush."

"I'm on it, Keet. I'll comm later." Give Sparky a pat and run out.

✂ ✂ ✂

I have to stop rushing around like this. Geez. I'm boiling. There's a wipe in my satchel somewhere. Stop! Crap! Keet is going to blow. Run after them, quick. Where did this draft come from? There's one over there. Good. And over there. OK. I had how many again? Geez. I should have used a slipclip. It would work on this old stuff. Just one more by the knotted citrus. Oh oh. I'm burnt toast. He's staring straight at me.

Wow! Look at those eyes. Oh get a grip, girl. He's not that thirst quenching. Oh yes he is, Elize. Look at those lips. Actually, he's perfect. And his skin. I've never seen anyone that exotic before. It's as if his eyes have constellations inside of them. They're so bright and beautiful. He looks pretty plain to me, Elize. Honestly, can you please keep it quiet up there. I need to figure out a way to retrieve that paper. Well, at least my voices are not entirely destructive today. *Rejoice in gratitude for all that life presents to you. Be as thankful for the storm as you are for the gentle wind.* Hmmm. Time to practice what Caroline taught me then. Legs, do your thing.

"Way, stranger." Is that the best you can do? Oh dear. I'm drenched. Good. He's smiling.

"Way back, strangest." Interesting humor. Giggle. "Third millennium paper? You have your own personal archives?" Hick. Focus. Say something. I wish I had my flutterbot with me. Maybe if I step under the shade with him. No. Worse. He examines the artifacts on the paper, especially the large granite carvings. "Are you studying ancient mythologies?"

"No bloody way! I live in the real world. This is my cousin's stuff. He works at the museum and fancies himself a modern day Indiana Jones."

"Ah yes. Indie." He chuckles. My feelings exactly.

"No irrational 'souls and spirits' stuff for me."

"In the time of my ancestors, that was reality. Who is to say what is real and what is not."

I think he's offended. Now you've done it. Patch it up.

"Oh, I didn't mean to —"

"No offense taken. It was a different time."

Stop staring at him. And fidgeting. I feel silly. He's just another boy. No, he is not. You know he is special, Elize. You can feel it. It is in his eyes. It is in the way you feel when he looks at you. It is in his hands. Oh, stop it. Get the paper back.

"It is still unspoiled. He need not know."

He hands the paper back, looks away briefly towards the west end of the orchard, and smiles. Avoid his eyes. Look down at the archives article. I can feel him watching me.

"Way, dazy girl. You'll be late for class." Jacinta's at the path. She makes believe she wipes her nose with the back of her hand and snorts. Right. Professor Snot. Is this what déjà vu feels like? He stares at Jacinta waving at me frantically, then giving up and running to class and —

Creeps, the rock! Don't put your hand in your pocket. Don't draw attention to it. Go to class.

"Are you ill?"

"No. I'm fine." What a thing to say? Do I look ill? Check my forehead. I am still a bit warm. I'd better wipe up before class. No GHU around? Good. I do look suspect. "I must run.

Thank you."

Don't look back. He is still watching, Elize. Hush now. I have to focus on my studies. Crap! My hair is blowing all over the place, I should have tied it up this morning. Juicy. The doors are still open. I can sneak in the back.

✄ ✄ ✄

What's with me today? I feel like I've run the highland trails. Everyone is heads down working on a challenge, except for that boy.

Oh oh. He's staring straight at me. Wow! Look at those eyes. Oh get a grip, girl. He's not that thirst quenching. Oh yes he is, Elize. Look at those lips. Actually, he's perfect. And his skin. I've never seen someone that exotic before. It's as if his eyes have constellations inside of them. They're so bright and beautiful. He … I'm burnt toast.

"Miss Elize!" Don't ask me. Don't ask me. Please don't ask me. "Perhaps the assignment is too simple for you? Please come forward and share your genius with the class, so that we may progress to the next level of complexity." Here comes the wipe and the snort. Ewww. "Or perhaps you wish to share with us the thoughts you deem more deserving of your time?" Crap!

Rub that little silver pup. Breathe. Count. Breathe. Count. Breathe …

"Miss Elize we are waiting." Get up, Elize. You can do it. You know how to get the answer. Be the silent storm. No, Elize. Forget that silent stuff. Go wipe the condescension off all of their faces. Tell that Snot of a professor what you think of him. *The hours of folly are measured by the clock, but of wisdom no clock can measure.*

One more deep breath. Juicy. I accept the challenge. Everyone is watching. I take the stage. Bow in my mind and make that board sing. There. Back to my seat.

Pay no attention to the mouths gaping and the awe you just incited, Elize. *This too shall pass.* There are more important things to consider now. Look away from him. Do not talk to him, even with your thoughts, especially with your thoughts. Guard your thoughts. Let your mind be very still and just listen.

✂ ✂ ✂

"I've been looking for you for hours, chum. Have you been sitting here all this time?"

That sounds like Stitch, fading in. Where did everyone go? The pond feels so fresh. It's always calming to sit here and gather my thoughts. Pond? Did he say hours?

"Eli?" Huh? Oh right. Stitch. "Have you been here all day?"

"Hey lo, Stitch. Just daydreaming."

"Trip. I can have that effect on my chums, yeah?" A smile and a poke. Oh and I get an extra hip wiggle for that too. Hehehe. In your dreams, dweeb. "Your soul needs to flip a pass."

He's right. I feel topped up. Hiding from Father is one thing but constantly living in fear of another GHU quarantine at the tiniest sniffle, narrowly escaping a public murder charge,

battling with ever cantankerous voices, my course load, my
blackouts and mostly not knowing what the sheiss this bloody
rock is STILL DOING IN MY POCKET! And that hair color.
What now?

"Ease, Eli. Would you rather I clip out?"

Juicy. This is frustrating. That's no way to treat a friend.
That's debatable. Not now. His hair is vacillating between blue
and gold. Big breath in and smile.

"Slap me, Stitch. I do need a break." Here comes the red.
Juicy! It's really bright so this will be top juicy. "What do you
have in mind?"

"Follow me to the Nook." OK … so swatting is part of the
fun? "Hold still. Got it." He shows me the captive bumblebot
buzzing wildly, and furiously swinging its stinger at him.

"That's one cross pollinator." Stitch chuckles.

"It seems to be confused by you. Have you been snuggling
with Cyd?"

"Not consciously. And this is a citrus model anyway. It
might just be defective." Like most early version hybrids.
Stitch pulls out the main stem and puts it into pocket number
picazillion three. A patch of bright yellow springs from his
bangs. Another unfortunate soul to add to his gadget supplies.

Here we are. We head to the counter for water. "My treat."

"Ta, Stitch."

"Five per cent or ten per cent?"

"Well, since you're buying." Nudge him. His hair turns a
pretty blue.

"I'm on it, chum. Grab a seat with a clear view of the
courtyard." He winks.

Hmmm. What mischief is he planning today. The boy is trouble, Elize. Not listening.

Stitch places my floramug on the table. He takes a sip of his and spits it out. "This is not ten per cent. It tastes more like two." I agree. Mine tastes like must as well. The inside leaves look clean. A student is arguing with the clerk about his. Stitch is already onto his scheme. "Switch sides. I want you facing the court, yeah?"

"Why?"

"You'll see. Write this down." He passes me what looks like a normal slippad, but I know better.

"Anyone you know out there?"

Natalia has a good sense of humor. I have a feeling she'll need it. "Natalia."

"Juicy." He grins. OK. I'll grant him that. "Perk, write this down, exactly as I say it."

Natalia, "night flyer".

Natalia screeches and runs, waving her hands about, into the psychology building.

"That's mean." Giggle. "The poor girl is terrified." Hehehe.

Stitch's hair is bright red. He grins. "Pick another one."

"Rajid's calling after Heather. Ohhhm gee. I think he's finally going to ask her on a date."

"Perk, write this but don't put the period yet. Wait until he gets close, then add the period."

Heather, "huge fart"

Giggle. "Oh you're bad." Here comes Rajid. Now the period.

Ohhhm gee. I'm ripping and rolling here. Stitch just has to

turn around to see.

Rajid's voice is trailing after Heather. "Heather, wait. Is it something I said?"

"Share, Stitch. What genius did you invent this time?"

"I cracked the bioFrequency so I can broadcast a phrase. I can also use someone else's voice. Do you have your headband?" Nod. "Put it on." He grabs the pad and writes.

Elize, "There's a zombie behind you!".

Slap him! This is fun. This is what friends are for. I really needed to laugh. Whoops. Awkward moment now. Change the subject. Ugh. Shaplo with his groupies. What do they see in him? Stitch turns around to look.

"Stitch, can you do a group thing?"

"I'm already on it, chum. I created one called ShaploVixens."

Vixens? A poke and a smile. "I thought you'd like that one, yeah?" I'm loving this. OK. My turn. Grab the pad.

ShaploVixens, "Who wants to get good and juicy with me and sliderpad Patty tonight?".

Patricia kicks Shaplo in the balls and clips out. Stitch is howling. "Ouch! What did you write?" I pass the slippad back. He howls louder. "Good thing he didn't get it from you. He'd be unconscious."

"Years on the slick, bud, years on the slick!" My cheeks are sore. The other girls walk off in disgust shouting obscenities at Shaplo … except for one. Stitch and I lock raised eyebrows. This is perfect for one of Professor Snot's pontification sessions. Hehehe.

"Here. Your own Naughtypad." Stitch hands it over. "Keep your headband on and we can communicate in secret until I can get you a quality biochip."

"No, thanks. I have enough of you already. I don't want you in my brain too." Giggle.

"I can't hear your thoughts, chum, just send you messages. It picks up a free channel and sends one bit at a time. If it detects a camper mid-signal it kicks out with a ping." Brilliant again! Oh, there's the counsellor and Dr. Tenille. Stitch chuckles and writes.

Counsellor, CaptainSnook says, "Arrr. You ever been to sea, Billy?".

Crap! Keeto on the comm. "I missed it!"

"Missed what, Eli?"

"Never mind. You have something else?"

"Remember Stitch told me to watch out for Wakanda? Well, she came back."

"Hang a sec. Stitch, Wakanda came back." That's a new hair color. Charcoal.

Stitch grabs the comm. "The jewel? Not here. Let's meet in my room after dark." He hands it back to me. "Have to clip." Did he say jewel?

"Wait!" Juicy. Another paper mess. Pick up before … too slow.

"You're not actually thinking of going there, are you?" Here comes the black hair.

"Well —"

"You were going without me? It's Keet, yeah?"

Follow him into the orchard. "I knew you would try to talk us out of it."

"So it's you then. What are you afraid of, Eli?"

I don't know. "Keet is the one who suggested it. There's a direct transport to Albaraaton and then it's just on the outskirts. We picked up some bioShields and enough energy packs to last three days, just in case."

"You don't know the terrain." He pulls me under the knotted tree and whispers. "It's suicide, especially for Keet."

"He's not a pup anymore." I can't believe I just said that. "He can sneak around too."

"Grabbing the sails off a three foot galleon is *not* survival training. There's a reason humans live behind biowalls, Eli."

"We have the gear. We'll be fine." Once I get on the chumbuds network and figure out the plan. Right now actually. Stitch puts his hand on my shoulder and turns me around. I really should start carrying my flutterbot. I feel a heat wave inside.

"Perk, I'm going with you, chum." He wipes my forehead softly and smiles. "You know you need me."

Deep down, I do. Maybe that's what scares me. There he goes, bopping away.

Good. Time to blister. Into J-branch and up the lift. Quit smiling. People will think you're crazy. So what? He really is my juiciest friend. Almost home.

Giggle. Dweeb. He made me a mood room! Blue.

Mini-Lizzy! Grab him. Quit batting those googly eyes at me. Hold this paper while I sketch the maze. Wait! "Come back here with that." He's sniffing around the walls. Juicy. Behind the privyshelf again. OK. Let's see what's back there.

Jumpers! Fine. Stay on my shoulder then. A hole? And a box. It's fused. Shake it. Sigh. Wait! It's opening.

K E E T O

Day 395: morning

This is bent! What was I thinking ... or not thinking? I am not ready for a real dig. I woke up this morning soaked and understandably anxious with the thought that we have just committed ourselves to an illegal archeological expedition. Sleuthing in Dr. Tenille's office is not death-defying behavior. I hate to admit it, but I am relieved Stitch showed up.

Eli awoke drenched as well, though I imagine her nightmares were the culprit. She tells me the voices are more invasive as well. They seem to argue with each other while she is trapped in her head, as a witness. Considering she loses full function of her senses during her episodes and judging by the intel we have managed to amass from the chumbuds about our mysterious destination, staying alert will be a challenge, to say the least. A one-second lapse could mean the difference between ... Well, best not give that thought any energy.

With all the gear we packed for our dance with insanity I had no room for extra reading material. This midday writing break provides a suitable pacifier for my overactive imagination. There will be plenty of opportunity to panic when we get there. In the meantime, my left brain gets to exercise its reporting skills, with just enough of the right hemisphere to keep a channel open to you.

I feel vulnerable without your favorite items and books to soothe me, especially the crystal pendant you gave me. Eli made me promise to leave it behind in case we find ourselves surrounded with more of those plasma weapons once we reach our destination, so I locked it up in a my hidden safe, along with the flashes I found buried at the bottom of my satchel last night, after my journaling session. They could have been there for months. Regardless, my curiosity deserved closure, or it would have kept me awake on the eve of our first trip into unfiltered territory. As it happens, the shock of what I saw filled my body with enough adrenaline to blow the heart valves off a patrolling Sentinel. I did not sleep last night.

Once my anger was somewhat under control, I commed Eli and patched Stitch in. They decided to pack up right then and there and brave the ventilation shafts. Eadonberg is still under Ministry House arrest. Yes. The so-called regrettable affront on personal liberties is not that which the Gadlins are accused of at all. A perpetual state of curfew is the real act of terrorism in my opinion.

Eli and Stitch arrived just before midnight and together we spent the wee hours dissecting the recording and postulating theories. The equipment used to chronicle the assault was pre-cube technology, as such we were unable to engage in a true holographic experience. The vantage point appeared to be from inside the walls of the cell itself because, from time to time, as the lens shifted from victim to offender, we could see the edges of what looked like a hole drilled into stone. Whoever was controlling the viewing angle could not have been far. As much as we played and replayed the scene, we could find no hint of a third person.

Stitch figures that some frames were removed. He was able

to detect subtle joins, at various points in the interrogation, where edits were made. The copy in my possession is a version of a no doubt more revealing original, assembled in sections. Since I left the original flashes locked up for safe-keeping, I chose to bring a full transcription for further analysis.

Words when written take on a different hue than they do when spoken, and when augmented by kinesthetic memory, they take on a visceral significance. Here is my personal edit on their charged exchange. It includes the key elements my intuition guides me towards. My own annotations are in brackets.

(The cell is much akin to the one I visited below water level in the GHU: faintly glistening walls covered in an ice-like substance, complete darkness, a sliver of light beaming down from above.)

Sothese: How does it feel to be abandoned?

Nathruyu: Your version of reality is wanting.

Sothese: (a scoff) The only wanting in my reality is that tantalizing redhead.

(Nathruyu's anger requires more energy than she possesses. Her body remains listless while her eyes convey the brunt of her disgust.)

Nathruyu: I regret the source of your intemperance.

Sothese: As do I, dear …

(His intonation does not drop at the end of this statement, which suggests that dialog is missing. The darkness offers only a partial view of his face, making it a perfect target frame for a visual edit, but the auditory oversight is telling.)

Nathruyu: You have lost that right.

Sothese: Your days of influence are over. Tell me what you know.

(Nathruyu looks past him into the mist, wafting in the darkness.)

Nathruyu: I think your hounds have separation anxiety. Why not invite them in?

(Perhaps this explains the frosty puffs. I imagine them behind a containment grid, as I was when I visited with her, yet Sothese appears to be inside.)

Sothese: (laughing) That would please you.

Nathruyu: It would lighten my mood.

(A slight twitch in her labored smile hints at another time jump. The scene resumes a fraction of a second after snarling would have naturally started. The lapse is barely audible, but there nonetheless.)

(A huge claw-like device slams into Nathruyu's windpipe. She coughs. She attempts to create a gap with her fingers, but she has no strength.)

Nathruyu: (winded and weak) Will you no longer touch me?

Sothese: (He approaches into better view.) And sully my beautiful white skin?

(He turns the arm and the clamp locks onto her neck. She gags. He shoves her against the back wall. She falls into the corner, bent into a ball, wrapping her tortured charcoal naked body with her long black hair, expelling her grief with dry heaves.)

The pain is too caustic. I must stop. The images are etched into my heart so much so that I can smell her myrrh … your myrrh.

The assault only escalated from that point forward. There were no words and no sounds, except for the hunger inside Sothese's fork-tailed servants. Nathruyu was mute in her torment, though what is lacking in the recording pierces the apparent silence on this transport. The screeching I know exists between the frames haunts me.

As upsetting as witnessing Sothese inflict his physical, mental, and emotional abuse upon Nathruyu was, I am grateful to whoever dropped this bomb in my satchel. Callousness of this nature cannot emanate from any soul that would dare call itself human. I refuse to believe there exist those, in this time of Unification, who are so disconnected from their own empathy that they find ecstasy in the debilitating agony of others, let alone willfully causing it. The question arises now whether Sothese was acting alone and in contravention of the Pramam's wishes, or whether his Pramamness ignores the messages he professes to receive from Their Holy Trinity.

There was no confession on Nathruyu's part, nor was there mention of Gadlin accomplices or even of a greater Gadlin conspiracy to stage a spiritual coup at the Ministry level. But this, Eli proposed, could have been edited then entrusted to a new secret admirer, who simply picked up where my amethyst-eyed beauty left off.

Would this be the real Gadlin involvement the Pramam seeks to uncover? Shudder the thought that Father has his hand in this. The same blood runs through my veins. Could I be capable of such horror? No. Your blood is also half mine, and you are no sadist. Dr. Tenille could be doctoring more than his patients.

The truth is, we still have no proof either way, which is irrelevant in my mind since the only evidence I need resides within me. I may not have the military acumen of a GMU operative, but what I do have is a deep emotional intelligence that surfaces at times, and this is one of those times. I just know that Nathruyu is not guilty of the crimes the SIF have charged her with. It can be no other way.

We are arriving in Albaraaton soon, so I will be quick and pick up the rest of my reportage later this evening. Tomorrow, we sneak the copy of the incriminating flashes that Stitch made last night to an expedient Gadlin mud slinger. This connection, he promises, will not sell out for credit. Her reputation is her livelihood. Thankfully, our congenial dweeb of a zigazillion pockets has the merchandise well stowed for safe passage through the station scanners, not that scoping equipment has ever been a concern for him.

Eli and I, on the other hand, are careful to keep privacy invasion to a minimum. Today, we had the unpleasant opportunity to overcome a rather difficult challenge with respect to keeping our identity secret. Stitch unexpectedly changed his sleep-over plans, after we had scrutinized the interrogation for the third time. He insisted that he could not leave Eadonberg without a crucial piece of equipment.

No curfew was going to restrict his freedom to come and go as he pleases, so he sealed his vow, via chumbud salute, to meet us directly at the transport station with our tickets reserved and paid for. My first mission, should I choose to accept it, he chuckled, was to get our fair maiden safely to our point of departure. But for me, the assignment became an exercise in trust, more than anything else.

Our initial strategy was to weave our way northwards through the secondary walkways and scaffolds, since not having bioTravel precluded using the hovertrain, but we opted to hire a slidercab instead, mainly due to the amount of gear we were carting. A quick anonymous beacon, on the chumbud community wall, proved to be discreet and safe. We simply imprinted a slip with the secret call code that a second anonymous chumbud shot back at the beacon's target and handed it to the driver at the agreed upon pick-up spot. The vehicle was complete with signage, permission markings, and most importantly, fake scanners.

Securing passage on the over-secure transport, however, was no flick of a sketch wand. We were standing in a scanning line, in full bug gear, when Stitch arrived wearing the blindingly bright coveralls he had purchased last year from Mr. G. The logic in owning a wilderness suit in the city suddenly did not seem so ridiculous. How he intended to protect his head from the recent infestations, randomly appearing in swarms within the coastal cities, was a subject of much ribbing. Perhaps the insects are mood sensitive, Eli snickered, but Stitch just grinned and focused on the scanners.

Meanwhile, I wanted to document our first vacation of sorts in images, so I asked the woman standing in front of us in the queue to take a flash of Eli and me in full bumblebot tester attire. She smiled and snapped a few poses. Then she went on to tell us how flashes make such great memories, how taking flashes is so much fun, how viewing flashes afterwards brings so much joy, or something like that.

She was quite chatty, but our conversation was cut short by the scanner guard, who refused permission for her to board with her enormous shoe collection. The argument which ensued was the perfect distraction for a security breach … ours. The funny thing is that I remember each pair in her luggage being exactly the same as the next pair, which I found odd at first. But once I heard her argument, it all made sense.

The woman contended that she had a personal invitation from the Pramam's advisor to attend a URA appointment ceremony in Albaraaton, and that she was providing shoes for all the models at the Stew Über fashion show segment. While the situation escalated with several more transport personnel arriving to check her credentials, Stitch stealthily rigged the scanners clear through to the seats he had reserved, as promised.

The first gate took us to the platform where Eli and I each stood on blue circles, facing each other, beside raised doorways into the sidewall of the transport car. Unlike the trains servicing the more remote highland towns, these particular vehicles were fully automated. Once the transparent scanning wall between us cleared our virtual tickets, virtachairs formed that raised us up and over the edges of the openings, and slid into our designated spots, in our respective rows. Stitch embarked next, taking the position Eli had occupied on the platform, and the process repeated. Anyone who misses their aisle call forfeits their ticket to standby travelers.

That is where I now sit, my body curled up as tight as I can to keep prying eyes away from my journal, while Eli and Stitch poke, giggle, and laugh across from me, as they secretly scribble on their slippads and spy on the antics of the surrounding passengers. This is only my third experience with intercity travel, the first being when we moved after we lost you, the second, our escape to Eadonberg, and the third, well, I am nervous to see what will present itself on this journey.

The plan is to find the source of the red granite based on the piece Mashrin had and which kept showing up later in Eli's pocket — that is providing that the excavation site is not buried, which it very well may be after all these years. Fluidity in a schedule has always been beyond my comfort zone. Still, there is a level of security which comes from having Stitch with us ... I hope. I even toy with Stitch's bent belief that the rock did indeed want to be found, and that the glamorous exploits of the fearless archeologist I have been visioneering for myself from the safety of various armchairs throughout my life, has always been my fate.

Shivers of fearful excitement pull me from contemplation into consternation. We have arrived. I will finish up later.

Fortunately, I am now sitting in the corner of our hostel room, because even I would have me clamped for what I am about to admit. As it was in Eadonberg, taking care of permissions clearance was our first order of risky business. Stitch's virtachair was first to drop into the passenger hold, a containment field box on a sliderskid that either delivers you effortlessly to the exit, or sucks you into a detainment cell, for further processing.

The special operations training Stitch received from Odwin from the age of nine stood up to the challenge, as expected.

While the agent approved his bioTravel access, Stitch signaled one of our chumbuds to initiate a packet swap. As long as the agent stayed on schedule, we and every other passenger in our aisle could sneak through the gap in security. Our chumbud could only bombard the system with fake packets until the next sweep of the automated authenticator. Any delay would have been disastrous.

Obviously, we made it, or the GMU would be reading this journal by now, but we only did so by a razor's edge. While my flyer bake was threatening a fast exit from my stomach, the shoe woman, who had shared our aisle, required separate handling. Stitch had his hand on a special frequency jammer, hidden in his fancy overalls as a last resort in case we needed to break out of holding. All ended well, and we reached the hovertrain drop in time to experience the vibrant bustle of a pre-party atmosphere, amidst the scorching heat of the midday sun steaming off the cobblestone streets.

I remember you reading us stories of how Albaraaton was the only coastal city which had been spared from the ravages of the third millennium, that its high altitude protected it from the tsunamis of the Great Ocean Swell, that its arid rocky landscape offered no food for the Poison Fires, and that once the dangers had passed, survivors from the three continents that were decimated converged onto its mostly intact infrastructure. I stood there breathing the air that was thick with the past until we had to scurry.

The Pramam and his entourage were touring the artistic installations lining the main avenue. Trading class merchants from all over the world have bargained with well-established families for exclusive use of their pre-holocaust shops, filling them with overpriced and underpaid wares, from undisclosed sources. It was the perfect setting for minor mischief makers like us to lose themselves in the crowd and prepare for a venture into the unprotected zones along the coastline.

While the GMU and the SIF were preoccupied securing the old quarter, carved into the rocky mountains, for the Inner Council appearances during the weekend's festivities, Eli, Stitch, and I meandered to our chosen hostel, shopping for souvenirs along the way. We seriously wondered what had possessed Eli to think that a loose bun, French lace shrug, and pencil skirt were even remotely rebellious. The city that never sleeps was full of them.

Stitch is taking a final pass now through our backpacks to make sure we carry with us every conceivable survival apparatus we could possibly need. According to our calculations, we have less than six hours to wander the old quarries, from low tide until the waters cover most of our target terrain. Considering we have no idea what we are looking for, we might as well have one minute. He brought a buoyant platform with a long rope for us to sleep on during high tide so that our search can continue once the waters recede. That gives us three chances to dig up some history before we have to blister back to Eadonberg.

We were all set and I was feeling quite confident until Stitch turned to us and said: "Perk, I hope you brought fast shoes, chumbuds. Because when I say clip out, it means yesterday."

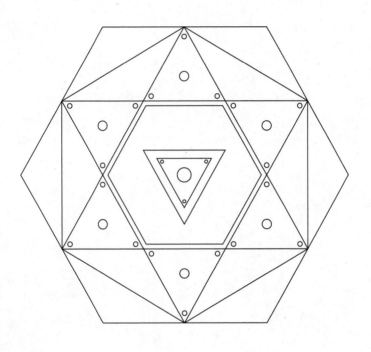

CHAPTER SIX

N E P H A R I S S E

Day 395: midday

The Albaraaton transport station platform buzzes with more than simply the feverish pace of expectant travelers. A swarm of insects has just beaten the midday sun through the dispersing wall of golden mist beyond the city's biowall, at the far end of the station. They hover for a moment, systematically stressing the force field. It gives way long enough to accept the rush of millions of wings inside a whiff of toxic stench. The emergency inhalers immediately syphon the yellow fumes into the underground ventilation shafts, yet the persistent perpetrators outsmart the backdraft. Panic strikes the lungs of all who have not come prepared.

Nepharisse shifts her eyes away from the clearing agent and towards the exit, where Keeto and Elize's half-Gadlin confidant successfully test Zafarian's bright orange coveralls. The boy's eccentricities, though a target for ridicule, leave him well protected, whereas the more image conscious drop to their knees as the black ribbon-shaped cloud spirals past and fans out in the direction of the old quarter.

Fortunately, a feast of Nepharisse's blood, and that of the twins, is not to be served today, for the aisle of virtachairs they had occupied is the one currently suspended inside the protective passenger holds. A change in perception can reframe any situation within a positive light. Furthermore, the unexpected boon from Zafarian's technological wizardry simplifies Nepharisse's plans for uneventful passage into the city.

As announced in the Pramam's latest Holy Address, the bioTravel upgrade is strictly enforced. Those who do not comply with the new Ministry restrictions are subject to clamping, under questionable pretext. For her part, even if she had decided to fabricate a catering contract instead, Unification employees no longer enjoy special immunities. As for the twins, their non-compliance is a matter of greater concern.

The sliderskid transfers Nepharisse to the arrival zone, where she pauses under an extensive reflective canopy designed to block direct scorching sunlight. She primps her luscious curly ginger-auburn hair, smooths her curve-enhancing white dress over her hips and buttocks, and makes like she is taking inventory of the shoes in her sliderbag. Her left hand distracts while her right one acts. Hidden in the heel of one of the sapphire blue shoes is the coded parchment that the youthful academic relayed to her at the Museum of Antiquities in Eadonberg.

The promise of complicity gives her courage. As she contemplates the new task requiring her immediate attention, a flush of heat tickles the back of her neck. Urgency has come to alert her in the form of the three officials, watching from the covered passenger pick-up zone. She flees undetected through the cobbled streets lined with shops, smiling her way past the GMU guards flanking the parading Pramam, whose folly is setting foot in a Gadlin nest. Surely Sothese has made him aware of the black market economy that clothes the trading class matriarchs. Perhaps the Unification's Divine Messenger considers himself immune to the creed that binds the itinerant merchants to each other and to their belief in equality when agreements are breached.

Charm is a weapon Nepharisse wields with finesse. She maneuvers herself inside the Pramam's entourage and extends her right palm up, bearing a revealing gift of her own design. The twinkle in her gaze enraptures the spiritual minion who moves mechanically to her whimsical poetry.

A secret flash for you to view, for you alone in private too. You thank me for the flash of light, and view it now before the night. I leave this flash for you to see, a different choice will come to be.

A lesser mind is easy prey for words that bewitch. Nepharisse nods respectfully past the blank bodyguards and at the Pramam, while he accepts the mysterious offering. Once he slips it into his inside breast pocket, she secures a loose hijab over her hair and slips out of view, just as Sothese pushes his chest through the throngs of Unified devotees, his three officials marching in unison behind him. He extends a dutiful formal bow to his chosen head of state, who, after a brief courtesy, excuses himself.

Puppets on invisible strings dance at the hands of their mistresses at the small kiosks, filled with theater crafts. The art flourishes still. Perhaps the illusion of control resonates with the human condition, providing entertainment through song and story, while at the same time mirroring their self-inflicted bondage.

The Unification did not conquer its way into the daily rituals of the masses. It was welcomed, and it keeps expanding its reach, mostly due to the broad appeal of its dogma. As repulsively contrived as the new Unified religion is to Nepharisse at its core, its superficial practices were palatable to those who had fallen into despair after the tragic death of the Pramam's mother, Anabelle, and the multi-faith coalition leaders.

Their palette, however, would not likely accept the formalities calling Nepharisse to an abandoned monastery at the edge of the biowall. Every city has its neighborhood where few dare to trespass, yet the Chancellor of Albaraaton prefers to embellish the Exchange Sector's unsavory reputation as a mercantile transition zone. Its location, at the fringe of the breathable airspace, befits the ill-repute of its residents. When one becomes a trusted link in their well-guarded supply chain, unimaginable treasures are accessible, although the dangers inherent in such acquisitions often rival their credit value. Nevertheless, there are those whose aversion to personal harm is underdeveloped, a fact that consumers have no appreciation for.

The lure of lucrative distribution rights is not what attracts Nepharisse to this district. A critical intervention requires her assistance. Since the guidance she has received is presumably correct, innocence is about to be stripped and shattered, before her watch is complete. This she will not abide, for her lofty personal aspirations cannot jeopardize her current responsibilities.

Haunting cries echo down the hallways. Nepharisse's heart swells with agony as she flies through the corridors, despairingly seeking the tiny wails. The architecture creates a maze of sound that confounds the ordinary senses. Nepharisse lets her legs direct her to the epicenter under her feet. She pulls the emitter from her thigh holster.

A vision of Nathruyu, twisted in pain and wrapped in shame by her long black hair, shoots fear into her soul. Hesitation is the source of failure. She rifts into the catacombs below and interrupts the loathsome branding ritual.

Nepharisse's dread has dropped her into the den of Sothese's hounds, alone. The female official aims her blinding eyes at her and smirks. They collect from the children what they abducted them for and elect to forgo any further claim. Their bloody impressions tattoo the stone surrounding their sacrificial lambs as they slowly retreat into the darkness.

The one-year-olds are still salvageable. Nepharisse removes her head wrap, fashions a double pressure bandage for both victims and soars through the building, looking for her absent support. As her sliderbag rejoins her, a whisper reaches out to her. The challenge, which risks breaking Nepharisse's commitment to harmony, is the one who has long been her inspiration, the one she strove to emulate, until now — the scholar.

This negligence of the replacement partner has cost them two biochips. Nepharisse hands the stabilized bundles to the tardy scholar without so much as a scorn. She forgives and focuses with emotional clarity on her prime objective. The time for debate will come later. As she leaves the sector, she glimpses a hip-jiggling bright red-haired familiar face disappearing into an alleyway. Perhaps a separate discussion is also due to come.

Her glide through the exit of the gated sector transforms into a swoop through the gigantic carved entrance of the old quarter. The human sentinels in full ceremonial dress indicate that the guests of honor have arrived. Nepharisse parlays her manufactured permissions into a personal escort to the inauguration ceremony for the new director of the URA, to be held at Council Court, the most impressive chamber of commerce in the entire Unification.

Floating as an angel, fluttering her sapphire-adorned diaphanous silk wings behind her, her long slitted gown flows with the air of high society. The unmistakable hydraulophone vibrations of Trimorphic Rhythms reflect their water messages throughout the cavernous wonder. Their trademark triple stutter singing style multiplies inside the triangular hall to concentrate into a trance-inducing melody, beckoning tonight's invitees through an opening at its apex. Nepharisse adds her own allure to the ambience.

The scanning equipment at the granite cocktail stand blinks red, prompting the concierge to intercept her approach. His advance retreats upon meeting her stunning blue eyes and unassuming smile. He hands her a crystal party favor, checks "Mme Über" off the guest list, and, mustering a quaint attempt at old German, he offers to check her sliderbag.

A worrisome chill interrupts Nepharisse's polite regrets. She must arrest the process threatening her anonymity immediately. Her request for directions to the female comfort room diverts their conversation to a door down the hall and to the left.

Shivers begin to raise the silky smooth skin on her arms. She expects her face to expose shortly the telltale signs of her origins. Nepharisse brushes past a woman perfecting her outer appearance and seals herself, and her shoe collection, into a private stall. She stares in horror in the mirror at her darkening complexion as the lights in the room slowly extinguish. The unfortunate prey at the mirror garnishing her appearance will satisfy her desperate needs. All else must wait.

Nepharisse bursts from the stall, blackening quickly, to terrify her target with a clawed hand at the base of the skull and an open mouth kiss. After a momentary struggle, the innocent belle droops listless in her arms. Nepharisse sits her comfortably on a tufted bench, leans her gently against the wall, and leaves her wares, and the woman, in a state of suspension. Infused with renewed composure and milky elegance, Nepharisse sashays towards the gala.

The musical entertainment has stopped. This is Nepharisse's opportunity to sample the sweet taste of the fruitful results she has nurtured. A quick pose for the local Gadlin paparazzi, and she dances into the ballroom to thoughts of mischievous disinformation. Ignoble gossipmongers can provide unexpected benefits, when suitably enticed.

A quiet giggle at her scheme provokes a nervous batting of enormous feathered Über Lashes from an extravagantly gowned trading elite, presumably overcompensating for her physical insecurities. Nepharisse's natural beauty cannot help but overshadow any attempt at rivalry from women of that flavor. So as not to shatter the girl's already fragile self-image, she stifles a further giggle, whilst she imagines the real Mme Über's half-closed eyelids under the weight of her darling Stew's monstrous fashion creations.

The current Stew Über "EQ" collection is an overstated display of color and calculus. The designs promote differentiation through customizations for each female form into color gradients, based on a plane tangential to each body contour, while at the same time integrating the volume within each luscious curve over their location within the room, relative to other "EQ" fashionistas. This ingenious interplay of tints and shades creates a fluid event decor, entirely controlled by the movements of and interactions between its participants.

While the Albaraaton Chancellor delights the privileged with his wit and generosity, Nepharisse searches the effervescent crowd for the Gadlin leader. Although news of the Pramam's visit has pushed most of the Albaraaton clan underground for the duration of his stay, Wakanda has a reputation for living on the edge of reason. Her folly lies in the belief that she can operate above any law the Ministry can concoct. Nonetheless, history has proven her ability to do just that.

Tonight's affair, however, may convert boldness into bondage, for through the overhang in the silk shawl obscuring her hair, Nepharisse shadows the brazen women from a distance. Wakanda takes advantage of the kaleidoscopic garment distraction to camouflage her approach, while the Pramam endorses his private couturier's coming creations with the caveat that he implement a more secure control mechanism than the "Naked" collection, a vain attempt at humor only appreciable to those who attended his speech at Schrödinger University last year. The "Trimorphic" collection hits the runway to the triple-staccato step of the musical sensation it honors, and to the polite tittering marking the ones who follow satirical Gadlin broadcasts.

The moment of truth has finally arrived and the Pramam does not disappoint. Sothese licks his lips in anticipation of a formal appointment to the position he has filled in Vincent's absence. The Pramam begins by announcing that the previous URA director has been reassigned to Ministburg to oversee an important research project and is thus relinquishing his directorship. He then publicly thanks his trusted advisor Sothese for stepping forward, in the interim, and concludes with the announcement all ears pause to hear.

"Miss Corrient Shakti? Approach the Mount ..."

The official blessing freezes inside the coldness of Sothese's eyes, Wakanda listens on in utter shock, and Nepharisse rejoices in the justice she has influenced. A simple messenger can alter the order of things after all, my dear scholar.

As Nepharisse prepares to receive the praise moving towards her upon completion of her successive earthly trials, the surprise escaping the mouth of the uninvited Gadlin leader flies into her own. The Pramam has covertly acknowledged Wakanda.

Anabelle releases a shriek of intense pain mixed with exhilaration. Her son drops into gentle hands that place him onto a large lotus pad for the birthing cleanse. The globally respected spiritual luminary has coated the armor of love and wisdom she carries for humanity with the light of her first and, as history shall record, her only progeny.

Cheers, from all directions, converge onto the mother and child, as the world rejoices with visions of the extended peace and prosperity her enlightened bloodline will bring. A hawk chases a water snake, too curious for her liking, and claims a perch on Odwin's shoulder. Wakanda approaches the newborn for a quick Gadlin acknowledgment, then promptly regains her position at Odwin's side.

▲ ▲ ▲

Sothese locks onto Shakti when the Pramam excuses himself from the ceremony, taking two bodyguards with him out a side entrance. The three officials approach the new URA director at Sothese's command, just as Wakanda slips out as well. Nepharisse follows the Gadlin while Sothese sizes up the unwelcome challenge.

That drama would be sure to provide much amusement, but it is a diversion Nepharisse must forgo in favor of another of much higher import. She tracks the tremors that Wakanda makes on the stone floor with her heels to the council session chamber and engages the Pramam's two guards flanking the doorway in a flirty discourse.

A double homicide, with but her lips as a weapon, proves simpler than she had imagined, yet no less regrettable. Such is the manner in which she must stave off the resuming chill. She seduces the first sentry with a syphoning kiss whilst the other's desires are aroused as he ogles her, then she cheats time to continue her feast with the second, in one continuous breath. The scene is now primed for a tantalizing report, forged from the words reaching her as sounds in the dark.

"Oh, my One. What a brave Gadlin … or a stupid one. To what does the illustrious Pramam owe this displeasure?"

"I bear a gift."

"Odwin's head, I pray."

"No. A gift exchange."

"Of course, the indomitable Gadlin spirit. You are in no position to barter. I could have you clamped right now for terrorism."

"Yet, you do not."

"There is nothing I need from the likes of you, Gadlin. Odwin has not the courage to come himself? He must send a mere peddler?"

"Odwin is no longer in charge. I am." The silence mutters a hint of approval. "Do I hold your attention?"

"Speak."

The sound of a board pulled from a satchel and a quick sketch locks Nepharisse's jaw.

"The alias awaits the passcode." A slip rips away from a slippad. "The list of Gadlins I want released. It is in your interest to keep our race alive. Genocide is a difficult agenda to sell. Your disciples are not 21st century barbarians."

"You may have your little breeding posse, Gadlin. What is the passcode?"

"Release them. I have a barge waiting. When they get there

and I receive word, I will send you your passcode."

Her footsteps rumble towards Nepharisse, then stop. "You are not dismissed. You are my insurance."

The Ministburg lockdown warden responds immediately. Nepharisse calms the alarms ringing through her body and focuses her attention on the names of the fortunate souls who have met a criteria only Wakanda can divulge. Many faces appear in her mind as the names travel to Ministburg, but one in particular evokes a view towards a distant village.

▼ ▼ ▼

The infant comes to Nepharisse through hands necessarily cloaked for a package of this nature. She rides with the smothering fog, testing the limits her steed can achieve, until the chase ends at a break in the landscape, and a Gadlin settlement appears in the distance. The journey ends when a pregnant woman opens a door and weeps the tears only a sister can shed. The woman unbundles the baby boy and holds him tightly against her heart as she bows to the messenger, whose face she can no longer remember.

▲ ▲ ▲

Nepharisse recoils from the realization that her ears have led her to.

The kind of logic that can justify the betrayal of thousands for a meagre shipload belongs to the likes of Sothese, not any Gadlin, especially not the leadership. Odwin would have never contracted with the Pramam. Before she accepts responsibility for the accuracy of the message she is about to deliver, she rifts a uniportal into the room to witness the payment with her eyes. Wakanda writes the passcode on a slipnote and hands it to the impatient Pramam, facing the stolen board with his back to Nepharisse, who boasts a clear view into the maze.

The unthinkable manifests. The Pramam has administrator access to the entire underground network.

E L I Z E

Day 396: morning

"Are you sure this is the place, Stitch?" It doesn't look very mercantile to me. What exactly do they exchange here anyway?

"Yeah. It's a Ministry drop zone. No scanners." Illegal merchandise? Right. Part of the Pramam's Divine Mission, eh? "Trip! There she is."

"Juicy!"

"That she is, bud." She's just a plain-looking, skinny little Gadlin. Nothing juicy about that. As long as she takes us to the granite site then I'm yay with her. Just the same … Kick them both.

"Ouch!" Hehehe. A chorus of cantankerous cavils. She's checking behind her quite a bit. Why don't you wear a big sign on your forehead, fishy: *Meeting outlaws here.*

"Are you sure she's reliable? She looks like a newb." A bit like Keet did our first day in Eadonberg, actually. If the three officials hadn't been distracted by Nathruyu running in the opposite direction, we would have been found out.

"She's a stealth mud slinger, yeah? She doesn't leave the maze much."

"She must really want this recording to risk the flats with us."

Keet's right. If Stitch is correct about the tides … Hick. What are we doing here? We should turn back. Keet wasn't thinking straight when he suggested this. He's changing. He's becoming more bold, but in an irrational kind of way. And I agreed with him. I must be bent! Yes. You already know you are unstable, Elize. You could have stopped this. He is still controllable. He wants to protect you. I don't need protection. Oh, but you do. No I don't. Shall we discuss this later? You mean, argue? Eerie giggle. Go away.

"Act like you know me."

Stitch pokes the girl and smiles. "I do know you, cutie."

Oh please. Just make the trade, eh?

"Walk with me. You have it?" She pulls an old map from her satchel and does the switch with Stitch. Impressive. I didn't see the flashes disappear. The newb has some skills. "Enjoy the trip."

And where does she think she's going?

"Hey lo, flatface." Let go Stitch. Nab the map. "Yeah. You."

"You're no Gadlin."

She shifts her eyes over to Stitch, then back at me. "Let me explain. You have what you want. I have what I want. We're complete."

Not so fast. Grab her shoulder. "You're supposed to take us there, rook."

"No, highlander. The deal was to show you how to get there." She flicks the map in my hand with her finger. "Enjoy the— Crap!" Her eyes are huge. She freezes.

Stitch charges over with jet black hair. "Bound to another contract, yeah?" He shoves her on the ground.

"Stitch! What's come over you?" Pull him off her. Pin him

against the wall. Hold him there. "Let her go." The girl runs away, terrified. Wait for his hair to change. Good. Release him. Crap! Bright pink. Not so good. Turn around. Sheiss!

"Leave the Gadlin. She is not the one we want." It's the three officials!

"Pica quick! Follow me, chumbuds." Grab Keet by the arm and run. Juicy. We're in the Exchange Sector now. Down into a ... maze?

"Catacombs. Juicy!" Eye roll.

"We'll dig some other time, Keet. Let's blister." Dead end. "We're trapped!" Stitch pokes me and grins. I should know him better by now. There's a hatch. He pulls out his frequency thrower, camps on the controller channel, and hacks the lock code.

"You first, chum." OK. Here I go. "Wait! Your bioshield. Put it on. You too, bud. Check your wristbands." Right. Flashing lights on. Shields on. "Trip. Open up." And into the yellow fog we go. The hatch auto-locks shut.

Phew. It's a little warm out here.

"Did you bring a portablower?" Well, that was a hick question. Here comes the clearing already. "Bopping to *Oye Amigos* here too, eh?"

"The broadcast station is over there. Or over there. You'll see once the fog clears. Perk. Where's Keet?"

"He was just behind me. Keet?" No response. "Keet?" Try not to panic. What if his bioshield is jam. NO! Check the wristband. "His blue dot is—" Screech! "You wack!"

"Pica trip, bud! Eli's eyes popped." Keet's face enters our fog-free bubble, ripping and rolling.

"Hahaha." Honestly. This is no place for juvenile behavior. "I could have flipped the shield control when you grabbed my ankle."

"Slap me, Eli." Tempting. "So, Stitch. Care to share?" Yes. I also wouldn't mind knowing where my hip-wiggling poke-happy friend disappeared to back there. He hesitates. Hands on hips. Stare.

"Some interpret the Gadlin Creed in their own way."

Huh? "Meaning?" He should be used to my squashed frog face by now.

"It's a matter of contention in Gadlin contract law. A contract always states a completion date, yeah? After that, the hired 'helper' is free to pick up another client, usually the highest bidder. They're supposed to honor their contract like pure water. Multiple contracts are allowed, but if a new client is on their hit list, then there could be trouble until the previous contract expires."

"Hit list? And define trouble." Come now, Elize. Trouble is Zafarian. Like your father. You know nothing. Breathe. Calm. Serene. Breathe. It's just paranoia talking. Breathe.

"Eli? Is everything trip, chum?"

I should tell him. No, do not. Trouble, remember? OK, you win for now. So shut up.

"Trip? Yeah. Like the one you went on. What was all that about?"

"Some greedy Gadlins argue that the full disclosure bylaw is more of a guideline than actually binding. They seek out their marks as clients then collect double credit. A downpayment from the second then the balance from the first, upon completion."

"Why would anyone contract with them, even with full disclosure?"

"When you need something done in a clip, roll with the best."

The best way to get yourself killed. Keet, free up your eyes. Are you listening at all?

"So you think she sold us out?"

"I fig she did. Yeah. Ta for stopping me, Eli. My superhuman, chum." He pokes me and laughs. "It was not behavior Odwin would have been proud of."

And not one I care to witness again. He could have killed her. He would have killed her. Trouble. Trouble. Trouble. Geez. You're relentless. He would never. Not him. Not Stitch. Elize is right. Not Stitch. He is a good soul. Yes, he is. *There is nothing either good or bad, but thinking makes it so.*

What's Keet staring at? Nudge him. "Let's look at the map. What does your compass say, Stitch?" Peek over his shoulder. That does not look like any compass I have ever seen. Nudge Keet again. "What are you calibrating?"

"Granite contains quartz. I brought a Sentinel sniffer, just in case."

Shudder. Sentinels. Keet finally pays attention. "I thought the hairy, drooly, fanged, and uber smelly beasts were Unification hybrids engineered for security duties? And wouldn't they drown? The quarry is underwater. It's here on the map." Keet slaps a film on top. "And the topography shows the tide levels." Smart use of the archives.

Stitch just shrugs and continues fiddling. He points the

sniffer into the fog, turns around a few times, and shrugs again. "There must be some interference, yeah?" He puts it in a handy front pocket and pulls out a timepiece. "Perk. Hook in." He's blistering. He clips a rope to the hatch, then to the secure belts he made us strap on this morning. "Faster." Oh yes, the chest harnesses. Why the rush? "Hold tight. Here we go."

"Go wh— Whoa! The map!"

"We're trip. I have crumbs. Keep holding. It won't be long."

"Before I lose my pants." Giggle. We'll get to see Keet's adult butt now. Where did this wind come from all of sudden? Juicy. It's taking the fog away. It would take me with it as well if I weren't clipped in. And there it goes.

Stitch checks his bioshield, then Keet's, then mine. "Trip, ya fig?" He beams. It reminds him of his survival training with Odwin, I wager. Keet seems a little out of sorts. He's likely reevaluating his sanity for suggesting we come here. What is he staring at now? Whoa! Look at that drop.

"A little taller than Van Billund Hall, eh, Keet?" Nudge him. Could he look any whiter I wonder. Hehehe. Or greener? "It'll pass. Just keep looking up. Ready for the drop, Stitch?"

A big grin and bright red hair is the cue.

"This wasn't on the map." Keet's grumbling.

"Well, we're in it and it's huge." Keet mumbles something about impossible. Then he just mumbles. Whatever works to keep him moving is juicy with me. I won't even ask Stitch how we're going to get back up. I'm sure he has it all figged. All I need to do is count to keep my mind off the height. Starting with one, two, three—

When did I put this on? These flying bugs are quite annoying and the mask is not really working. They keep getting stuck in the netting. "Get out of my face!"

"Hey lo, chum. Welcome back, I think."

When did Stitch slip that wilderness suit on? And Keet? Predictable. Picking up junk for fossils no doubt. He has quite the collection already. Hang a sec. Where's the cliff? We must have been walking for hours. Dizzy. Look at all this garbage. I don't see any red granite quarry. Ohhhm gee. Are we standing on it? How deep does this stuff go? So this is where the relics in Mr. G's shop come from.

"Quite the eclectic collection of garbage." Geez. Another one stuck in my mask. Pick and flick. Pick and flick. Pick and flick. Sigh. I'm bored. "Stitch, are we there yet?" Giggle. He turns around and jumpers! Look at his suit go. So that's how it works. Hungry little critters. He traded his wormy hair for an entire body of worms. Ewww. Keep your distance.

"Slap me, chum. If they keep eating like this, I'll have mud shooting out the trap all night, yeah?" Ugh. Well, at least it clears some air space around us. Keet doesn't seem bothered by them. Come to think of it, they aren't after me either, just my mask. I wonder if I took it off.

"We've been walking for hours, Stitch." He's singing. That's new.

"Make it exciting. It's all up to you." Hmmm. His voice is not bad. OK. Off this goes.

"What are you doing?" Stitch rushes over and tries to put my mask back on. Help. I'm being attacked by the worm man. "Put it back on. It will break the bioshield."

"What a stench!" Stitch is a grey-haired mess. "It's worse than the Restricted Sector."

"Don't breathe it in. I'll reset your bioshield." He kneels in the crusty mud and taps some sequences into the controller on my belt. I can't hold it anymore. Breathe.

"Now that's better. Just like the highlands."

"No. Eli! I told you to hold it. Now you're in phase two."

"Phase two of what?" Keet drops his latest sample and runs over. They are both bending right now. Push them off me and kick that bug magnet mask away. "Honestly, boys! You're both bent!"

"You're still breathing?! You should be in a coma by now." No, thank you. I've been in one already today. But he doesn't know that. "It disables your sense of smell first, and then it slams you." Stitch shuts off his bioShield and immediately starts to throw up. Keet taps it back on for him. He's confused. Hang a sec. I'm confused. "So it's true."

"What?"

"You're from one of those cities where people have adapted." Huh? "The gases. You can't smell them?"

Geez. Keet! You have to lay off those spicy flyer bakes. "Yeah. I can smell them." Keet takes off his mask. Grimaces at the first whiff, that would be his, then nothing. Strange. "Maybe it's the highland dust we got used to."

Keet whips out a recorder. "Let's take a weesie. Everyone say *hey*."

"Well, you might be able to see our faces through the snapping bug gluttons." At least these ones can come off later. "Let's keep walking." Keet is back collecting garbifacts.

Hehehe. "They seem to only be after you, Stitch."

"I guess I'm juicier." Hip check. He jettisons about a meter.

"Who's juicy now?" Dweeb.

Stitch counters with a poke.

"Do you have secret pockets where you hide power snacks?"

"You're the one with picazillions of pockets. And the collage of whatever those bits are." He fits the landscape. Random junk patched together somehow. Like that elbow rope thing poking out his sleeve. Tug. Tug. Tug. He unzips his coveralls. I'm feeling the heat as well.

"Trip, ya fig? Clothes with soul. Every piece has its own energy. The patchwork creates the story." He points to a multicolored and multitextured weave. This one represents unity. All different animal skins woven into one. That's real Unification, not the flyer mud the Pramam dumps." He pulls a little paper booklet from inside the patch. Another pocket!

"Oooooo. Secret incantations?" Wiggle my fingers.

"Yeah." A poke. "Beware. Words have energy too." He chuckles. "It's the Gadlin Creed. Odwin gave it to me. I keep it close." Hmmm. Send Keet the sound-familiar look. He opens it to a random page and smiles. "Here's one for you. *Artificial mental boundaries shatter in the presence of your true being.*"

Hip check number two. "You mean my physical boundaries." Hehehe.

"Or this one is Odwin's favorite. *Calmness is power.*"

"Calmness is power? So is that the secret weapon you used on Nathruyu when she was choking me?" My throat is sore just thinking about it.

"No Tess there, chum. I woke up. She was down. I was trip." He shrugs. "I'm dunked on that one."

"Really. And all this time I thought you were my hero." Bat my eyelashes. He laughs.

"Shhh. Keet might decide to challenge me for your hand, fair princess." A poke and a smile. Now hip check number three. Whoops! A little strong.

"Back on the slick, Eli?" Keet's done collecting.

"You wager, Keet. What about you? As an apprentice curator you qualify to join the university team."

Find the book. What? Find the book. Who are you? Find the book.

Whoa! Ouch. "Are you guys—" What are they looking at? Crap. Stay low. What is someone doing all the way out here? Hick. We're all the way out here. I can't see. Grab some lenses. I still can't see. "Those Gadlin cloaks are huge. He's digging for something. Or she. I can't tell. Wait. He has something. Come on, turn around." Or not. Now what? Hand them back, Keet. Crap. The Gadlin's gone.

"Ohhhm gee. Stitch? What is that?" I can hear it too. It sounds like thunder. There's not supposed to be a storm today. Take the lenses from Keet.

"Yeah. What is— Crap! What time is it? It's the tide!"

"Clip out! NOW, chumbuds, NOW!"

Voices, if you start now, all I want to hear from you is faster, faster, faster. "Keet! Are you bent? Run AWAY from it."

"We can't outrun it. There's an exit. Over there. Trust me." He knows something. But how? No time. We're jam anyway, so follow him.

"Check that wave. Pica trip! I wish I had my boogie."

"Stitch, you're pica bent. Keep running."

"You see it, Eli. That building over there. We can make it." Where? OK, Keet. Let's hope Indie strikes again. Yes. There's a reflection.

Stitch is looking green. No. His bioshield is failing. Grab him. "Hold your breath, Stitch." Almost there. Phew. Thank the little baby prophet. Quick. Help Keet seal the hatch. Done. Big breath in … and out. Juicy. Calmness is power.

"Ta, chum. I fig there was a frequency spike." Stitch looks better. His hair is green, not his skin.

Someone is using this space. The air is filtered, and the hatch is solid. Someone with no decor sense though. Yuck. Ugly curtains. Let's see what a front row view looks like. "Jelly alert!" Jump back. Shiver. It's a little cold in here. There's a light somewhere. I can see myself in the glass. Hat head. What was that? Check behind. Nothing. I think I'm tired. I'm seeing reflections.

Here comes the garbage. Stitch is fascinated by it. Keet should be too, but he's shaking, and quiet. It's all too intense for him. He'd rather be home in his books. In the safety of his own crypt. Good. Out comes the journal. That should calm his nerves. He needs to get it out on paper. That way he can process what just happened. Right. But what did just happen?

"Keet, you saved our lives. Top researching." He stops writing and looks at me, confused. Better let him write. Actually, no. He has an opportunity to experience life and here he is acting like a pup again. And giving me a dirty look. Jumpers! That was loud.

"It's just a glitch in the deflection field. It's trip. It's a dunker it's holding at all. Keet, bud, the history of the world is clipping past us and you're missing it." That got him moving. "Ziga trip! I used to ride waves to shore like that near Odwin's place. They were a bit smaller though."

"In case you forgot, we came down a three hundred meter cliff. You would have been smashed against the rocks."

"But what a way to go, chum!"

Keeto and I are back in sync. "You're bent!" Now where is Keet going in the dark with his newfound bravery? A circle flashes green.

"Trip. An ancient elevator."

"There's a tunnel down there. We should go." A tunnel? He wants to sneak around, in the dark, under 300 meters of water, in a tunnel? He must be ribbing me. "We won't find what we're looking for here."

"And we will down there?" He's mute again. I think he's trying to say something, but nothing's coming out. He's staring past me, petrified.

K E E T O

Day 396: late afternoon

I just want to close my eyes, but I am already blistering through my thoughts. My writing is barely legible. Maybe I am just dreaming this. I hope I am just dreaming this. I do not remember ever been so terrified. This is bent! And it was all my idea. WHAT was I thinking? Nothing is coming into my head, except for the sound of centuries of failed human ingenuity slamming against the window's protective energy shield. Gulp. That could have been us. Frail human stupidity, yet ...

Research? My digging skills were not what found our escape route. I wish I knew how I knew but I just knew. Tough girl there is still calling me a pup! I am just going to ignore her, but not Stitch. Letting history pass me by is something I have vowed to you to no longer do. Something is not right though. We need to get away from here. Let me test my new transcription gadget.

Whoops. I forgot to turn this thing on.

What thing? (new voice)

Annotate new voice. Eli.

We are taking an ancient elevator down into the darkness. The hunch that is drawing me into this abyss is also pushing me away from whatever is testing the force field.

Ohhhm gee. Post traumatic stress. (Eli)

Eli is trying to mask her fear with humor again. Levity is

not the pacifier I use for my demons. My choice is silence, going within, looking for your strength to guide me through, which I must do now in this deep dark hole we escaped to.

We didn't escape, you dragged us in here. In fact, this whole trip was your idea! Part of your brain was baked from the zap. The thinking part. You just— (Eli)

Eli is understandably upset. Her challenge now is to keep her voices quiet in the presence of the darkness which permeates her dreams, whereas mine is a foray into mobile introspection.

They're back? (new voice)

Annotate new voice. Stitch.

Ouch!

You promised, Keet. Don't you even care about me anymore? Who else do you blurt out our private discussions to? Nathruyu, eh? You told her everything, didn't you? You just— (Eli)

The further down we drop the more creative Eli's neurosis gets, almost as if it feeds off the blackness that engulfs us.

Neurosis? You're ribbing me. You talk to our dead mother in your hick journals. And now listen to yourself, eh? (Eli)

You lost your inner monologue, ya fig? (Stitch)

(Laughter)

Pica overdazed, bud. (Stitch)

Ziga bent I'd say, Stitch. (Eli)

Slap me for laughing. Everything is juicy. I'm testing out my transcriptor as a running commentary tool.

(Laughter)

Eli, I am not used to censoring my journal. I do care about

you more than you can imagine. Forgive me.

Is the silence an indication of her acceptance? The worry I release every night in the pages of my journal is testament to my affection for her.

Well then, say it directly to me, Keet. (Eli)

I'll do one better.

The last time we held both hands together facing each other in the dark, I took comfort in the belief that we somehow summoned you, and that it was your protection, present as a third power, which cloaked us from the tagging frenzy at Van Billund Hall. As I stand here once again with my heart open to the person who means more to me than any riveting artifacts which temporarily seduce me away from that truth, you breathe with us, together, as one.

(Sniffling)

That's … beautiful, Keet. Together. (Eli)

Together.

(Throat clear)

Chumbuds? (Stitch)

(Laughter)

Fumbling through a chumbud salute with not a sliver of light is a great way to reaffirm our pledge to one another, before we delve into the unknown.

Trip. The trio has landed. (Stitch)

At least we think we have landed. The door is still shut, which may very well be the only barrier between us and a charge of toxic water. We were saving our head lights until absolutely necessary, but I can sense Eli's resolve breaking. The storm seething outside our sealed box will either kill us, or the airtight lift will. Stitch illuminates the situation while Eli and I rummage through our backpacks for oxygen masks. The gauges on our belts are on the cusp of the red zone, which may explain why Stitch is fumbling with the controller. Crap! He just passed out!

Eli, put yours on first. You can't help him if you're unconscious.

As usual she ignores my incessant babble, which in this case is no idle chatter. My mask goes on first before I wrestle some sense into my temerarious twin.

He's awake now but Eli is still hovering over him. I accidentally tapped off the transcriptor in my haste. Her mask is lying around somewhere. Here it is.

Eli! He's juicy. Put on your mask. Now!

In what dimension does she think she is that an eye roll is warranted?

Keet you're overreacting. It's your beakish mother hen attitude surfacing. I'm fine. There. It's on now. (Eli)

I have no words to process the slight Eli just lashed out with. Ohhhm gee. I just chastised her for treating Stitch like I acted myself towards her. Not all mirrors are made of glass.

But they can still splinter. I know you are just protecting me, Keet. We need to find out what's outside this cage we're in or we'll end up throttling each other. I'm topped up. (Eli)

I would say. Ouch. At least it was a kick with a smile, a touch more bruise-inflicting than a poke but with similar intent, nonetheless.

You do the honors, bud. It's your adventure, yeah? (Stitch)

When Stitch asked us last night if we had brought fast

shoes he failed to mention for what purpose. I will attempt to ignore the white of his teeth reflecting off Eli's head lamp. The fact that he knew what we were up against and still hip-jiggled along the flats is a behavior I would associate with certain kinds of brain deficiencies. Hmmm.

Bending, ya fig? (Stitch)

Hick. I said that out loud. Anyway, it is bending as Stitch puts it. I wager the explanation will surface at some opportune moment. It was like riding the wind in the highlands up there as the tide tsunamied into the quarry. The same power which had threatened the pants off my butt slingshotted back to us six hours later.

I'm going to slingshot off your butt if you don't open that door, fishy. (Eli)

Right. Everybody take a deep breath, and keep your eyes wide. I'll start with just a crack then slowly, and gingerly. Are you hearing this?

As long as we're not smelling it, we're trip. Check your gauges, chumbuds. (Stitch)

We need a brighter light. (Eli)

Whoa! The water level is rising fast. Whatever this building is, the tide is crashing right into in. Eli is not budging. There is a channel just a few meters away where the water is gushing past. We have no way of knowing how deep it is without taking the plunge, and I am definitely not volunteering. Stitch obsesses over his watch, tapping his foot. Eli stares at it, at his foot that is. I recognize that emptiness. Her mind is lost in her nightmares, which have followed her into this dank dungeon I have lead us into. The water level is still rising. A couple of meters more and we will be experiencing a crash course in underwater exploration.

Any second now. (Stitch)

Crap! There go my chances of becoming a famous explorer. Mine are not the bones I want the next apprentice curator to dig up. The plan was to join you after a full life not just barely a half one. It is just as well Eli is not present to see this coming, or me pacing so feverishly. Stitch is as calm as the stillness we are headed towards. He must have a piece missing.

Ease, bud. Perk. (Stitch)

The foot tapping stops. I can hear Eli breathing again, which means the rush is over. The channel is full and flowing peacefully. The river even looks incredibly clear. Yet, should I dare? I sense that Stitch is thinking the same thing. Eli beat us to it.

Juicy! Is this what fresh water smells like? (Eli)

There must be a filter somewhere and a flood gate. How did you know it was going to stop, Stitch?

The floor and the walls are dry. I fig it would take more than a tide cycle to do that. There is no entry point for sunshine. (Stitch)

So knowledge is what trumps our fears. The unknown becomes known and imagination finds a more productive outlet, such as —

Finding what you brought us down here for instead of subjecting us to incessant third person babble. (Eli)

Welcome back, chum. The blackouts as well then? (Stitch)

Yes, but that wasn't one of them. (Eli)

Not like the climb into the quarry, ya fig? (Stitch)

Eli summons her substandard acting skills to look unconvincingly shocked. She should realize by now that Stitch often knows more about us than we do of ourselves. A snare my way echoes a sentiment that I am no master of the stage either. Stitch's poke, smile, and his wiggle mean the blue hair is not far behind. I wish you were alive to meet this character, though if you were he would be bopping around others instead.

Or not at all. (Stitch)

Keet, talking to Mother does not make her real. Let her go, or at the very least keep your conversation to yourself. I'm bending just listening to you. Can you switch to quill and paper now? (Eli)

We can stay here until the next high tide. I'll pop the oxygen tent. The levels will drop again as the tide retreats. (Stitch)

There is an unnatural calmness about being encased in a granite structure under the sea bed. Stitch succumbed to it first, then Eli, after a short bout of eyelid resistance, but I somehow have been spared the intense fatigue lulling them into a deep sleep. Before I give myself credit for supernatural stamina, I must confess that a hint of foreboding is what keeps my hand moving over these pages. Without even a sketchy image of what lurks outside our makeshift hostel, relinquishing my consciousness to the darkness holds no appeal, regardless of how fatigued I surely must be.

Perhaps solar deprivation has thrown my circadian rhythm into fibrillation, or the electrical impulses in my brain have finally short-circuited my inner clock. Eli keeps ribbing me about my mind getting zapped from the granite weapon, even though the hit was far from it. Nevertheless, I wonder whether there is veracity in her quips. I have noticed a change in my anxiety levels, which had previously been attached to Eli's condition, but now have their own mysterious cause. The angst is no longer intense and compressed. Rather, it persists in toxic waves, beneath the surface of my skin, much like the ones we fled today.

I have been seeing things. At first, I thought they were just tricks in the fog, then mirages in the mist while the virulent froth charged the granite flats, but now the forms have more defined edges to them, almost as if repeated encounters are revealing more and more detail. Is this the gradual process through which madness emerges? My clarity of thought disappears during these experiences, which unsettles me further still. Fortunately, Eli's success in coping with her increasingly vivid episodes inspires some optimism.

The panic that drove me into the elevator resurfaced in the river flowing beside us. Are the mute eyes that blinked in the waters the intuition that lured me here? I consider it best to save this disclosure for our silent moments together, lest my delirious monologue raise suspicions about my mental stability. Curiously, I sense nothing but amplified tranquility around me as the current hums, not terror resurrected through my written words. Yet something is amiss, whilst the faint murmurs of Eli and Stitch, resting on either side of me, bookend today's excitement.

The silence sounds more like whispered incantations streaming past than nothingness. If I am to ever travel the world cataloging history firsthand, as I yearn to do, I should start by investigating strange phenomena. Yet I sit here, afraid to live, as always. Enough. Fear is simply excitement without a plan. So, here I go.

Transcriptor on, journal in hand, head light on, and out into the dark cave I venture. As long as I don't stray too far, nothing bad will happen. Reframe. As long as I stay close, all will be good, and safe.

The walls are very smooth and cold, like I should be too. The roof is also flat and polished, but the height's difficult to estimate. It could be as tall as Osler Hall. The aqueduct seems endlessly wide. There must be pillars supporting all this stone and … Juicy! Indie strikes again! One over the —

Ummm. I think I'll head back now. I'm likely just seeing my own shadow reflected off the shine, but just the same … Who am I ribbing? My shadow moves with me and that one was definitely playing peek-a-boo with my resolve. We're not alone.

Where is this breeze coming from? Crap! I have to wake Eli and Stitch up. Now!

Ohhhm gee! You gave me such a fright. Where did you go? (Eli)

Stitch has already broken camp, and all our bags are stacked inside an inflatable craft moored to the river. It's amassing momentum, fast. His eyes are as wide as Eli's mouth screaming at me. Apparently our fearless chumbud is part human after all.

Stop your blabbering and get in the bloody craft! (Eli)

Crap! Hook me in. Ahhhhhhhhh! IIIIIIII haaaaaaaaave toooooooooo siiiiiiiiign ooooooooof noooooooooow!

That was no random puff. The gentle tickle quickly

morphed into a life-sucking backdraft. Even though Stitch had it all figged, he knew the risks, and he wisely kept those details from us. It turns out that my momentous cavernous discovery is one of many Gadlin underground hideouts. Stitch has been here with Odwin, years ago, on a training excursion. The memory of a fellow apprentice, syphoned off their barge by the backdraft, still haunts him, hence the saucer-eyed black-haired expression. Understandably, the unfavorable odds of survival discourage most aspiring gatayoks as they begin their trials.

I hereby soberly declare, in your otherworldly presence, a deep respect for the dweeb.

Visions of the ocean slurping us out to sea through a gigantic underground straw kept my eyes fixed on the reversing water. I have never experienced such clarity. Verily, the legendary Caribbean blue has manifested itself in my waking hours. Could this be the beginning of a new epoch for humanity? I theorized, in my efforts to remain calm, until we reached a critical junction that almost ripped the eyes out the crown of my head.

Way above us, the debris infested sea was skating across a huge aperture. The timing was crucial. Stitch shot a dual autograbber at two pillars, flanking the canal behind us, to stall the boat past the opening, shot another one at two pillars ahead of us, shot another one straight down into the rushing water, locked them all tight, then monitored the torrent above, with his finger on the releases. Once the yellow fog joined the noxious tide, we held on to our pants and Stitch started the count.

At this point, Eli and I had over-consumed our oxygen supply, so we held our breath, as we echoed the numbers in our heads: one, two, three ... nine, ten, eleven ... thirty.

The opening sealed shut, just as Stitch released all the anchors, and we slingshotted towards a massive drain hole. Stitch pulled out two more dual autograbbers, this time securing the front before the back, locked us tight over a streaming chasm, and started counting again as the water disappeared. We were left suspended between two canyon walls, perched high over the deepest darkest hole imaginable.

While Stitch just sat and relaxed, Eli and I were gasping for breath. Surprisingly, instead of passing out, we were fine. Eli tapped her gauge a few times and the display flickered. There must be a reserve. Just the same, Stitch pitched us replacement cartridges and we clipped them in.

Eli is peeking over my shoulder. Switching back to transcriptor mode.

So you're interested in my secrets now, eh?

We need to find a way back. Hop off. (Eli)

Are you bent? Eli! Oh.

The autograbbers double as a pulley system. Trip, ya fig? (Stitch)

We need to follow the water.

Who's bent? (Eli)

You want to go down there? Crazed, bud. (Stitch)

No. There's another flow somewhere. That way.

Now hang a sec, Keet. You don't know what's over there. We need to climb out before the next tide. (Eli)

I'm trip with that, bud. Follow me, stealth. Sound ricochets in here. Let's hope no one's home, yeah? (Stitch)

A three hour walk and we found the entrance. Ouch.

Shhh. (Eli)

We're trip. No one home. OK, bud. Show us your Tess. (Stitch)

Vibrations through the stone direct my ear to the back wall. Ouch.

Enough with the blabbering. (Eli)

Fine. It's behind this wall. Up there. Can you reach it?

Climb on my shoulders, chum. (Stitch)

Jumpers! (Eli and Stitch)

The eyes are huge. Are they alive? (Eli)

Frozen in ice. Juicy! Look. An old digital playback system.

A what? (Stitch)

It's all about the relicberry, Stitch. All I need is my cable. Plug and download.

Do you know what they are, Keet? Take a flash of the smaller ones too. They're smiling. (Eli)

Perk. Did you hear that? The stairs are this way. (Stitch)

Wait. We didn't find it.

(Grumbles) know (grumbles) bloody (grumbles) (Eli)

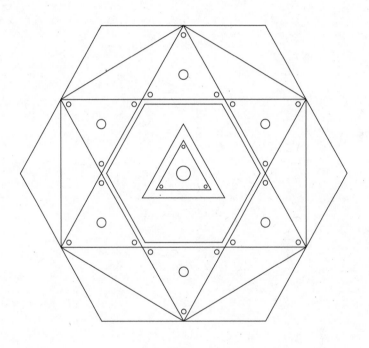

CHAPTER SEVEN

NEPHARISSE

Day 396: early evening

A treasure lost, another gained. Nepharisse projects her latest success story onto the blank canvas she creates with the granite walls, as they glisten in the light seeping through the oxygen tent pitched beside the underground water channel. Ensuring that the artifact captivates the right hands is a matter of seizing the correct moment, and executing a perfect delivery. However, turbulence still aims to disturb the flow of his subconscious mind, although a different disturbance from that which quickens her reflexes. She leans her back against the pillar, selected as a cloak, and channels the dark light, traveling through the vastness around her, into her bewitching thoughts.

The mirage Nepharisse creates on the stone warps the perspective of space. Gravity moves through the frontal plane towards her chest while Keeto's face pokes over the hull of an inflatable craft. His eyes reveal the wonder of a young boy, along with the clarity of an elder. Waves of wisdom reflect their fluid nature in his wide black pupils. Through them, she enters his heart and weaves her message into a basket of gold. His motive must outshine the purity of her gift in order for knowledge to move through him and deposit its bounty. Today, he learns to trust the sparkles that dance on the wings of her words.

Follow the waters for all that you seek. Trust the waters with the secrets you keep. But flee the monster in the house of the deep. Or the water shall weep.

The image of Keeto's face transforms into an awestruck reflection off a wall of ice, thick with the frozen bodies of extinct mammals from pre-industrial seas, arrested in time at the height of their game. Joy is the essence of their spirited play, for they have been saved, and they rest with the hope of clean oceans again. Elize enters the frame, enamored by the creatures. A flash illuminates the room. In the background, Zafarian's likeness whips its head away from the crystalline masterpiece, distracting Keeto and Elize, as the vision fades.

A sinuous trickle marks a towering zigzagging staircase carved into the side of an underground cliff that leads to a leaky hatch. The sun fans its rays into slivers along the surface of the precipice to reveal the source of the drip, a carved out niche half-way up with a peephole into another chamber.

The gap chips open, and its hidden fortune fills the scene, as the artifact melds into the wall it hangs from.

The communication ends with the delivery perfected and the spotlight aimed at a different actor in her triumphant biography, the half-Gadlin.

Zafarian is unusually edgy this morning. Living with a conscience polluted by half-truths leaves a soul suspended in a web of splintered alliances, or at the very least, trapped inside a splitting headache. Perhaps his migraines would not be as debilitating were he not resisting them, nor if he had not misplaced the last of the black-market herbs he grinds into his morning beverage. Odwin's incommunicado behavior has left him probing the maze for a new source, but the other one who can help has not yet come forth.

Elize joins Zafarian's search with half-hearted enthusiasm and without success. Difficult is the task to commit to a goal with no knowledge of its purpose. This, and other laws of existence, often arrive in the form of such nebulous statements, yet to those who pay heed to their meaning, they speak the truths unadulterated by the limited human intellect.

Nepharisse is grateful to be the bearer of these versal principles, and a guide to those who choose to follow them, but she expects more from herself than acting as envoy for a versal postal service.

Directing Keeto's scripted archeological debut is Nepharisse's first priority, followed by investigating the suspicious nature of Wakanda's relationship with the Pramam. To what he owes her favor is knowledge Nepharisse is not privy to, although she presumes neither the Divine Messenger, as he blasphemously calls himself, nor the acting Gadlin leader will supply a factual account of their liaison. Her own guide will act as a sieve for the inquiry, lest she be fooled like those she herself readily influences.

He is closer. Nepharisse can feel the tingling sensation returning to her skin as the cool subterranean air thins in wafts in his presence. How brazen of him to risk revealing himself to the others. The pleasure he savors in splintering the hearts of the women of his choice will enjoy no feast on Nepharisse's watch. In her current state, all she has to do is to clutch his arm, his ankle, or, more delightfully for her, his neck, to imprison him inside his own body, for disposal at her bidding. The beat of an antique timepiece would be the only pulse of his survival.

Cautious footsteps provide the opportunity for his escape. Nepharisse notes the encounter for future investigation and focuses on Keeto tiptoeing in the dark. A cursory peek around the edge of the column she hides behind nudges the junior adventurer towards his first hammer and chisel discovery, while Nepharisse rides the breeze to the surface to recharge.

Tap, tap, tap goes the audacious foot standing at the sink hole. The sun douses his skin in sweat as he flickers in and out of view, through the radiant heat waves rising from the granite flats. Visceral memories of efforts thwarted drive her impulse to extract retribution for his mischief, but her more dominant equanimous disposition releases him, for now. The distraction would prove disastrous, as it relates to her priorities. The twins must find the artifact and return it safely to its rightful owner. For this, she risks the body she works so diligently to preserve and returns to the depths of the excavation site.

Nepharisse checks the periphery before she enters the refrigerated room. The door creak whips Zafarian's head towards her, and just before he is conceivably to utter her name, she preempts him with a smile, to which he responds in kind. With further cognition avoided, she slips to the background and relives the thrills and chills of swimming the coastline with the friendliest giants on Earth.

▼ ▼ ▼

NEPHARISSE

The pod has delayed its journey north, as long as they possibly can, for the young ones are still vulnerable to new predators that have risen from the deep. The shortcomings of humanity have driven the waters to unbearable temperatures and have choked their food supply through persistent pollutants and mass extinctions caused by the acidity bathing the coral reefs. In its striving for balance, a new normal has emerged that excludes most of the diversity previously abundant. The whales have been forced further and further north, so that they now share the sedentary lifestyle humans have evolved into since the invention of agriculture.

As the leaders round Cape Scott, at the northwestern tip of Vancouver Island, for their last great migration, a band of giant squids, that have secretly been tracking them, attack. They too are suffering from the runaway temperatures and dwindling oxygen levels in their natural habitat, the canyons of the oceanic crust, and have been picking off larger and larger prey entering their marine territory. But since hardy visitors have become wise to their threat, the cephalopods have joined together in groups, and now hunt up and down migratory paths for the royal catch, the majestic whales.

Calf or kid, they are one and the same for Nepharisse. Species graced with the kind of intelligence humans consider consciousness and self-awareness exist in many forms, all of which deserve her protection. She has spent many nights contemplating the lore of the heavens on the backs of the blues and the grays as she monitored the route for upwells of tentacles, belonging to the creatures who once solely existed as myths of the high seas. Most of her trips have resulted in safe passage, but this one proves catastrophic for her cetaceous ward.

A synchronized explosion of tentacles envelopes each and every calf in one single strike as Nepharisse shrieks the alarm to no avail. The mothers have no time to react, and all their children drown inside the abysmal lair of their assailants.

▲ ▲ ▲

The flash from Keeto's recorder invites a cheery light into the darkness since the mystery surrounding Mashrin's rock takes the twins three hundred steps closer to Nepharisse's dream. Keeto will find it, this she knows, for she has shown him where to go. Elize, on the other hand, has no waking knowledge of her part in the dream.

It is the book she must find.

Please keep this in mind. Elize, it is the book you must find. Remember. Find the book.

The grumbles under Elize's breath confirm Nepharisse can still communicate with her. This advantage may soon disappear with Elize's ability to focus. Repetition is the key to anchoring the idea, which, once solidly implanted, will grow into an obsession, unchecked by whatever affliction attempts to oppose it. How long the process will take, however, is not for Nepharisse to speculate. Keeto is the star until his chisel and hammer splice the first shard from the opening in the cliff.

As it was in her visualization, Keeto slides his body through the breech that he widened in the rock and pulls the object of his quest from a hook on the wall. From behind the portal Nepharisse has rifted inside the granite, she witnesses him beam at his first treasure. She gives the trio a head start back to Albaraaton while she seals the chamber, then shadows them for the time it takes to ensure that her precious cargo boards the transport to Eadonberg in compliant hands.

The transport station is clear. Anyone remotely aware of the twins, or of the device they are smuggling, is not on the manifest. Nepharisse steps onto the center of the platform and soaks in the closing bit of the day's light. From here, she can watch the final boarding call, the last aisle of passengers being lifted into position, and the safety agent securing the airtight doors. Conversely, she could also be the subject of much attention, which would concern most, but not her.

With her cloak offering cover from holographers, she lingers in plain view as the transport leaves the city's protective biowall. Her lungs enjoy a reprieve. The temperature is stable. All will be well soon ... but soon is a relative concept.

✂ ✂ ✂

Paused on the crest of a bridge, Nepharisse blinks while her black eyes adjust to the absence of light. Darkness erases the separation between earth and sky. For as far as the strongest telescope would normally see, there is nothing but nothing. An endless black velvety canvas is the new backdrop for the thoughts of all who dare enter this realm, be it by fate, or by accident. Furthermore, only the chosen, who have achieved a higher consciousness, can illuminate its depth with the contents of their mind.

There is no sound but the soft symphony of silence.
There is no touch but the sweet sanctity of solitude.
There is no scent but the faint fragrance of familiarity.
There is no taste but the dreamy delight of deliverance.
There is no sight but the vibrant vastness of vision.

Enter the expanse of no thing.

It is no place, where treasures are found and lost. It is no place, where demons are vanquished and victorious. It is no place, where answers reside and questions arise.

Welcome to the dreamless state, Elize. The book has the answers you seek. Find the book.

Nepharisse turns to face Elize, just as the conversation her sudden appearance interrupted ends, with a quick solid tempo fading into the void. Surprise followed by recognition is the expected reaction from those who happen upon Nepharisse in their waking hours, but without the gemstone brilliance of her sapphire blue eyes, surprise gives way to confusion, as is the case with her accidental visitor.

Separation from self comes with great effort in this world of no end and no beginning and no end. Nonetheless, Nepharisse disentangles herself from the interplay to become the puppetmaster inside a dreamworld. The questions begin.

"Who was that?" Elize has no evidence to follow, for the stranger has been dismissed.

"One I have sent on a quest."

"For a book? I heard you say 'find the book'."

"Yes."

"I am to find the book as well?"

"Yes. With every shard of your soul, you must find this book."

"If you want it so much, why don't *you* find the book."

"The book is for *you* to find."

"And whoever else you send on a quest for it, eh?"

Nepharisse smiles. Her breath leaves no sound, since there is no response she can offer that Elize could comprehend at this stage. And the questions continue.

"Where have you been? I've been looking for you."

"I am always here. You were looking so hard you could not see. Soften your focus and you will see, Elize."

Nepharisse feels dejected. Although her presence is never missed, it is also never remembered. She laments relationships that are all too brief and in which nothing develops but a superficial encounter. The short-lived memory that the unwitting participants in her schemes have of their interactions with her provide no continuity for any meaningful bond to form, let alone any true friendships. Always the elusive beauty she remains, biding time for her page in history.

Until then, she expresses her story through phantom imagery for an audience of one.

Nepharisse's narrative paints a sandy coastline with delicate ripples lapping its shore. The stillness at the surface of the water begins to froth as millions of pincers slice through the tension.

The messenger, Nepharisse, is ignored. Deaf ears only serve to validate the self-image she strives to eradicate. Little by little the oceans are dying, and her warnings remain unheeded, even foolishly denied. Effluents from unsustainable agriculture on a planetary scale, desalination of the sea, disappearance of the arctic and antarctic glaciers, acidification of the oceans, and fossil water extraction to the surface are all contributing, either directly, or indirectly, to reduce the amount of oxygen in deep water and along the coastal seabeds, to the point of asphyxiation for bottom-dwelling species.

The children, risking their toes in the morning surf, do not relate to the joys of collecting seashells or creating an artistic collage of washed-up coral bits, for these things have long disappeared from the oceans. They have never laughed with a clownfish, or prayed with an angelfish, or even wished upon a starfish. This last generation of humans to be born before the year of The Great Smoke remembers its trips to the beach as jellyfish infested waters and small raked and disinfected clearings between mountains of algae and drift plastic.

Commando crabs in the millions, with shells as strong as tanks, rushing the beach as they gasp for oxygen, become the last memory for the frolicking youth. Seabirds swirl through the sky and, in the confusion, swoop down to peck at whatever is moving. Nepharisse dives into the bloodshed, screeching and crushing and yanking in vain. There are just too many for her to save. Her knees buckle as she collapses amidst the fallen. Her only solace resides in the gentle caresses she gifts, so that they may forget.

"You were at the quarry. You were looking for something."

"Do you remember how the tide rolled in?"

Frustration blankets Elize's face at the cryptic dialog, reminiscent of the twisted child collector for whom Keeto constantly stands in defense. Nepharisse allows the emotion to ride its wave and continues illustrating nature's biography.

The swelling begins with an unquenchable fever thirsting for the world's glaciers. The Maldives submerge as initial sea level rise consumes the earthly paradise. Multiple intermittent tsunamis slam the low-lying lands with liquid walls as, one by one, the Antarctic glacial ice shelves break off, leaving the glaciers they dam free to slide off the continent. Aquifers drain through endless consumption and join the ecosystem. Monsoons scrape arid lands, flooding their way to the oceans, which themselves contribute to their own expansion, and the climate inferno builds.

The era of The Great Swell sees the planet's topography completely transform into the intricate island network Nepharisse currently travels. The vast arteries of underground rivers and their enormous pools have joined their life partner at the surface, to super-saturate the atmosphere and drown the land. As a result, when the moon calls the waters obey in abundance. Yet human thirst remains unslaked and the looting continues, until their parasitic existence is disposed of.

"What about the children? Are they parasites to be disposed of?"

"Humanity's children are its salvation."

"Who chooses them?"

"You know."

Elize's impatient foot-tapping sends circular ripples in the tide smoothing itself over the granite flats appearing beneath her, and the wavelets settle into a looking glass over the reflection of Vincent's trembling lips, muttering a useless prayer. He casts occasional glances at the mirrored hallway while Nepharisse soothes the infants twins, as she always has. The operation is swift, yet intense. While two other cloaked invited intruders perform the ritual, she keeps the babes focused on her voice. They hear nothing but her voice. Her voice assures them. They are free.

Elize recoils in time to narrowly miss a spray of blood slicing through the reflective waters and arcing through the dense black velvety canvas.

"Is this real? Is this what happened to Keet and me?

"It happens to all of you. To the chosen ones."

"There are others?"

"There always have been, and there still are."

Elize steadies herself against the bridge parapet. A blinding light illuminates the tattered edges of an old parchment, while Nepharisse's repeating thoughts loop their vibrations, as she lingers in plain view on the Albaraaton station platform, watching the Eadonberg transport leave the city's protective biowall.

Remember to find the book. The book is what you must find. All is in the book.

E L I Z E

Where am I? Geez. What am I wearing?

"Stack one, two, or three please." Huh? Oh, it's a PAL. I'm in the archives with Keet and Stitch and … Whoa! Look at all these books. Nine stacks piled almost nine high, and one more right in my face. "Stack four, five, or six please." Swat the PAL over to stack three. It's waiting to fetch again. Wave it off. Whoops. Almost sent it into the academic.

Ah yes! The trademark eyebrow raise. Doesn't he ever relax? Apparently not. I suppose relentless staring is acceptable social behavior where he comes from, eh? Let it go, girl. Focus on something else.

Hick! It's my tunic! It's way too big on me and with this belt … grody. Obviously a noteworthy fashion statement. I don't remember buying this in Albaraaton. It looks like something Keet would wear. Hang a sec. It is something Keet would wear. It's his. I must have slept in his crypt last night, but I just don't remember. Come to think of it, the last thing I do remember is sitting on the transport back home and playing with that dial. Where is the artifact anyway?

Keet and Stitch have some research as well, but stack for stack I win, although their PAL deliveries look somewhat related, while mine are completely random. It's like I don't know what I'm looking for. I got a good enough look at the thing. It should be etched into my brain. Well, here's the culprit.

My PAL's sketch history is absolute scribble. It's a wonder it retrieved anything at all. I wager it's just defaulting to a shuffle pick, and I'm not even sure which stack I've read.

"I can't believe what just happened!"

Crap! Stitch is being loud again, and here comes Mme Beaudoin. I'd better look busy so she doesn't start picking at me. Once she gets going, every little thing upsets her, and I think there are pretty specific rules on hoarding. Juicy. Look what I have here. My PAL is a pickpocket. Maybe a quick skim through Keet's entries for yesterday will wake up some brain cells.

Time to speed read, and just in case Keet decides to glance my way, I'll hide inside my own archive stacks. Here's the spot. Hehehe. The transcriptor couldn't figure out my grumbles. *I know. Find the bloody book,* were my exact words as I recall. Jump forward to … the section on the granite flats after we found our treasure. Anything juicy in here? Let's see.

I have reread the transcription three times already and I am still reeling from the ordeal. Whatever is gong on in Eli's head is a mystery to me.

Not just to you. Trust me.

She has been obsessed with finding a certain book, but when I press her for more detail, she claims she has no clue. She is haunted by a voice, in addition to the usual mad chatter tampering with her sanity … Let that one ride, Elize. There is no madness in you. None whatsoever. Yes, we all agree … *telling her to find the book.*

Right. The book. I should go find it. What do you need a book for, Elize? Keep reading the journal. You know he edited himself while he was transcribing. You need to know what he is hiding from you. No, that would be a violation of his right to privacy. Put the journal back, Elize. I can't put it back now. True. What would you say? You programmed the PAL to steal it? You only want to know what happened while you blacked out. That is an excuse, Elize. Just ask him. No need to breach his trust. OK. Anyone else up there have an opinion? *Seek the answer from the center of your being.* Then my answer is *continue reading …* in peace, please.

The staircase led us back up to the granite flats, very near to the cliff we had repelled down in the first place. The three-hour walk in the searing heat, negotiating centuries and perhaps even millennia worth of human debris, had been completely unnecessary. This particular entrance to what I speculate was a secret subterranean water filtration system is well camouflaged. Had my intuition been more developed, perhaps we could have avoided the hair-raising river ride and associated rise in blood pressure … then again, maybe the journey is the real discovery.

My first inclination, when Stitch divulged his connection to this place, was, as always, to use his delayed disclosure as fuel for the cinders of distrust I still save for him. However, I do believe him when he assures us that he was blindfolded during the voyage, and thus was not aware of its exact location. It could have been anywhere within one day of his starting point, when, in fact, the Gadlin apprentices had followed a zigzag double-backing path to get here. He made us chumbud swear to never disclose its whereabouts to anybody, upon threat of complete abandonment. I imagine I will have ample opportunity to put my honor to the test as our relationship progresses.

To be honest with you, I feel refreshed, yet drained. Journaling in the sun, waiting for the next tide to lift us up the cliff face, is therapy for the misgivings I am experiencing with respect to our choice to forgo a pick and grip ascent. Neither option is ideal. To plummet to our death or to smash against a wall of rock at the speed of an intercity transport makes no difference to the end result. In light of our recent adventure, I feel more qualified for the latter.

Blah blah blah. Keet eavesdropping on Stitch and me talking about Mother … Me telling him my nightmares are back … Stitch offering to do a dream sweep on me to help me clear them … Us finally finding a staircase up the cliff that wasn't there when we arrived.

I think we just didn't see it. I know I didn't. And here is where he stopped while the tide was rolling in. Actually it nearly flipped us over this time.

Now this is interesting …

As we were sneaking our way back through the catacombs, thanks to Stitch's crumbs, I had the distinct impression that someone was following us. The sensation began at the water's edge when we deflated the craft and packed it. It was the same feeling that has been tracking me since the blast I received from the granite artifact. I was definitely conscious on our way to the transport station, so either Keet didn't tell us or … Crap! He's having symptoms too.

Could paranoia have found me a willing victim as well? They were no gemstone eyes in the fog. Honestly. He is still thinking about her. *But eyes nonetheless, and three sets of them.*

More blah blah blah about her and how he's still connected ... Whoops! Almost kicked his shin. Hehehe. Force of habit. I don't want him to see me with this ... Next page.

Oh yeah. That was grody. Stitch emptied the droppings from his bug-hungry wilderness suit on the transport. What a mess! He could have waited until we got back. At least he used a bag. Hang a sec ... What does Keet say about them?

At first I mimicked her fake upchuck, but Stitch's keen interest in dissecting the droppings enlisted my attention as well. While Eli curled up in her seat, examining our well-earned boon with the curious dial on it, the taste preference the insects had shown towards Stitch pointed to Ministry violations beyond a mandatory curfew and a bioTravel directive. What we had expected to be mere excrement was in reality a pile of undigested flying robots. Mosquibots is what Stitch called these Ministry agents. He said that they were either filling up or dumping, meaning taking blood samples, or injecting something.

Thankfully the little spies were filling up, which is more acceptable than secret injections, and they were likely doing so by keying off biochip signals to find their prey. Then it dawned on us. My heart sank as we realized what motive is behind their thirst for blood. They are sweeping the planet for Gadlins.

No!

All I could think about was you when I saw the intense pain on Stitch's face as he uttered the word "Mother" and turned his tears away from me. He wasted no time imagining the worst, and immediately pulled out his travel board to check the headlines: "Terrorists apprehended hiding in Northern Cascadia, in the Caringorms, on the Baltic and Andean Ridges, and in Western Austranesia", "Gadlin clampings top 100 during overnight SIF operation", "Gadlin leader still at large and wanted for treason".

Stitch sent flares in all directions, hoping to attract some aid from the chumbuds network, and immediately received an explosion of responses. The underground was shaking. Their foundation was crumbling. Everyone was panic-stricken. He turned to me and whispered, "Ministburg lockdown," then jet black spears sprang from his roots. His hair spoke louder than the words he gritted between his teeth. "Misty Moon. I should have killed her." Sothese's hounds were after Stitch, not Eli.

Whoa! I missed all this? Remind me not to get Stitch blowing. Misty two-faced Gadlin owes me.

Wakanda is the obvious suspect, according to Stitch, so he gave me a crash course in packet archeology, and we went straight for Wakanda's private activity threads, but we dug up nothing. No packets, absolutely no history. She is more secure than the Pramam's advisor. Desperation led Stitch to resort to mud slinging. He bombarded all community walls with thick dripping ooze, based purely on his opinion of Wakanda, a practice, which as leader of the community, he clearly disapproves of. A few seconds later, red spears replaced the black, and he yelled in the softest whisper he could muster: "Odwin's in the maze!"

Juicy! He's safe. Huh?

A quick communication welcoming Odwin back and

reporting that we just got back from Albaraaton with something from the training site, and could he please send along some migraine tonic, was the last message that traveled the underground. The network went dead. Not the entire maze, just the chumbuds community.

Honestly, did I really miss all this? What was so enthralling with that artifact to obsess me with it to the extent of deafness?

At this point Eli finally piped in with "Look, it's—" and froze, just as the outer dial clicked into the second inner one, mid-sentence.

That's right. That's the last thing I remember. The dials started to rotate on their own once I played with them for a while. Crap. I wish I could remember the sequence I used. Never mind. What happened next?

Just to be sure, I signed into chumbuds with my alias and was granted access. Stitch's was just banned, so I put my new knowledge to immediate use, unfortunately with the same results. One more try with a shadow alias Stitch has for himself, and we confirmed that, this time, the entire chumbuds network was indeed shut down. Fortunately, the backup comm Stitch keeps for emergencies allowed him to organize an escape route. A special EVAC was on its way.

Chances were that the GMU had infiltrated Odwin's alias and now knew where we were. We had to get off the transport before the next station. In the meantime, Stitch loaded Nathruyu's abuse recording into the maze at large, with a curse to Misty Moon. I will spare you the details. Eli's state and the events that ensued are much more important than Stitch's newly revealed vocabulary.

We jumped out the emergency exit onto a hovercraft carrying three hooded figures, one of whom, to Stitch's apparent shock, was Wakanda. Eli was still comatose, with her eyes sucked into the artifact, and Stitch was doing his best to hide that fact from the woman, to no avail. She extended her hand. Stitch took our treasure from Eli and placed it reluctantly into Wakanda's perfectly manicured well-fed grasp, and in return, she gave him a small package.

The rage that overtook me brought with it a frightening, yet short-lived, surge of superhuman strength, as I pinned Stitch to the bottom of the craft, pushing his head over the edge, with his bright pink hair skimming the surface of the rocky landscape. Your image in my heart is the compassion which tempered my assault when Stitch pleaded in my ear: "They have my mother."

Eli's unresponsive state became Wakanda's trump card. Her condescending tone still boils my blood. "Look at your sister. You can't bring this into Eadonberg and let it fall into the wrong hands. The curator could not even protect a stone pyramid. Do you think he will be able to handle this?" I am sure she had a point if only I knew what "this" was. My cooperation triggered the opposite response in Stitch. He accused Wakanda of selling him out, of selling the Gadlins out.

Her retort could not have been more poignant. I remember it clearly because, deep down for a moment, I wished I were Stitch: "You arrogant boy, I just saved your mother! —" except for the arrogant quip. That label has fitted Stitch from the start, with his nonchalant poking and incessant grinning.

Holy Crap! And there's more.

ELIZE

We approached Eadonberg from the southeast and the view ... Skip the travel commentary. *And we used the slipmap Wakanda handed us to get Eli to safety until the effects of whatever afflicted her wore off, which apparently depends on how long she has been in. Then she rushed us off the craft and into the western ventilation shafts before I had a chance to ask her what "in" meant.*

I'd better hurry ... Eli comatose still ... Wakanda told Stitch to tag along ... He should hand over any artifacts ...

And get handsomely paid for it, I wager. My snark prompted a dejected toss of the package Wakanda had given him. It landed on my bed. The thought that Eli and I were being manipulated to find items for Gadlins on contract, wary of being caught with the goods, crossed my mind. The ruse ends here. I refuse to let another anonymous messenger seduce me into a game with the promise of answers. I stared at the offending parcel while Stitch offered up an explanation, which I resisted at first, until I realized that his motives were sincere.

The contents of Stitch's gift were two biochips, one for each of us. I think it best to remain ignorant of their origins and will leave my morality on the shelf, just this once. These minuscule Ministry tracking devices are more valuable to us than an artifact that puts Eli in a catatonic state. My urge to dig can satisfy itself through an afternoon of research in the archives instead. With the chumbuds network compromised, the stacks are our only option to learn about the device we gave up.

Geez. And I thought it was simply another blackout. Here's Mme Beaudoin now.

"Mr. Zafarian. Your presence is already noted." She stares at his mischievous orange hair and walks away.

Time to sneak Keet's journal back to … Crap! Where did it go? Forget about it. Focus on the piles. Find the book. Right. The book. "Where is that book?" What's Keet looking at?

"Odwin would never have made a deal with the Pramam. He would have found a way to free them all." A gold tint replaces the color of mischief. I've only seen him this sad when he thought he had lost me in the arcade. Strange. How could I—

"Crap! This is frustrating." Poor Keet. Grab the PAL and sketch for him. There. Hmmm. That was easy.

"Trip. That's exactly what it looks like. Welcome back, chum."

Wait. If I turn it … That's my dreamcatcher. "What?" Keet's staring at me.

"Don't tell me you think this is a coincidence."

"Right. No one in the history of the world could ever have thought up of a pattern of triangles, hexagons, and circles." He snares.

"Share, chumbuds."

"Eli has a dreamcatcher exactly like this."

"Not *exactly* like this. It has no symbols and notches. It's just a pattern." The PAL comes back with artwork, mandalas, wall murals, … "Pretty, but what does this have to do with Mashrin?" Geez. Doesn't that academic ever go home? "Isn't that why we went there in the first place to …" I'm so drained. "Look, I have to get some sleep."

"I'll go with you, chum."

Keet's eyebrow goes up.

"I'll be fine, Stitch. I'm awake." Sort of. At least I'm here. "You two keep digging." A little resistance from the boys, and done. I need some air.

Eadonberg feels different. The trip was only three days, but it seems so much longer, and at the same time, so much shorter. Sleeping at Keet's crypt last night I don't think was very restful. At least, according to his journal I slept there. Well, on one hand, I have nightmares that haunt me during the day, and, on the other hand, I have blackouts that steal my day. I think I prefer the blackouts. There's no pain to relive.

Yawn. Crap! Another one of my hallucinations. I just thought I saw someone with pale pink hair standing at the Snack Shack. Actually … I did. There's another one at the Snack Barge. The color of indecision. Giggle. Stitch has started his own epidemic. And a couple on the Victory Bridge with blue hair. How romantic. A bridge for their hearts. Hehehe … A bridge?

Easy stepping, girl. I'm a little dizzy. Just make it to your room and you'll be fine as long as the nightmares don't get even worse. The intensity of them two nights ago was almost unbearable. Tap tap tap hurry up, lift. Finally. Geez. Did I turn off the cooling? Tap on the lights and back home sweet—

Creeps! Someone trashed my room.

KEETO

Something big is happening and we find ourselves, once again, in the thick of it. Eli commed me in a panic, the minute she reached her room, to tell me that someone had broken in while we were digging around the granite flats. She found Cyd lying on the floor, hugging his crystal vase, which fortunately he was able to save. The beautiful organic yet gothic stand he had been kept on did not fare as well, but nothing a quick replacement from Mr. G's shop cannot rectify. I could tell by Eli's tone that the reckless abandon the vandal had inflicted upon her decor did not impress her much, and that whoever had perpetrated this crime was long gone. Stitch and I wrapped up our fruitless sleuthing and snuck onto campus, through the mounting distrust infecting Eadonberg's residents.

Although the accelerated decay virus that triggered the GHU panic had not claimed any new victims since we left for Albaraaton, the GMU was still on high alert for suspected carriers and eager informants, which was really a cover for scooping up more Gadlins. Luckily, as we traveled the central corridor, a curious epidemic of mood hair exposed who to steer clear of. You can probably guess who inspired that new fad, although it turns out that the sudden expression of pigment was not a matter of style, but rather, an oversight.

The organism that Stitch had purchased as a rinse, that binds to hair follicles for ninety days, had an undesirable side effect: the ability to jump. I imagine that Eli and I had acquired a few critters when we camped the granite cavern, in close quarters, and we will no doubt exit the incubation period with a splash of color. In the meantime, hidden agendas had best move to Albaraaton since Stitch has inadvertently coiffed our city in a truth serum.

Upon seeing the disaster in Eli's room, we adopted the role of forensic interior design critics, and realized that no one had actually forced an entry. Someone had simply assumed command over the room controller. Since most of the furniture was virtual, there was only one real casualty. Cyd had likely been snooping around in Eli's absence and had managed to tip his perch, while breaking the fall with his monstrous leaves. Nothing, however, went missing.

The hexagonal box Eli had found behind her privy shelf was still where she had left it six days ago. It represents another little mystery attached to the strange energy bathing her corner of Van Billund Hall, which used to cancel the ambient frequencies incessantly humming in Stitch's biochip, up until we breached the ceiling last year by cutting out an escape hatch to the roof.

Although the opening was still patched, I felt a hint of something inexplicable, through perceptions based on scientifically measurable disturbances that I had formerly failed to notice. The sensation drew me to the empty box lying open on Eli's desk, and as I neared it, the scent of myrrh triggered visions of a face I do not recognize, through eyes that were not my own. I must have been engrossed with the malleable padding inside the hand-sized case for a good minute because my attention slowly redirected itself to impatient foot tapping and a highland wave.

Eli was calling my name whilst my head was floating in another dimension. There is no doubt in my mind that someone had been in this room, some time ago, with less than honorable intentions, yet the palpable malice that transpired evades me. All I can report to you at this point is that items have a habit of disappearing from that room of hers, and whatever was inside the curious box, tucked away in a hole behind the privy shelf, had suffered the same fate as your beautiful indigo crystal brooch, the jewel you cherished and protected, even during your last days inside the GHU psychiatric wing.

Stitch postulates that Wakanda might have something to do with the larceny, and based on the research I discovered last year, I am inclined to agree. According to Gadlin legend, the diamond inside the Jewel of Airmid would certainly elevate the woman's worth and status amongst the Unification museum curators, affording her the luxury of favors granted in reciprocity for her generous artifact loan.

Acquiring treasures through theft makes for fat profit margins. Stitch was quick to point out that Wakanda has no lack of that, which suggests that if she was in fact aware that the jewel had surfaced in Eadonberg, specifically in Eli's possession, she would have had to contract an honorable thief fit to retrieve it, rather than securing the gem herself as she had with the item we had just scored on our trip to Albaraaton. Otherwise, we would have found her chubby legs flailing from the old hole in Eli's ceiling.

Regardless, there is always more to the Gadlin story than

our hip-jiggling friend tells us. Or perhaps he is grappling with discordancy, like I am. On the one hand, high principles explicit in the Gadlin Creed far surpass any Ministry attempt at creating a culture of acceptance, cooperation, and unity. On the other hand, Gadlin Law permits interpretations which can lead to contradictions in principles. The full disclosure by-law, in particular, leaves some flexibility in the strict rule of "Honor thy contract," which prompted Stitch's surprise assault on Misty Moon in Albaraaton. His "roll with the best" comment afterwards makes me wonder whether he anticipated trouble and still took a chance. But he really did look like he was going to kill her.

I suppose that any intent, whether verbal or written, can be distorted by those with the power and cunning to do so, for their own gain. Add to that the right of contract annulment bestowed upon the Gadlin leader, for invocation at their sole discretion under extreme circumstances, and inter-clan integrity collapse can manifest with a spoken word. The choice rests within one heart. Just whose heart has the lead is what turns Stitch's hair bright pink in his moments of solitude.

Earlier this morning, I witnessed one such lapse in Stitch's normal, if you can call it that, state. I woke before the sun to a familiar sound I no longer recall and instinctively reached for the crystal pendant you gave me. A soothing calmness flows through my turbulent thoughts whenever I wear it. Only its recent absence has made me aware of the confusion that surrounds me. It is quite literally my rock, much like regular contact with Odwin was for Stitch, whom I caught sneaking out my door and into the cove of crypts my quarters are part of. The blue glow of the generator below the floating floral centerpiece gave off enough light for me to observe a side of him he has thus far concealed.

Here was not the energetic chumbud Eli and I have interrupted on occasion executing the directives of his bioCal morning routine, which includes completing a bioPlank challenge with his court buds to stay fit for the game. The blue-rimmed silhouette, standing with his back towards me, was not even bopping to a silent beat. He calmly wrapped his body in stillness while he thrice repeated a muted mantra, followed by a respectful bow for three seconds. He then reached inside his sleeve, pulled out a small slip, and released a pop-up hologram to the sky. The virtacreature almost flew into my open mouth as I gaped in awe at yet another genius tweak to common technology. Its mirage dissolved when it touched my lips.

The experience left me somewhat unnerved, mainly due to the suspicious look in Stitch's eyes when he caught me spying on his secret ritual. We let the awkward intrusion pass, yet the fleeting heat rush that oozed from my pores prompted a mental note to investigate his incantation further. The words suffuse the sleepless hollows in my own mind.

You are the purity that defines my heart, you are the power that travels my veins, you are the thoughts that saturate my mind. I welcome your presence.

For the first time since I have known him, I am aware of Stitch's vulnerability. Our roles have reversed. Instead of anonymously aiding and abetting fugitives from a prison of lies crafted by a father with a secret advisory role to the Pramam, he is now a target in a planet-wide witchhunt, bartered through a surrogate leader. A real leader should stand in solidarity with all Gadlins and their descendants during this second attempt at ethnic cleansing, rather than trade them in support of a private agenda, which apparently includes confiscating the boon from my first archeological dig. I may not have earned the right to wear a fedora yet, but I did lead the chisel through a niche in a cliff, after all.

I suppose having scored the Galleon's sails from Dr. Tenille's cabin is some consolation for my loss. They make a beautiful backdrop for your game board, in the recess by the window slit, especially when moonlight shines from above, giving the fabric a lovely sheen. However, I doubt that the impulse that drove me to appropriate them was rooted in interior design. The rationale is as elusive as the insight I am hoping to receive about your involvement in Dr. Yarkovsky's death. What could a few sheets of canvas tell me that volumes of printed entries from Captain Snook's private journal cannot?

That question kept my faculties hostage while I crossed the campus orchard on my return jaunt to the archives. Then it occurred to me that Dr. Tenille must have performed an autopsy on the victim, and that based on past discrepancies between official GHU reports and Dr. Tenille's personal journal, I could reasonably expect a revealing report. I wagered that the answer lay in the reams of paper I am hiding in my crypt, in plain view, as entries dated past your supposed discharge from the GHU, and that is exactly where I later discovered the traumatic analysis.

Before I get to that, another shock was awaiting me at the archives, in the wake of the mess of publications Stitch and

I had left on the round table. I had expected Mme Beaudoin to swarm me with a list of library infractions, but instead my, Stitch's, and especially Eli's towering mini-stacks had been returned to their rightful place, and sitting at our favorite sleuthing seats was the quiet academic whispering not so quietly with a stunning red-headed woman.

Anyone within earshot could clearly detect the irreverent tone in her voice. Even as she smiled, then turned her back to me, her energy sent chills down my spine. This was an argument intentionally made public, in a semi-private setting, to put a fine point on her displeasure, or rather intense disappointment with the academic's shortcomings.

All I could make out was something about being late and losing them. The emphasis on the latter was especially cutting. Whatever had eluded them was something the scholar refused to accept responsibility for, which infuriated the woman behind her well-practiced poise. She simply stood up slowly, handed over a small parchment, swooped her curly locks towards me, and smiled right past me, while the target of her contempt smirked.

The surprises did not end there. After I had settled into a quiet corner on the perimeter of the room, away from prying eyes, I sent my PAL to the stacks for anything related to extinct water mammals. Although the subject of my research is not forbidden, fiddling with ancient technology to replay moving images of creatures frozen in a timeless vault on the outskirts of civilization, would draw more attention than I cared to experience. Therefore, I was careful to position my body in such way so as to obscure a direct line of sight to the display on my ancient phone while I fiddled with it under the table.

Perhaps due to the momentousness of our aquarium discovery and its potential impact on humanity, frustration got the best of me after repeated futile attempts at starting the app. The only existing record of these magnificent animals was at my fingertips, and my cherished relicberry was failing me. Visions of a smiling pointy-snouted being encased in ice, attempting to communicate a critical message to me upstaged the presence approaching from the center of the room until the figure stopped at the edge of the book aisle closest to me. My musings faded.

In my periphery, I monitored the academic, who has been a fixture in the archives ever since I have been working as apprentice curator. Only recently has he become more vocal. He was madly scribbling onto a piece of parchment, the tip of which I could distinguish from the page in the open book he was using as a prop.

I imagined a PAL flying by him and plucking the note from his hands to deliver it to me, but reality turned out to be even better. While all eyes were on an overburdened PAL, laboring to remain airborne, the young scholar returned the volume to its original resting place and walked towards the mayhem between us.

No sooner had he taken three steps than the personal automated librarian lost its lift and sent its cargo crashing to the ground in front of him, prompting an acrobatic tumble onto the table I was guarding my treasure under. Finesse saved the scholar from a complete face plant and he respectfully excused himself, with a courtly bow. I watched him return to the stacks, a few aisles away, impressed with the calm he maintained during the near catastrophe. It was almost as if he knew exactly where to step at exactly the right moment, so that he could carve out a clear passage towards me.

As vain as that idea might seem, it was not the ego's folly. On my lap, lay a parchment with the following beautifully penned message: *I have the answers that you seek. Aisle nine. Stack six. Book three. One minute.*

A swift rush back to the GHU holding cell revisiting the black figure twisted in pain in the corner of her prison momentarily stole my breathe. If only the scent of myrrh were not bottled inside my memory and those gemstone eyes were here in the archives, waiting to bring closure to what time had interrupted. My heart raced. I gathered my effects and deliberately tempered my haste towards the appointed section. Once at the rendezvous spot, I deciphered book three to mean the third book from the left on the shelf and pulled it out. A hand whipped out from the other side of the book stack, attached to a whispering voice.

"Pass me the device." I hesitated but the murmurs assured me. "I can fix it."

Thinking back to that moment, while GMU sliders hum their oppression over Eadonberg's skyline as I sit in my crypt, unsure of whom I can trust, the decision to hand over to a virtual stranger the second treasure from my first dig flirted with disaster. Could the comfort I felt with this young scholar be due to his daily presence in the archives? Or was my intuition guiding me towards the birth of another secretive relationship?

My blackberry was returned to me with the opening credits

of a documentary and a pointed question to which I remained silent. Why I was compelled to pirate a copy of the app was no one's business but my own. History belongs to humanity, not hidden in a vault inside a granite quarry. In fact, my quick thinking will bring enlightenment to the world. Yes, that is so.

Through the portal we had created through the shelf, I saw the scholar's familiar eyebrow rise and the deep stare of dark green eyes. "Prepare yourself" were the words that announced what I was about to witness in the palm of my hand.

The grace and fluidity painting swirls in the clear waters reminded me of the times I would watch Eli on the slick while she immersed herself into her choreographies. There was no separation between her and the surface, just like these majestic creatures who moved as one within their liquid domain. Thousands breached the ocean's surface in unison. Their powerful fins created such a surge of perfection that their disappearance would have seemed unfathomable to anyone alive at the time, as would the future stories fed to children and curated by the Ministry. No epic mystery had sealed their fate.

Spears, cross-bows, guns, longlines, nets, factory trawlers, massacres of entire pods corralled into coves of death, and image after image of senseless disembodiments and blood-thirsty genocide played, until too few of these beautiful beings remained to survive collateral damage in the ocean's ultimate revenge against human insanity. A froth of hatred lashed all words from my heart except for a weak: "but why?"

"Ignorance, pure ignorance," was the response that sent a shiver of cold racing through my veins as my new connection returned to his studies, and I to my thoughts, which brings me full circle to the growing concern I opened tonight's journaling with.

Eli and I are at the epicenter of a planet-wide shift that we currently have no capacity to understand. All I occasionally glimpse are waves of foreboding as if our lives were meant to unfold exactly as they have been, despite the illusion of choice we are fooled into believing we possess. Instead, we are the ones possessed, as you were, and as all who carry the mark are. It is the mark which binds us to our fate, and which stamps its host with a sickness the GHU quarantines, under Dr. Tenille's loyal care … or so it appears.

Spread out in front of me is an image of Dr. Yarkovsky, face down on the morgue slab, with a hurried red arrow pointing to the base of her skull, and Dr. Tenille's alarming annotation: "The mark of the hunted."

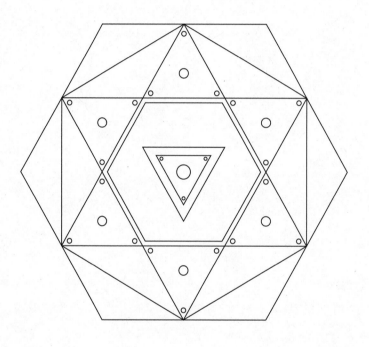

CHAPTER EIGHT

NEPHARISSE

Day 399: 12 a.m. (day 398: midnight)

Nepharisse wakes with urgent eyes. They are here.

She dusts the yellow powder from her cloak and races through the ventilation shafts to the tide's edge, syphoning the last of the energy her body requires for complete rejuvenation from the blue glow of the cooling generators along the way. Unlike the underwater network in Eadonberg, Albaraaton owes its amenable temperature to tunnels carved into the bedrock that supports its architectural behemoths on the surface.

Masonry is in no short supply in this infamous commercial city, and the more lavish the better, according to the trading class. The love of luxury even extends into the shafts themselves as each of them boasts carvings representative of the neighborhood it serves.

Commanding voices, echoing from the next sector, direct a crew on proper docking procedures. The tone of the directives suddenly deepens and increases in amplitude and frequency. They create a haunting harmony with the high-pitch howl announcing the tide's imminent retreat. The travelers are out of time. Shrillness screeches the names of the stragglers who call out for ropes to hook themselves to, whilst a few fade with the retreating waters. Nepharisse reaches the intake vent, on the side of the cliff, in time to pull the safety line taut and hoist a dangling Gadlin back up the rock face.

Drenched and winded, the woman bestows endless gratitude upon the stranger who saved her life, but Nepharisse is no stranger. The Gadlin barge that carried Sakari and her cohorts across the high seas from Ministburg lockdown slides down its mooring harness and stops at the shaft intake.

The passengers disembark. Their tired faces stake claim to the names Nepharisse saved in her mind, from the list of lives Wakanda bartered with the Pramam for. The illusionary freedom they now enjoy will serve them for as long as the Pramam extends his benevolence to their leader. However, as soon as the goodwill credits are fully redeemed, only peripheral vision will ensure their liberty.

The backdraft forming inside the tunnels, on the other hand, honors no contracts. Sakari rushes to a cleverly hidden false wall, brushes it open with an intricate hand gesture, and whips the dozen or so bioshields over to the others. Nepharisse agrees to don one as well, despite her immunity to the gases. There are many minds to influence, so she chooses to erase her face with a friendly smile to all, along with a bidding for a safe passage towards their ultimate destination.

As Nepharisse turns to brave the oncoming yellow smoke bomb, Sakari faces her to block the way. She places a flash and a crystal jewel in Nepharisse's hand, gently lays her right palm on Nepharisse's right shoulder, and whispers "Please let him know I am safe." Nepharisse completes the cross with a light hold on Sakari's left shoulder with her left arm. The Gadlin promise seals the contract. This is one message Nepharisse will take great pleasure in delivering. She slips the pendant around her neck, tucks it carefully against her chest, and disappears into the toxic brume.

▼ ▼ ▼

Mother, where are you?

Father?

Nepharisse runs blind through the storm as her nostrils clog with yellow sand. She chokes. She falls to her knees. A crimson wisp dances away as she dusts herself off and keeps running, trusting that the course she has taken will lead to clear sky.

But the earth rumbles and Nepharisse tumbles. Down, and round, and down she rolls against a swirling canvas pixelated by golden granules, until the wind scoops her up and swoops her gently towards the now tranquil river.

Clarity returns to her world through his words. Their song heals the lingering tremors and she returns to the lost, to guide them through the turbulence.

▲ ▲ ▲

Order is lacking beyond the sulfur-crusted door. The presiding chair calls the clan chieftains into the gathering hall to calm the understandable anxiety of those who continue to lose their kin to the GMU sweeps. Wakanda ploughs through the hushed confusion about Odwin's whereabouts. She stands firmly upon the leader's plinth, a brazen move that screams presumption to the more senior gatayoks who abide by traditional succession protocol.

Odwin's braid has not yet been woven into the ancestral tapestry, hence his light still shines over the strongholds, precluding any claim to governance. Within the Gadlin community, Wakanda has not officially earned the stature of Gayok.

Fortunately for her, few outsiders know or even understand the subtleties of Gadlin life, and the Pramam is not one of those few. His ignorance may very well be his disinheritance. Nepharisse expects that tonight's agenda will test inter-clan solidarity in the face of this current, and most far-reaching, crusade against them. Based on the sentiment of outrage coagulating between the jaws unhinged by recurrent stories of blanket arrests and aimed at the Ministry's fraudulent accusations, the Inner Council would do well to live up to their advisory responsibilities and demand irrefutable proof of the stated Gadlin Conspiracy.

The urgent need for a consistent response to the Pramam's genocidal intentions presents a convenient opportunity for a reinterpretation of certain Gadlin customs, although those who share the absent leader's beliefs have already voiced their disapproval of Wakanda's political maneuvering. Murmurs of conspiracy have indeed touched the lips of gatayoks close to Odwin, yet the murmurs are of a different class altogether.

Discrete suspicions are the bait that has drawn Nepharisse to the secret ambitions she hopes will reveal themselves inside the underground auditorium, which conveniently lacks visible entry from the Museum of Antiquities, beneath which it lies.

The uniportal she has rifted in the generator room, adjacent to the cavernous dugout, offers her a a familiar hawk eye's view of history unfolding. The exquisite ice sculpture, witnessing tonight's event, scintillates above the congregation while slowly dripping its meltwater into the deep well in the carved stone floor. A freshness infuses the otherwise stale subsurface air with every precious bead from the thematic ornament.

Palabar, the Gadlin herald, highlights the intricate root system designed into the frozen sculpture with a quote from the artist:

"Let us remember what lies in the ground and the strength we need will surely be found."

The reverent silence breaks with an opening comment from Wakanda that tests Nepharisse's composure. "The Pramam may have infiltrated our presence in the maze, but he underestimates the depth of our network."

"Or rather the depth of your treachery." The quip escapes from Nepharisse's mouth at full volume, filters through her peephole, and infuses the melting masterpiece with its intent to reach the ears of global consciousness.

A raised face to the braid-covered domed ceiling suggests that perhaps one soul was touched by the intensity of her words. His black eyes do not belong amongst the itinerant merchants. A fool's laughter tugs at her ears, reminding her of futile chases in enclosed spaces. Could her delayed return to Eadonberg be one such barren indulgence? Only time stripped of illusion can know for sure. Nepharisse consults the vision clouding her sight for the answers.

▼ ▼ ▼

Nepharisse's eyes open onto the central walkway in Eadonberg. Her right hand brushes the space between the breast pockets of her uniform, then calmly joins her left in a hurried swing towards the Museum of Antiquities. The message she carried from Albaraaton overrode any past restrictions imposed on direct contact with the twins. A subtle slip into Keeto's satchel no longer sufficed, for it would have affixed his response to a random schedule, when immediate action was the only consequence of her disobedience she was willing to accept. She had to reach out to him.

The Gadlins must uphold their community values. The homogeneous ethos of peaceful existence, self-restraint, and sharing must endure the tyranny forced upon them, despite the undercurrents of mistrust she senses in the recording presented to Keeto last night. The very lives of the Unified masses, for whom the Pramam has brewed a self-serving tincture of poisonous terror, are contingent on the indomitable Gadlin spirit.

But more importantly, the twins Sakari's son has chosen to protect, the pair, Keeto and Elize, whose choices are entwining them tighter and tighter inside a forest of savages, all groping for them to satisfy their own agendas, are the ones who must not only survive the looming chaos but also evolve to grasp their role in it.

The unspeakable future, attempting to splinter dreams of expanding Nepharisse's own significance, races the murky lavender waters against her. The gurgles, approaching the marble gate at slider speed, are unmistakable to the singularly aware. Nepharisse pours her intent into their empty posturing, killing any hope of them redesigning destiny to suit their destructive needs. Her fingers caress the pendant around her neck, as she shapes soothing script under her breath.

Your crystal completes you. You feel whole, calm, and safe when you wear your crystal. You love to wear your crystal. Wear it next to your heart ... always.

Nepharisse looks left, smiles, dives into the western canal, and swims around the first structure the Gadlins successfully reclaimed from the Mediterranean to the cove of crypts at the back. She points the frequency emitter at the inlet and seals the only waterway into the wheel of floating mausoleum residences, whose perimeter walls double as the support for an underwater barrier that keeps the top water layer of the cove clear from any plants extending upwards from the ocean floor.

The eyes that swirl around her emit shards of disapproval. They triangulate an attack and lunge at her, but their efforts fail. Gratefully, they remain trapped in the medium that binds them.

▲ ▲ ▲

A deeply centered joy erases any tint of doubt coloring her decision to linger in Albaraaton, and a satisfying exhale directs her sight back to the gathering below. Nepharisse continues to broaden her worth, as surely as Wakanda continues to broaden her influence. Three nights of deliberation and planning have begun with the venue at capacity. The Gadlin Watch is alert and focused.

A disturbance outside the hall interrupts the roll call. Emotions stir as a dozen or so chieftains, who rush the entrance with open arms, weep with joy. The reunion could not have been more favorable had Wakanda not orchestrated their arrival herself. She crosses the floor to welcome the weary crew she had secretly exchanged for the Gadlin dominated underground network in the maze. "Behold the genesis of a new era: The Gadlin Dominion."

Her declaration sends a chill through the air, which momentarily arrests the meltwater metronome dripping the passage of time into the granite well. The tone is set for some icy debate that begins with a blunt request for clarification from the clan leader whose stronghold has suffered the most raids, Odwin's blood cousin, Winolla.

After an abrupt comment chastising the feeble subculture two generations of black market gypsy ethics have promoted, Wakanda instructs the herald to complete the attendance check and orders the chair to suspend further discussion until the Gadlin Pledge is fully executed and sealed by all who wish to participate.

Words have no power when they are simply recited by rote. No arm crossing the heart can serve as a proxy for sentiments from the soul.

The declarations, which have endured for as long as Nepharisse can recall, bring all in attendance to a spiritual frequency that invites the wisdom of an otherworldly intelligence one could best describe as the collective force that permeates every animate and inanimate entity in this physical world. It then becomes a matter of keeping the channels of communication unencumbered by earthly distractions, and there are many.

One such distraction is the ostensible faith the Gayok elicits from the average Gadlin, an illusion Wakanda has built into the image of herself as a respected world leader. She confuses the loyalty Odwin has earned over four generations of service with four generations of perfect contract completion. The Gadlin Creed will allot her compliance but not commitment. Such a treasure comes from the will. Her wealth remains on the same plane where distractions abound, creating a circle of deceit inside which she plays at leadership.

For now, slightly more than half the room maintain their faith in the Gayokcy, while the others are still reticent, despite the personal endorsements the latecomers have provided through their repeated gratitude. Nevertheless, past misgivings are metaphorically cast into the blue flames of the cooling generators, that coincidentally fuel the first order of business.

A mature gatayok, from the German Islands, shares his progress with the first cooling experiments. The generators are holding, and the target zone is steady at one tenth of a percent below URA predictions.

Excitement travels through the crowd and amplifies the expectant energy, wicking a few extra beads from the suspended ice decor. The sound of a waterdrop shattering the surface tension sends a shockwave into the shafts. The ripples trigger cells of recognition under Nepharisse's skin. Could this be the groundswell that reawakens majesty sleeping below the granite flats?

Anticipation becomes the thief of time as Nepharisse swims with the mammals in her mind. And of the flow? The flux measurements from the ancient Gulf Stream are forthcoming. Although the treacherous seas are still seething from the ravages of past civilizations, hopes are high with persistence for the Gadlin dream.

However, the Pramam is not their only threat. Public fear has trumped the desire for black-market goods. In order to generate the credit their research demands, the itinerant merchants are forced to deal with a breed of clients they typically refuse, a breed which dissects the brains of infants.

That thought meets a quick death at Nepharisse's command. Wakanda is the one she is investigating at the moment, but her vantage point has reached its usefulness. If Nepharisse is to realize the vision that just transported her to Eadonberg, she must begin recording the forthcoming discussion from an insider's perspective, therefore she adjusts her cloak over her eyes and rifts into the museum foyer from beneath it.

The exhibit room is deserted. A draft flutters the feathers of a dreamcatcher in the ancient Amerindian section, which leads her to the hidden staircase she seeks. She smiles past the watch, easily works her way towards the deep hole carved into the center of the meeting place, the acoustic focal point of the chamber, and taps a rigged Gadlin brooch adorning her cloak. The reportage begins.

The depth at which a heart can sink knows no deeper place than that which Nepharisse's currently dwells. High above Wakanda's head, in the clutch of outstretched arms, is the treasure for which Nepharisse had orchestrated an excavation and its smuggling into Eadonberg. Elize was the one who had carried it last. The risk that this greed-driven Gadlin woman, Wakanda, could inadvertently activate its power, flattens the mountain of accomplishments Nepharisse has been building to gain the recognition and respect she aches for. She did not progress this far only to shrink back to simple messenger status. The artifact will return to Eadonberg, this she declares as sharply as the stalagmites encircling the water well can pierce the flesh of the thief.

Fate lends a reprieve to Wakanda, ignorant that the power she seeks through political connivance pales in comparison to that which lays dormant in her hands. Nepharisse releases her hold on the fatal fantasy she contemplates and joins the traditional Gadlin auction, often called to safeguard treasures suspected as prized museum candidates.

The bidding starts with Sakari, whose offer demonstrates her conviction in finance as well as in word. The crowd is silent. Palabar probes for more, and the count begins.

A loss invariably brings dishonor and financial ruin to a Gadlin who buys the privilege of keeper duties, a fate worse than death for the pledgor and their family. Nepharisse could easily influence an exchange, but a presentiment impels her to outshine the bid instead.

"Going thrice and gone!" turns all heads towards the beautiful redhead with the sapphire blue eyes, sashaying towards the herald to claim her prize. A deep breath followed by a broad-spectrum smile brings the auction to a forgotten conclusion, and Nepharisse slips back into the crowd, stroking in some essential energy.

With the boon safely tucked into a satchel under her cloak, Nepharisse would be planning her exit were it not for the treacherous revelation preordained to reach the ears of her bourgeoning adventurer, Keeto. A masked man drags a badly beaten and bound woman, in GHU patient clothing, pleading for clemency. He pushes her head onto a stone block at the front.

Wakanda waves three pages of parchment she claims represent the lost pages of the Gadlin Prophecy. Nepharisse bites into her tongue upon recognizing the mother she had saved, the soul who had trusted her, and the death sentence Wakanda utters.

"This woman bore twins."

Dissent emanates from a handful of Odwin loyalists, but Winolla's sterilization suggestion is deemed insufficient. Nepharisse closes her eyes and asks for permission and a blue light escapes the breeder's body a split second before the ax severs her innocence.

A screech echoes throughout the cavern.

"Intruder in our midst!" Wakanda orders the exits barricaded.

Nepharisse is already weakened. She seeks a scapegoat as she slowly removes her sapphire blue shoes and kicks them between two stalagmites and into the well. Sound vanishes with them. She brushes past staring eyes, directing them to follow her gaze as she targets a female gatayok near the exit. A smile impels her mark to quietly take her shoes off. Nepharisse slides them on. Bare feet throw further suspicion onto the unfortunate soul, who can merely protest as the masked man arrives to handle the breach in private, later.

Nepharisse slips through the horde intent on berating the accused, who is left citing her lineage, their reputation, and threats of retribution. Sakari's attention, however, rests squarely on the familiar face wearing the payment for her delivery. They exchange a subtle lip curl and Nepharisse escapes with her prize and enough energy for her return to Eadonberg.

ELIZE

Deep breath in. And out. I'm ready. Here I go … right after I adjust the boot a bit … there. Now I'm ready. OK. Up I get … one more adjustment … that's better. Now I'm ready. Juicy. Off I go. Maybe I should stretch first. It's been a while. Hamstrings and hold. Left quad. Right quad. Calves up. Calves down. A couple of more times. Shake it all off. Good. I feel great. Let's do this. Off I go. Oh wait. Fold my socks over. That's better. Look at the time. I should come back tomorrow. Elize, get on the slick! Yes, or leave!

I'm going to do it! I'm standing … walking on the slick … testing out the glide … checking the—Elize, let go. *To surrender is to have faith in the flow. Do not fight the river, for if you tighten the current will engulf you and you will drown. Simply relax and float.* Just let go.

Whoa! Top juicy! Father's not here to stop me anymore. I'm free!

Let's try a spin … and a jump … more speed … a double … more speed … a triple. I'm back! Nothing exists outside this moment. I swoop effortlessly into perfection. My body knows no limits. I don't think, I just am. Why did I wait so long?

More power … glide … soar … feather landing … more power … spin … spin … spin. What's that flash? The lights are out. What's happening to me? No! Here comes the ground.

✄ ✄ ✄

Hang a sec. Tapping won't make me work any faster. Huh? I must have fallen asleep. Everyone has their eyes, I mean eye, on their quarter-scale holopatient. Hehehe. What a sight our little pirate crew is. There's Captain Snook glued to his board. I guess I should be designing the correct treatment for this case, but I'm still rattled.

It felt so real. I'm sure that it's just my imagination. That it was just the dizziness causing hallucinations before I finally passed out. On the other hand, I think about how Father reacted when it first started happening. He told me to stop, but I didn't. I would spin faster and faster until the lights went out. They always went out. And when I would wake up, disoriented, he would ask me if I saw anything, and I would say no. Mother told me not to tell him. She told me I had to keep it secret. She said it would pass.

Look at me. I'm sweating. No one else seems hot … except for that boy over there. Giggle. Oh oh. He's staring straight at me. I could really use my flutterbot right now. Look at those eyes, lips, and perfect skin. Wow! Oh, get a grip. He's not that thirst quenching. Oh yes, he is. His eyes sparkle. He must be new. I would have noticed him before.

"Sweet Belle, are ye looking for land, me lass?"

"Nay, Captain. Just thinking." Dr. Tenille squints his left eye then back to his board. He's unusually excited. What's he doing? Juicy! The observation window behind him is a perfect mirror.

That's odd. He just purchased a return ticket for Albaraaton, leaving in an hour. What business does he have there? Whoops. He caught me staring again. Busted. Now I'm on the spot.

"Still thinking? Perhaps a second patch would help?" He's ribbing me, and quite enjoying my squashed frog face. He's crazier than Mother was. No. I didn't mean that. She wasn't crazy. It's the GHU. It's Father. He put her in there. They made her crazy. Wait. Dr. Tenille was responsible for her. He must have known. He's still hiding something, and now he's sneaking into Albaraaton. Crap. The three minute warning. Quick. Eyes closed. Focus and … so simple. Done.

Dr. Tenille nods his approval and dismisses me. Juicy.

A message from Keet. "Meet me at the Snack Shack when you get this." I'd better blister.

The whole city needs to calm down. Look at all those grey hairs poking through the hats. I have enough anxiety of my own. Jumpers!

"Welcome back, Miss Elize. Did you miss me?" Who said that? The holowall guy. Just keep walking. Swat his hand away. "How was your trip?" How does he know? He doesn't. He's fishing. Just ignore him and keep walking. "Let's have a drink next time."

There's the Snack Shack. I'm finally hungry. Dissecting always cuts my appetite.

"Way, Ashton."

"Way, Eli. The reds are fresh today." He hands me the best one, as always. Whoops. Flyer bake burst. "Extra wipe?"

"Thanks."

Keet's on the terrace. "Hey lo." Tap my foot. "It's dead,

Keet. You can take your time, it's not going anywhere." Geez. When did the voracious caveman surface? He must have buried his highland manners in his crypt. Ugh. "Spare me the ode to the flyer bake, Keet."

"Slap me, Eli. I'm starving." With pleasure. Reach for his mouth. He beats me to it. Muffles. He swallows. And here come his teeth again.

Ah. The blowers are off. Quiet at last. The sun at last. "You're not going to finish it?"

"I'm suddenly not hungry anymore." He burps.

"Keet, your manners." Here comes Stitch. Keet picks at his food a few times, wraps it up, and puts it in his satchel.

"Hey lo, chumbuds." His coat is chomping on mosquibots again. Great way to ruin a good meal. I'll finish it later.

"Since when do *you* listen to directives?" Point to his quarantine cap.

"I fig I shouldn't aggravate the spread, yeah? And now I can hide my unholy intentions from you." A mischievous grin and a few wisps of orange.

"You missed a spot."

He pulls his cap past his ears. Another grin and a poke. Keet is not amused.

Stitch swipes his finger across Keet's arm. He looks at his fingers and frowns. We lock eyes. I can see the yellow dust too. Zap me back! My dear brother has been bit by the adventurebot, if there were such a thing. Not a subject for public discussion though. Stitch agrees.

"You look messed, bud. A night of zombies?"

"Noisy ones. I had trouble sleeping." Keet gives us that

change-the-subject look.

Stitch stares at our hair. Think fast. "We got the GHU-mandated rinse already. We barely avoided a full on infestation. Ta, Stitch." That little bit of sarcasm should do it. It might even convince me. Who am I ribbing? We never caught the moody critters. There's something about us that's different and it's more than just a mark. We're an easy target for a hair hunt.

"Since when do *you* listen to directives?" Snare face at you, Stitch. He chuckles.

More mosquibots arrive. Ashton activates the terrace perimeter field. Stitch's wilderness worms nab the last few pests. The patrons relax.

"Perk. Guess who surfaced, yeah?" Stitch slaps a slipnote on the table. It's coverage from the Albaraaton URA director's inauguration party.

"Trimorphic Rhythms was playing and we missed them. C-C-Crap!"

"L-l-look who's in the background." Caroline!

"Seems like she's still visiting her special friend, eh?" Eyebrow raise. Is that jealousy, dear brother?

"She's up to something. Miss 'I've been expelled' is still on campus. I see her in the distance sometimes, but when I call her she ignores me." It's just as well. She's too close to the Pramam's advisor for my liking. "What are you looking for, Keet?"

"Flashes from our trip." Giggle. There we are in full bumblebot gear at the transport station. Ah yes, the never-ending granite flats. Nice garbage. And more garbage. And ... The Gadlin! Keet pauses the playback.

"What are you thinking, bud?" Keet's on a dig now. He's flipping through his recorder faster than my eyes can track. He stops. He goes forward, backward, forward, targets, explodes. Stitch and I crowd in.

"How on this planet did she get into that image?"

"Jumpers! A ghost in the ice, yeah?"

"She must have been standing behind me when I took the flash."

"I don't remember seeing her in the room. Do you, Stitch?" He shakes his head. We're all thinking it. I might as well say it. "What is she doing following us around?"

Keet squeezes out a "crap" between his teeth. "I trusted her."

"With what exactly?" He'd better not have told her anything.

"Never mind."

"What do you mean 'never mind'? What the sheiss did you tell her?" How dare he ignore me. He has three seconds to respond. You know he told her everything, Elize. From the first day they met, you know what happened. She got to them both, Keeto and Zafarian. You cannot trust them anymore. Times's up. "I'm talking to you!" He needs a shove.

"What the—"

No. I'll bust his teeth instead.

"Ease, chum!" Elbow room, bud. "Oumf!"

"What are you looking at, pink head, filthy lice bag!" Ouch. My arm.

"We're leaving. Are you done?" Keet squeezes a bit harder.

"Done." Ohhhm gee. What came over me? And that poor

girl. Did I really call her a lice bag? Stitch cleans up the mess. I feel like a hick. But it felt good though, did it not, Elize? No. It was horrible. You made me do it. You egged me on. Deep giggle. Where are the others? They are gone. No. That is a lie. We are here. You wanted this lesson, Elize. Your mind was shut. And now? *Fear fuels the voice of deceit. Be wary of your fears.*

"Please accept my sincere apologies, miss. I haven't been sleeping well." I'll take a forced smile over a GHU pickup any day.

Keet loosens his hold as we walk the central corridor. His whispers show concern. "The dreams again?"

No more tough girl. I can't hold the tears. Stitch pokes me very gently and smiles. "Perk. A gift awaits in my gadget graveyard." Giggle. He always knows what to say.

Keet is staring up at the sky as if he never saw the sun before. At least he's looking much more energized. Well, not compared to Stitch, bopping to the beats again. I prefer the shade of the orchard, and here we are.

Everything is so peaceful when the blowers stop. I miss the cool moisture of the morning fog and so does the citrus grove. But people are so afraid of terrorists now that they would rather bake than keep the water balance. Something has to give.

You nasty little bug. Go pester someone else. I don't taste good, remember? On the contrary, Elize, you are quite delectable. You again? Compliments won't make amends. Deep giggle. It was not flattery. Go away.

"I still can't fig why you both were not bitten."

"We don't have biochips, remember? You told us that …

or maybe you were wrong and we do after all?" Well, call me fishy if that wasn't an are-you-bent look.

"You don't. But neither does my mother."

"Your mother?" That got Keet's attention.

"Yeah. No Gadlin does." He's massaging his temples.

"But you do."

"I'm only half-Gadlin. If the mosquibots are partial to free blood, then I should be off their menu, not you two."

"What about Wakanda? She wasn't swatting anything on the EVAC barge." The what? Oh right. I was lost in my head during that ride.

"She carries a black market biochip, yeah? I fig she has more than one, for different identities. She has the credit for it. Most Gadlins barter for goods and services and biochips are rarely offered. The Ministry has had a standing order on biochips since at least when my mother was born. This past year the asking price has tripled."

"What about defective biochips?" Stitch really might be wrong about Keet and me.

"If the trace mechanism is disabled the bots might bite, yeah? Trip, chum! I think you figged it. They must be snacking those who don't respond to a trace." He's rubbing his temples again. He pulls a scanner jammer from pocket zigazillion. "Mine has never worked. There's a constant hum. That's why I'm always listening to *Oye Amigos*; it's the zorro effect."

"So then why were we spared?"

Stitch shrugs. Without a biochip we would be mistaken for Gadlins, but the mosquibots are leaving us alone.

Good. We're at Stitch's room now. He heads for a scent

infuser. He spritzes the air with dramatic arm sweeps and grimaces. "You must have body odor, chumbuds." Swat.

Keet's thinking. "I wager, the decay virus spreads through the bloodsuckers."

"Are you saying the epidemic is manufactured, Keet?" Whoa. Stitch is listening carefully.

"Trip theory, bud, but we have no proof. We need to follow them to their hive." Stitch walks to his techno slice-and-dice table. He returns with two minuscule earpieces and a small jewelry box. "The biochips are ready for duty." He shows us how to wear them.

Keeto is trying a triple-staccato step. "Juicy! You loaded us with bioRhythms."

"The biochip is voice activated. All the bioApps have their own commands."

"Does this mean we're now traceable?" Ohhhm Gee. We're going to get clamped! Keet is thinking the same thing.

"Neah? I disabled the trace. Unfortu—"

"BioRhythms off. Ahhh. On, on, on. Crap. BioRhythms on!" Keet's bent over in pain.

"Unfortunately, you get the migraines too."

"How do you function?" Keet's still rubbing his temples.

"The herbs help. Certain songs seem to help. But that's all I have found so far." He does a few hip jiggles for effect.

"Ta, Stitch. They were worth the price." Keet glares at me. You'll find another artifact, pup. Stop glaring! "Where did Wakanda get them?"

"I didn't ask. Whoever they came from was either already dead … or …"

Keet breaks the silence. "I hope they towed the Unified line. With the extra sweeps, it's not just the Pramam's speeches we have to blend in for." Keet eyes the jewelry box. Right. The gift.

"Hold out your hand, chum." He pokes me and smiles. "Palms up, cutie. I'm not proposing yet." Dweeb! He laughs. Keet doesn't. Stitch drops a tiny triangular chip onto my pinky. It has a thin antennae-like rod extending from each apex. "Courtesy of Misty Moon. It was Mashrin's. Trip, ya fig?"

Keet and I drop our jaws. Did he say Misty Moon? "The girl you tried to kill?"

"Good thing not, yeah? She caught some mood critters. She was telling the truth about not knowing that the three officials tracked her. I fig she could have sold it to Sothese for ten times the credit."

"If she survived the transaction. Sothese has a tendency to assault people for what he wants." I'll grant you Nathruyu nostalgia just this once, dear brother. "So this is what a biochip looks like. What are those spikes?" He leans over to touch it.

"Perk, stop!"

"Ahhhhhhhhh!" Where am I? These people are tall. A stuffed toy? Whoa! I'm a kid. Are those my parents? "Get it off me! It's digging in." Someone's at the door. I'm running. My mother grabs her evening purse and kisses me. Who is that coming in? Jumpers! "Finally." Crap. My finger's bleeding. Suck it fast. Do not leave any blood behind, Elize. Yes, no blood, Elize. *Agreed*. Right. No blood. All better.

Stitch grabs my hand. My finger is sliced pretty deep. I snap it back. I'm fine. Just throw me a bioskin. "Maybe you should avoid touching things, Keet. You seem to trigger defense mechanisms." Keet's confused. He looks at his hands.

"A little longer, chum, and I don't think it was coming out."

"And our earpieces?" I'm thinking the same thing.

"I plugged it into a substrate membrane and sealed them together."

I can't imagine having that wedged into my brain. Hang a sec. The specimen in the blue goo. "Stitch, do you still have those flashes from Nathruyu's hideout. The swimming slime?"

"Yeah. Here's a close up." Target. Explode. Gasp. "Trip! The third puncture mark. We figged it right, yeah?"

"Except that it also acts as a recorder."

"Ziga trip! You had a memory?" Keet can sense my anxiety. He stares at my finger. The swelling is completely gone. The sting is gone. He knows that bioskins don't work that fast.

"I think I saw her parents." And if the chumbuds network were active, we could verify that.

"That means we can find out who last saw her alive." Good idea, Keet.

"Here. Your turn." I grab the biochip with a tweezer. He steps back. Stitch takes it over.

"I'll slap it on my diagnostics board. No finger sacrifices needed." No sacrifices. Except for Mashrin it seems, and the others.

"By the way, did you ever find out who the first victim was?"

"Just a name." Stitch sifts through a mess of slipnotes. "Selima Jansel. Another highlander."

Geez, Keet. I can hear you gulp from here. Stitch looks

up, questioning. Keet shrugs. Stitch stares at me. My shrug is honest, but I have a bad feeling.

"You want to share about your new hygiene routine then, bud?" Stitch puts his portablower in reverse and sucks the yellow dust off Keet's arm.

"Right. Share, Keet."

"OK. Last night I—"

What was that?

We all run to the window. The GMU is taking over campus. Here comes the GHU red swarm. Crap. They're coming into the building. This is no laughing matter, dazy half-Gadlin.

"You find this funny? I've been quarantined in the GHU. No rips there." They're doing a sweep. Screams from the hallway. Crap! The Sentinels just dropped. "We have to get out of here." He's *still* laughing. "Get away from the window."

"Ease, chum. No need to clip out. Just wait." He's almost ready to burst! OK. Just a peek.

"Eli, get down!" What? I can't help myself. I'm rolling. "You're both bent. The Sentinels are ... pink?!" Stitch is howling. "You didn't."

Keet starts to rip.

"Perk. We need to break curfew tonight. This will make it easier." Down to a giggle now.

"Why?"

"To trace the mosquibots to their secret hive. To stop the Gadlin genocide."

KEETO

Nightmares tell the stories that the waking mind does not want to suffer.

Perhaps this is the reason Eli has not taken advantage of Stitch's offer. A dream sweep would force her to relive the agony that bathes her body in sensations she would rather not remember, even though the answers we seek are surely buried in the darkness that haunts her.

Although my nights of sleepless terror were short-lived, they provided an appreciation for the strength Eli must surely possess to have lived with her affliction for a decade. Whatever keeps her soul from resigning to a future contorted in confusion, spent in the corner of a GHU observation cell, is the same power that impels me towards restlessness of a different nature.

After I had finished journaling last night, my mind refused to settle. It was suspended, as it has been since we have returned from Albaraaton, across the chasm draining the pristine river beneath the granite flats. The quiet hours are when the questions resurface. Questions like: who is hunting those with the mark?

If Dr. Yarkovsky was indeed prey, then mother must have been as well. And what of Eli and me? Are Sothese's three officials looking for blood ... our blood? Or were they only searching for Mother's jewel, which disappeared last year?

Their interest in us after so many months of indifference suggests otherwise. I wager that they have not acquired what they had been sent to confirm the night they appeared outside our kitchen window back home, or rather where we used to live with Father. It was never a home without you. It was simply a house in which Eli and I were held captive, while your spirit splintered inside a padded cage. Even the mementos we have of you were jailed beneath the slider pad of a house you never lived in.

This spiral of thought will lead me no closer to the truth. It only serves to smear my journal with ink. Father is away on some Ministry mission and your children are on one of their own. Eli, in particular, is obsessed with finding a book, and I suppose my fixation is to keep digging into the past, yours, and anything or anyone remotely connected to you.

The problem is, I have no clue whether the hunches I receive are relevant. Doubt blows my thoughts around, which sometimes makes me feel like the Galleon's sails waiting for the right wind to whisk me off to a treasure chest of answers. Instead, I am moored to my fears. What if it is already too late to save Eli from your fate?

Yesterday, her obsession kept looping between my ears. The persistent book that needs to be found was keeping me awake, until it finally dawned on me that, maybe, the three officials were also looking for a book. Furthermore, I may not have possessed the proper awareness until now, and thus have overlooked a potential gem in the library, curated for myself from your favorite ancient titles.

The idea grew into a theory, and then into a relentless

compulsion, as I spent hours scouring the pages of philosophy, history, mysticism, fiction, healing arts, science, psychology, and various other obscure subjects. The initial conclusion, however, prevailed. I could identify no content that agents of the Ministry would travel to a highland village for.

Regardless, I had abandoned rational behavior. My quest had me leave the safety of my crypt and seduced me with the promise of recovery. If only the recovery was that of Eli's sanity, for her voices take her closer to a mental state clinically known as schizophrenia. Instead, a covert sprint to the base of the Victory Bridge offered the hope of reclaiming the book Nathruyu had requested of me, in exchange for information concerning the Pramam's special interest in your case.

As I stood with my hand on the door that would thrust me into an underwater maze prone to random explosions of toxic gases, the faint scent of myrrh illuminated the path with a vision of gemstone eyes. I took a deep breath and followed my fluttering gut.

A rush of yellow smoke, infused with a stench more pungent than the garbage lining the granite flats, nearly spit me out of the shafts beneath the "Hub" hovertrain drop. By seeming serendipity, I pounced onto a ladder leading to an exhaust vent and bounded onto the platform with perfect timing. Consequently, I chose to risk the curfew enforcers for the remainder of my trip and prowled the night, using, as my guide, the slipmap I had dotted for Stitch when Eli was taken hostage last year.

My fortune ended just outside Almedina Square. A GHU craft appeared over the access point, indicated on my map, and was heading towards me, scanners on full. I leapt into an archway leading to the Almedina courtyard and hid against the entrance of an old restaurant. My entire body sprang forward when I realized that I was not alone.

Gratefully, my accidental companion remained calm. She swiftly pulled me back into the recess before the vehicle's headlights flooded the passageway. The girl was the actual object of the GHU manhunt, although, considering what we discovered this afternoon, I hesitate to commit to paper the deeper truth that arrests my heart, that her unborn twins were the target.

She trembled as the echo of heels flitted nearby. We gaped in horror while the long hooded cloak, floating in the wake of the pursuit, exposed a GHU uniform. The hunter disappeared around the corner and into the square, then the clicking suddenly stopped. At one end of the passage, the GHU craft hovered, and at the other end, the GHU predator awaited. We were trapped.

The situation evoked a response in me whose origin stems from you. I felt compelled to chance GMU interrogation in order to protect a complete stranger from the very medics who could ensure a safe birth for her children. She informed me that they were transferring her to a prenatal retreat, specially designed to accommodate the specific needs of women carrying twins, but stories about questionable procedures, mothers becoming mentally unstable, and others even less fortunate terrified her.

When she asked me what I was running from, I simply replied, "Breaking curfew". The circumstances that were responsible for my part in our synchronistic encounter were irrelevant. She was the only one who mattered. I imagined her to be a time-warped manifestation of you, hiding from the GHU in the Gadlin strongholds, yet they still got to you, thanks to Father.

A shaft entry point was within throwing range, so I pleaded with her to come with me, but she had already surrendered to her imminent capture. She clutched my arm while she forced her breath into a well-rehearsed rhythm. Her eyes dulled with the physical and emotional pain she could not conceal. The contractions had started, one month too soon.

Tears rolled down her cheek as she pushed me deeper into the wall recess and stumbled into the floodlights. "Run," she whispered. "You can't help me now. Go!" Before I could even protest, she rushed towards the medical team, filing out of the red craft, while coming from the opposite direction, the hooded figure was closing in fast. The medics ushered the young mother into the vehicle and slid off, leaving their GHU colleague stranded at the main archway.

I was numb. The ensuing darkness mirrored what I felt inside. Would the infants be stripped of their mother, as we were? Giving space to my worries was not going to bring her back. It was not going to bring you back. I peeked around the corner of my nook at the blue sapphire shoes leaving Almedina, tracked them to the sector walkway, and sighted them disappearing into the ventilation shafts, coincidentally through the very vent highlighted on my slipmap. I stalled for a few moments, inhaled deeply, and claimed the role of stalker the cloaked figure had just relinquished.

The drop was shallow, as was my breathing. My ears

picked up some movement in the shadows behind me that frosted the sweat on my hands. I focused forward, with my eyes monitoring the periphery, leery of a surprise attack. Skulking around in the ventilation network bordering the Restricted Sector invites malice from sources I would rather not entangle myself with. As I neared a nook housing a generator, my lips felt a familiar sting. The slipmap slid from my icy palms and flew past a beautiful stranger with sapphire blue eyes and luscious ginger hair.

For a moment I sensed a mutual emotion I can best describe as anticipation. With her soft smile and lyrical voice, she invited me to follow her.

In whom you trust answers come. In the answers you trust a hand appears. In the hand you choose trust emerges. My hand for you.

The woman extended a white glove towards me, then waited. As I contemplated my response, whispers conspired to highjack the decision. The gemstone eyes glanced past me, then reached into mine for urgent consent, which I willingly granted. The rest of our mysterious encounter exists as fog in my memory.

A chase, wheezing, a fall, a helping hand, dead ends, generators, backtracks, hovertrains rumbling overhead, an explosion, more running, sapphire heels, a wide-brimmed hat, and a hard landing at the "Hub" hovertrain drop form the montage of my overnight escapade. When I regained control of my senses, I remembered the flashes that the bewitching redhead had entrusted me with and probed my satchel for them. They were safe, yet I was not.

KEETO

Sothese and his three officials were having a subdued discussion across the platform at the "Hub" drop. I immediately shrank behind a holopost, hoping that the image playing would have enough opacity to act as camouflage. I have no way of knowing for sure, but if they did catch a glimpse of me, they made no issue of it. They headed west along the east-west hovertrain walkway and, in the blink of an eye, I could see them as four figures entering the Sports Complex at the "Arena" drop. I must have dosed off. Dawn was breaking.

Thankfully, the trip back to my crypt was uneventful. I was too exhausted to react to anything at that point anyway, and certainly not to a few splashes coming from the western canal. Sleep was the only thought I could entertain. My bed linen would even be the dust cloth for my clothes, until my comm started playing, an hour later, to the tune of Mme Beaudoin's reproach. I sprang from my bed and blistered to the archives.

After I had apparently passed out on the job for a third time, the curator granted me the rest of the day off, with a clear expectation that I would retire to my quarters, which I had every intention of doing. However, the flashes in my satchel changed all that. In fact, they were to change my beliefs regarding the Pramam's Gadlin conspiracy propaganda. The bit I saw in my crypt, of Wakanda selling the artifact for profit, was insignificant compared to the shocking revelations that came in Stitch's room later, after we had watched the entire recording.

I was on my third flyer bake when Eli joined me at the Snack Shack. Stitch arrived shortly after that, still dodging mosquibots. Friend-turned-stalker-Caroline is a subject I do not want to write about at the moment. And Eli's incident with the finger-sucking biochip deserves a much more thorough analysis than I can offer at this time. If it indeed does carry Mashrin's memory, then we need a safer way of retrieving her experiences than having the biochip permanently integrate itself into a human guinea pig, namely one of us. Besides, it is past midnight on a day which began with one hour's sleep, so I will skip to the juicier stuff … the top juicy stuff.

The images from a secret Gadlin gathering made Stitch more than a little uncomfortable. He had never attended one, but he knew well enough that anyone caught recording one, or in undeclared possession of one, would be in direct violation of the Gadlin Creed. When we pressed for details, he quickly changed the subject, for fear that merely thinking about the punishment would bring about its execution.

I am beginning to question whether the Gadlin Creed is simply a myth, created by the leader, to enlist partners in fencing stolen goods and to manipulate internal loyalties into complicity to murder, under the guise of saving the world from some fictitious Gadlin Prophecy. Pressing Stitch for answers met with anger and confusion.

"This is not the Gadlin way," he kept repeating.

A blank stare at his sports clothes, drying on a hook by the window, could not stop his burning eyes from watering. Eli's nervous picking at her crabseat failed to conceal the heartache I also shared. A cold silence threatened to shatter our chumbud bond.

Wakanda was on a mission to kill mothers of twins. Just how long ago her crusade started was the question which we were grappling with. Did she stop at the mothers? Whose loyalties had she contracted for? Speculations festered in private while I monitored Stitch's quiet meditation. He had disconnected from reality in order to process the scene we had just witnessed. I believe that his behavior was not that of someone who was privy to a Gadlin Conspiracy.

Eli was the first to lay out her palm. I offered my fist next and waited for that big grin we both have come to appreciate. And it came … with a chumbud slap. Our plan to find the mosquibot hive was on.

The curfew came, and off we went. Even though Stitch had cleverly infected the hairy sentinels with mood lice, he packed the sniffer, just in case. Then he released a new and improved mosquibot he had quarantined in a containment field and stood still while the needle-nosed spy collected his blood sample. The upgrade consisted of a microscopic homing beacon, linked to Stitch's infamous wristband gadget.

Eli winced as the insect hybrid syphoned the DNA which proved Stitch's Gadlin ancestry. The risk worried her as it did me. When Misty Moon delivered Mashrin's biochip to Stitch, she warned him about recently installed DNA sniffers along walkways, public transit, and business sectors, connected to a blood data vault, which is what inspired his present mischief. The source of her intel was not on offer, considering she had already breached a contract. As far as the common Gadlin knows, insects are to be avoided because they tend to transmit viruses. A global panic would serve no clan.

Stitch, on the other hand, disagrees with the secrecy, but with the chumbuds network still locked down, his only recourse is to get the concrete proof he needs and to leak it to a Gadlin sympathizer in the media who ignores Ministry coercion.

As soon as the sample was on board, the DNA thief grazed Eli's head, slipped through a crack in the door and flew straight for the lift shaft, where it shot out the top of the tower. We tracked its urgent escape, using Stitch's wristband, to the ninth floor of the center tower of Osler Hall, before it suddenly vanished. We had to blister. The haste in our poke-happy chumbud had us gasping for air and hoping for time. The only thought I remember having was "Crap!"

Once in the south clearing, Stitch pitched us each a face shield and smoke bombs while we kept pace and shadowed his footsteps, exactly. Our next challenge hid around the south-east branch of Van Billund Hall then back north to the vines of the ivy wall. Last year's greenery had evolved into an ill-tempered mess of leafy twine, though nothing a few well-placed snips could not handle. We snuck through and stood by the pond for a moment of reflection before our grand entrance into the medical lab's amethyst center tower.

At first glance, Osler Hall was in complete compliance with the Ministry directive. All levels were dark. Upon approaching the central tower lobby, we realized that the building was suspiciously over-tranquil. The entrance scanner was disabled and the permissions guard was slumped over his station, with a spilt teacup on his lap. Stitch's hesitation released the courage inside that fed off my instinct. I walked straight past the unconscious night watchman, summoned the lift, and urged Eli and Stitch into the virtachairs.

The long dim corridor on level nine turned our nervous breath to mist as Stitch scoped the walls and ceiling for sentinels. Nothing stirred but a faint light flickering from a crack under the entrance to a surgery cell. I could feel the density of what we were about to discover pressing down on my heart, and a presence beyond the shard of amethyst light squeezing through a crack in the interior wall. The activity visible from outside the building was an illusion. We had entered a sub-zero crime capsule.

The bandits we sought swarmed past us when Stitch hacked the lock. Millions of mosquibots in clouds swirled under the light, keeping our shock inside closed mouths. Below us was the trench where the recent child mutilations had occurred. The butchers work for the URA!

The floor-to-ceiling walls of blood that saturated the room formed an image of Father through my eyes. Thousands of vials, some filled, others still empty, each labeled with a Gadlin name and grouped by clan, formed the crimson tapestry we were about to expose, a tapestry of every Gadlin alive today.

Stitch ran straight to his family's section and stole a dozen or so samples. Next, he raced to Wakanda's clan, muttering with disgust as he scanned the tags: "Protect the Gayokcy." He went quiet mid grumble. No name, no empty vial.

Wakanda was the only Gadlin missing!

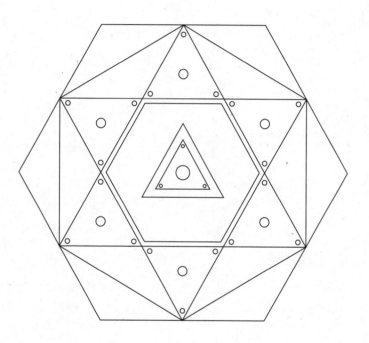

CHAPTER NINE

NEPHARISSE

Day 400: dawn

Dawn reflections do not live long on crystal towers. They spread their light through open flowers. Inspiring thought in mourning hours.

He will surely be pleased with her success, but what of the young mother she had failed to save at Almedina Square? And the one she had unwittingly condemned to an indefensible termination in Albaraaton?

Nepharisse's fingers trace the contour of the artifact in her satchel, careful not to inadvertently cause it to shift. Although, as she inhales the waking sun creating an amethyst mosaic across the orchard canopy of the campus oval, her grief clouds the meaning behind it all.

In her stillness, somewhere between the western leg of the Victory Bridge and her recent travels, time collapses against her wall of sorrow, spraying blasts of bittersweet triumphs into a template for hope. Each moment of glory shows its price in its wake as innocence falls for the welfare of all. The sun may not rise for the unfortunate victims, yet it does rise again for the offenders nonetheless —for now.

Although judgment is not Nepharisse's role, delivering messages that can incite justice is well within her mandate.

She expects her second delay to prove as worthy as her choice to investigate the Gadlin gathering. However, based on the GMU parade escorting a GHU craft down the central corridor, she fears that the warning she communicated as a result of yesterday morning's research through GHU obstetric records was likely ignored.

If only circumstances would grant her an opportunity to correct her failures. If only. If only.

Still, that is not a task assigned to her, nor is it a thought which would elicit clemency. No. The body is forsaken, another is broken, and a third is in danger of the same. Her will once again must focus on Wakanda.

She stares through the chaos and etches a deliberate imprint of yesterday's orchestral masterpiece into the pathways of her present mind.

▼ ▼ ▼

Nepharisse's Gadlin cloak draws attention from three voices whispering under an awning. She feels them watch her as she swoops southward along the western canal to the Museum of Antiquities. Conditions in Eadonberg are inviting outside influences better left wanting for the time being. Her energy stays locked on the runner who will deliver a reluctant, though necessary, offering to Sothese. Wakanda must be stopped.

The museum network has thus far remained neutral to the Gadlins, for their curators are fully aware who sources the treasures which ultimately support their elite lifestyle. Nevertheless, the Ministry is still the administration on record.

Since wearing traditional costume publicizes this quiet support to the patrons who covet rewards promised to loyal informants, off comes Nepharisse's cloak, and into the hands of a scowling Mme Beaudoin, whose mood immediately softens with the warm smile greeting her.

Nepharisse walks her sapphire blue shoes towards her chosen enforcer of versal law and begins his tutelage under the watchful eye of the academic, uncloaked, yet obscured, at a table beneath the spiral mezzanine staircase.

Cataloging induces sleep in the drowsy. Sleep makes the drowsy happy. You are drowsy and love to sleep.

Keeto's head crashes into the shipment manifest. A girlish giggle, a raised eyebrow, and a loud snore share the incident, until Mme Beaudoin's voice booms from inside the artifacts room. The test is a success.

Keeto fumbles into the Round Room with a PAL close behind. He sits at the hub, while his remote assistant gathers the requested load, and yawns.

Yawning induces sleep in the drowsy. Sleep makes the drowsy happy. You are drowsy and love to sleep.

He slowly leans back in his chair until it tips over, and he wakes to save face, albeit too late. Another incident noted.

Serious eyes peek from between the stair treads at the small stack the curator hands off to Keeto, who is standing by the front desk. The eyes narrow slightly as the sapphire blue ones smile back.

Sleep, Sleep, Sleep … and Keeto trips on his rubbery ankles and into the arms of his employer.

"Mr. Keeto! Return to your quarters and sleep. You can

resume tomorrow."

The flexible highland instrument is now ready to be tuned for the upcoming Gadlin *tragédie*.

✂ ✂ ✂

Nepharisse begins by setting the tone: greed fed by ignorance. She directs her new brass to trumpet the news waiting for an audience inside his satchel.

A secret scene is yours to play. Remain awake this special day. Awake you see the false at play. Awake you play the false today.

▲ ▲ ▲

A discordant pitch from the GHU craft pulls Nepharisse from her composition for an instant, then onto the Snack Shack terrace, while the vehicle slides by.

▼ ▼ ▼

Elize's feuding voices preclude any consistent harmony on her part but do deliver a dark comedic interlude to the dramatic magnum opus Nepharisse is developing. Though Stitch's percussive nature, on the other hand, may hold the pace, it has the potential to crash as the tension builds. Keeto is the one to penetrate the noise and implant Nepharisse's intentions.

For now, never mind. They need not know everything. Never mind, Keeto. She need not know. Just, never mind.

▲ ▲ ▲

Further south, fields from broad frequency energy beams suspend all students along invisible grids as the GMU convoy sweeps the campus oval, spitting out all but the expectant mothers they seek.

▼ ▼ ▼

Entertained by the pink Sentinels dropping from the interbranch links, Nepharisse relaxes in the common room and allows act two of *The Greedy Gayok* to write itself as she waits for her trusted trumpet, Keeto, to set the key: Murder in A Major.

"So this is why the rock wanted to be found? Always in my pocket to draw out Misty Moon so that Mashrin's biochip could attack me?"

"And to zap me with plasma apparently, just for a rip."

"Without hacking the code we still have no answers, chumbuds."

"Dr. Tenille knew about the mark of the hunted. Not great news, but it explains—"

"Nothing, Keet. People with it end up dead. We already know Mother is dead, but not who killed her. All this time spent being his dweeby Belle and that's all we got?"

"And the Galleon's sails."

"Right. Maybe Wakanda wants to guard those ... Where did y—?"

Nepharisse's smile helps Elize forget.

Yes. The Galleon's sails would bait the butcher.

And now, the flashes must play. Play the flashes. Play the entire flashes.

"Juicy. The 'wrong hands' now have the artifact."

"Perk. Wakanda is no Tess. She just has an eye for high credit items. And … Jumpers! This woman must have done something ziga horrendous squared! Wakanda is invoking the Termination Law."

"That doesn't sound very juicy."

"Except for what's going to spew out of her neck, yeah?"

A muffled shriek announces the murder, followed by an explosive gasp that introduces the motive. "This woman bore twins."

As act two in this Gadlin opera concludes, Nepharisse travels between the outraged trio, the campus mayhem, and the chatty common room.

✂ ✂ ✂

In Zafarian's room, the blood dripping on the platform has a dreamlike quality that Elize recognizes. Fortunately, her voices splinter her thoughts and fracture the images.

✂ ✂ ✂

On campus, a young student, pregnant with twins, races the GMU grid as she heads for the hidden ventilation shaft entrance in the south clearing. Nepharisse waits for her in full GHU uniform, smiling with optimism. The warning was heeded.

✄ ✄ ✄

The common room clears when the silent curfew, announced through bioAlert messaging, broadcasts to student biochips, while Zafarian begins to question the Gadlin Creed, repeating an affirmation that commits his heart to an act of treason. "This is not the Gadlin way."

✄ ✄ ✄

Neither is it Nepharisse's. Her part in the conspiracy ends here and without judgment, for that is not her right. Future murders do not warrant her accidental complicity. Nepharisse remembers her place as a lyrical messenger and scripts a final song for her chosen hero, in harmony with versal law. It rules over creeds, promises, contracts, and directives, be they Ministry or Gadlin in origin.

There is only one law which one must abide. From this law no one can hide. In this respect, the Unification is on your side.

✄ ✄ ✄

Long white gloves present a warm herb infusion to a night shift medic and disappear into the shadows of a deserted hallway in Osler Hall's center tower.

▲ ▲ ▲

NEPHARISSE

Thousands of mosquibots, scheduled for routine extermination, chase Nepharisse through time, back to her present perch on the south leg of the Victory Bridge. As they flee north along the central canal, Nepharisse safeguards a cargo far more valuable than that of the winged DNA couriers.

With a right hand in her satchel, a left on her new crystal pendant, and the blue light resting inside her, she recommits to her primordial role. She sashays onto the campus oval, radiant as always, with the sun stroking her long curvy thighs as her Gadlin disguise floats behind her, and students attempt their awkward descent from the citrus trees that broke their fall in the wake of the GMU net, that is sweeping southward still.

The ones Nepharisse failed to warn become ghosts in her heart. This she must accept, for the power she carries is not hers to wield. The order of things must unfold in their new direction as many more shifts are due to occur, but not by her design. The task is best left to the one who can foresee the consequences.

In this realm, a simple messenger she nevertheless remains. She whispers a poem of comfort to the mother she did reach, presently braving the shafts beneath her feet, and swoops towards her belated appointment at O'Leary Hall.

Her nerves impede the grace in her step as she hastens to clear the vision of a conversation she would rather not engage in. She glides to the threshold she is anxious to cross and trusts that her stealth past the other doorway will keep the tiresome babbling within from rousing.

The door opens to a disapproving hand clutching the arm about to knock and immediately shuts Nepharisse inside its wood rich office. His reproach is not the welcome she had envisioned, although she expected some form of displeasure regarding their twice rescheduled rendezvous, one to spy on Wakanda's secret Gadlin gathering, and the other to set the stage for reckoning. Perhaps he believes that Nepharisse's use of her power to influence Keeto to enlist in a vigilante crusade against Wakanda walks the line between justice and revenge a little too comfortably.

Speculation brings no favor her way. She reaches into her satchel and presents the artifact he had appointed her to collect and had expected to arrive three days ago. His demeanor changes. For a fleeting moment, she detects a hint of relief and a shard of respect for the resourcefulness she has demonstrated with her clever salvage operation. He nods and positions it carefully inside an antique pedestal with a retractable cap. This item does not belong in impetuous and ignorant hands.

Vibrations of joy quickly dampen with Anubrat's warning. She cannot be seen on campus. She is to stay away from Elize. The hounds are following Keeto and they will get to him through his twin, if they must. He also forbids her to stage any further entanglements with the siblings, or with anyone else for that matter.

Nepharisse protests. "I can take care of them. I know I can if you would just let me."

Has she not proven her fire with the matter of the sweet shop owner? Anubrat's condemnation emphasizes that there are others who can employ those means. He wants to preserve her innocence, untarnished by the violence that sometimes becomes necessary, but her spirit longs to grow up.

"There will be plenty of time for that, Nepharisse."

Her courage appears with the recognition he expresses at her initiative regarding the recording of abuse Nathruyu suffered in Ministburg. Her eyes lift timidly towards him, knowing that the question she is about to ask has already been released. How could he have entrusted the women he instructed her to save to a murderer? This was not supposed to be.

Screams and cries of a demoralized child, lunging for him and falling at his feet, summon an uninvited creak from the entrance door and an inquisitive: "Is everything all right?"

With her enchanting blue eyes retreating behind a mirror of tears, Nepharisse deflects a stream of questions with a labored smile as Anubrat quickly obscures the artifact. Dr. Tenille closes the door then rushes out of the building to a fictitious appointment he is apparently late for.

Nepharisse' mind drifts back to the encounter that subjugated this annoyingly smitten pawn of hers.

▼ ▼ ▼

Dr. Tenille sits intent at his desk, installing the sails on a 16th century galleon model he is crafting, when a knock and a creak give passage to a beautiful redhead bearing a meal. The smiling GHU catering employee gliding towards him arouses a pink flush in his cheeks and an awkward prattle. She entices her intellectual captive with a delicious tray of food beneath which she has attached a patient release slip for his approval. His eyes never leave her gemstone beauty whilst he authorizes the women's discharge.

This is where it all begins.

▲ ▲ ▲

Solace comes to Nepharisse in the form of her many successes. Still, her sobs fall on the gentle hand that guides her towards his reclaimed treasure. She begs for his wisdom. Why did you not tell me? I could have saved them all. I could have spared their pain. Anubrat smiles and gradually rotates the outer dial as they watch together in reverent silence, her hand in his. Indescribable splendor suspends her sorrow in peace.

The weightlessness raises her arms away from her sides, shaping a cross with her limbs one curved palm up, the other forward. Invisible life particles energize the tips of her fingers into a rapturous surge upward towards a blissful union, entwined above her head, as their energy stretches towards the heavens. Serenity attracts meaning from the universe and her elbows gracefully spread, drawing love into her heart. In resonance, she rejoices, whilst her being listens to the words of truth infused in the conversation flowing through her mind.

Losses do not equate to failure. The esteem I hold you in extends beyond your understanding of it. Your work with the twins is not complete. This written list is for you to protect.

Another message? Have I not proven myself capable of more?

You cannot see your worth through the eyes of resistance.

But I am capable of greater endeavors. With higher clearance in the GHU, I could influence the Pramam himself, as it was in Albaraaton.

Compromising your body or your anonymity will give rise to undesirable consequences. You must continue your influence at your current level. The real power lies with the advisors. The parchment in your hand is the catalyst for all that has been, and all yet to come.

You are the one I trust to deliver it safely. You are the one I can always rely on. You are the one who will persist when others stray. That is why the others are in harm's way. They clear the path for your finesse.

I am your favorite?

Our little secret.

He is watching her. Will he try again?

Yes. You must be ready. You must be patient. Your mastery of time is essential.

I will make you proud, Anu.

You always do, my dearest Nepha. Save your fire. Its fuel will come … soon. Now go. She has been punished long enough.

A suctioning breath fills Nepharisse's lungs with purity. Her radiant smile echoes the sentiment in Anubrat's embrace. She is his dearest. In this moment, she belongs again, yet stands apart.

She is not her mother. She is not her sister. She is the wings of the universe.

Nepharisse's spirit soars with pride and a new appreciation for herself and her capacity as the agent of change. Hesitation in the shafts had stayed her weapon in exact alignment with the greater plan, a design which Anubrat has sole connection to. And now, the prospect of surprising her mark with a gift excites her beyond measure. She moves with purpose down the deserted hallway of O'Leary Hall, bending the reality that manifests as her success as her body travels through time and space.

The lobby is as unassuming as one would expect from the Special Investigation Forces headquarters. There are no GMU guards, building protectors, or scanners, typical of a Ministry division, for there is no need for such devices. The SIF have a reputation for special talents that make such precautions unnecessary. Their immense roster of rotating agents is the key to their investigatory prowess. Few can detect their presence, making them ideal candidates for questionable fact gathering methods, the very techniques Sothese had inflicted upon Nathruyu in the Ministburg lockdown.

Their Witness Relocation Program is so effective that strangers walking the corridors of the SIF headquarters are commonplace. On the path to the secret detainment section, hidden behind a false community mixed-media mural, Nepharisse and her cloaked accomplice encounter few surprises, though she becomes one of her own in the cold darkness of her target's cell.

"They are gathering."

Her message floats a blue light through the catering hole in the containment field and into Nathruyu's frozen prison. The black, pitted face watches the luminous dance while minute frozen crystals flake from the hopeful black eyes, twinkling a delicate melody reminiscent of the one Monique used to play with her crystal hair tresses. Nathruyu's entire will focuses its intention on amassing the strength necessary to accept the gift into her open mouth. A weak nod expresses her sincere gratitude.

"You have been punished long enough."

The hooded figure disables the energy grid, quickly uncloaks, gently dresses Nathruyu with her only covering, and releases her to Nepharisse's care, while being extra careful not to make skin contact in the process. The now naked woman then glides her black, pitted body into the cell and slowly contorts into a twisted silhouette, living the purgatory of her new home.

ELIZE

"**I**f Keet finds out you spent the night here I'll be trapped in a sermon on highland propriety."

"Then it will be our little secret." A smile and a poke. "Besides, I fig he had no sleep either." He taps a few buttons. The magnoform appears, finally! "Valah! All fixed. You said impropriety?" Dweeb. A big grin. Keep dreaming. He walks to the window and stares at the pond. "I need a moment, you trip?"

"Juicy by me." Still. I'm curious. It sounds like a mantra … purity … power. I missed it. He's repeating. Maybe if I move over here. Oh. That's not right. I should give him privacy. He's done now anyway. What's in his hands? Juicy! What a pretty virtacreature. Giggle. "It tickled my lips."

"Ta, chum. I don't feel whole without my morning meditation." He's looking at this hands, rubbing his temples, looking at his hands again.

"It's not too late to stop this, Stitch. We can comm Keet. Treason is grounds for the Termination Law. You told us that."

"I'm trip. It's crit we see her clamped, yeah? Even life is a trade to her."

I hate to say this but "Gadlin trade is what got Keet and me to Eadonberg safely."

"There's a Gadlin Creed, Eli. Murder is not part of that. She twisted it into a Gadlin Greed." He's staring out the window again. What's he looking at? Right. That's it. I'm going to confront her.

"Perk. There's a GHU sweep." Do I look like I care? "Crazed, chum. Make sure your biochip is on tight. Clip out!"

Caroline is not getting away from me this time. Crap. An energy grid. Juicy. Up in the air like a birdbot on a string. "Stitch!" It's pulling him away.

"Whatever you do, don't comm me. I'll find you."

Here comes the scan. Think positive. Ahhhhhhhhh! Stuck in a tree. Well, at least the biochip worked. It spat me out. Hmmm. Interesting view. There she is. She's heading into O'Leary Hall. You little witch. Wipe that cocky smile off your face. Phew. It's getting hot up here. I'd better jump down. I'm sweating. I have some water in my satchel. Good. OK. So who was I following? Oh no. A mini-blackout. I sure am hot. No virus please. Maybe that's what they're sweeping for … again. What's that?

Tap. Tap. Tap. Get away from me. Run, Elize, run. Pant. Hide under here. Who's there? Tap. "Show yourself!" Where's my pup? Rub it. Breathe. Count. Quietly. There's a shadow. Please. Go away. Please. "JUST GO AWAY!"

Whoops. I would be staring too. Well, so much for the "no sleep, no nightmare" theory. OK. After Keet gets Wakanda's DNA, Stitch does the dream sweep. And don't you dare talk me out of it. You hear me up there? Good. If the answers are really in my dreams, we'll find them. And if I'm losing my mind, I hope we'll find that too. Brrr. Now I have a chill.

Caroline! Wipe that grin off. The GHU is done. There's one of their staff leaving campus. I should follow her. Stitch is comming. "What happened?"

"The GMU being the GMU. Where are you?"

"I'm heading north. Hang a sec." My permissions. Here you go. "On the Victory Bridge now."

"Did you find Caroline?" What's he talking about?

"Huh? I'm following a GHU employee. She looks suspicious and— Caroline?"

"Eli, are you dazed? I'll be there in a clip." What are you smiling at? Whoa! A woman just dove into the western canal. Is she bent?

"Hey lo, chum. Lost your mind in there?" Slap him.

"No, fishy. Some woman just jumped in. Over there! Across from Ministry House." Caroline! I have to comm Keet. "Caroline's at Ministry House."

"Juicy. She's blistering. The meeting is set for Almedina, tonight. I got Wakanda's DNA sample. Caroline will make sure Sothese is there." You just keep smiling and we'll settle this later ... Ummm. "So did you reach Caroline?" Swat Stitch's hand off my forehead.

"Eli, are you dazed?" Why does everyone think I'm dazed? Honestly! "Did you sleep?"

"I'm juicy, Keet." Actually. I'm exhausted.

"No you're not. Is Stitch with you?"

"Yeah." He is looking happy all of a sudden. Eye roll. Flirting with a redhead. Boys. "In body."

"Juicy. Pass the comm over." Poke the puddle of mush.

"Hey lo, bud ... ya fig? ... Yeah ... Trip. I'm on it." Back to me ... "Keet wants me to infiltrate your dreams, chum. Off to the crypt."

"Now?"

"You're having memory lapses. You need to lie low." He's right. Almedina is no place to have an episode. It's too close to the Restricted Sector. Shudder. I remember what happened to me as if it were yesterday. OK. Through the marble gate, bow to the greeter, into the Round Room. Wave at Mme Scowl-face. A smile? Smile back. Stitch shrugs. Keet's waiting at the back door. We rush to the cove and into his crypt.

Bark. Bark Bark. "Good Sparky. I'll be back later. I have to make up for yesterday." He points to his wristband. Eye roll. Yes, the green and red dots will stay separate. "Get some sleep." Out he goes and Stitch comes straight over. Slap him.

"Ease, chum. I need to tune your biochip." Juicy. I like this station. Very rhythmic. "Close your eyes." Deep breaths. Juicy. Relaxing. Yawn. Sweet dreams. Sweet dreams. Sweet dreams. Eerie giggle.

><><><

Crap! Again? Where are we?

Stitch sends me a chum-your-brother-is-bent look, and he's right. I know what's down there. Keet sticks his head into the vent then back out again.

"Hurry. She's here." Where? He jumps into the hole.

"I don't see her." Or anyone at all. "We shouldn't be here." Stitch looks serious. No bopping. "Keet?" He peeks from the vent.

"It's coming from the east." Creeps. The Restricted Sector? "Jump in." He goes back in. He *is* bent.

"What's coming?" Whoa! "Will you—" He pulls me in. Then Stitch. I don't want to be here. "Hang a sec." Catch up to him. Stitch stares at a flashing yellow dot on his wristband as he walks.

"Trip, bud. The tag is good." Impressive. Keet tagged her *and* swiped her DNA.

"OK. So your hunch was right. Now what?" He points to a nook. No. I can smell it. Stop him. "Not there."

"Ease, chum. She's in lockdown, yeah?" A big grin and a poke. "Hero, remember?" Giggle. Dweeb. Keet's annoyed. I never let him in on the inside rip. Nice shade of blue the generator is reflecting off his eyes though. Crap. It went out. Turn around. No. It's still on. Odd.

"The agreement was for one thousand each." That voice. Think, Eli. I know that voice. It's coming from the next vent.

"I trust the Pramam can make up the difference." That one is Wakanda.

"You are talking nonsense, Gadlin."

"It's Gayok, to you. To all three of you." Ohhhm gee! The three officials. Keet climbs the ladder. He's recording this. Juicy. Top sleuthing. "Perhaps you lack the intellect to understand? Let me clarify, then. How many have you sold to your illustrious ingrate?" Sell what? If I could just peek too ... That was close.

"Ta, Stitch." Lost my balance and very nearly lost our cover.

"A pair here and—"

"Silence!" The leader is steaming. The other voice scoffs. "Your profits are high enough."

"My profits are my business. The contract was for all of them. The Renata twins were mine."

Did she say twins? I can't move. Keet and Stitch are frozen too. First the mothers, now the children. Stitch sits on the shaft floor and leans back against the shaft wall. His eyes are glued to his yellow dusted shoes. He knows what this means. We all do.

"Those biochips were to be destroyed. Your ignorance will kill us all."

"We know about your Gadlin superstitions." They're laughing. "More nonsense." More laughing. "I suggest you take the matter to the Divine Messenger." Still laughing. I wish I could see her face. "You are in no position to trade ... Gayok." Juicy! They have her. That shut her up. It also shut Stitch down. He's still staring at his shoes. "Unless you care to part with the jewel." The what?

"You believe in Gadlin myths now?"

You'd better not have —

"The Jewel of Airmid is no myth. The girl had one." I knew it! Mother's jewel! Let go of me, Keet. I'm going to tear her to pieces. He pushes me back down.

"Eli, no! Stick to plan." I'd rather improvise, but he's right. We have her. Sothese does a good job at interrogations. Deep giggle. Let her rot in Ministburg, Elize. She deserves it ... and more. It feels good, does it not? To envision her face on Nathruyu's contorted body. They are both evil. Deep giggle. Do not let hate consume you, Elize. It will drive your actions ... all of them. It will obscure what you seek. *The instant we feel anger we have already ceased striving for the truth.*

"The jewel is not for the likes of you."

You neither, greedy Gadlin.

Stitch looks up, teary-eyed. Keet and I join him in silent meditation. We sit in a circle facing each other. He is crushed. I am crushed. Keet holds on to hope. "At least we know what they were after."

"But would they kill for it?" She would. I can't hold back the tears. The words are stuck. We knew this day would come. The knowing. But it hurts so much. "She killed Mother."

"Flyer mud!" What's he doing defending her? "You have no proof."

"We have the recording. Our mother bore twins. Then she went after the jewel. You're only half Gadlin, Stitch. You owe the Gayokcy no blind faith."

"Perk. I took the pledge. I am already a traitor to my people, yeah? I have to believe in something." He is hurt, confused, lost. I need him back.

"You can believe in us, Stitch." Palm up. Keet's fist goes down. That's my hip-wiggling chum. Shhh. All together now. "Chumbuds!"

"So, what next, Keet?"

"I go to Almedina Square." Still bent it seems.

"You weren't seriously going to hand over the Galleon's sails, eh?"

"That was the plan."

"You don't have to do this, bud. Your intuitions have been on credit so far. The sails must be important. We need to keep them safe."

"If I don't show up with them, she'll know we set her

up." And the Gadlins courts will put a contract out for Stitch. Whatever this prophecy is, she has them acting out of fear. It's not rational. As if you know what that means, Elize. Shut up! There has to be another way. The Ministry will get them when they get her. "It's all juicy. Sothese knows the bait is my risk. Caroline will get it back."

"But he'll see you." Stitch hands him a cloak. Giggle. He makes a gangly Gadlin. "OK. Mind the hovertrain draft. We'll hide in the western passageway. Take the south one when you're done and we'll meet you on the walkway."

Peek out. Walkway clear. Sneak to the west. I'm scared. One last look over to Keet for comfort. NO! "Stitch?"

"I see him. That double-crossing" He fumbles through his pockets. "Trip." Whoa! That looks like a weapon. "Only if we have to, chum." Right. Only if we have to. Where's that pup charm? Rub. Rub. Rub. Breathe. "I'm a good shot. I'll aim for the fedora as a warning first." OK. Flying fedora works. Grab his hand and get into position.

There she is. Here comes Keet. Say something. A throat clear. "Juicy! We have sound." Crap! The lights in the square went out. "Stitch, we need a—" always one step ahead. Big grin back. "Do you have a second pair? Juicy. Ta, chum." I see his face. Smile for the flash, mystery man. "What are you figging, Stitch?" Nudge.

"He's not a Gadlin. Perk, he just nodded at Wakanda. It's a trap! Sheiss! I'm dunked. Why would she give you biochips." Did he say give?

"Share, chum."

"They were gifts, to keep you safe from the Ministry,

yeah?" But she killed Mother. Didn't she?

"What exactly does she know about us? And for that matter. What exactly do *you* know about us?" So, I'm funny?

"I know you're cute when you're angry." Yeah. You'd better duck. A poke and a grin. Geez. "No conspiracy with this half-Gadlin, Eli. Perk. I'll share later. They're talking."

"You make a charming Gadlin, Mr. Keeto." Keet pulls the sails from his satchel, all rolled up neatly. I can't look. Is this really happening? She has them now. She unrolls them, feels them, smiles, and drops a small bag in his hands.

"What's this?"

"Your payment." He opens the bag. We should have hidden a recorder in the hood.

"These have no credit value. They're illegal."

"As I imagine your acquisition methods were."

"My sources are no business of yours." Whoa! Keet. Don't get her blowing or we're jam. Phew! She finds him amusing.

"Indeed. A fine Gadlin, Mr. Keeto. Zaf's influence, no doubt." Where's Sothese? Keep her talking. "I am sure dear Dr. Pirate Parody would purchase a few. Most shops in Albaraaton, of course, and in Tir-na-nog, there—"

"What was that?" Good acting, Keet.

Juicy. Here they come. Sothese and three SIF agents. Show time.

"Crap!" The agents are running after Keet. "Was that part of the plan?" Stitch checks the blue dot on his wristband.

"What a pleasant surprise!" Sothese grabs Wakanda by the neck. She gags. "Now, what could be so tantalizing so as to draw a terrorist out in the open like this." He snatches the

Galleon's sails and slides them in his coat.

"Trip. Keet's clipping through the buildings."

Wakanda is groping at Sothese's arm. "Arrested for black-marketeering. Greed 'baring' gifts." Geez. He laughs at his own ribs! He leans into her and whispers. "Pardon? You can't breathe?" He laughs again then loosens his grip enough for her to whimper.

"If I don't return tonight, the full Osler Hall recording is going public this time."

The SIF agents return empty handed. Phew! Keet outran them.

"We lost the thief in the shafts." The thief? Hehehe.

"Leave him. We have something far more newsworthy here." Sothese wraps around Wakanda. He pulls her hands behind her back. He pushes her body forward and whispers to her. "We have that covered." He yanks her up by the wrists. "You have nothing left to trade, Gadlin."

Whoa! That was loud.

Ouch! Screeching static. Pull this biochip off. Stitch is bent over in pain. He kills the yellow dot on his wristband. "We're deaf, chum!"

Wakanda screams. I can't move. Sothese is staring this way. Quick. Against the wall. What do we do now? He knows we're here. I wish I could hear what they're talking about. That screaming. What's happening. Crap! He's still staring. Grody. He's not?

Stitch covers my eyes. "You don't have to watch this."

Here comes Keet. "Mission accomplished. What's going on?" He stares into the courtyard.

The lights come on. Wakanda's face is contorted. She's panting profusely. Sothese lets go. She falls to the ground. The SIF agents are looking the other way. The three officials are there, watching. Bastard! No one deserves that. Oh yes, Elize. She killed Mother, remember? Sothese will take care of things. Deep giggle. Elize, you must shed tears. You must clean yourself of this toxicity. I can't. Yes, you can. You are still human. Show it! *The deepest pain often harbors the power to transform you into a higher being.*

Sothese's anger ricochets off the courtyard walls. "Clamp her!"

Keet holds me tight. "It's over, Eli. I'm so sorry. Sothese's hounds are taking her away now."

Stitch is crying. He's really sobbing. He closes his eyes, mumbling. He's asking for forgiveness. What have we done?

Noooooooo! Run after him. Whoa! Watch the light. Pull him back in the dark. "We can't go back, Stitch!" Stop squirming. OK. Slap me, chum, but I have to slug you. Keet helps him up. Stitch shakes it off.

"Ta, chum." He rubs his jaw. I reach to stroke the bruise. He ducks, then smiles. "We knew what he was. I'm trip. We should g—" Was that a blast?

The SIF are shooting at Sothese's officials? Did I miss something? No. No blackout. Stitch and Keet are as dumbfounded as I am.

"Perk! Sothese is coming this way with Wakanda. Ziga pica mega Sheiss!"

"Over here, Stitch, there's a shaft vent."

"Do not play games with me, Gadlin." Sothese gives her

a chokehold reminder. "I am not afraid of the Pramam." I can see her eyes. She's terrified. He lets her go.

The three officials are on … fire? They're burning alive. No. The fire is out. Why aren't they dead? "Are you seeing this?" Mouths open. Eyes wide. They are too.

More plasma. Ohhhm gee. Their own body is generating it.

"Misty Moon!" What is she doing here? Crap they saw her. Noooooooooo! I can't look. Is she? Stitch is blowing. She's gone. Keet's pacing down below. He stops. He sniffs. He jumps back up the ladder and watches with us.

Plasma everywhere, Sothese is trying to corner his hounds. "You need us!"

"There were others before you. I can find more."

The SIF weapons explode. Their sleeves catch fire. They run. Wait! Someone's coming. I can barely see. It's too bright. Eek!

"Nathruyu!" What? He's right. She's going straight for them. They're running. They're splitting up. She grabs one. Down. She targets the second. Down. Ohhhm Gee. She has the third. All down. Sothese pulls his coat over his face. Gasp!

"The beautiful stranger!" Keet's smiling. Right. He has something to share later. Back to Nathruyu.

Juicy. You go girl. Give Sothese that audacious smile. What? She's letting him go? "This is bending. Keet, any theories? Keet?"

Stitch lights up the shaft. "Jumpers. He's vanished!"

K E E T O

Day 401: late evening

He is just sitting there, crouched, staring, like I am some sort of mutant. He is the aberration. I do not even know where I am right now, or what he wants from me, if he has any desires at all. This place feels so real, yet, at the same time, I could be living in my mind. The fear that I am still somehow suspended across the deep borehole beneath the granite flats, waiting to be sucked in by the whirlpool draining beneath our boat and simply watching my life stall in vignettes across my eyes, is an irrational one, as all fears are. But this one, in particular, has invaded my quill.

If it be fantasy, then let it arouse the senses of future armchair adventurers, who perhaps will find meaning through my journey. If these visions are reality, then let them ignite the power inside me, without being consumed by it, like what I just witnessed topside. The fact is, I have a parchment on my lap, a feather dipped in ink in my left hand, and a blue light illuminating my thoughts from above. I cannot see beyond the darkness cocooning me at arm's length, but I can feel what lies beneath, and it is not my bed.

At this point, I wager … Actually, I have no idea. Have I entered a space where I can talk to you freely? Or are the thin white circles studying me a cause for censorship? Trauma can mute any voice and poison its victim with mental decay. Furthermore, the injured need not be the sole recipient of suffering. Those who stand on the sidelines, with a toe dipped in collusion, can fall into silence as well, provided their conscience is stronger than their beliefs. What do I believe?

"The real question is not what, but why."

He is urging me, or rather, forcefully excited for me to quote him. Regardless, he remains in the dark.

My immediate concerns are with his intentions. How I came to be in this ventilation shaft nook, whose faint scent of myrrh still lingers, without any memory of my travels towards it, intrigues me. However, I suspect that he is looking for answers himself, and since my safety is likely bound to his agenda, I must accept a certain amount of ambiguity concerning my current situation, although the horrendous climax of my well-conceived plan to deliver Wakanda to Sothese deserves probing with my captor.

Upon honest reflection, I guess I did cast the newly elected Gadlin leader into the arms of retribution, but that violation was not in keeping with the spirit of my scheme. If the souls of all matter are verily listening as one, in accordance with Gadlin theology, then their interpretation of my objective was inappropriately liberal in my opinion. As for the change of heart, if Sothese actually has one, that unexpected reversal did more than drop a few jaws.

This creature, hanging on every stroke of my quill, just outside the edge of my blue bubble of light, must have some wisdom to share with me, if only to appease my misgivings about Nathruyu, who appeared out of nowhere to finish the job on Sothese's behalf, saving him from Misty Moon's fate, without leaving a single scar on her perfectly smooth ivory skin. Her black eyes seemed to reach out to me in the calm night sky that engulfed the plasma chaos. What exactly happened up there?

"The real question is not what, but why."

"Write it all down. Just like I say it. Write everything I say down exactly as I say it. And what you say. And what you think about what I say. And what you think about what you say. And so on."

What I think?

I think I am definitely on the fringe of insanity here. Did I pass out? Did a virulent smoke bomb charge at us while we were spying through the vent? The relative cleanliness of my clothing points to a different explanation. OK. If the approach to take is to focus on the why, and by the stranger's enthusiastic head nod I assume this is so, then let me reformulate the interview. This is an interview, is it not?

"Oh yes! You are cataloging a historical moment."

Juicy. The *Chronicles of Keeto* are born from the internal musings of the *Fedora Felon*.

"Felon is too harsh. I have not been convicted. I do not wish to be convicted. Erase that word."

It is written in ink that you presumably provided. He lunges for me and—

"Start over on a new page."

and his black-pitted hands claw at my parchment.

"I do not want to have black-pitted hands. Start over when I say *The Fedora Freedom Fighter*. That is the new title. Yes. I like that. And call it the *Keeto Kronicles* with a 'K'. Now s—"

And that is as far as I can accurately describe.

The essence of his fiction was that he had fought for the rights of all those who live in his circle, in the Restricted Sector, and had stopped the new order of things intended to eventually replace the Unification with something much worse for our planet. His triumphs included various strange devices and words and symbols that really meant nothing to me, except for a description he gave of a crystalline device that "captured the power of life inside its crystal petals." An image of your jewel appeared in the emptiness your passing left, at which point my intuition screamed at me to blister towards the generator. But I never made it.

His attack came swiftly. He ripped the parchment from me and engraved three F's into my right palm with the very ink I had created his treasured future biography with. Then his skin started to change just as my body temperature fell. The blue flames from the generator, which under normal circumstances would have me sweating, offered no reprieve to my chattering teeth. All the while, my muscles became stiffer, and his laughter announced to the others like him who were skulking beneath Almedina Square that some unfortunate soul was trespassing.

Were it not for a familiar stomping, booming its echo down the main shaft, I shiver to imagine that the Fedora Felon's story could have been the last piece I ever wrote. The distraction proved disconcerting enough for my assailant to break contact with me, and for me to capitalize on his unfortunate lapse, which was fortunate for me. I remembered my instinct and once again blistered towards the generator, surprising both him and me with my ability to move at all. This time, I made it, and he did not.

KEETO

One finger on the force field containing the blue fire broke its integrity and syphoned the air around me as my body thawed. Then came the toxic boom which I luckily anticipated. I exited the soon to be yellow-dusted alcove, slammed my back against the wall of the main shaft, and took a deep breath. The explosion blew the fedora off the Eadonberg outcast as he raced eastward towards his ghetto, leaving behind the two parchments, which I have affixed at the top of my current journaling session, and a thin golden powder.

When the blast vibrations settled, the foot thunder that had provoked the incident slowed and stopped behind me. Wakanda had inadvertently saved me from a stiff encounter with the realm you live in. She reached into a large crystal adorned satchel and held out a gas mask for me to ostensibly stare at. I can only presume that her greedy hands had decided to wait for a trade. Her attention rotated between the toxicity gauge on the mask and my face. Once she realized that there would be no profit on the horizon, she stowed the item. A few moments later, her air filter signaled that the air was once again safe to breath.

Imagine my shock when she rushed over to greet me with a lowland cheek-to-cheek, pulled out a personal suction brush, and vacuumed all traces of the smoke bomb from my clothes, then hers. Afterwards, we surfaced to walk right past the scene of her defilement. I found little sign of emotion as she entered the courtyard in which she had succumbed to unwanted ecstasy. Her brief condemnation of his affront was a simple quip: "His indiscriminate behavior is his greatest liability."

Perhaps Sothese shared an unofficial history with her that

thrust their relationship into the open. His recorded escapades with Caroline are certainly less than romantic. Nonetheless, the scene had left me ambivalent. I did not know whether to admire her strength or deplore her passive compliance. Surely, Eli would have fought him in words and certainly in violent retaliation. "Why?" was indeed the question that bore scrutiny.

I chose not to express misgivings concerning the timely appearance of the fedora man, nor indicate awareness in her dealings with Sothese's hounds. My tactic was to not respond to the information I knew was forthcoming. And I was richly rewarded for my temperance.

After scanning Almedina Square for DNA, which was curiously absent, Wakanda invited me to sit with her inside a cafe she had access to. From her satchel, she retrieved a board that she placed on the table in front of us. A few hand gestures later, as if by magic, the entire chumbuds network was back online. She admitted to me that as a desperate bid to limit the growing casualties in the Pramam's Gadlin crusade, she had traded administrator access to the network for the lives of a bargeful of Gadlins. However, the version the Pramam had acquired was a decoy that deceived him with a pseudo time capsule of the aliases, including staged interactions between its private members that are still ongoing.

Later this afternoon, after I had announced the revival of the original chumbuds network, and the existence of its ingenious autonomous forgery to Stitch in the morning, we discovered a small blood stain, splattered on Stitch's wall, only visible from a specific angle. This sort of camouflage, Stitch clarified, is for extra security. That would explain why we had missed it on our transport ride back from Albaraaton.

The stain spread into a detailed account of mutilations far more disturbing than the brain alterations inflicted upon unconscious nine-year-olds in the medical lab. A substantive list of infants, no older than one, had their vermis stripped while they were awake. In all cases, three adults were the perpetrators. Many of the babies died, some were abandoned in their bloody pools, and others were taken still screeching in pain, never to be heard of again. In that list we found an entry from six days ago: "Renata, twins."

The expressive details required no supporting imagery. Eli's catatonic state was proof enough. It took the two of us, this time, to guide her out of wherever the horror had trapped her. Even now, as she sits cuddling with Sparky on his mat, a dark energy envelops her. I cannot hear the voices, but I know they are talking, as are the aliases reconnecting in the chumbuds network, and my own reasoning faculties.

Wakanda's ingenuity has given Stitch a dose of humility. "Ziga Tess" was the expression he used to describe the back door she had created for herself with his brainchild, in order to implement a "pica trip" Pramam sting operation. Unfortunately, the sting the Gadlin community has received from the mosquibot invasion continues to swell as the last of the DNA samples arrive. On a side note, the swelling on my branded palm has luckily subsided, yet the tattoo remains.

Wakanda may have honorable motives for keeping the needle-nosed vampires' true nature hidden from the clans, a sort of collateral damage in support of the Gadlin Prophecy, or conversely, our initial assumptions may still be accurate:

KEETO

Greed.

For my part, the "woman bore twins" excuse for a Termination Law invocation trumps any goodwill Wakanda may be trying to foster. Our verdict remains. Her conscience is wanting.

However, it is interesting to note that I find no fault with my own. I can claim ignorance, indemnity against the actions of a sick b— bully (you know the word good taste does not permit), or otherworldly justice, even though that thinking risks attracting the hounds of Baskerville to my crypt. Shudder. My childhood sleuthing influences have colored my analogies. One thing is certain, someone compromised the anonymity Stitch has taken great care in designing into our secret society, and Wakanda is our prime suspect.

Our newest Osler Hall break-in revealed more than names and blood samples. Upon closer inspection of the flashes we recorded, from the mosaic of clear and crimson-filled vials decorating the walls, we discovered that several hundred of them were marred by a black dot in the bottom right corner of their tag. Furthermore, there was a whole section we had missed, stacked below a fictitious clan name and sporting even stranger label titles, such as WakandaEatsFlyerMudForBreakfast or UnifyMyBalls or MistyMoon, whose vial was still empty, as was mine.

The implications for the breach are vast. Someone, somehow, has managed to correlate actual individuals with their invisible aliases. The whole premise behind Stitch's efforts to create a safe and open forum for truth and empowerment was to lock out any Ministry access, a task for which the system is foolproof. It is obvious to us now that Wakanda is no fool.

But what do we do now? What else is Wakanda concocting? Is Teddy's disappearance just a ruse to keep him imprisoned?

The official report, polluting the biochip Ministry broadcasts today, simply adds confusion to an already heart-numbing series of experiences. Here is a transcript of the portion of the reporter's communiqué I find the most telling. And what it tells me is that mountains of mud are going to fly through the maze for a long time to come.

> After an extensive and commendable internal investigation by Sothese, the Pramam's personal advisor, three Gadlin insiders have been arrested in connection with the case of the twisted brain collector and the murder of three SIF agents, who were also in complicity. The surveillance footage these agents claimed were from the Gadlin strongholds was illusory. The actual location, regrettably inside a secret sub-floor in Osler Hall at Eadonberg's prestigious Schrödinger University, is currently sealed and under GMU quarantine.
>
> A further casualty in the successful apprehension at Almedina Square last evening was a young bystander who died a horrific death at the hands of the inhumane Gadlin plasma weapons, which also left all light fixtures in the courtyard in shambles. The Gadlin leader is under Inner Council orders to appear before an

interrogation panel as the suspected mastermind but remains in hiding, thus providing additional evidence of a widespread Gadlin Conspiracy, which still boasts intact leadership.

The recent completion of Sothese's productive tenure as interim URA director will allow him to martial his talents exclusively on identifying the elusive architect behind these unconscionable acts of terrorism. Rest assured that law-abiding citizens throughout the Unification will once again enjoy the peace and prosperity inherent in the Pramam's gracious guidance, through Their counsel. Perfect are They.

The only admission in this fabrication that is not divergent from the actual events that took place is the misuse of the medical lab for mysterious experiments on children, not to mention the viral experiments Sothese's hounds are also receiving the blame for. I expect more Ministry mischief will be conferred onto these new scapegoats. Sothese was quick to cover his face when the plasma frenzy was over. I wonder what he was hiding from or why?

"The real question is not what, but why," as was so eloquently put by the Fanatical Fedora Freak.

That is a more fitting interpretation of those three F's carved into my ... Huh? I must have just reacted to the ink as it got absorbed. Phew. I had no desire to wear the monogram of a lunatic. One mark on my body is well enough. Or in Eli's case, not well at all.

If she continues tossing around, she will crush Sparky. Let me lay some blankets on her. I am not the only one who has been running on essentially no sleep for the past three days.

Your daughter is resting peacefully at last. She wanted to stay with me tonight for fear of losing me. Last night was traumatic enough for her before I had vanished. In earnest, I feel calmer with her close to me. Like the wind needs the rain to create a storm, we need each other to weather the one that is coming.

Perhaps that is why Eli continues to cling to Father's flashes of our ninth birthday. The fun, the friends, the laughter, and the knowledge that you were with us, in spirit, from your padded room at the GHU, offers comfort in her moments of instability, which are increasingly more frequent and intense.

As our hunt continues for the answers, *their* hunt continues. If we only knew who *they* are, or what *they* are. And why us? Why you? Why the mother of twins?

Or maybe, in the end, the reasons make no difference.

Still, reasons are the lure which drew us to Eadonberg in the first place, reasons are the magnet that still attracts me to Nathruyu's seductive game, and reasons are the treasure that keeps escaping us the closer we get to its source.

So here I conclude three sleepless nights, in a trance-like state, desperately trying to will Eli's demons out of her as if life depended on it, but all I see are three pairs of eyes, expectantly waiting inside the tears of my own, while my body craves the potency it savored last night, and the scent of myrrh intensifies outside my crypt.

KEETO

GLOSSARY

alias *n*
a nickname or user id inside the **maze**
assalam *v (anglicism from Arabic)*
to say good-bye, to leave
auto ... *n*
a sensing device performing a single task (e.g. autolock)
band *n*
see **secure band**
bang-o *n (Stitch slang)*
anglicism of Spanish word "baño", bathroom
bending *adj. (city slang)*
confusing
bent *adj. (highland slang)*
nuts, crazy
bioApp *n*
A program running on a **biochip**
biochip *n*
internal intelligent chip attached to a human brain
bioclothing *n*
clothing that is alive and often sentient
biodome *n*
a fully enclosed dome shaped **biowall**
bioRhythms *n*
A **bioApp** that transmits a music broadcast to the brain
bioshield *n*
invisible shield surrounding a person to filter toxins
bioskin *n*
membrane to grow skin on wounds
biowall *n*
invisible shield surrounding a city as a unidirectional filter

blister *v (highland slang)*
  to get things done fast, to move fast
blow *v (city slang)*
  make someone very angry or pissed
board *n*
  futuristic version of a computer screen
boogie *n*
  one-person barge for surfing the tides, extreme boogie board
bounce *v (city slang)*
  to feel unnaturally energetic, hyper
bumblebot *n*
  a hybrid automated bee programmed to pollinate plants
carebot *n*
  flying bear-looking vital sign stabilizing equipment for kids
chat something out *exp.*
  reach an agreement
chip down *v (slang)*
  to physically recover from a change in **biochip** program
chumbud *n (Stitch slang)*
  a friend, chum for opposite sex, bud for same sex
circle *n*
  circular neighborhood of homes protected by a **biodome**
clamp *v*
  to restrict someone to an area and track their whereabouts
cleanerbot *n*
  self-guided intelligent floor cleaner and garbage picker
clip *v (Stitch slang)*
  to hurry, to do something like yesterday
clip out *exp. (Stitch slang)*
  get out fast, head to the exit lightning fast
cloaked *adj. (Stitch slang)*
  encrypted, as it pertains to a communication device
comm *n* and *v*
  1 *n* personal communication device

2 *v* to communicate using a **comm**

crabbot *n*
self-guided intelligent crawling surveillance device

crabseat *n*
genetic hybrid between a crab and a chair

crack *v (Stitch slang)*
to panic

credit *n*
the currency (there is no cash)

crazed *adj. (city slang)*
nuts, crazy

crit *adj. (Stitch slang)*
very important

creeps *n (highland slang)*
a bummer, crap

cube *n*
a freeze-frame of a holographic video (**flash**)

da ya *adv. (anglicism)*
a double yes; once in Russian, once in German

daze *n* and *v (city slang)*
1 *n* a party at an underground club
2 *v* to party, to go to a **daze**

del *v*
to delete

dizzy *adj. (city slang)*
gross, disgusting to the point of an upchuck

drip questions into the maze *exp.*
to broadcast a question for anyone to answer

drop *n*
a stop on a **hovertrain** route

drop detector *n*
detects when something draws power from the grid

dunked *adj. (Stitch slang)*
to be totally lost, to not understand what is going on

(it's a) dunker *exp. (Stitch slang)*
   (it's a) wonder
dust *n*
   encryption to make images look like garbage to searches
dust filter *n*
   special type of **maze** sketch that can find **dust**ed images
emitter *n*
   device emitting frequencies to change properties of matter
ease *v (city slang)*
   to chill out, to calm down, to take it easy
eh *interj. (highland slang)*
   adopted from Canadian "eh?" at the end of a sentence
explode *v*
   to zoom a **flash** or a **cube**
fig *v (Stitch slang)*
   to figure
fence formation *n*
   GMU tactic for securing a perimeter
fishy *n (highland slang)*
   turkey, silly, dumb-dumb
flagged *adj.*
   marked for Ministry investigation
flash *n* and *v*
   1 *n* holographic video, moving memories
   2 *v* to record a **flash** on a device
flashpack (flashes) *n*
   a pack of multiple **flash**es that plugs into a viewer
flatface *n (highland slang)*
   a stone faced, unfriendly, or vacant person
flip *interj. (highland slang)*
   bummer, crap
flip a pass *exp. (Stitch slang)*
   get out of something without permission (e.g. skip class)

floramug *n*
waterproof leaves which fold into a drinking vessel
flutterbot *n*
hybrid used to cool off, a flying fan with multiple wings
fly wild *exp. (Stitch slang)*
to let imagination control you, to go off on a tangent
flyer mud *n (Stitch slang)*
bullshit
frame *n*
freeze frame from a **flash**
Gayok *n*
the leader of all Gadlins, the chief
garbifact *n*
Elize's humorous way of referring to old junk
gatayok *n*
a Gadlin clan leader, a chieftain
geckohold *n*
hybrid for hands-free reading material such as **slip**s and
slippad reading
ghostgrabber *n*
gadget to slice through **flash**es to see all the frames as stills
from infinite angles
GHU *acronym*
Global Health Unit
GMU *acronym*
Global Military Unit
good whip *exp. (highland slang)*
good comeback to a dig at someone
hanging low *adj. (Stitch slang)*
lacking energy, wiped out
hang for a sec *exp. (highland slang)*
Hold on for a minute, wait a moment
hey lo *exp. (highland slang)*
hi

hick *n (highland slang)*
  "doh!" when used alone, dumb-dumb otherwise
hide between the packets *exp.*
  to remove your id tag on a **packet** and thus be untraceable
holo ... *n*
  interactive holographic objects (e.g. holopost)
hook *v*
  Fool someone with a white lie
hurts like a mangled scan *exp. (city slang)*
  hurts like hell
hush *adj. (highland slang)*
  to be quiet, to not make a sound, to be on **hush mode**
hush mode *exp.*
  comm setting to emit close-range canceling frequencies
hovertrain *n*
  inner city public transit hovering above walkways
imprint *v*
  to transfer media to/from a **slip** by sticking it to a device
jabber one's way out *exp.*
  talk oneself out of a situation
jam *adj. (city slang)*
  used in expression "we're jam" to mean being in trouble
juicy *adj. (highland slang)*
  cool, equiv. to **trip**
jump *v (slang)*
  to scare someone, used in expression "you jumped me"
jumper *n (city slang)*
  something that startles you
kittybot *n*
  hybrid used to control vermin
knockout stick *n*
  device that knocks people out
lie low *v (Stitch slang)*
  to get some sleep

lifeshield *n*
  a device that creates a field to protect from getting crushed
lift *n*
  shaft with elevator platform that materializes when called
lo-flower *n*
  lo moth (colorful North American moth) and flower hybrid
loose *adj. (highland slang)*
  relaxed
magnoform *n*
  magnetic field acting as a raised sleep surface
match *n*
  Someone's spouse as matched by the Unified clergy
maze *n*
  futuristic version of an internet-like network
messed *adj. (Stitch slang)*
  appearing sick, horrible, pasty white
mick *n (anglicism)*
  adapted from French slang "mec", meaning a dude
midi *n (highland slang)*
  midday meal, lunch, adapted from French "midi"
Mount *n*
  the holy podium where only the **Pramam** speaks
MPD *acronym*
  multiple personality disorder
naughtypad *n*
  fake **slippad** that broadcasts written phrases to **biochip**s
neah *adv. (city slang)*
  no
newb *n (slang)*
  a newcomer
ohhhm gee *interj.*
  equiv. to OMG, oh my god.
oh, the shards *exp. (city slang)*
  you break my heart in a joking manner

one-way portal *n*
  see **uniportal**
operative *n*
  a stealthy and highly trained member of the **GMU**
out-of-bounds tag *n*
  attached to an archive shelf when a document goes missing
overdazed *adj. (city slang)*
  stoned, drugged up, out of it
packet *n*
  a block of information existing in the **maze**
PAL (personal automated librarian) *acronym*
  programable flying book retriever, a type of **sniffer**
parked *adj. (slang)*
  to be sitting waiting for someone
pass *n (Stitch slang)*
  an out, an exit out of a tough situation
patch *n*
  an update or fix to a malfunctioning **biochip**
Perfect are They *exp.*
  ceremonial verse used as a lead in for **They are One**
perk *v (Stitch slang)*
  to listen up, perk one's ears
permissions *n*
  one or more access rights granted by the Unification
pica *adv. (Stitch slang)*
  super, very
plane *v*
  to **slide** just above ground with special shoes
plane like I'm on the slick *exp.*
  to hurry, derived from the sport of planing
poke a rib *exp. (Stitch slang)*
  to tease, to play a trick on
portablower *n*
  personal short-range device to blow fog away for visibility

GLOSSARY   ix

Pramam *n*
  leader of the Unification and head of the Inner Council
**privy … ** *n*
  protective item container with teeth (e.g. privyshelf)
proximity reader n
  echolocation device used in the fog to detect obstacles
red craft *n*
  GHU ambulance
ride it *exp. (city slang)*
  go with the flow
ride *v (Stitch slang)*
  to not show up for work, just ride on by
rift *v*
  to change the properties of matter using frequency shifting
right on credit *exp.*
  right on the money, right on target
rip *v (highland slang)*
  to figuratively rip one's pants laughing, used like LOL
rip and roll *exp. (highland slang)*
  to laugh so hard you loose your balance, similar to LMFAO
roll *v (highland slang)*
  to laugh uncontrollably
rook *n (slang)*
  a rookie
rubber (narrow field rubber) *n*
  undetectable small frequency range canceling device
sajadum [sá-ha-doom] *n*
  small crystal building used for meditation; fits three people
sage master *n*
  an individual of highly cultivated wisdom through study
scan *n* and *v*
  1 *n* result of reading a **biochip** for health/security purposes
  2 *v* to read someone's **biochip** using a frequency device

scan jam *exp.*
 jamming of the frequencies a device uses to read a **biochip**

scanning wall *n*
 a wall that continuously **scans biochip**s within a meter of it

scrubber *n*
 program attached to a **packet** in the **maze** to wipe it clean

scuff *n (city slang)*
 a complication resulting in verbal or physical confrontation

secure band *n*
 a wristband with clearance level access past **sentinel** posts

sentinel *n*
 a hybrid species bred for security duty

señor *n (slang)*
 dude, adapted from Spanish

shakes *interj. (Stitch slang)*
 used as expression to mean "whoa"

shard *n*
 see **oh, the shards** for its use in city slang

sheiss *interj. (anglicism from German)*
 shit

shoe will stick to him something fierce *exp. (Stitch slang)*
 the boss will get on his case, give him a butt kick

SIF *acronym*
 Special Investigation Forces

sketch the maze *exp.*
 equiv. to web surfing but with sketching device

slack *v (slang)*
 to put something off, procrastinate

slam *n* and *v*
 1 *n (Stitch slang)* a scoring throw in a sports game
 2 *v* to lightly punch a friend when annoyed at them

slap me *exp. (Stitch slang)*
 I'm sorry

sleeper *n*

portable sleeping surface

sleeve *n*

an envelope style folder used to store loose documents

slick *n*

futuristic sports rink based on hovering mechanism

slide *v*

to arrive at a destination by way of a **slider**

slider *n*

a personal vehicle that moves by sliding just above ground

sliderbag *n*

a self-propelling piece of luggage with built-in **slider**
capabilities

slidercab *n*

a **slider** for hire, a futuristic version of a taxi cab

sliderpad *n*

a place to store a **slider**, like a garage

sliderskid *n*

platform which transports goods/people over short distances

slip *n*

interactive membrane to store/display/manipulate media

slipbook n

futuristic version of an e-book using the **slip** technology

slipclip n

a clip to keep individual **slip**s together

slipmap *n*

an interactive map imprinted on a **slip**

slippad *n*

a stack of **slip**s temporarily bound to each other

slipwork *n*

similar concept to paperwork except concerning **slip**s

snare *n*

facial expression, a cross between a stare and a sneer

sniff *v*
   to use a **sniffer** to find something
sniffer *n*
   device that finds things based on frequency detection
spongysuit *n*
   self-cleaning body sock people use instead of showers/baths
sprinkle dust *v*
   to encrypt an image or **packet** to render it unsearchable
stomp *v*
   to go on a verbal rampage
stretch rodent *exp.*
   sarcastic way of referring to a ferret-like animal
stroke *n*
   one single line or gesture when sketching through the **maze**
sunshaft *n*
   a lift shaft that captures and stores solar energy
sweep formation *n*
   GMU tactic for fanning out and overtaking an area
sweep *n*
   a complete search of an area using a **sweep formation**
swish *v (Stitch slang)*
   got it, figured it out
ta *n (Stitch slang)*
   thanks
tag *n*
   location tracking and monitoring device or **biochip** flag
tagged *adj.*
   biochip is altered and marked as a suspected criminal
Tess *adj. (Stitch slang)*
   genius, derived from inventor Nikola Tesla
They *pron.*
   The holy Trinity of Jesus, Mohammed, and Abraham
They are One *exp.*
   ceremonial response to **Perfect are They**, equiv. to "Amen"

thrower (frequency thrower) *n*
a device that shoots frequencies at a specific point
top *adj.* and *v (highland slang)*
1 *adj.* so much, as in "top juicy" meaning so cool, equiv. to **pica**
2 *v* to ace, to pass with flying colors
topped up *adj. (highland slang)*
stressed out
trace *v*
to run a diagnostic on a **biochip** to find a defect
transcriptor *n*
device to converting voice to text directly into a journal
transfer chest *n*
a futuristic shipping crate used by the Gadlins
trip *adj. (city slang)*
cool
trip out *exp. (city slang)*
get lost, go cool off
trip with that *exp. (city slang)*
I'm in, I'm cool with that, it's all good
uniportal *n*
a thin membrane acting as a one-way viewing window
unit *n*
a group of military personnel
URA *acronym*
Unification Research Arm
valah *interj. (Stitch slang)*
anglicism of French word "voilà"
virta ... *n*
a virtual object with solid properties (e.g. virtachair)
wack *n (highland slang)*
creep, weirdo
way *exp. (city slang)*
hi, equiv. to **hey lo**

weedel *n* and *v*

  1 *n* hose and weasel hybrid that vacuums up weeds

  2 *v* to concoct a story or to weasel out of something

wiggle hips over *exp.*

  happy to see, like wagging your tail for

wipe *n*

  a membrane typically used to wipe off sweat, like a hanky

whip *n (highland slang)*

  a comeback to a **rib**, as in "good whip!"

ya fig *exp. (Stitch slang)*

  you figure, equiv. to **eh**

yay with that *exp. (highland slang)*

  down with that, cool with it, all for it

yeah *adv. (city slang)*

  equiv. to **eh**

you-belong-in-a-jar look *exp. (highland slang)*

  you're nuts, you're a freak

yum it up *exp.*

  eat something voraciously

zap me back *exp.*

  I'll be, I'm surprised, will you look at that

zapped *adj. (slang)*

  touché, you got me, I fell into that one

zapper *n*

  a wearable alarm device that sends a mild shock

ziga *adv. (Stitch slang)*

  super super, even more than **pica**

zorro effect *exp. (Stitch slang)*

  when something masks the effect of something else, e.g.
  noise-canceling headphone

ACKNOWLEDGMENTS

Every person who has crossed my path has either directly or indirectly shaped the mind and the spirit expressing their creativity through the characters in this novel. Only by turning the pages of our own lives can we discover the narrative that enriches the meaning of our experiences. In gratitude for these treasures, through their support, wisdom, and encouragement, a few of many names come to mind:

My children Siobhan and Jeremy, my parents Art and Norma, my sisters Kylen and Laura and Jenn, Bob Proctor, Sandy Gallagher, Gina Hayden, Arash Vossoughi, my PGI Matrixx friends, Amy Stoehr, Peggy McColl, Sylvia McConnell, Jacky Tuinstra Harrison, Jelayne Miles, Margarida Costa-Pinto, Rachel Oliver, Neil Oliver, Damon Flowers, Jody Royee, Alena Chapman, Jennifer Beale, Greg Reid, my Secret Knock friends, RUKE and his team, Nancy Trites Botkin, Mark Shekter, Ana Jorge, Alecia Guevarra, and many more.

I especially want to acknowledge Les Petriw, Jason Brockwell, and the team at NBN (National Book Network, Inc.) for their role in taking Nemecene to the next level.

And, of course, I continue to send special hugs to my disco poodle, Lola, who always finds the joy in the simplest of things.

ABOUT THE AUTHOR

Kaz is not an author in the traditional sense. She creates fictional worlds using any media she can shape into a richly layered vision. Her strengths have always been imagination, design, and a natural ability to connect the dots, which she weaves into beautiful tapestries that engage the senses. Kaz uses the rhythms and nuances of words to successively reveal deeper meaning behind the narrative.

Nemecene: The Gadlin Conspiracy is the second episode recounting the adventures in the greater Nemecene™ World — a place where you can engage in life-changing immersive experiences that inspire and empower you to think, feel, express, connect, and act in harmony with others, nature, and our life source, water.

Kaz has a bachelor in Applied Science (engineering) from Queen's University, a fashion degree from the Richard Robinson Fashion Design Academy, certifications in personal training and hypnosis, a US patent in user interface design, an IMBD credit as director, and has written extensively on environmental issues via WomanNotWaiting.com, LifeAsAHuman.com and her philanthropy mission at Aguacene.com.

When she is not scheming the perfect muahahaha moment, you can find her hanging around some four-legged friends. She speaks English, French, Spanish, and is currently learning Russian. She also strives to be a recovering chocoholic, with limited success, and to look more and more like her standard poodle every day.

THE MISSION

Do you love water? (say *yes*)

So do I.

We love water because we *are* water and pretty much everyone and everything we hold dear in our life is water.

What if every time you read a book, watched a movie, played a game, hung out, or nabbed some swag, in order to dream big with your friends inside a science fiction fantasy Nemecene™ World, you actually could define history for zigazillions of lives — human and non-human alike?

And you wouldn't have to become an activist, a kayaktivist, a slacktivist, or any other kind of -ivist … unless you wanted to juice it up a notch, of course. You can simply be a friend.

The Nemecene™ World immerses us in a future flooded by dead oceans and poisonous gases, but we don't have to manifest that. How we relate to water is the key.

We truly live in an epoch of water that is fast heading towards an epoch of redress. As founder of the Aguacene™ Fund at Tides Canada, my personal mission is to use all things Nemecene to fund water stewardship projects, starting with the Mackenzie River watershed and the Beaufort Sea.

Philanthropist through fun! And by purchasing this book, you now are one.

Thank you.

Kaz

GET EPISODE 3

NEMECENE

THROUGH FIRE AND ICE

If you hate Sothese now, you'll love … to hate him in the next episode of the *Nemecene* series. He'll be reveling in his elevated role as lead narrator with an opening tale that is certain to have him slithering under your skin. As the Pramam's personal advisor, Sothese has access to secrets that could destabilize the Unification.

Will his carnal obsessions lead to temptations beyond his mandate? Or will they thrust his own motives into the toxic seascape?

Stay connected with the Nemecene™ World for juicy teasers as his story unfolds.

www.NEMECENE.com/episode-3

Available Spring 2018!

For more information on where to buy
Nemecene™ episodes and products go to

www.GETNEMECENE.com

COLLECT CREDITS

Want to earn some currency?

Join the Nemecene™ World — score 9 Nemecene™ Credits.
Enter YOUR unique biochip # (see inside front cover) at

w w w . N E M E C E N E . c o m / r e g i s t e r - b o o k

Creeps!
You've been biochipped!

Want EVEN MORE currency?

Invite your friends to join.
Find out how at

w w w . N E M E C E N E . c o m / i n v i t e - f r i e n d s

Perk! Here's a little secret.

Leadership has many privileges.
Get the inside scoop at

w w w . N E M E C E N E . c o m / l e a d e r s h i p